Hope by the sea

Tessy Braun

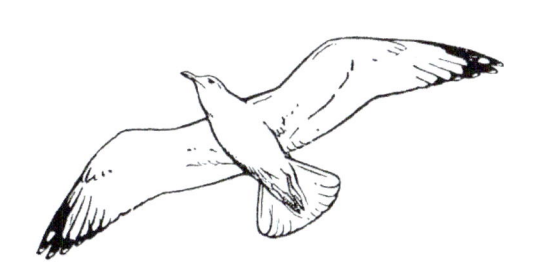

*For Marie,
Thank you for choosing my book!
Best wishes,
Tessy Braun x*

Copyright © 2024 Tessy Braun

All rights reserved.

This book, or any portion thereof, may not be reproduced or used in any manner whatsoever without the written permission of the author, except for the use of brief quotations in a book review

This novel is a work of fiction. All the names, characters, events and incidents in this book are either the product of the author's imagination or used in a fictitious manner. Any resemblance to actual persons, living or dead, or actual events is purely coincidental.

ISBN

979 833837251 7

Dedication

To my mother, who always believes in my writing. Now, brought to life with your unfaltering encouragement, **Hope by the Sea** is finally here for all to enjoy.

Furthermore, to my dear sister, who has always taken great care of me, regardless of what life has thrown our way.

No better remedy would I prescribe
so to cleanse your spirit and your mind,
than to take a walk by the ocean-side

Noise of waves crashing over rocks
helps confusion become unblocked,
clears a cloudy, muddled brain,
and makes you feel alive again.

Sea Doctor by Tessy Braun

PROLOGUE

The flame twisted with orange hue as the edges curled up and turned to ash in an instant, the image disappearing into a state of oblivion. Without care, she tossed the burning photograph into the fireplace before igniting another, which followed the same fate. She watched, not expecting the exercise to be anywhere near so liberating.

Some say there comes a time in life when no choice remains but to take a firm hold of your own destiny, and when the time arrives, you will know. It will be one of those 'now or never' crossroads, the very moment to gamble on your dreams, and you will know when the opportunity presents itself. It is true, however, that our personal circumstances can hold us back, perhaps it is the need to put others first before our own wolfish ambitions. Yet when an inherent thirst has grown within, in such a way that passion spills from every corner of your heart, some like to think that eventually we will arrive at a time to make those changes happen for once and for all, a time that is right for you, a time that is right for the universe.

The one that tastes like fruit

The time for escape had surely come for Lorelei Logan, who was nearing her fourth decade, though where the time had gone, she couldn't quite say. What was certain though, was she was soon to set sail on the voyage of her lifetime and her next chapter would be her most unfamiliar yet; for at its core revolved one word and one word only, *freedom*.

Enduring eighteen years trapped by what could be described as a terribly unfortunate misjudgment of character, had taken its toll on Lorelei. It had been two decades wasted in a toxic marriage, like an aircraft that had experienced turbulence too many times. In fact, *this* aircraft had dropped right out of the sky and, on more than one occasion crashed completely; its engine oil spilled like marbled blood, all purple, yellow, and blue. Yet, Lorelei, like the forgiving individual she was, kept handing over her boarding pass, taking her window seat, only to keep watching her happiness slip further and further away.

"One day," she had dreamed. "One day, I'll escape, but that day is *not* today."

Lorelei perched on the edge of her bed for a moment and recalled how exhausting the marriage had been, and how she had quite forgotten what it was like to live an ordinary life. She had at one point wanted her marriage to be a success, of course, and had tried relentlessly to salvage what was left of it. The truth was that no amount of patching up could save it, and as the years rolled on, the abuse was more and more tangible. Lorelei began to realise the cycle she was in and became under no illusion that it was ever going to stop. His pathetic crocodile tears now meant nothing and were just a part of his 'act' after each frenzied rage. No 'sorry' could make it better because all expectations had been exhausted that Jay had a hope in hell of changing his behaviour, his routine, his 'set'. Even after couple-therapy, anger management and counselling, the manipulation would always return, stronger and evermore persistent.

Despite ending in such bitter divorce, when the couple first met at university, they had fallen so quickly (and deeply) in love. Jay was charming; cheeky, yes, and a little roguish, but always with good intention. He was dark-haired, with hints of green in his unfathomable eyes, always clean shaven and well-groomed, and he spoke with a strong Somerset accent. His bone structure was good, with a strong pronounced nose. He was always popular among his peers and sporty, too. Lorelei was smitten from the start and there was no doubt that Jay had suitably impressed. It had been the sporting events he took part in, which caught Lorelei's attention in the beginning. He often ran half marathons, and obstacle races became a frequent vocation of his. Even mountain biking came to be a favourite pastime. In fact, it was

Jay who eventually encouraged Lorelei to start running herself, nurturing her own journey from couch to 5k.

Before long, they were firm running buddies, regularly participating in races together, but after a short time those activities morphed into romantic weekends in the countryside. He would come to show her that he was quite the perfect lover, proving himself to be gentle and attentive. Their relationship developed and seemed so promising in those early years, and it was not long after their graduation that Jay proposed. Lorelei enthusiastically (yet somewhat hesitantly) accepted, perhaps because part of her had anticipated how the future would unfold, but she was too young and too naïve to listen to her own honest intuition.

She traced her finger over the words written on what she now considered to be the most sacred document of all time — *the Decree Absolute*. It was the long-awaited legal document that finally put an end to their marriage, although it had ended long before this document had even been printed. Yet there it was, in black and white, *dissolved*; and just like an aspirin dropped in water, it had fizzed away into nothing — and this was worth celebrating. With a glass of Sauvignon Blanc in her hand (the one that tastes like fruit), she raised her glass to meet the air in front of her, then brought the rim to her lips and supped generously. It tasted good. It tasted like honeyed relief after a burdensome divorce and quite frankly a disastrous union. Although it was long lasting, *did that count for something?* Lorelei sighed, thinking that if only she had someone to celebrate with, then perhaps she wouldn't feel so flat.

Friends were not in abundance, for over the years she had been forced to lose contact with many of them. Jay hadn't liked her close-knit circle of friends, so put an end to her socialising many years ago. Lorelei texted Janey, her older sister, who had planned to come over to join her that evening, but disappointingly for both, a domestic issue had led her to cancel with short notice.

Of course, Lorelei had called her mother briefly with the good news, and Iris had sobbed uncontrollably upon receiving the word that her daughter could finally move forward in her life, although because of a nasty cold she didn't have the energy to talk for long. Lorelei would have called her dad if she could, but she could no longer reach him, for he had taken his leave of this world less than a year earlier, though she knew he'd have been pleased for her. In any case, she liked to think that he was watching over her and had received the news in his own celestial way.

Lorelei reached into a cupboard in her bedroom for a decorative box and pulled out dozens of photographs, letters and little cards that had been sent alongside flowers (all from Jay, of course). She pursed her lips. There was no reason to keep any of it. A few months ago, she had read some articles about 'burning ceremonies' and how the process could help to symbolise a final goodbye. It had been her intention to get rid of it all, and one by one she set the papers alight and watched with pleasure as her history with Jay, quite literally, went up in smoke.

That evening after her little ritual, Lorelei's way to celebrate was to have a long soak in the bath and change into her nightclothes (the comfortable ones that made her feel relaxed). How safe it felt; no longer forced to look sexy when she didn't feel it, or just wanted to lounge around. She then retreated to the sofa to cuddle into her blanket in front of the television to get lost in a documentary about how everyone was made from stardust. Only she didn't quite manage to stay up for the whole sixty-minute episode, as so often was the case.

A monstrosity of a hospital

The time was nigh for dreams to materialise, and Lorelei was more ready than ever to take the plunge. It would indeed be a giant leap that would change the course of her life, propelling her into a bright future full of possibilities and opportunities. (Or at least this is what she kept telling herself.) With almost two desperate and miserable decades well and truly left behind, Lorelei knew exactly what direction she was to travel in, and her compass was pointing due south to the Cornish coast. It had always been an aspiration for Lorelei to end up there one day. She simply adored the memories she held of her family holidays in the south of England; the abundance of long summer days that they had spent exploring the wild and rugged coastlines (not forgetting the desolate moorland nestling in the county's heart). On many occasions she had fantasised about a life in Cornwall, longing to call this curious land her own home, and over the years her desire to do so had only grown stronger. Bristol wasn't a million miles away from Cornwall, but it was still far enough.

  Lorelei woke up with an unusual spring in her step. She'd dreamt of this day under the watch of a hundred new moons. Longing for the time that she'd skip through those hospital doors (the same ones that she'd trudged in and out of for eighteen years, *every* morning), and now, finally it was the *last* time she'd ever have to walk down that dismal whitewashed corridor *ever* again. It didn't feel like a hospital that day. The open space more closely resembled an airport, for today it was a runway stretching out in front of this soon to be re-born child. There she was, adorned in her blue uniform, like an air hostess (yet not as glamorous), about to start her shift as 'Lorelei the nurse'. She stood straight in front of those sliding doors and, with an ambitious smile creeping into the corners of her mouth, she was ready for take-off, and nothing was going to keep her on the ground.

As Lorelei approached the lifts, she looked around and gave thought to whether she would miss her life as a nurse. Of course she would. The sense of purpose was sometimes overwhelming and, although the long shifts were a disadvantage, it was safe to say that her profession was always, well, *mostly*, rewarding. Pondering whether or not the fresh sea air and ocean views would be a fair payoff for a much less demanding role, she didn't register the lift door opening and her colleague Lucy calling her name from inside.

"Good morning, Lorelei, earth to Lorelei!" the enthusiastic thirty-something year old chimed. "Come on, in you get, are you daydreaming again?" Lucy made contact with Lorelei's arm with a comforting squeeze. "Well, you've got lots to dream about now, haven't you lovely? A whole new magical dream lies right ahead of you. I'm *so* envious!" she squealed.

With that, the lift jolted to a stop, and the two nurses scuttled into the ward.

That last day turned into a whirlwind with so many farewells and best wishes showered upon her, along with a striking display of autumnal flowers. The burnt orangey brown hues were comforting, along with a beautiful sunflower centrepiece. Lorelei adored flowers, but not roses. Never roses. Tulips, yes, and autumnal arrangements were always so very much appreciated. Although true friends were scarce in Lorelei's life, there had been a small number of colleagues who had been there to support her during those dark days. The ones when she had not been able to hide her tears (or her bruises) for long. These women had some understanding of how deep the scars were, and how much Lorelei needed to heal herself by making this momentous relocation.

Lorelei had hoped to stay in contact with some of her work colleagues, therefore, since the breakdown of her marriage she'd made the brave decision to rebuild her social media account. For now, her circle was dismal, but she hoped she would stay connected with the few friends she did have, for she intended to maintain some sense of connection with her life in Bristol, or at least the few positive parts of it. Jay had never liked her being connected with the world or having any sort of relationship with anyone other than himself. It was a tedious game, and she grew weary of defending herself when it came to relationships with male friends. Frequently he demanded that she completely remove from her friends list anyone of whom he was suspicious. Over time Lorelei grew tired of the constant need to respond to his preposterous accusations, so the easier option was to just eliminate the need to be subjected to his green-eyed jealousy. So leaving social media had been the easiest option, the option that minimised the stress, and anything she could do to minimise stress was a bonus in her book.

And so, the time had come to take the final walk down that clinical concourse. She handed in her security pass at the reception that had greeted her morning after morning for what seemed like an entire lifetime. Sadness was not abundant but perhaps a small trickle of nostalgia creeped through the cracks, but it was mostly a feeling of relief that engulfed her, and of course excitement at what was to come. With a final glance behind her, Lorelei stepped through the sliding doors, letting down her long auburn hair from a neat ponytail as she passed through. For the very last time, she strode away from that building with an air of confidence, quite ready to start the beginning of her new, prosperous, and most importantly, *free* life.

She walked up the concrete steps which led into the car park and slumped herself into the driver's seat of her little yellow city car. Lorelei could not help but think of her dear father and how sick he had been at the end of his life just a short time ago. She knew that if he was still here, he would be proud of her, and he would be pleased that she had escaped the turbulent marriage that she had been trapped in for so many sorrowful years.

It was November and although the sun was shining, the air was cold. This was Lorelei's favourite type of weather. The kind where long boots and furry coats came out of the wardrobe, along with woolly tights and knitted hats. The ironic part of all of this was that without the inheritance money that Lorelei received, she probably would never have been able to make this mammoth relocation across the country. She had been lucky beyond belief, for she and her sister had not understood their father was sitting on such a fortune.

It was happening now, though; it was *really* happening. Her new home was already waiting for her in St Ives, in the far west of Cornwall. The apartment was a stone's throw from the beautiful St Ives harbour and, although it was going to be somewhat of a downsize in terms of space, the one-bedroom flat would be a piece of paradise for Lorelei. It was just a short stroll to the shops, beach, and other amenities; how she loved walking around the island and the cliffs. It would be such a privilege to have all of this on her doorstep. The little flat was cosy and sat above one of St Ives's many art galleries scattered across the quaint cobbled streets. She'd travelled down a few times throughout the last eight weeks to decorate and move a few bits and pieces, in advance of the official move date.

Sitting still in her car looking over at the monstrosity of a hospital, Lorelei thought back to her father's last moments. She closed her eyes softly and thought how he was lucky enough, if you can call it luck, to die at home, in his own bed with both Lorelei and her sister present. Their mother, Iris, had also been there. At the end of a stoic battle with cancer, her father finally succumbed to the disease almost a year to the day. One might hear about people passing away peacefully in their homes, but their father's death could not be described as such. Terminal restlessness had presented itself the night before, although neither Lorelei's sister Janey, who had been staying with her father in his home, nor their mother had realised.

"We had a terrible night. He kept trying to get up," a concerned Janey had explained upon her sister's arrival in Devon.

The girls' mother nodded. "Yes, dear, it's been a particularly exhausting night. Neither your sister nor I have had a wink. Your poor father. I really can't bear to see him like this." Although they hadn't lived together for thirty or more years, Iris had been involved with his care and had seen her ex-husband more often in the last six months than she had in many years. A bond had been built once more, and it had all been very difficult indeed.

The doctor had given him weeks only, but as soon as Lorelei arrived at her father's house, she knew it would not be as long as that. He had clearly deteriorated since she had seen him just a few short days ago. Lorelei gestured to her sister and whispered, "You're not going back to Bristol tonight, are you? I *really* don't think you should…"

It didn't take long for death to come. From Lorelei's arrival, it was just mere hours before he left them. Sensing the dying process was progressing, the girls made a frantic call to the 'end of life' nurses. There was sickness, wailing, and restlessness. Lorelei and her sister lifted her father as he vomited into a bowl which Janey could not cope with rinsing after each use. Janey had problems dealing with anything involving germs or uncleanliness. She worried excessively about minor illnesses, and what was happening to her father really gave her the heebie jeebies. This year she had been especially anxious about the big C. However, Lorelei's service as a nurse had stood her in good stead for dealing with the end of life, and of course, sick patients. Though to note, despite being aware of the merciless cruelty of death — nothing — just nothing, could prepare her to witness her father's last breath.

It wasn't peaceful. It wasn't a serene or a 'spiritual experience' (at least not for the three witnesses, for who could tell what was going through their father's mind despite how he appeared). Their father, Gerald, had again become extremely restless, and was once more persistent in trying to sit up and move around the room, though clearly he was unable to do so. He seemed disoriented, and the sickness had become intense. When he lay back on the bed, an all too familiar sound was heard from his chest. Upon hearing the distinct rattle, the girls exchanged knowing looks. *This was it*; it would have been perfectly absurd to think otherwise. Lorelei was by far the calmer of the two siblings. Her composure was indeed commended in the immediate time; admiration for her ability to remain focused was not short of praise, though later her cold reaction to grief was questioned somewhat, but Lorelei was to learn that grief can present itself in all manner of ways.

The nurses performed their duties with grace and delivered their services with a bedside manner that Lorelei didn't always witness in the city. They referred kindly (and with love) to the patient as 'flower' and were continuously reassuring him in an attempt to dispel his very apparent fears. He was frightened, and the girls' hearts ached for him.

"I've always…" Gerald croaked, struggling to get the words out. "I've always loved… Iris." These words, Iris had not expected to hear again in any of their lifetimes. Gerald thrashed around again and groaned in pain. "I'm sorry, I'm sorry," he cried to Iris. Their marriage had ended, for reasons that she didn't care to revisit, but it was clear he loved her still, to this day, and it broke her heart to know it. It was time for the *'just in case'* medicine. The nurses explained it would be just a couple of injections that would stop their father from experiencing pain.

"Dad," Janey said. "They're going to make you feel better. Just a little injection, and the sick feeling will go away."

Little did the two sisters and Iris know what would happen next, for instead of soothing their dying father, the injections seemed to have quite the opposite effect. In fact, he immediately changed his posture, became tense and in what seemed like mere seconds (possibly minutes in reality), his eyes became wide like a rabbit in the headlights, his jaw locked open and down he went like a plank of wood on his bed. *Not* relaxed, *not* sedated, but now with an absolutely terrified expression on his face. Was he there? Was he not?

Janey cried, "Dad!" Turning to the nurses, she painstakingly begged them, "*Is he gone?! Is he gone?!*"

They couldn't say for sure, explaining that sometimes the dying process would take a further breath or two, and no sooner had they muttered those undecided words when suddenly there was an almighty gasp from their father, accompanied still by a petrified expression. More gasps. All three hurriedly reached out with words of comfort.

"Remember all those summer holidays down in Cornwall, the Isles of Scilly, how beautiful it is!" cried their mother.

Then Lorelei frantically exclaimed, "Dad, we love you, we're here, we're *all* here!" The girls desperately continued to reassure him.

Janey wept, clinging to her father's arm. "Don't be scared," she said. "Dad, we're here. You can let go; you can go…"

And then he was gone. As simple as that. Seventy-eight years old and only six months ago, he was walking for miles on the beach every day. How rapidly things can change, how quickly cancer can rip a family apart. They stayed with his body for some time before retiring to the kitchen for a cup of tea, not knowing exactly what was supposed to happen next. Still feeling somewhat numb and surreal, the impact of what had happened had not fully hit home for Lorelei. It didn't seem real, and to Lorelei's bemusement, strangely, there were no tears rolling down her cheeks. In contrast, Janey hadn't stopped sobbing and was falling hopelessly apart, while Lorelei remained level-headed and unemotional. Lorelei asked herself why she felt so numb and wondered if it was because subconsciously, she was relieved that her father was no longer suffering.

The undertaker was called around two hours after their poor dad had died and before then, Lorelei and Janey spent some more time with their father. A daughter sat at either side of their father's body, which by now was stiff with rigamortis and cold to touch. When the professionals arrived, they treated the family with the utmost respect.

"Take as much time as you need," they reassured. Lorelei stroked her father's cheek, and the girls both laid a kiss on his forehead.

"Goodbye, Dad," Janey whimpered.

"Goodbye, Dad," Lorelei sighed, leaving the men to their work of tending to the dead. Lorelei pondered on how exactly they would manage to carry their dad down two flights of stairs, because the lift surely would not be big enough for a stretcher. It was later she realised her dad would in fact have been carried vertically inside the lift, which is an image that never quite left her mind, even almost twelve months later.

It was two o'clock in the morning. They stood in the cold communal entrance to the apartment and watched as the undertakers solemnly carried their father outside and into the private ambulance parked on the green. It was beyond emotional, yet still Lorelei did not cry. The two daughters naturally stayed at the apartment with their mother, who that night sat up till even earlier hours alone, trying to somehow process the loss of her ex-husband and his final words.

Curled up together in the guest bed, the girls attempted to fall asleep for the remaining hours of the night. Of course, neither managed any quality rest, for they were both hideously tormented by what they had seen and haunted by the journey they had been on over the last six months. To see it all come to a crescendo in a few hours that evening, they now lived with the realisation that they were fatherless and would never see their dad alive again.

Lorelei turned the ignition and the engine started. Moving the gear stick into reverse, she took a deep breath. With one final glance towards the hospital, she pulled away and headed to the car park barriers where she jubilantly handed in her yellow parking token for the very last time. Despite the mixed up and jumbled memories that plagued her as she relived her father's last moments (which in all honesty she did rather often than perhaps was healthy), and despite the years of manipulation in her desperately unhappy marriage, *she finally had hope.*

In the shade of a hawthorn tree

Boxes lined the hallway, but they'd soon be making their way into the removal lorry that was waiting on the street outside. Lorelei's belongings were ready, and so was she. It was time to say 'goodbye' to the bright lights of the city and 'hello' to sweet smelling fresh country air. Though, in fact, it wasn't the most idyllic time of the year to move to Cornwall with the weather teetering from autumn to winter.

Janey would join her sister on the drive to Cornwall, and would hop back on the train from Penzance a few days later, just to help her settle in. Lorelei wished her sister could stay for longer. It was a shame she had to rush back, but she was grateful for the company for the time being. God knew she could do with the moral support, and not to mention help with the unpacking. Janey's role as 'older sister' meant she was always very supportive of Lorelei and had been there for her at various times over the years, taking care of her emotionally (and sometimes financially) in her teenage and young adult years.

Though sharing the same parents, like many siblings, the two girls were rather different in nature. Lorelei was a wild, free spirit at heart, and Janey was the *slightly* more sensible one.

At least Lorelei's nature *was* a free spirit, before she had been so terribly suppressed by Jay, but regardless of his force over her, she still possessed her spark.

Despite Janey's level-headed approach to life, this could only be said regarding matters not concerning herself, for she was plagued by irrational worrying about her health. These panic attacks would often develop quickly and were so devastating, leaving her completely debilitated. Janey was married to Robert and was in a perfectly stable partnership. She held a senior position in an information technology firm and did very well for herself indeed. Robert was a head chef in a prestigious hotel, and his occupation sadly demanded long hours and late nights. He cared a lot about his work and took great pride in it, having cooked for celebrities and even royals, including Prince Charles. He was known to everyone to be an honourable man, caring and attentive and a real 'softy' at heart. He'd never let Janey down and supported her through thick and thin, trying to understand as much as he could about her mental health. One thing was for sure, no matter how tedious Janey's all-consuming anxiety became, Lorelei had no doubt that Robert would stick by her side, no matter how poorly she got. Health anxiety was truly the misery of her life and restricted her in all ways imaginable. Pregnancy with her daughter Ruby appeared to be the trigger.

What was supposed to be an enlightening experience became nine months of excruciating hell. The entire pregnancy had been exhausting for everyone involved, and it was certainly not a time that Janey thought fondly of. She only narrowly survived, in a state of distress during each trimester, fearing that she had contracted some sort of terrible illness that would harm her unborn child. Unfortunately, Janey's health anxiety still spiraled out of control even after the birth.

Janey was a sophisticated-looking woman with dark brown hair fashioned in a short pixie cut. She had warm Mediterranean looking skin all year round, which her daughter, Ruby, inherited. Often complimented on her perfect complexion, it was a stark contrast to how Janey felt on the inside. The sisters took in the last sights of the empty property before heading out into the street.

"So, little sis, it's the big day! I'm so proud of you for making this move." Janey squeezed her sister's hand. "Even though you're almost forty, you'll always be my little sis."

Lorelei wiped away a tear. "Thank you, I think I'm going to be really happy in St Ives, but I'll miss you," she sniffed. "You can come and stay as much as you like, as long as you're okay on the sofa."

The sisters climbed into Lorelei's car as they watched the removal lorry leave ahead of them.

"I hope I'm making the right decision Janey," Lorelei swallowed. "I mean, what if this is all a terrible mistake — what if I can't find a job?"

Janey sensed the anxiety in her sister's voice, and anxiety, she understood. "Look, you have a place to live, and you still have, what, over £15k left from your inheritance. You've got enough to keep you going until you find a job, and let's face it, all the pasty shops of Cornwall are going to be fighting over you!" she laughed.

Lorelei rolled her eyes at Janey. "Well, I'd rather work in a pasty shop than look for a nursing job. I've had enough of it. This is a fresh new start from *all* angles."

Janey nodded. "Yes, I do understand, but are you not going to be totally bored out of your brain serving sausage rolls and cheese twists all day?" Janey chuckled.

"I may not do… erm…retail. Maybe I'll find an

office job or something?"

Janey smirked. "This is the far west of Cornwall you're moving to!" she teased, knowing that in remote Cornwall, opportunities might be scarce. Both sisters were in fits of laughter. They strapped themselves in, and with the air pressure topped up and oil checked, they were ready to hit the road.

The journey was straightforward, mostly on the motorway, and soon the city was left far behind, leaving only the beautiful green English countryside stretched out in front of them like a giant patchwork quilt. They passed the occasional river and cattle in roadside fields, and above them, the occasional bird of prey soared. An autumn mist hung low as they veered onto the A30 across Dartmoor where wild ponies and sheep grazed, before finally meeting Cornwall's spine, passing by Jamaica Inn, when the end of the journey was at last in sight.

It was early afternoon when the sisters arrived in St Ives. In November, the holiday season really had come to an end, and the streets were eerily quiet. It was a blessing, for in the summer months the narrow lanes would bustle with tourists. People had a habit of straying into the middle of the road, and it really was quite a feat to get through safely by car. Though today it was a breeze, and they could navigate the pretty seaside town with little difficulty.

Most of the houses in the town were holiday lets, so Lorelei had been overjoyed she had been able to purchase a property in her area of choice. They pulled up, squeezing the car as tightly as possible into the little space by the side of the road.

The two sisters emerged from the car and stood looking at the facade of an elegant-looking art gallery called 'Penwith Moor Art'. From a blue side door, Lorelei could gain entry, and a flight of stairs would lead her up to the first-floor flat that she would now call home.

"Oh, I'm so excited!" She beamed with delight, her heart beating and anxiety rocketing in a positive way. With Janey by her side (as she so often was), she approached the blue door and with ease slotted the silver key into the lock. "Dulce domum!" exclaimed Lorelei. The flat smelt clean and fresh and the two sisters eagerly bounded up the stairs, heading straight to the kitchen for a cup of tea before any unpacking was to begin.

"Honestly little sis, you've done well, I'm rather envious!" Janey paused. "If I didn't have commitments, and the challenges with Ruby, I'd be tempted to move to the countryside myself, although I quite fancy the Lake District." Janey sighed a somewhat heavy and laborious sigh.

Lorelei gave her a sympathetic look. "I know it's hard with Ruby, but Robert is a good man and you're *successful*. There are so many positives." Lorelei comforted her sister, although in reality she knew it wasn't easy for Janey. Her high-pressure job didn't help with her mental health, and although Robert was honourable, he had a tendency to be lazy around the house, which meant that Janey ran the home mostly on her own. Yet, she had a five-bedroom house in a nice area with two cars on the drive, and in so many ways, life was so comfortable.

"Yeah, I know, but she's fourteen now, and really not showing *any* signs of calming down," said Janey, a look of sadness swept across her face. Janey and Robert had struggled with Ruby's behaviour for most of the young girl's life. She had always been oppositional and difficult to manage, but since hitting her teens, things had gone from bad to worse. Janey poured the tea, and they sat together at the breakfast bar.

"The years go so quickly Lorelei, I'm getting older,

only five years to fifty!" she gulped. "In some ways I *want* them to go, because it's so hard and I want Ruby to mature and grow up." Janey blowed her tea. She sometimes felt so overwhelmed with the kind of child she'd been blessed with. The last ten years had been a constant battle of fighting for support for her daughter and their family, but it was so difficult to access any kind of help. For one, because Ruby was so intelligent and excelled academically, and secondly, the system was so difficult to get through. Although in one sense Ruby was clever, and could present well, at home her behaviour was a different matter altogether.

"No one doubts it's hard. We all know you do your best." Feeling nostalgic, Lorelei added, "and yes, I can't believe we're so *old*. I still remember being small and running around Granny's lawn, playing with the dogs. It's a lifetime ago, but happy memories."

Looking out the kitchen window, they saw the forecast mizzle was moving in. Expecting the removal company to arrive soon, they were keen to get moving before the weather really took a turn for the worse. What Lorelei really wanted to do was throw on her rain jacket and hurry down to the harbour beach. She loved to see the moored boats wedged into the sand; it was such a typical Cornish sight. Since childhood, St Ives had always been a very special place for her. It was where her parents had taken the two girls on holiday. For many years, they camped or stayed in a static caravan, but in the later years they had stayed in St Ives. She even remembered which cottage, however, it was now a privately owned home, much to Lorelei's disappointment, as she would have loved the chance to stay there once more.

The apartment was adorable and perfect for one person. Though small, did not feel cramped or claustrophobic, but instead cosy and snug. The space would be perfect for

Lorelei. She looked forward to starting up painting as a hobby and could just imagine sitting at her table on a Sunday afternoon with her canvas and mixing palette.

The living room was decorated in a nautical theme of pale blue and white, with a soft long pile rug and cushions scattered over a very inviting grey-blue corner settee. Lorelei had enjoyed furnishing the flat over the last few months, and as always, her sister had been a great help with the furniture selection and colour schemes. Much of her furniture was being brought down from Bristol, including the fridge and tumble drier, but Lorelei had really wanted to redesign the living space and a new sofa was simply a 'must'. She'd keep her bed, table and chairs and a glass cabinet, all of which she inherited from her father, as these items brought her great comfort.

There were other miscellaneous bits and pieces that she had taken when his possessions were shared out. She loved the little trinkets from her father's travels around the world. These also brought much comfort to Lorelei, and she couldn't wait to unwrap them all over again and perfectly position them in their new home. With that thought, the removal lorry arrived, but being far too wide to fit down the quaint St Ives Street, the vehicle had to park a few hundred metres away. The removal staff certainly had their work cut out for them.

Some hours later the gruelling job was completed, and Lorelei's flat looked less cute and cosy now it was cluttered from floor to ceiling with enormous brown boxes. The job ahead seemed incredibly daunting, and suddenly the flat felt smaller than ever before. It was lucky that Lorelei had a lot of time to get stuck in with the task of unpacking before her next arduous undertaking, which was to find herself employment.

"Janey, we need to go down to that little shop; we *need* wine, and shall we treat ourselves to a takeaway tonight? Pizza? Indian?" Feeling quite pleased with her feat so far (having got down to Cornwall with no hiccups, and successfully had her belongings transported, with nothing going missing), Lorelei smiled. Things were really looking positive for her new start. It really was like being reborn. She had no commitments, no financial worries, and was ready to start enjoying life.

"I second that! It's been a long day, and I'm starving, so…" With lips pursed in deep thought, Janey swiftly concluded. "Let's get pizza!"

Pizza was a firm favourite with Lorelei, so she was happy with the choice and got on the phone to a local takeaway without delay. The delivery would take no less than forty-five minutes to arrive, so the two sisters had enough time to nip down to the convenience store for their desired bottle of wine, and of course it would have to be Sauvignon Blanc, a particular type. Actually, it was Jay that had first bought it for her as a birthday present a few years ago.

"That's one good thing that came out of the relationship then!" Janey cheeped, whilst chuckling to herself. While Janey laid the table, Lorelei, glancing out of the living room window at a seagull perched on the telephone wire, paused, and then remembered for a moment the day he asked her to be his wife.

It was a scorching mid-summer's day, going back nineteen years. She was so desperate for his love; she'd have done anything for him (Some may have even said she was obsessed.) When he popped the question, it wasn't too grand or extravagant, but even so, it had been perfect in Lorelei's eyes. In the meadow, partly covered by the shade of a hawthorn tree, they lay together in the sticky July heat. She ran her finger up and down his arm, thinking of how much she wanted to kiss him.

It had been a happy day walking in the countryside. Lorelei loved getting out in the fresh air, and that summer they had been blessed by the most prolonged heatwave. Lorelei concluded she did so very much miss those kinder moments in the relationship and perhaps she was indeed looking through rose-tinted spectacles, however, she felt somewhat still fond of those happier times.

"No!" she cried out loud.

Janey, upon entering the room, turned to her sister in surprise. "*What is it?!*" she asked with a streak of concern in her voice.

"Oh, it's just my mind wandering to Jay and the good times…"

Janey stiffened, and for a moment a degree of tension filled the air between them. "I really don't want to hear that man's name spoken in a good light…"

"I'm sorry, I know you and him didn't get along…"

"Lorelei, *you* and *him* didn't get along, and why was that? Because he's a manipulating conniving rat, not to mention an abuser."

"You don't need to remind me — I *am* aware. I've just been through a nine-month divorce. I know why I divorced him. I know he was a pig," she said, rolling her eyes at her sister.

Janey gasped in disbelief. "A pig! He was a dirty fucking viper fish, a pathetic excuse for a human being, not a pig, Lorelei. Pigs are *cute*!"

"Well, if anything, Jay was cute, right?" Lorelei teased.

"*No*, he was *not*! Actually, maybe he looked a bit like one of those red river hogs at the zoo…" Both sisters burst out laughing and fell playfully into each other's arms.

"Right, come on, you stay here," Janey instructed. "I'll pop down to the shop and get that Sauvignon Blanc you are so very fond of, but if there is any more talk of that bloody cretin, then I will be going back to Bristol tonight *with* the wine and Pizza!"

It wasn't long before Janey was back from the shop, and the pizza delivery had arrived not a minute later than promised. In the wake of their father's death, Lorelei and Janey had both turned vegetarian to keep their bodies healthy, intending to reduce the risk of suffering the same fate that befell their late father. Nevertheless, they enjoyed their new diet. Their pizzas were topped generously with sweet red peppers, mushrooms, onions, and buffalo mozzarella, and accompanied by the most flavoursome garlic bread that either sister had ever tasted. The wine went down beautifully, perhaps a little too well, because by nine o'clock they were both wrapped up in their respective blankets trying not to fall asleep in front of the TV, and in all honesty not doing a very good job of it at all.

My dear friend, anxiety

The winter sun glared through the small gap in the curtains straight onto the two sisters. The light stirred Lorelei first, who squirmed around uncomfortably while trying to hide her face from the unwelcome sunbeam. Before long, she had no choice other than to wriggle unenthusiastically out of her snuggly bundle of blankets to pull the curtain closed. With the light finally shut out, she attempted with resolve to return to slumber, yet regrettably was without success. Lorelei stretched her arms and yawned, taking in the shadows of objects strewn across the floor, which included the open pizza boxes along with two empty wine glasses, and the tomato ketchup which had not been returned to the fridge.

     Glancing over at her sister, still peacefully asleep, she sighed. Janey looked so pretty, with her short hair all messy. She looked young; sleep seemed to conceal her never ceasing worries. However, Lorelei was pleased to see that the move had been a significant distraction, helping to take Janey's mind off her own all-consuming problems. This was especially well received at the weekends when the welcome Monday to Friday routine wasn't there to keep her worries at bay. Compartmentalisation was an incredible concept, and when

Janey was focused on her busy role, she could shut her anxiety out to some degree.

It could be something quite trivial to trigger her dear friend, Anxiety, who never liked to stay away for too long, like when Ruby came up with a cold sore for the first time causing a tumultuous affair. The common virus had been a beast that Janey had feared for years preceding the birth of her daughter, and even though life threatening it most certainly was not, and *even* though it really wasn't a big fat hairy deal at all in the grand scheme of things (a minor annoyance at the most), for Janey it *was the end of the world* as she knew it. The big nasty cold sore was sure to furiously spread over the entirety of Ruby's face, starting from her lip, upwards to her nose, then making its evil way to her eyes, or *worse*, to other parts of her body. It made Janey shake and shudder and spun her into an irrational state. Ruby had been just five years old when she first developed one, and Janey, who researched every kind of infectious disease in preparation for its eventual arrival, was immediately on the case. Janey's heart had begun to beat faster than usual, and a sinking feeling creeped over her, like all her blood was draining out (or in) and she might have fainted at any moment. Of course it had come to her, this bad luck, which she would be destined to endure for the entirety of her life.

It was absolutely inconceivable that now Ruby got cold sores that this meant that she would have to deal with the herpes virus for the rest of Ruby's childhood and *what if she touched it* and it spread — or worse, what if Janey caught it from her daughter? *What if she already had?* A myriad of questions would run through her wild mind and there was absolutely no rationalising Janey's thoughts.

Another not so dissimilar occurrence was over Ruby catching a verruca from the pool, the ones that she couldn't get rid of for years and years. Bath times and showers would never be the same again, and would now follow a strict military operation, and *God forbid* if Ruby didn't put her socks on, or if they fell off in bed leaving the infected foot exposed. Once Ruby gave great pleasure in rubbing her foot all over her mother's towels, cleverly channelling into her mother's weakness. Of course, this intense anxiety would rub off on her young daughter, and it very much did from an exceptionally young age. It was one of the reasons why the health professionals felt Ruby was '*the way she was*'.

Naturally, that was just another disaster to add to Janey's list of failures. In addition to minor ailments, Janey would also become distressed and frightened about the more serious health conditions, even more so after the dramatic death of her father. In fact, this was Janey's newest apprehension, and she lived in a very real fear that she had the disease herself. She'd always had irritable bowel syndrome, but now, of course, every niggle, every pain, every time she had a bowel movement that wasn't quite the same as usual, every time she felt bloated, this was *of course* a sign of cancer. It goes without saying that Janey had cause to be astute to symptoms, given the family history, and Lorelei too had become aware of her body and what to watch out for. No one could deny it was indeed a sensible approach to take, but Janey became obsessed.

Though that morning as Lorelei spent a few minutes gazing lovingly, but at the same time in anguish at her sister, she saw how the everyday stresses of raising a child with anger issues, juggling a full-time job, and worrying excessively about health had all but vanished with the escape of peaceful sleep. She pondered over whether going to sleep is much the same as dying, but without the dreams.

She would miss her dear sister, who was scheduled to leave later that day to return to the city. She wished so desperately that Janey could find contentment one day. Lorelei reflected on how her sister always felt her life had been sabotaged by some sort of unearthly curse of misfortune, having been born on Friday, 13th. Janey was convinced that she would die young; bad luck seemed to be attracted to her.

At least Lorelei knew that Janey would be looked after by her husband Robert. He was such a caring man and Lorelei had always been envious that Janey had found such a kind and considerate companion. Although Lorelei was saddened that Janey would be leaving her later that day, she would not be lonely because her mother was coming to stay for a few nights. That in itself was worrying, though. The relationship between her and her mother could be somewhat tricky, with both Lorelei and Iris having strong personalities, Iris having been born under the sign of Scorpio and Lorelei Aquarius. Iris was a stoic woman, and like Lorelei, had been a nurse before she retired fifteen or so years ago. Lorelei had been profoundly inspired by her mother, and the stories she had been told about community nursing in the 1960s very much influenced Lorelei's career choice. She certainly had a lot of admiration for her mother, but regrettably, they didn't always see eye to eye.

Janey turned over and stretched her arms out high over her head, slowly awakening. She lifted her head a fraction and glanced at the clock then, noticing it was before nine am, descended back into her fluffy bed of cushions once again. Lorelei, however, sprang up and made her way to the little kitchen with unforeseen energy to make a cup of tea for each of them. In fact, she would make a *honey* tea, which was what their father liked to drink before he died, and it had somewhat stuck as a rather reminiscent morning drink.

Flicking the radio on, Lorelei enjoyed the upbeat

tunes of Pirate FM, which propelled her into a cheerful and productive mood for the rest of the day. She was excited, for this new life was what she had been waiting for, and now it was here, and *all hers*! For almost two decades she had yearned to escape and wished for a chance to start again, and now she was really free, no longer with anyone to answer to, free to make her own choices, free to do whatever she wanted to do (within reason she supposed). Lorelei rejoiced in the fact that she was her own woman *at last*, and nothing, absolutely nothing, was going to stop her finding happiness or halt her success in any way whatsoever. Stirring the clear squeezy honey into their hot tea, she hummed along to the tune on the radio. *Is it Taylor Swift?* she thought to herself; she was far from in touch with current chart music.

"Wakey-wakey, Janey!" she cooed in her sister's direction in a jovial and melodic way. "It's time for your morning cup of tea!"

"Oh, you were always an early riser, ever since we were kids. Whatever happened to a lie in on a child-free weekend?" Janey moaned, rolling her eyes. She turned over, but only briefly. "Well," she grunted, "I suppose that we *do* have a lot to do. What time is my train?"

Lorelei shrugged as Janey grabbed her bag and dug around in the bottomless purple leather sack for her tickets. "Where are they? I had them here earlier…" Janey whined.

"Don't you have electronic tickets?"

"Yes, but I *printed them out*… you know I like the old-fashioned way." Finding the crumpled piece of paper among biscuit crumbs and bits of, well, even she wasn't quite sure what, Janey moaned. "I really need to clean this bag…" she wailed, and with that, she emptied the entire contents all over the rug. Packets of near empty pill cases, hand sanitiser, a hairbrush, mints, lip balm among other possessions had fallen out alongside the ticket. Lorelei noted it seemed her sister was still taking her anti-anxiety tablets.

"I can't stand it when my bag gets like this, I can't stand it Lorelei." Huffing and puffing she read the information from the paper ticket. "Okay, my train is later this afternoon, I need to be there at the station at five, in Penzance, so leaving here no later than four please."

Lorelei looked aghast at the mess on her beautiful cream long pile rug where the contents of Janey's bag were rudely strewn. "Okay, that's fine, but come on, *clean this up*. I'm going to have to get Dad's vacuum out again," she sighed.

Shortly after their father's diagnosis, he had made an impulse purchase of a Dyson Cordless vacuum at the hefty cost of a few hundred pounds. Lorelei remembered at the time wondering just why he was thinking of making such an acquisition. She had made a remark to Janey at the time. "Why is he thinking of buying a vacuum cleaner? Does he not realise the seriousness of his cancer?"

"He's probably just trying to be normal."

Lorelei felt a pang of guilt when she recalled her selfish thought on that terribly sad day. She had contemplated that perhaps one day that soon to be purchased vacuum may actually be *hers* (and it looked like such a nice vacuum cleaner too). Well, here it was, taking its grand residence in her cupboard in her little flat in Cornwall.

"Of course I will clean it up, Lorelei. I've tipped it out because I can't stand the mess I've been carrying around; can you get some kitchen wipes and a carrier bag? I need to drink my tea..." Janey wrapped her slender fingers around the vintage mug that was adorned with pretty blue and pink flowers. She brought it towards her lips, and took a sip. "Hmm, you've put honey in it; it's so nice, it reminds me of

Dad." Placing the mug back down on the table she whimpered, "Oh Lorelei, I still can't believe it sometimes, what Dad went through, you know?" She remembered those horrible last moments and a tear rose to her eye.

"Yes, I know. Dad wanted to die though, at the end Janey. He kept saying so. He was weak. He was ready to go."

"I know, I remember telling him he could go, that he could…*let go*…" More tears rolled down Janey's blotchy face. She was a sensitive soul, perhaps more sensitive than her sister, despite the professional bravado Janey often masked her insecurities with.

Lorelei moved closer to her sister and rubbed her back affectionately. "I know, come on, I know it's hard, I know. Try to remember Dad before he was poorly."

"I'm sorry. Right, I need to pull myself together."

"I'll get you those wipes sis, let's sort your bag out."

Janey was a complicated character. She was so terribly obsessed with cleanliness around the house, yet often exceptionally unorganised, frequently leaving things to the wayside, for example, her life admin. She'd always get there in the end, but it seemed to be the response to her anxiety, yet ironically, letting things get out of control caused her so much more angst, and on this occasion, it was the handbag. However, now it was wiped down inside and out, all crumbs and bits of unwanted paper removed, having a lovely clean and organised bag felt wonderful.

They got to work around the little flat, opening boxes, unwrapping ornaments and photo frames that had been asleep in bouncy bubble wrap. A little box containing a few tablespoons of their father's ashes was next. It was left over from the sample they had used to make cremation jewellery.

Delight was taken in lifting out each treasured book from the big brown boxes and positioning them in perfect order in the freshly polished bookcase. Lorelei had a diverse taste in her literature but scarcely had time to read these days, and it had been many years, decades even, since she had immersed herself into any sort of fiction. Janey, on the other hand, was quite the book worm. Despite this recent lack of interest in reading, Lorelei did have a nice collection of books, including non-fiction publications about yoga, tarot, and horoscopes.

Janey admired her sister's home, but had a nagging feeling that something was missing. "I really love your new place, but what about some house plants? Don't you feel terribly sad you don't have a garden any longer?" Janey was quite the keen gardener, nurturing plants from seedlings in her greenhouse, and her outdoor space was beautifully presented. In particular, she loved wildflowers like tansies, verbena, and foxgloves. Janey had often given her sister young plants to grow in her own garden and felt sure Lorelei had got pleasure from them.

"Yes, I do. I hope one day I'll have a garden again, but house plants sound a great idea…" Lorelei beamed, imagining a trip to a garden centre soon.

The living room glass cabinet was coming along so nicely, and every item was positioned with love and care, each little trinket preserving a memory of a period in Lorelei's life. Little scarab beetles and basalt figures from Egypt, Russian Dolls from, well — Russia, among other sweet items like shells, bottles of sand and figurines that she had been given over the years.

The sisters then moved on to the many kitchen utensils, pots, pans, and cutlery, with the heart of the place gradually taking shape and beginning to feel like a true home. Though the sisters' father had been in the accountancy trade, he had always had an overwhelming passion for cookery and Lorelei had a pocketful of fond memories of preparing tasty and nutritious meals with her father. He had taught her much when it came to her acquired culinary skills, and a particular favourite was slow-cooked lamb with redcurrant jelly and rosemary. Although there was now no way that even a tiny morsel of that delicious tender lamb would pass her lips from then on, and she didn't really miss it, in fact, she embraced her new vegetarian lifestyle wholeheartedly.

They worked relentlessly to unpack a good number of items, but the job would sadly not be complete that day, and as the hours passed quickly, this became more and more apparent. Before they knew it, it was time to make the short journey down to the market town of Penzance on the southern coast.

Janey stretched and yawned. "I'm so glad we got so much done, but I do feel bad to leave you with so much more to do!" she yawned again. "I really wish I could stay longer." Janey ruffled her own hair, giving it some natural volume, adding to the 'messy' look that she wore so well.

"You have a life to get on with, and I'm sure you have missed Ruby?" Lorelei twitched her eyebrows, and then added, "Maybe…" Lorelei comforted her sister.

Janey took a deep breath, in preparation to face the cold fact of the matter. "Not *really*, to be honest," she pitifully admitted. "Isn't that a terrible thing to say?" she said, awaiting reassurance from her sister, who, of course, gave her an understanding look. "Ruby has really been pushing the boundaries," Janey picked up their teacups to be washed. "She's *so* difficult to manage." Pausing on her pottering, she turned to face her sister. "So, actually, no, I haven't missed her one bit, and I've rather enjoyed this weekend away. It's been nice to have a break and I wish I could have more!" with that brutally honest reflection, Janey's phone rang.

"Oh, it's her, oh no, *what's happened now?*" With trepidation, Janey answered. "Hello darling?" she warbled, but the response she got from her daughter was not so welcoming, to say the least.

"*Mummy*, when are you coming home!?" Ruby shrieked down the line. "Daddy's not letting me have *any* sweets, and I *need* something for pudding!" Before Janey could respond she went on. "He's being such a *fucking* bastard, I need my sweets, I *need* some pudding, Mummy, just do something!" Janey was about to form a response, but Robert came onto the phone instead.

"Janey, she's not listening, in fact she's been absolutely awful all weekend, I'm about to lose my rag and you of *all* people know that's unusual for me." Hearing Robert's voice was gratifying. She'd missed him, at least.

"Yes, I know, you're usually the one that stays cool," admitted Janey, concluding to herself that he didn't sound very *cool* right now, however she wholeheartedly sympathised with him.

"Janey love, how do you cope when I go away for work?" It sounded like Robert was exhausted, and again, there was not one part of Janey that did not empathise. Who could blame him? *Ruby is quite honestly a child from hell*, she thought.

"I *don't* cope," snorted Janey, with a hint of jest. "That's why I'm so bat-shit crazy." Ruby's raging and roaring could be heard in the background, with insult after insult thrown at her father, and Lorelei could hear the commotion remarkably well, despite now not having her own ear to the handset.

"Look Robert, I'll be home later. Hopefully she'll be asleep by then, but if not, I'll deal with it, or try to, at least." She tried to give him reassurance the end would be in sight.

In the background, Janey heard an almighty thud, followed by an unusual hot-tempered yell from Robert. "*Ruby!* Don't you dare!" Then turning his attention back to the phone call, he revealed. "That *little* — she's just thrown my cup of coffee down the stairs."

"Oh gosh, darling, dare I ask why she was not allowed the sweets in the first place?"

"If my fourteen-year-old daughter thinks she can speak to me in the way in which she does, then she has another thing coming. I would never have believed a daughter of mine could be so destructive and hateful. Honestly, *she needs help* Janey…"

"*We all do.* I'm going to contact the doctor again, and speak to the school again, heck, maybe I'll call social services *again.*"

Murmuring in agreement, Robert continued. "We may have to. We don't seem to have access to the kind of help other families get. Just look at Lauren and Steve and their son, Thomas. They've had him referred to an educational psychologist!" Janey could hear the state of despair in Robert's voice.

"But their son has academic issues too and fits the profile of being severely autistic. Ruby, however, presents as an intelligent and neurotypical child, in front of the doctors anyway, if only they could see what she was like with us…" She recalled the countless tantrums resulting in Ruby breaking things and causing so much distress and damage. "Okay, I hope you can manage to diffuse the situation, darling. Remember, if you can, ignore her *as much as possible*, she'll likely calm down and say sorry, then things will settle."

Tears of frustration could now be heard in Robert's voice. "I'll try. Maybe I should have given her the goddamn sweets and not tried to enforce the boundaries…"

"It's hard; there's no easy answer. Don't beat yourself up. She doesn't respond to normal discipline methods. We know this, but does that mean we don't give her consequences?"

"I don't know. When will she learn? Things are getting harder every day!" He paused. "And by the way, the weekend's outbursts were triggered by her extremely rude behaviour, demanding this and that, and not listening to any of my requests; just *normal* everyday requests, Janey."

"Yes, ones that other children would listen to and respect." She felt for Robert, she really did, but she was glad he was facing these problems as it demonstrated it was not just herself that Ruby had a lack of authority for. "I'm really sorry, it sounds like it's been a tough weekend. Just hold on in there." And with a hint of regret in her voice, she comforted her husband. "I'll be home soon."

"Bye darling, I love you. Have a safe trip." Before Robert had a chance to disconnect the call, Janey heard the screech of further abuse hurtling towards her husband, and the sound of something large crashing in the background. She clicked the end call button herself and turned to Lorelei.

"*Oh, I wish I could stay*, I wish I could run away, like you've been able to."

"Come on now, it's not exactly running away. I mean, what am I running from?!" Lorelei raised her hands in bemusement.

"Well, whatever it is, I wish I could do it too." She could so easily swap a life of parenting for the free and single life. She envied her sister. "Do I want to go back to Bristol? No, of course not. Do I love my life as a parent to an aggressive and violent child? *What do you think, Lorelei?* Okay, I love Robert, I do, but if there was a ticket out of here, if there was an escape for *me, I'd take it.*"

It was time to go. Janey had a train to catch. She flung her grey sports holdall over her shoulder and took a last look around Lorelei's flat. "Bye bye, little St Ives flat, until next time, I shall miss you."

The two sisters shot down the staircase and out the blue door before jumping into Lorelei's little yellow car.

"We'll just head down southwards directly. It won't take us long," Lorelei explained. The road was narrow, with fields on either side, some of which contained charming countryside ponies with brown and white coats. There was minimal traffic on this rural route as Lorelei had anticipated and they quickly proceeded along the edge of the Penwith moor with its imposing and eerie outcrops of rocks. Such myths and legends surrounded the area, which was gloriously haunting, and most certainly atmospheric. Moving onwards, they advanced alongside infrequent clusters of houses on the side of the road graced with whitewashed stone walls. Then, travelling further south, they saw the ruins of an old engine house (one of the many that clung to roadside verges or steep cliffs around Cornwall). They were a prominent reminder of the county's mining heritage.

Janey and Lorelei arrived at the train station with plenty of time for a coffee from a nearby café. The station itself was poorly equipped, with just three platforms serving the town of Penzance. Janey wrapped her arms around her little sister in an affectionate cuddle. "Oh, I feel heartbroken to have to leave you here, my little sister, all alone…"

"I am *fine*. I'm a big girl now. I will be perfectly fine." She paused before adding, "And happy."

Giving Lorelei's shoulder a gentle rub, Janey established her understanding. "Yes, I know you will be, you're so brave and I admire your strength through this whole divorce, and I truly applaud you for making this life-changing move." and referring to Jay she added, "It's about time you led a life free from *his* clutches."

Lorelei gave her sister a look with perplexity, for she had not considered herself brave at any point of her journey. "Strength? It's taken me years to escape from an abusive marriage! I haven't been strong at all. In fact, I've been quite the opposite — I've let Jay manipulate and oppress me for years. I haven't been strong, my darling sister, although I appreciate your sentiment."

Janey took her sister's hand in hers and squeezed her fingers. "Yes, but I understand how suffocating it has been for you, and *you've broken free* when you never thought you could."

Nodding with a growing sense of accomplishment, Lorelei replied with gratefulness. "Thank you, it means a lot, I suppose I should be a *little bit* proud. Listen, I really hope that Ruby's asleep when you get back and you can have a restful sleep yourself. If I can help, in any way at all, with Ruby, I will. You know that, right?"

"I'll manage, Lorelei, but yes, I know you would help. I do love my daughter, I really do. I'm sure everything will be okay in the end."

Lorelei smiled. "I'm sure too, and I don't doubt for one minute that you love her at all. I'll always be here for you both. I want to help. She does respond positively to me, more often than not."

"True. Thank you so much for this weekend. It's been a really lovely opportunity to spend some time together, just me and you. It's been special."

Lorelei concurred. "It has, now go. That train is due to leave any minute now. I love you."

"I love you too sis, I'll send you a message when I'm home."

Lorelei waved to her sister as Janey passed the ticket barriers and boarded the green and yellow cross-country train before it snaked off into the countryside. It would be a lengthy journey back to Bristol, and a journey that Janey reluctantly took. Lorelei padded glumly back to her car, with newfound resolve to help her sister. Surely there must be some help for them out there? She did worry though, because a family like Janey's had a tendency to slip through the net because they appeared so 'perfect', even to the professionals. Ruby did not come across as 'a child in need' compared to others. Snapping out of her thought-train on how to fix her sister's problems, right now Lorelei decided she had to focus on herself and settle into her new life in St Ives, and although she was desperately sad to see Janey leave, she had to stay *positive* about the future. Disturbed from her busy mind, Lorelei's phone buzzed loudly from within her pocket. It was Janey! *What did she want now? She only just left?*

"Janey?"

"It's Mum! She's been trying to call you! You need to call her — now!"

Saffron cake

"Lorelei, where *are* you? I've been trying to call you for the last forty-five minutes. What's the point of having a mobile phone if you *never* answer it!?"

Rolling her eyes, Lorelei *tried* to respond.

"—Lorelei, I'm outside your flat, there's nowhere to park, it's *very* narrow. I thought you'd be here to help me negotiate the space!" The sense of frustration in her mother's voice was evident.

"Mum, I wasn't expecting you until six thirty. I'm still over in Penzance. I'll be another twenty minutes or so."

"Dear Lord, Lorelei, I'm absolutely dying for a piddle, I can't park the car, even if I could, I can't leave the car anywhere *anyway,* with it being full of my belongings. This is ridiculous!"

It appeared that Iris was in one of her flaps, where she momentarily found it impossible to process anything with logical thinking.

Lorelei took a deep breath. "Mum, there's more parking up the street. Just make your way up the road and try to find somewhere. I'll be there really soon, promise."

"I hope so Lorelei. It's getting dark and I'm all on my

own. I've got valuables in the car. I'm not happy about this at all."

Lorelei was determined to avoid an argument, for that would be the last thing she needed. She was sure that her mother had said she was arriving in the early evening, and since when was early evening at five o'clock in the afternoon? She rushed to the payment machine and pushed a fifty pence piece into the slot for the short stay. She was reluctant to rush the journey because the country lanes weren't easy to navigate, and even more difficult to do so in the fading light.

It wasn't long before she was approaching St Ives town, and then the hill where she had expected her mother to be waiting, yet as she drew closer, she couldn't see her dear mother anywhere. Feeling a little agitated and panicky, she blew air out of her mouth. *Where had she gone?*

Lorelei was lucky to find a space to reverse into, squeezing in between two parked cars, which was fairly easy with her little vehicle. Immediately checking her phone and realising that there had been no messages or missed calls, Lorelei began to panic even more.

She put her phone to her ear and called her mother's mobile phone, which rang and rang with no answer, over and over again. It was dark now, and all sorts of things were running through Lorelei's mind — had she had an accident and been taken to hospital? What could have possibly happened in the last twenty-five minutes since they last spoke on the phone and just *why* was her mother not answering?

Lorelei threw the phone down on the passenger seat in exasperation. Should she stay at home and raise the alarm, or drive around the town to see if she could find her mother? She wasn't quite sure what the most logical course of action was. She called Janey and after a short ring, her sister picked up.

"Janey! Have you heard from Mum in the last twenty-five minutes?"

"Uh, no, why?"

"I've got back to my place, and she's not there, but she said that she *was* there about twenty-five minutes ago."

"That's really strange. You know what Mum's like, has she gone off to the shop in search of some Cornish saffron buns, thinking you'd be a lot longer?"

"It's possible that she's gone somewhere, but nothing's open here Janey, it's almost six now, it's November, it's dark. I mean, Tescos will be open but not a lot else, and I'm not even sure that Mum knows where the supermarket is!"

"Okay, it's a bit strange. You've tried calling her, I assume?"

"Of course, several times, but no reply. Should I drive around, or wait here?"

"Look, she won't be gone long, I'm sure of it."

"Yes, but what shall I do in the meantime?"

"Just hold fire for another five mins and then give her another call. She's probably just ventured to the supermarket, worried you don't have enough milk or something!"

"Hopefully it's just that!"

In the midst of Lorelei's foreboding uneasiness over her mother's wellbeing, Iris sat snugly inside a warm cottage on Tregenna Row, which was a good few miles up the road from Tregenna Lane, where Lorelei lived. It seemed there had been some confusion over the address. When Eleanor Trevarthan had peered out of her bedroom window, she had noticed a somewhat distressed lady outside on the street, having difficulty manoeuvring her rather smart looking metallic blue Land Rover Discovery on the small windy street. She became interested, not in the least because the lady was getting precariously close to the bumper of her own car, which was not quite as fancy as the Land Rover but nonetheless precious enough to force her to don her winter coat and brave the elements. Eleanor was in her sixties and lived with her husband Jago. He was reading the Echo in front of the fire when Eleanor came down the stairs announcing she was going out. They both had lovely Cornish accents.

"Dear, there's a lady out there parking, well *attempting* to park, and I'm a little worried she's going to bump our car."

"Oh well, what are you going to do, Ellie?"

"Well, I'm going to help her, of course. Put the kettle on, will you dear, and do we have some of that saffron cake left?"

"Well, I should think so, dear. Are we expecting guests?" He chuckled, the friendly soul he was.

Eleanor zipped up her jacket and stepped out of her front door, observing the woman, who was becoming increasingly distressed. Now outside of her vehicle, observing with disgruntlement the space that she was trying to fit her sizable four by four into.

"Excuse me!" Eleanor called.

Looking up at the friendly, well-meaning lady, Iris paused. "Erm — yes?"

"I can see that you're having some difficulty there. Let me help you," Eleanor said. Between the two of them, they managed to inch the Land Rover back and forth until it was perfectly nestled between the two cars, and once finally in, a sigh of relief was let out by both ladies.

"Oh, thank you, I am so very grateful. I'm coming to see my daughter. She's just moved down here," explained Iris.

"Oh, how lovely!" Eleanor exclaimed with delight, whilst wrapping her scarf back around her neck, for the wind was strong and it had blown off.

"Yes, she's had a difficult time, you see. She's making enormous life changes, you see."

"I see."

"So, yes, I've come to stay with her for the next few days." Iris continued to give much more information than necessary, as she so often did.

"Which number on the street does she reside in? I must admit, I haven't seen any new neighbours move in lately."

Iris looked around and struggled to make out the house numbers in the dark. "It's number twenty-six."

"It can't be number twenty-six."

"Why on earth not?"

"Because this is number twenty-six…" Eleanor pointed to the front door of her own property.

"Oh *super*! I've arrived right on the doorstep. Lorelei will be so pleased I've found it with no problems, but she's out at the moment, she's coming back from Penzance, I'll just wait here in my car."

Eleanor raised her voice just slightly, in order to make it heard just a little more, as it seemed to her that the lady was not understanding the message she was trying to deliver.

"No," she said, her accent unmistakably Cornish. "I don't think you understand. It *can't* be number twenty-six because number twenty-six is where *I live*."

Iris sighed. "No dear, my daughter lives here, at number twenty-six Tregenna Lane. I remember the blue door."

"Tregenna Lane? You're on the wrong street, this is Tregenna Row!" exclaimed Eleanor, now understanding the lady's confusion. "Listen now, you look as if you've had a long journey, and need a nice slice of saffron cake and a cup of tea, won't you join me and my husband Jago?"

Now, at the mention of saffron cake, Eleanor had Iris's full attention. Saffron cake was an undeniable favourite of all teatime treats — how could she refuse such a kind offer, after all, the lady rightly observed, it *had* been a very long journey.

"I would be delighted, that's very kind of you, I should like that very much, indeed!"

Iris was shown into the lady's beautifully rustic cottage which was warm and welcoming with the fire burning. In front of the flames, on a red leather chair, sat Jago, still reading his newspaper.

"So, my name's Eleanor, or you can call me Ellie, and this is Jago, my better half, and I didn't catch your name?" She turned to her husband. "*Jago* get off of that there old armchair, and get our guest some tea and cake!"

"My name's Iris," she said, passing her coat to Eleanor. "Thanks terribly for your help this evening. Haven't you got a lovely home!"

"Thank you. A lot of these are holiday homes now, but we've kept it on. It's hard in the winter; can get cold, and it's rather isolated."

"I can relate to that. I live in a small village on the edge of Dartmoor on my own." She looked around at the wonderful wooden beams in the cottage and the delightful paintings that clung to the wall. "My older daughter who lives in Bristol keeps begging me to move to the city, but now that my youngest daughter is down here, it's a difficult decision to make. They lost their father last year. It's been a tough time."

Nodding, Eleanor sympathised. "I'm so sorry for your loss. I don't know what I'd do if, God forbid, I were to lose Jago, I hope I go 'fore him! But I do know what it's like to lose someone…" she trailed off and for a moment her bubbly expression faded, and she looked numb.

"Are you alright?" Iris asked.

"Yes, yes, just caught for a moment in a memory. Grief is a funny thing, never really leaves you."

Iris explained how silly she had been to confuse the two addresses, for she knew very well it was an art gallery that Lorelei lived above. "It's been a long trip. We can just put that down to a senior moment," she laughed.

Jago brought in a metal trolley on wheels with a white lacy cloth laid on the top tray. Upon it lay a pot of tea with matching teacups, and a generous portion of sliced saffron cake with what looked like *real* butter.

"Oh, look at that. What hospitality!" approved Iris with much satisfaction and newfound admiration for her new 'friends'. "Did you make it?"

"Oh yes, I don't usually, but over the winter months the little bakery in the town is closed, but your own baked goods don't compare to the likes of the big superstores."

"It looks very good; may I use your lavatory before I tuck in?"

"Of course, 'tis just at the top of the stairs."

Iris gratefully took a slice of cake and placed it on to one of the little plates on the trolley. Eleanor smiled; it was nice to see her guest appreciating the food.

"I have a son, you know," said Eleanor, out of the blue. "He's a writer, lives in Hayle, a town a few miles away."

"I know Hayle well; we stayed many times at a holiday park there when the girls were growing up."

"Ah, so you did, wonderful stretch of coast up there, a beautiful beach. Yes, he lives there. He's a lovely boy; he comes to see us quite often, I couldn't imagine having a child so far away like you do, even if they *are* grown up."

"Well, my Janey, she moved to the city a hundred and twenty miles away when she was just sixteen — she's done ever so well for herself."

"Just sixteen? My!"

"Yes, my other one left for university only a few years older than that, studied nursing."

"Must have been hard."

"Yes, it was." Iris was inquisitive herself. "So, you say your son's a writer?" Iris asked, and Eleanor nodded. "Is that his main profession?"

"Sadly not, it's hard to earn a living writing poetry. There's not that much money in it, but he does attend local events and has had a poetry book published."

"How lovely. You must be so proud of him. My Janey, she loves books, was always writing stories as a child, and oh my, the diaries that girl wrote …"

The ladies exchanged more pleasantries and stories about their families whilst drinking their tea, while Jago retired to his newspaper in front of the fire. Iris had not realised the time ticking on, and by now it was approaching seven o'clock.

"Oh, my goodness, look at the time, Iris. Hadn't you better contact your daughter, won't she be wondering where you are?"

"Oh, I'm sure she's not worried about me — she's probably at home preparing some food for us."

By now, Lorelei was becoming frantic with worry. She had still not been able to reach her mother by telephone and now, having waited a good twenty minutes or more, she decided to drive around the town to see if she could find her. Perhaps she'd fallen asleep in the car, perhaps she'd broken down somewhere, or got lost?

Perhaps she'd had a heart attack and been taken to hospital! Janey had suggested when Lorelei contacted her for a second time — she was always quite the optimist. Lorelei tried to call her mother again, and this time the phone went straight to voicemail.

Before calling the authorities, Lorelei would have a further drive around herself to see if she could find her mother, but if she had no luck, she would have no choice but to call the police.

Iris reached inside her handbag for her mobile phone.

"Perhaps you're right Eleanor, I should get back, but I'm sure my daughter would have called me by now had she been worried." She retrieved her handset from the zip pocket in her bag and pressed the button at the front of the handset to activate the screen, but nothing happened. Iris shook the phone, as if that really was going to help. "Something's wrong with my phone — I think the damn thing's run out of battery."

"Oh no, do you know what her number is from memory?"

"I'm afraid I don't, but I must have it written down somewhere in my diary."

"I think we need to get you back to your daughter, Tregenna Lane is not too far away. She could come here and collect you; you could leave your car here."

"Oh no, I can't do that; I've got all my bags in there!"

"She could always move them into her car for you. I think it would be best."

Iris continued to search her bag for her diary,

muttering, "I know it's in here somewhere...."

Lorelei scanned the parked cars as she drove past. Her phone began to ring, but she couldn't reach it on the back seat, and besides, she was driving and therefore couldn't take a call legally. When the ringing did not cease, she thought it could well be her mother calling, so she stopped the car in the middle of the road and reached for the telephone. A missed call was displayed that came from a St Ives area code. She hit the call return button, and a lady answered.

"Hello, Eleanor Trevarthen speaking."

"Oh, hello, I just had a missed call from you."

"Oh yes, dear, your mother just called you." Eleanor passed the phone over to Iris.

"Darling! I'm so glad you called back!"

"*Mother, where* are you?"

"Well, there's been a mix-up dear, and I've ended up at twenty-six Tregenna Row and not Tregenna *Lane*. You should be clearer with your directions, darling—"

"—Me?! I should be clearer!? You never listen. I've been worried sick about you."

"Oh, you shouldn't have worried, Lorelei. I've been fed and watered and had some lovely company."

Ignoring her mother's pleasantries, she confirmed the address. "Tregenna Row, you say? Number twenty-six? I'll be right there, and mother, *I am not* happy!"

Before proceeding towards the address where her mother had been having a 'lovely time', she sent a quick text to Janey, giving her an update on the situation. Then, keying the address into the sat nav, she set off to the destination to retrieve her mother. It wasn't long before she spotted a perfectly parked metallic blue Land Rover, recognisable as her mother's by the number plate which concluded with MMF, which she always remembered as *My Mad Family*!

Lorelei had no choice but to park some distance away and had to walk a few hundred yards towards number twenty-six. She then knocked on the door, which was painted blue, just like her own front door.

To her surprise, her mother answered the door, which was quite surreal. Iris wasted no time and went on to introduce Lorelei to Jago and Eleanor, before taking it upon herself to offer her a cup of tea and some saffron cake.

"Oh Mum, I would love to, but it's so late now and we should get you back." Turning to Eleanor, Lorelei smiled. "Thanks so much for looking after Mum and sorry for any inconvenience."

"Not at all, love, and your mum has told me all about you. I'm sorry for the challenges you've faced, dear, and I hope you'll be happier down here in St Ives."

Lorelei shot a fleeting infuriated glare towards her mother. What on earth had she been telling this couple about her personal circumstances? Surely, gossip would spread around this small town like wildfire. She certainly didn't want her reputation being tarnished from the offset. Returning her eyes to Eleanor, she thanked her profusely once more, and they politely said their goodbyes.

Lorelei did decide to take Eleanor's advice and left the Land Rover where it was. She lifted her mother's luggage and transported it into her own car. Of course, the weekend bag had to go on the back seat because there wasn't much room in the boot of these little city cars.

Soon they arrived at twenty-six Tregenna Lane. Lorelei would give her room to her mother for the duration of her stay while she would sleep on the sofa.

Over a further cup of tea, they held a conversation

about the importance of answering your mobile phone, carrying a power pack, and making sure correct information is taken down to avoid mix-ups such as the one that happened this evening. After the tears (from Lorelei) and the frustration (from Iris), mother and daughter hugged and told each other that they loved one another.

They decided to make a nice cottage pie, with meat free mince and broccoli, and then watch 'Countryfile' followed by an early night. Lorelei was so pleased to have her mum there for a short stay, despite the unfortunate start, and looked forward to spending one-on-one time with her over the next few days. That evening Iris retired to the bedroom before nine and Lorelei had neither the will nor energy to stay up any later herself, so instead, she closed her eyes and tried to think of a vague plan for the beginning of the week, but her mind kept on thinking of things she really didn't want to think of. Images of Jay kept flooding to her mind's eye. She just couldn't seem to shift them and then, when she finally did, images of her poor dad replaced them. Oh, how she wished there was a switch she could flick, so she didn't have to be plagued by these moments in time each night. As an antidote she tried to think of her father before he was poorly, to counteract the less pleasant imagery that so often tormented her, and luckily in not too long a time her tiredness overcame her, and she fell into a deep and nourishing sleep that was so thoroughly required.

The holed stone

To Lorelei and Iris's delight, the West of Cornwall had been blessed with a spell of clear and dry weather for the week ahead. The pair were delighted, for it was perfect for a few days of enjoying the fresh air and visiting some favourite and much loved locations. It was just like a mini holiday, except Lorelei wasn't on vacation — *she actually lived there*, finally, in her most treasured, most magical Cornwall. A county saturated in myth and folklore, and one which had a unique energy. Cornwall never ceased to invigorate her imagination with four hundred miles of rugged coastlines and tempestuous oceans, and of course, full to the brim with charm and all the Cornish Piskies you could wish for. Not to mention cream teas and Cornish ice cream too, oh, and fudge and rock. Although Lorelei wasn't too keen on rock, unless it was of the fruity kind rather than the traditional minty variety. Though crumbly fudge was her overall weakness, walnut and honey, or perhaps just plain clotted cream. Lorelei was looking forward to spending some quality time with her mum and just taking pleasure in all that Cornwall had to offer.

After a tasty breakfast of tea and poached egg on toast, the strategy for the day ahead was formulated. As young children Lorelei and her sister had been dragged around the antiquities of West Cornwall and the fascination had somewhat rubbed off on Lorelei, although it had been a while since she had paid a visit to her old friend, the 'Men an Tol'. In fact, it had been a long while. She had once come down with Jay in the youth of their relationship, where she had playfully pushed him through the 'holed' stone. More happy memories came flooding back through those rose-tinted spectacles.

"Are we not so lucky with this weather?" Iris remarked. "I know it's cold, but at least the rain is going to stay away. It's quite perfect for this time of year, is it not?"

Agreeing, Lorelei chirped, "Isn't it just! I can't wait to drive along the coast road towards Land's End."

"Absolutely, it's really one of the most spectacular roads in the whole of Britain!"

"It is. Don't be fooled by the blue skies, though," Lorelei warned. "Wrap up warm!"

"Of course, you don't have to tell me that. You know me, I'm always prepared!" Iris nodded towards her pile of winter wear, including a winter coat, gloves, hat, and a scarf, all looking very woolly and sensible.

They set out into the fresh crisp morning air with walking poles too, for if they were planning on finding some of the standing stones they would be treading on uneven footpaths, and as Iris always said, "Don't walk the moor without a stick! And wear long socks to protect from scratches and ticks!" Although there wasn't much chance of tick activity in the winter months.

"I'm worried about your sister, dear," Iris suddenly exclaimed. "She's really not been herself lately, and ever since your poor old dad passed away, well, she's been crippled with anxiety."

"I know, and the additional pressure with Ruby doesn't help."

Iris nodded, and her expression saddened as she reflected. "I'd offer to have Ruby over the holidays next year but I daren't. I mean, ever since she had that tantrum when we all went to Paignton for the day, when she pushed me over. I honestly daren't spend any time alone with her." As sad as it was to say, it was true. Iris, although not exactly a frail old lady, was now in her seventies, and Ruby's unpredictable personality was a real worry for her grandmother's safety.

"Yes, I know, but I don't think she realised she would actually knock you down."

"What are you talking about, Lorelei? She's a fourteen-year-old girl, not a four-year-old. She's got a real temper, that girl, and I don't see it getting any better anytime soon."

"Perhaps Ruby can stay with me for half term, or in the summer holidays for a few weeks," contemplated Lorelei. "She tends to behave reasonably with me, well, most of the time."

"Well, that would certainly provide a welcome break for your sister. I can't understand where she gets it from, love. Yes, Janey's a worrier, to say the least, but growing up she never had an aggressive or naughty side, and Robert, well, he's placid in personality."

"It's a mystery."

Quite into the journey by now, Iris enjoyed the view as Lorelei cruised down the wonderful coast road towards Lands' End, the most westerly point of Britain. To their left, the haunting Penwith Moors stood with its dramatic granite stacks, looking less foreboding than usual in the lovely sunshine that they were being treated to. To the right of them the Atlantic Ocean, blue as if it were the height of summer, stretched out for thousands of miles, not stopping until the shores of America. It was so incredibly beautiful.

Lorelei's heart fervently belonged to the ocean. She had always felt at peace when close to water, finding it a very comforting place to be. Of course, not for one moment underestimating its power. She remembered a shipwreck upon the rocks at Lands' End, HMS Mulheim, which had been there for nearly twenty years, slowly rotting away, and the many more that served as a merciless reminder of the relentlessness of the sea.

They bimbled along the narrow road, past abandoned farm outbuildings where a ginger tabby scampered around the occasional cluster of houses. Stone walls lined the inhabited areas, and one had a red post box built into it. They continued past the ruined engine house of Carn Galver Mine, where one could enjoy a breathtaking walk down to the cliff edge for stunning views across the sea and coast. Iris had her ordnance survey map in her hand. It filled the entire passenger seat and was ripped in several places, not to mention coffee stained, and it would be fair to say it was in dire need of replacement.

"Right, we're going to be taking a left turn any minute now, so slow down now Lorelei," instructed Iris to her daughter. Despite having visited the Men an Tol on various occasions, it was still always somewhat of a palaver to reach it. Many of the left turns looked the same, and it would be easy to make a mistake.

This day the gods were on their side, and they arrived with no problems at the lay-by where just a small number of cars were able to park along the verge. Strangely, today the lay-by was in fact empty. At the height of the summer, getting a moment alone with the stones was quite rare with the constant stream of visitors. Lorelei and Iris had not visited in late

November before, so were not quite sure what they might expect, but thus far, the area was an isolated spot for their pleasure only.

They passed through the metal gate onto the track that would lead up to the part of the moor where the stones were located. It was a relatively short walk, perhaps fifteen minutes or so over a stoney track. The ground was cold and stiff beneath their feet.

"Ooh, isn't it a bit eerie at this time of year, Mum?" Lorelei remarked, buttoning up her coat right to the collar.

Iris agreed, also doing up her own coat, for there was a sudden nipping bite to the air. "It is a bit; no sign of anyone else around. Rather spooky!"

"Rather spooky!?" Lorelei was surprised by her mother's description given the fact that in recent years she had become quite the atheist, very much in favour of scientific explanations for any and all abnormal occurrences.

"Yes, well, this part of West Cornwall is notoriously queer."

Undeniably, the wild stretch of moorland was devilishly haunting. Stretching out across the peninsula of West Cornwall on a bedrock of granite, there were many ghostly tales passed down from generation to generation.

"I remember a story from when I was nursing from a dear old chap who once lived out here…" Iris began to recount the tale with an air of mystery in her now quite theatrical voice. "He wasn't the type that would make things up Lorelei. He was a respectable man. He was a relative of Lord Barnley, I'll have you know."

"Okay…"

"So, when he was a young boy, he saw something that would stick with him for the *rest of his life,* and it did Lorelei, until his dying day."

"Go on…"

"He was walking home from school one winter's afternoon. It was later than usual, as he'd been kept behind to finish some work."

"*He had a detention?*"

"I'm not sure, Lorelei, it was just later than usual, and it was therefore *dark*…"

"Ooh," mocked Lorelei, in a spooky voice.

"Stop it, will you! I'm trying to tell a story here."

"Okay." Lorelei bit her lip and tried to be serious.

"So, yes, the young cousin to Lord Barnley, was walking through the village somewhere on the edge of Penwith Moor. It was early evening, and the sun had set, leaving a peculiar ambience about the air. He noticed a woman with even more old-fashioned clothes on than what they themselves were wearing back then. She was struggling with her pram, and of course, being the fine young gentleman he was, he offered a hand, but the young woman disappeared into thin air!"

"What, simply vanished in front of his eyes? That's very spooky."

"Yes, apparently so…"

Lorelei shivered. "That story is very eerie; I wonder who she was."

"Indeed."

"I thought you didn't believe in all that, mother?"

"Dear, just because I've turned away from God, doesn't mean I am not open to other realms of possibilities. When it comes to spirits and what have you, one must have an open mind."

With that thought, the two of them walked in relative silence, breathing in the energy from the scenery, deep in their own thoughts until they reached a small stone style and some steps to the right of the path. Alongside the steps lay a wooden post with the words 'Men an Tol' carved into it, and once they had hopped over the little stone crossing, the enigmatic ancient stones were almost in sight. Lorelei and Iris eagerly continued along the path that had been beaten into the moorland over the years where tourists had trekked back and forth.

A few steps onwards, and the curious site came into their view. It wasn't very magnificent. In fact, the stones themselves were small, yet entirely intriguing. Two upright stones stood on either side of the celebrated holed stone, which looked like a ring doughnut. The local legend told that those who passed through the stone would be cured of illness, particularly children if they were passed through three times, for according to folklore, it would cure them from tuberculosis or rickets.

Quite unlike the summer months, the site was deserted. The air was still; it was peaceful, yet something in the air felt heavy, strange even. Lorelei walked between the stones, then ran her hands over the unusual, holed centre piece. It is said that the stones were not in the same position as they were originally, having been moved several times over the last six hundred years.

Iris took a moment to rest her legs by sitting down on one of the many stones scattered half buried into the ground and watched her daughter as she crouched down and crawled through the hole herself. Upon crawling out, she felt something tickle the back of her neck and she reached around to flick away whatever was causing the irritation, which had caught her quite by surprise. Upon feeling something on her hand, she jumped around hysterically, quite disturbing the peace on the quiet moor.

"Ahh! Something just landed on my neck! I think it's

a creepy crawly!"

Iris rushed over as quickly as she could from her seated position to see whatever was the matter. Lorelei was still jumping around in a panic over what had landed on her neck.

"Keep still," demanded her mother, as Lorelei continued to flap around uncontrollably. Her mother retrieved the item, which happened to be a black feather. Iris identified it as 'probably' a crow's feather. Lorelei held the feather in her hand and held it up at an arm's length, examining it carefully.

"How strange this feather landed on me. What could it mean, Mum?"

"What can it mean? It means a feather just landed on you, dear, because of the way the wind was blowing."

Lorelei sighed with confusion. "Just a minute ago you were all superstitious about ghost stories, and now you think it's a total coincidence that a black feather landed on my neck on Penwith Moor?"

"Actually, come to think of it, I think there is a superstition associated with black feathers. Can you look it up on your phone, Lorelei?"

Lorelei pulled her mobile phone out of her coat pocket and typed the question into Google, and read what she discovered out loud to her mum.

> *Someone you loved and lost is watching over you and protecting you. The appearance of a black feather may suggest that a little negativity is heading your way but, with the help of this special someone, you'll get through any rough patches and emerge stronger than ever before.*

Iris tilted her head. "Hmm, or a black feather just happened to fall on you for no particular reason, just chance, but nevertheless it's nice to suppose your dad is here with us."

With that sentiment Lorelei was just about to toss the feather back into the air but then unexpectedly felt the urge to keep it as a souvenir from the day, so carefully placed it behind the case of her mobile phone for safekeeping.

The two of them spent a few more minutes at the stones and Lorelei took some 'arty' photographs before heading back down the rural track back to the lay-by where the car had been happily waiting for them. The entire time that they were at the ancient site, they saw not one other visitor. It had indeed been a special time, and Lorelei felt altogether quite spiritual, especially because of the feather that had 'found' her. She tried to forget about any negative association that occurred alongside black feathers, because in general, she felt closer to her father after the occurrence. The more she thought about it, the more she believed that the mystical offering that was sent from above was mysteriously relevant in some way or another.

Iris and Lorelei enjoyed a drive further west, stopping in St Just for the customary Cornish Pasty (well, Lorelei had the cheese and vegetable variety, which was equally delicious). The rest of the day was pleasant, and both women enjoyed each other's company. They drove around the whole peninsula, stopping off at a few more favourite spots, including Porthgwarra, a picturesque fishing village with a small, secluded beach at the end of a cobbled slipway. Porthgwarra was complete with man-made tunnels and a cave. It was a charming location and had been used in several scenes in the popular TV adaptation of Winston Graham's books, Poldark. Iris knew all the little treasures to visit, and Porthgwarra did not disappoint.

The following days passed by quickly and before Lorelei knew it, it was Tuesday and time for her mum to return home. Iris could not leave her cat, Tilly, for too long. Even though the neighbour was popping in to feed her, Iris didn't like to be away for more than a few days. Lorelei wept as she watched Iris drive away, down the windy road, for now she was quite truly on her own, and she would miss the company of her dear mother. Yet it was now time to build her new life, and to stand on her own two feet. She looked forward to meeting new friends within the community, but her next number one priority was to find herself a job because, although she'd have quite liked to remain as free as a bird, reality had to prevail.

Reason Five Thousand

Some weeks had passed, and Lorelei was feeling comfortably settled in her new home. It was now moving into December with Christmas fast approaching, and she had still not been successful in securing employment. Lorelei was enjoying a lie in, which was a luxury she had not afforded to herself much over the years. It was dark and she was still very much in the land of nod.

    Her phone was ringing, in fact it had been ringing for some time, but Lorelei had turned the phone on silent during the night. The gentle buzzing of the handset therefore woke her where it was vibrating on her bedside table. She reached out to retrieve the phone. *Six missed calls!* She noted the number and realised it was Janey. "Oh no, what's happened now...?" she murmured out loud, still half asleep before answering.

    "Hello Janey..." she said, letting out a yawn, but all Lorelei got in response was an uncontrollable sobbing noise emanating from her clearly very distressed sister. She pulled the handset away from her ear because Janey's screeching was so very deafening, and certainly not welcome, especially at this hour.

"Janey, what's going on?" Lorelei asked, knowing only too well it could not possibly be anything other than one of Ruby's infamous meltdowns.

"Ro-Ro-Robert's away…" Janey struggled to get her words out, stuttering and blubbering as she tried.

"Janey, *breathe*…" Lorelei, in attempt to calm her sister, repeated slowly. "Breathe…" Lorelei had become rather accustomed to this type of telephone call over the years, and their occurrences seemed to have become even more frequent of late.

"I *can't* cope anymore. Robert's away, there's no one to help, she's gone off on one. Oh Lorelei—" Janey turned her attention to Ruby. "Get upstairs now! Get away from me!".

Lorelei pulled the phone away from her ear again to avoid being deafened by her sister's screams which, although directed at Ruby, were travelling down the phone with resonance.

Part of the reason Lorelei had never desired children of her own was because of how Ruby had turned out. She had seen in close enough proximity how crippling it could be to raise a spirited child, and no doubt it would be just her luck that any child of hers would be just as spirited. No, Lorelei just couldn't take the risk, not after seeing how parenting had dealt her sister such an unyielding hand.

"Janey, put her on the phone to me." A concerned and somewhat frustrated Lorelei sighed. Sometimes Ruby would listen to her aunt and Lorelei felt that there was a chance that she may get through to her.

"Ruby, Auntie Lorelei wants to speak to you."

"No! I don't want to speak to *her*!" came the reply. Ruby was a stubborn creature with an oppositional and reactive personality. She was also extremely changeable, often going from naught to sixty in the blink of an eye. Those who were close to her, who witnessed first-hand her frequent emotional eruptions, would often describe her as unpredictable. Janey's little bubbling volcano had always been this way, since she was only twelve months old. At nursery she was labelled as the 'biter', the 'hitter' the 'pincher', causing Janey much anxiety, for she always had dreaded the daily pickup, fearful of what her daughter had done to the other children that day. Everybody said, "she'll be better next year," but next year came, and she never was.

"I can't cope anymore," Janey moaned in desperation. She was slumped in the hallway with her knees drawn up to her chest in some sort of sorry fetal position.

"I know. I know it's really difficult, but tell me, what triggered this meltdown? What *actually* happened?"

Janey thought for a moment whilst digging her long nails into her shins. She started scratching her legs until white scratches turned to red lines. Her anxiety was getting the better of her. She sobbed while trying to structure a reply. "I-I don't even really know, she just explodes. It escalates so quickly!" Janey's mind was racing as she tried to retrace the events. "So, I made her breakfast; it was 'Shredded Wheat' because the 'Cocoa Pops' had run out. She turned her nose up at it, and demanded something else," she sniffled. "Well, I'm not doing it Lorelei, I'm just not. Mum wouldn't just throw away good food because we didn't like it. It's a waste, and she's eaten it before…" Janey felt exasperated, and this reflected in her tone.

"Okay," Lorelei prompted, "and then…?" Janey went on in a state of hysteria.

"Well, she just refused, and when I told her there's nothing else and it was Shredded Wheat or nothing, she picked up the bowl and let it all slide out onto the floor! What does she think she's playing at? She's such a spiteful little bitch, I mean, thank goodness we have laminate, but still…"

Janey continued to explain how Ruby had refused to clean up the spilled food, instead spreading it around the floor even more with her foot with a look of pure satisfaction on her face, knowing how much this was annoying her mother, who she knew was very house proud.

"I told her, if she didn't get the kitchen roll and start cleaning this mess up, she'd not have her mobile phone for the rest of the week."

The threat of having her phone taken away had really set Ruby's temper into full swing.

"*Yes, I am!*" she had said. "*You can't stop me!*" She had then bulldozed past her mother into the kitchen to reach her phone. In doing so Janey had blocked her daughter, holding her arms to restrain her.

"Then, Lorelei, do you know what that little bitch did? She only went and *spat* in my face!"

Lorelei glanced at her bedside clock — it was only just gone half-past eight in the morning; all this drama and it wasn't even nine o'clock?! *Reason five thousand to not have any kids of my own*, Lorelei thought quietly to herself. Just when she thought things may be calming down, there was an almighty bang, and her sister screamed.

"She's just thrown the bloody bathroom scales down the stairs! She's got no respect! I can't stand this!" Janey growled at her daughter, "*Look what you've done*! They're broken! These were my dad's! What do you think he would say if he were alive?!"

"I don't fucking care," came the reply. "*He's fucking dead. He doesn't know!*"

"Okay, calm down," Lorelei guided her sister. "Walk away into another room. Is she dressed and ready for school?" asked Lorelei, to which Janey confirmed she was. "Good. So, you need to just get her out of the house to the bus stop. Good god, haven't you normally left by now? You need to be at work at, like, thirty minutes ago."

"Ruby, downstairs *now!*" Janey hollered up the stairs to her daughter. "You need to get to that bus stop *now!*" Ruby bounded down the stairs, pushing past her mother on her way through and shot out of the front door, slamming it with unnecessary force behind her. The tornado calmed with the exit of the eye of the storm, and Janey could finally breathe.

Dreadful as it sounds, this kind of start to the day wasn't unusual for Janey and Robert. This morning had been slightly more challenging, given the fact that Robert had been away and was not there to help. Janey found it much more difficult to deal with Ruby's behaviour when he wasn't there to back her up.

No one could deny that Janey and Ruby had what some may describe as a toxic relationship. They loved each other fiercely, of course, but with a build-up of years of dealing with Ruby's outbursts came much friction, and their relationship was clearly damaged, perhaps beyond repair. Janey tried hard with her daughter, always with good intentions to manage situations as best she could, but parenting Ruby wasn't easy, to say the least. Throughout her life, the persistent rows had on more than one occasion resulted in Janey shouting and screaming at Ruby and saying things that no rational human being would even dream of.

"Oh Janey, I don't know what you're going to do about her. You need to speak to the school again, she seems to be getting worse." Lorelei paused to think for a second. "You know… you need to try to avoid these situations. Just make sure you've got the cereal that she likes. You need to be more *organised*."

Janey began to wail uncontrollably again. "I know, it's

just she goes through the food so quickly, I was working late last night, and didn't manage to get to the shop…" Janey knew in her heart that she did indeed need to become more orderly but often felt so hopeless with the demands of being Ruby's mother (as well as her professional commitments), that organisation outside of work sometimes seemed practically impossible.

"Okay, just make sure you get some later, and maybe buy a few packets. You better get to work."

The girls wrapped up the conversation and Lorelei curled herself up snuggly in her warm feather duvet again knowing that really, she should get up soon, as she had to try to find a job for herself, but for now another twenty minutes of shut-eye was the next item on the agenda.

Twenty minutes became a couple of hours and by the time Lorelei rolled out of bed, the hour was approaching ten thirty. Stretching out her arm towards the little bedside table, she reached for her mobile, cradling it like a rescued baby bird. No more messages from Janey — that was a relief. She checked her social media, eagerly scanning through her news feed and liking a few pictures posted by her family and a few work colleagues from back home. It was nice to see some old faces, although she wasn't missing life in the city, not even a fraction. Lorelei had high expectations that her friend list would grow and grow and keep growing in the near future as she met new people in the town. She was absolutely delighted to have ventured back onto the social media platform, having no one other than herself to answer to, regarding the amount of time she spent browsing.

Noticing a new friend request, Lorelei clicked on the little red icon to see who it was from. Susan Davis. *Susan Davis, Susan Davis…* The name was vaguely familiar, but she couldn't quite put her finger on it. Clicking on the profile for more information, she noted an occupation listed, NHS in Bristol. "*Of course,*" Lorelei muttered. She must be that nurse from Paediatrics that Lorelei sometimes met in the cafe before her shift started. *Ah yes, Susan. How nice that she found me and wanted to stay in touch*, she thought as she happily accepted the request, relishing the fact she had no one looking over her shoulder, and nobody controlling who she became friends with. Scrolling a little more down the feed, she saw her mother had posted a picture of her winter bird feeder with a pair of gorgeous bullfinches pecking at the seed. Her mother loved nature, especially birds, and fed them all year round. Iris loved the seaside in the same way Lorelei did, and that had been the reason Lorelei developed her love of Cornwall in the first place.

Today was the day that Lorelei was going to *seriously* start looking for a job. To a certain extent, there wasn't too much of a rush to find employment, but for now Lorelei wanted to fill her days and, more importantly, she wanted to meet new people. A reality hit her over the last few weeks that she didn't know anybody at all and was completely alone. Lorelei thought she would start by looking online to see what jobs had been listed, but before she could even start to think of sifting through job vacancies, she needed a cup of tea, and what would go so perfectly with that would be a nice pain au chocolate! A guilty pleasure, but such a delicious way to start the day. Bringing the breakfast refreshments back into her bedroom, she slurped the tea and enjoyed the pastry, and licking her lips in an attempt to motivate herself, she said out loud, "Right, let's do this!"

Typing the credentials into the search engine, much to her surprise, results appeared. "Maybe this won't be too difficult after all. Let's see. A waitress position, could I really do something so demanding as this?" she contemplated, continuing to scroll down to where more bar and restaurant positions were advertised. Then she spotted something else and said out loud, "A receptionist job in a hotel, that could be more like it. Fast-Food restaurant — *No, definitely not*!"

It was clear that hospitality jobs were plentiful, but she kept looking in case something special caught her attention. Of course, Lorelei knew that options for employment would be limited in a small Cornish town and the opportunity would be a fraction of what it was in the city.

It was eleven o'clock, and it looked dry outside, which was a welcome change from the recent downpours. Lorelei decided she would escape the confinements of the flat and walk down to the town shops to look around; Perhaps pick up a local newspaper and see if there were any positions in the shop windows that may interest her. She could have stayed in bed so easily, but if she didn't get some fresh air, and ended up spending her day at home, it would only make her feel miserable and depressed. She needed to speak to other people, to get to know the neighbourhood, and she wouldn't be able to succeed in this if she stayed cooped up inside the apartment, (regardless of how tempting that seemed).

After a refreshing shower, Lorelei left her little flat through the blue door and onto the quaint St Ives Street. After her father's death, his clothes had been mostly donated to charity, but Janey and Lorelei had kept some of his nice quality sweaters, and it was one of these that Lorelei had chosen to wear today. It was a yellow knitted jumper with pleats, and having it against her skin made her feel close to her dad. It was certainly the right weather to wear it being cold and wintery that day. After all, it was early December. As Lorelei stepped into the street, she saw the place was all but deserted, apart from a few locals going about their business. A stark contrast to the summer months in the thriving and busy town filled to the brim with tourists from all over the world. She remembered a time some years ago when she and Jay were at the Minack Theatre, which was an auditorium cut out of a granite cliff. They had met a lady from America who was on a European tour. She had just come from Glastonbury in Somerset and now stopped in Cornwall before heading on to France. It was just incredible to think how people from America came to little old Cornwall on holiday, although on reflection perhaps it was not surprising at all. The scenery was stunning beyond comprehension; the atmosphere was unique, and to be sure if the weather could be guaranteed no one would leave the country in search of paradise shores because it would be right by your doorstep. The problem was that Britain's weather could be so unpredictable and, even in midsummer, you could well be greeted with a wet and miserable climate.

Yet today, in early December, the air was crisp, and the rain did not show its miserable face. Of course, a chill to the air was apparent given the season, but popping outside for a short while was no inconvenience. Lorelei stood outside a newsagent that she hadn't yet popped into since moving to St Ives. She stood reading the cards in the window. A lost cat, holistic therapy services, a local writers' club, but no jobs on the notice board. With a sigh, Lorelei entered the store and wandered over to the newspaper stand. She stood there staring at the options. The St Ives Echo and St Ives Times seemed to be the two local papers, so she scooped up a copy of each and made her way to the till.

"Hello love!" said the lady behind the counter. She was a slender woman, perhaps in her sixties, with her grey hair tied behind her head in a loose bundle, and a purple streak tucked behind her ear. She had a pair of wide brim tortoiseshell reading glasses around her neck and wore a rainbow knitted jumper that looked to be a size too small. A warm smile crept over her kind and generous looking face.

"How are you, my deary?" The lady spoke as if she was already quite familiar with Lorelei, yet in fact, they had not had the pleasure of each other's company before.

"Hi, yes, I'm good. Thank you, and you?" Lorelei replied in a manner just as warm, for it was her nature to be polite and courteous.

"It's just, I've not seen you around, my deary. Are you new to the town?" she said, taking the newspapers from Lorelei. Although presenting outwardly considerate, Lorelei began to wonder if all shopkeepers would be so nosy in Cornwall.

"Oh yes, I moved not long ago, all the way from Bristol."

"Ah, I see… so what do you do, deary? You work local, do you?"

Lorelei smiled and shook her head regretfully. "I'm afraid I'm yet to find a job here. That's why I'm picking up these papers to see if there's anything around."

The lady smiled and scanned the papers. "I see. So, what is it exactly that you're looking to do, my love? That'll be £1.40 please." Lorelei handed over a twenty-pound note.

"You don't have something smaller, my love?" Lorelei shook her head.

"I'm sorry, no. I can use my debit card if you don't have the change."

The curious lady replied compassionately. "It be best, deary, but there *is* a fifty pence surcharge, my love, as it's under five pounds."

Lorelei presented her card to the machine, and quickly

Hope by the sea

realised there was a problem.

"Oh no, my love, we're not contactless, not yet, pop the card in, deary."

Probing again, the inquisitive lady asked, "So what line of business are you in, my love?" Lorelei ran her fingers through her long hair, perhaps to comfort herself from this well-intended interrogation. However, she supposed she really should be grateful for the friendly conversation.

"Well, I've actually been a nurse for eighteen years." The lady's hazel eyes widened quite incredibly, and she took a sharp deep breath in, as if Lorelei had proclaimed that she was a famous Hollywood a-lister from America.

"A nurse!" she exclaimed. "Oh, my *dear*, what a tremendously valuable occupation you have!" Nodding her head with great admiration she went on, "Well, I'm *sure* you could find something in nursing down in Penzance or Falmouth. Do you own a car, dear?"

"Yes, I do, yes, but actually I've moved down to the countryside to pursue a different kind of lifestyle to be honest. I think I've done my time in the NHS… You see, I'm looking for something with a little less responsibility…"

The eccentric looking woman behind the counter failed to hide her disappointment. Her excitement and admiration for Lorelei swiftly nose-dived at a dramatic pace, although she did manage to hold her tongue despite her obvious dismay. "Less responsibility, dear. Hmm, okay. Well, that's understandable, I'm sure. Your husband, though, he can keep you? I'm sure you'd have been earning a lot more than what these 'ere jobs will pay you."

Lorelei almost choked. Her salary had certainly been modest enough, and a husband keeping her? The lady was starting to tread on dangerous ground here with her assumptions about Lorelei's financial and marital status.

Lorelei inhaled in preparation to address this ridiculous speculation. "Oh no, I don't have a husband…"

Realising from Lorelei's tone that perhaps she had overstepped the mark, she apologised profusely. "Oh, I'm sorry my dear, I shouldn't presume, I really am sorry lovey, I'm a nosy old so and so sometimes!" The lady looked genuinely horrified that she may have offended the newcomer.

Lorelei reassured her. "I'm divorced. It's okay, you don't have to apologise. I'm on my own, and I'm proud of that, believe me…"

Suitably embarrassed, the lady quickly changed the subject. "Well, I'll keep my eyes and ears out for you, love. I'm sure something will turn up for you, always does, doesn't it? And what a brave thing to do, coming down here, you know, all alone. Me name's 'Mousie', used to live down in Mousehole, a bit of a nickname what stuck, deary."

Lorelei smiled. "Well, it's nice to meet you, Mousie. I'm Lorelei. I will see you again soon." With that, Lorelei walked out of the shop feeling pretty good about herself and ever so proud that she had made an acquaintance with a somewhat eccentric local lady, and also with the hope that she was that one step closer to finding a job.

She tucked her papers into her hessian tote bag and gently strolled down the near deserted street. Many of the shops had closed for the winter since trade was so minimal at this desolate time of year. The arcade was shut too, as well as the ice cream parlours lining the seafront. Lorelei thought to herself she'd have been better off staying in bed and searching on the job websites after all, rather than trying her luck in the town. So instead, she found herself on the harbour beach, sitting on a familiar wooden beam, gazing out towards the vibrant display of boats.

The cold air began to nip at her slender neck, and she

realised she should really have worn a scarf. She shivered and then took a deep breath in, feeling a little peckish again, and thinking it must be lunchtime soon. Lorelei unexpectedly felt rather lonely. She so desperately wanted to make new friends. A familiar hollow feeling creeped over her, and she had a sense of emptiness sweep through her heart, knowing she'd be going back to an empty flat for the rest of the afternoon.

She thought back to the prying yet agreeable lady she had had the pleasure of meeting in the shop and recalled the noticeboard in the window. *Was there not an advert for a writers' club there?* she pondered. In all honesty, Lorelei had never been a keen writer. It was her sister, Janey, who had kept diaries over the years documenting every little piece of history, some of which were probably best not remembered at all. However, a writing club could be the perfect way to meet new people — and she liked books. Lorelei tried to remember the last time she had picked up a book…Well, she *used* to like books. Lorelei mused the idea around in her head and concluded that, in a sleepy out of season town, this may be an opportunity she couldn't afford to miss. After all, it might be the gateway to building a social circle for herself. In haste, she jumped up and rushed back to the little newsagents on the corner of The Terrace. Standing outside the window (again), Lorelei retrieved her phone out of her bag and took a picture of the faded card in the display.

St Ives Poetry and Writing club are looking for new members to meet weekly. Anyone who enjoys the creativity of words is very welcome. Contact Hazel on…

Lorelei exhaled with disillusion, for woefully the part of the little card where the contact number had been written was sun damaged, and therefore Lorelei could not quite make out the number, which was frustrating to say the least. How was she going to make contact with her brand-new circle of friends without a contact number?! Interrupting her train of thought, Lorelei caught from her peripheral line of sight a frantic Mousie waving enthusiastically, and she was beckoning Lorelei inside with a perceived urgency. Moving away from the counter towards the door, Mousie came bounding over like an excited child.

"Oh, deary, I was praying you'd come back, else I wasn't sure when I'd see ye next." Smiling with great exhilaration, Mousie handed Lorelei a little note of paper. "I told you I'd be keeping my ears and eyes out for you dear, and my friend Hazel popped in this afternoon, and guess what?" she beamed in anticipation. "She's *only* looking to employ someone to help with *Molly*!"

The next portion of ginger biscuits

The Cornish mizzle came determinedly from the west and Lorelei hurried back to the flat, which was warm and smelled of cinnamon. After preparing herself a chai latte and a little plate of ginger biscuits, Lorelei made herself comfortable on the sofa among the array of soft and fluffy cushions. Lorelei pondered on the little slip of paper Mousie had given her. She held it in one hand, admiring Mousie's perfectly neat handwriting, and started to punch the number into her mobile phone for safekeeping. It just couldn't be a coincidence; Hazel, 'dog mummy' to Molly, *had* to be the same Hazel from the writing club. She was sure of it.

She laid her head down on the sofa and admired the light fittings. They were like little clear glass bowls with decorative silver balls inside of them. She cast her eyes across the lovely walls adorned with paintings of the sea, of which in the main she had inherited from her father, who was a massive artwork fan.

Dog walking? she mused. Surely, she won't become a millionaire in *that* trade, but like Janey said, she had enough savings to see her through for a good while, and all she really needed was a little cash to get her by. Perhaps it wouldn't be so bad. It would certainly be an active vocation, and with all the chai lattes, pain au chocolats and pizza she was indulging in, she thought that surely that couldn't be a bad thing. She'd not normally struggled with her weight, but now she was getting to a certain age, she knew it wouldn't be as easy to shift as it once was. So yes, she would give Hazel a ring. Things were really looking up.

She thought of Bristol and the hospital and wondered how Lucy and her old colleagues were getting along. She thought of the city and how everything was in reach up there. If you wanted to go shopping, there was a choice of the city centre, or the Mall, and there were so many places to buy all sorts of things. It was so easy in Bristol, and everything was open *all the time*. A choice of cinemas, escape rooms, the theatre, and so much more, all at her fingertips. Of course, these things weren't completely out of reach in Cornwall, but it was all a bit harder. Thinking of the theatre, she recalled how much she loved the arts, and how it was on her bucket list to see a show at the Minack, the outdoor theatre carved into the cliffs by a lady called Rowena Cade. She'd hoped she could tick that off next year! Despite all the amenities the city had, what it didn't offer her was *escape*. The world was her oyster in Cornwall, a new start, a new life. She felt so lucky to have this second chance.

Thinking then of her dear dead dad, she pondered whether she may like to see a psychic medium. Not that she was really into that kind of thing, but she was open-minded and secretly longed for more signs that her dad was watching over her. Shaking the thoughts away, she reached for the remote control and channel surfed for a while before settling on a documentary about Britain's greatest myths, which kept her occupied for the next hour, and for the next chai latte, and the next portion of ginger biscuits.

Molly, sit!

Lorelei stood with trepidation on the doorstep of a Victorian town house in Hayle. The town was a historic world heritage site famed for its three-mile stretch of golden sand as well as its estuary, which was highly regarded for its variety of wetland wildlife.

After Lorelei had made contact with Hazel regarding the role, she had kindly been invited to her house to meet Molly. Hazel knew that anyone she was going to trust with Molly would have to demonstrate a special connection with her darling pride and joy.

Lorelei silently admitted that she had never been a 'dog' person. Not to say she didn't *like* dogs, but since chasing around Granny's border collie on the lawn when she was a child, she'd not had much to do with the canine kind and had never had much of a desire to do so either. Lorelei rang the doorbell and nervously awaited an answer. She could hear Molly already barking like mad behind the door.

"Down, Molly!" she heard Hazel instruct in a firm voice and then the big heavy door opened, and a young bouncing black labrador came bounding towards Lorelei, almost knocking her sideways.

"Molly, *down!*" Hazel attempted to calm the overexcited pup, doing her very best to restrain Molly by pulling her back into the house, at the same time beckoning Lorelei inside. "Come in, come in! It's so lovely to meet you, Lorelei. Do come in. Mind the step."

The hallway was large and spacious, and Lorelei admired the flooring, which was planked with a fashionable dark oak. Lorelei was shown into the living room and sat down on a deep-seated tan leather sofa. The room was warm and inviting, with the scent of orange peel emanating from an impressive looking candle on the mantelpiece. In addition, what could certainly not be missed was the enormous Christmas tree dominating the corner of the room. It was a real tree in its pot, standing with the aid of an expensive-looking and intricately designed cast iron stand. Twinkling with clear lights, red and gold bows, and trailing silver beads, it looked truly enchanting, and for the first time in the season, Lorelei felt Christmassy.

"Right then," Hazel chirped, "let's get a cup of tea, or coffee if you'd prefer? I'll just leave you here to get to know Molly. Milk and sugar?"

Lorelei gratefully replied, "Oh, I would love a coffee, thank you."

"Great, I can try out my new coffee machine!"

"Milk and sugar please, that sounds lovely," confirmed Hazel's most appreciative guest. Hazel was a slender lady, perhaps in her thirties. She had thick sandy blonde hair which bounced over her shoulders with vintage charm. Her clothes were comfortable in style in the form of a long-knitted cardigan and stretchy black leggings. On her remarkably neat little feet she sported colourful knitted slipper socks with a turned-out white sheepskin lining.

"Great, I'll just get that prepared. You just make

yourself comfortable!"

Hazel left Lorelei alone with Molly, who hurtled over to her and jumped up onto her knees.

"Steady Molly, mind my tights with those sharp claws," said Lorelei.

Molly crooked her head to one side and paused for just a fraction of a second, before jumping up again in a playful manner as though she'd just been reunited with a long-lost friend.

Lorelei looked briefly around the room again. She noticed an array of books on wooden shelves across the alcoves of the room and, in addition, some beautiful notebooks on the coffee table, along with a few poetry books. It seemed that Hazel was fond of literature and her interests appeared somewhat cultured and definitely intellectual.

Lorelei reached out to ruffle the side of Molly's head, much to Molly's pleasure. Her tail wagged at a rapid pace, and she playfully gnawed on Lorelei's hand. Before long, Hazel re-entered the room with a tray of hot drinks and some delicious-looking chocolate biscuits.

By then Molly had settled somewhat, sitting herself calmly on the rug by Lorelei's feet, but when she saw the tray that Hazel was carrying, she was captivated and not least because of the lovely smell of the biscuits.

"Oh no, these aren't for you Molly!" chuckled Hazel, "I'll get you a little treat. You just wait right there." Hazel passed an exceedingly appetising barista-quality coffee into Lorelei's hands.

"Ooh, that looks lovely, very professional!" remarked Lorelei in admiration of the pretty swirl that Hazel had left on the froth and, of course, not to mention the chocolate dusting.

"Well, I've got this wonderful new coffee machine. I was excited to try it out, and you're the first one to give it a go,

Lorelei!"

"Oh lovely, what an honour!"

Sitting down on the tan leather armchair adjacent to the matching tan leather sofa, Hazel got herself comfortable and took a sip of her latte.

"Right, so down to business. Thank you *so* much for getting in touch. As you are aware, I'm looking for someone to look after Molly while I'm at work," said Hazel. Sipping her coffee, Lorelei smiled and nodded, and Hazel continued. "The last lady just couldn't handle Molly. She's an energetic pup, just six months old and poor old Lilith found it all a bit, well, overwhelming."

Lorelei raised her eyebrows. "Oh? How so?"

"Especially when they were out and about. She's a bit of a handful, you see, and Lilith, well, she wasn't the most *robust* of women, in fact, she was quite frail. She was coming up to sixty to be fair." Hazel reached down to stroke Molly, being careful not to excite her too much. "She was doing me a favour, having retired from the local post office. She wanted something to do to fill her time, and she loves animals. Bless her, she's got a house full of them. Mostly cats, but also African Land snails, guinea pigs, and a hamster I think, or was it a gerbil, one of those ratty little things. *Anyway*, what I'm saying, Lorelei, is that despite her striking and quite indisputable love for animals, looking after Molly was too much of a challenge for her…"

Taking it all in, Lorelei nodded to show her understanding and verbally confirmed her interpretation of the matter. "I see, yes I can imagine Molly could be a bit boisterous which may be tricky for someone like Lilith."

"So, my question for you *is*, do you think you can handle Molly?"

Drawing in a deep breath, Lorelei knew she had to be

unreservedly truthful, for she was indeed completely inexperienced with any sort of dog-handling altogether.

"Well, I won't lie to you Hazel, I've never really looked after a dog, or been around dogs since I was seven or so," she admitted hesitantly, "but, I really *like* dogs, and I think I could give it a good go, she seems a friendly soul!" Lorelei had absolutely zero expectations that Hazel would consider her as a suitable candidate, so was flabbergasted when Hazel went on to describe in more detail what she was looking for.

"Okay, so I have to work from Monday through to Wednesday, and I really want someone to come into the house when I leave so that Molly is not alone." She paused and then reiterated, *"She cannot be left alone."* She pulled out from behind the sofa a pair of slippers that had been ripped to shreds and dangled them in front of Lorelei's nose. "Not for one moment, Lorelei." She chucked the ruined slippers back behind the sofa. "I leave at eight-thirty sharp. I need someone to feed her, take her for a few walks a day and just generally keep her company until I come back, around about four."

"Okay, I could do that. I must stress to you though that I haven't had experience, but I'm sure I can do it. Of course, you would have to run through Molly's routine for me, and it goes without saying that you'd have to show me where everything is, and so on, but it sounds great!"

Molly started beating her tail on the rug, which Lorelei liked to think was Molly's way of sealing her approval of Hazel appointing her to the job. Lorelei reached down and rubbed Molly behind the ears.

"Ahh, look at that, you're a natural. Here, take this." Lorelei held out her hand and Hazel placed a dog treat in her palm. "Ask her to sit."

Suddenly, under unforeseen pressure, Lorelei took the treat and did just as she was asked. "Molly, sit!"

To Hazel's surprise, Molly obediently did just that and flashed her brown puppy dog eyes at Lorelei with that little sideways head stance once again. Lorelei glanced at Hazel for reassurance.

"Go on, give it to her!"

Molly took the treat from Lorelei's hand and let out two little barks as if in appreciation and to say thank you.

"I *am* impressed Lorelei! She has really taken to you! When can you start?" Hazel beamed at a dumbstruck Lorelei.

"Seriously?! Are you serious?"

"Yes, why not? It looks like you and Molly have bonded so well already. I've had a few other *'interviews'* and Molly hasn't been so relaxed with any of the other candidates."

"No?" chirped Lorelei in disbelief.

"No, not at all. The last lady that came over was not happy! Molly ran off with one of her shoes and chewed it up! The person before that, Molly kept nipping at her ankles and whining the entire visit. I really think she likes you!"

Feeling quite pleased with herself, Lorelei beamed. "Well, I'm happy to meet Molly, and yourself, and if you think it would work, I can start as soon as Monday!"

Hazel was so relieved to have found a dog sitter that she and Molly both felt comfortable with.

"That's great news!" she responded. "Isn't it, Molly!?" Molly looked up, and Hazel could just make out a little twinkle in her eye. Yes, she approved, it was official.

"Oh, Hazel, I meant to ask you — I noticed in Mousie's shop that there was a business card advertising a writing group. The card said to contact Hazel, but the number had worn away. It wouldn't happen to be you, would it? It's just I couldn't help but notice how you are quite evidently a lover of books. Maybe I'm putting two and two together and getting five, but…"

"The writing club! *Yes*, that's me! I'm the founder of it!" Hazel expressed with great enthusiasm. Lorelei had realised that despite her small frame, Hazel was quite the extrovert. "I forgot about that little note I left in Mousie's store! So, you're a writer too?"

"Not exactly…"

"You like to read?"

"I used to…"

"That's brilliant! While you're looking after Molly, you're more than welcome to have a browse of my bookshelf, that is, if you get any downtime!" Hazel pointed up to the impressive display of novels and nonfiction books. Lorelei had already spotted a few she thought she might have an interest in, particularly some classics that in recent years she'd seen made into TV adaptations, like the Jane Austen novels she had noticed sitting on the shelf.

"Oh lovely, but I'm sure Molly will be keeping me very busy!"

"Well, if you find time. So, back to the group. Are you interested in coming along to our meetings?"

With no ounce of hesitation, Lorelei replied. "Well, yes, absolutely! I must admit, I've never tried my hand at writing, and it's been a while since I read a book, but literature does interest me, and I would love to meet new friends in the area."

Hazel reached for another chocolate biscuit and held the plate out to Lorelei. "This is perfect!" Hazel flung her arms around Lorelei's shoulder. "You know, I feel like this is fate, Molly is so fond of you already *and* we could really do with some fresh blood in the group!" To some, Hazel's manner may have felt somewhat over friendly, after all they had only met that very morning, yet her familiar nature did not seem out of place or make Lorelei feel uncomfortable, in fact it seemed so natural, like they had known each other for years.

"Thank you, it's really exciting! So, you meet once a week?"

"Yes, we do, on a Wednesday evening at eight o'clock. We meet at 'The Barrel of Blood' here in Hayle. However, we're looking to rent a caravan to use as our 'writing haunt' soon. Danny has a friend who owns a caravan park up on the Towans. They're mostly holiday lets, but they keep one or two for the family who run the business. It's so exciting, the views across the bay are wonderful, and it would make the perfect little retreat for us. We're looking to change our meet up to a Saturday morning so we can enjoy the view."

"Sounds perfect," said Lorelei.

"You'll love the group. They are such a friendly bunch, and Danny, well, *Danny...*" she swooned. "He's quite the looker and such a talented writer. He's published, you know, he writes poetry." It was clear that Hazel was very proud of her friend, and probably had a bit of a soft spot for him.

"Oh wow, that's amazing. I will have to get his book. What's it called?"

"Just search for Danny Kemp on Amazon. The book is called 'Shipwrecks & Driftwood'".

"Great! I'll look it up and order it!" *Do I even like poetry?* Lorelei asked herself.

"So, you'll join us this Wednesday?" asked Hazel.

"I'd be honoured!" So that was settled, and Lorelei felt a warm, fuzzy feeling inside. Hazel jumped up in a way almost as excitable as her gorgeous little puppy.

"Would you like to join me for a walk with Molly now!?"

"Yes, that would be great!"

"I can show you the route I like to go. I guess having

only moved down here recently, you're not familiar with the area?"

"I am a little, as I used to come here as a child on holidays, but I don't know it *really* well, so it would be perfect to come out with you now."

"Wonderful!"

Lorelei was looking forward to a phone call with Janey later to tell her about her new job, and her lovely new friend Hazel, and of course, Molly! Life was looking really positive, and Lorelei was genuinely excited to see what lay ahead of her. She felt silly for having been so nervous when knocking on Hazel's door because she now felt so relaxed and perfectly at ease. However, Lorelei was under no illusion that it would be easy and she knew she would need to go home and start researching what it was like to look after a dog, especially a young dog, who would need training and would be unquestionably challenging.

They buttoned up their coats, including Molly, who had a lovely little padded fleece jacket with a waterproof outer material. It was a royal blue colour and looked very smart indeed.

"She probably doesn't need it," said Hazel, "but I don't want her getting cold. Bless her Lorelei, doesn't she look cute!"

Lorelei agreed wholeheartedly, and giggling, she replied, "Indeed, she does!"

Molly bounced around energetically with the knowledge she was going outside for a walk. She jumped up yet again on Lorelei's legs, her poor knees now ripped with ladders where Molly had torn her tights. Noticing the holes and scratches on Lorelei's legs, Hazel gulped. "Oh dear, maybe don't wear tights next time."

"Hmm yes, not sure why I chose them anyway, in this weather. Not the most sensible decision I've ever made, but there we go!"

Once all wrapped up and ready to venture outside, Hazel took Molly's lead, which Lorelei was rather pleased about because Molly pulled and it was clearly quite a strain on Hazel's arms, but while Molly pulled, Hazel simply stopped walking.

"See Lorelei, what we need to do is stop. She wants to go, but while she pulls like this, I won't walk."

"I see." Lorelei started to note the similarities in this concept to discipline tactics that Janey had tried with Ruby and hoped that Molly was not quite as strong minded as her sister's daughter.

"Molly, sit," commanded Hazel. Molly just stood, wagging her tail in a picture of vivaciousness, and she was not listening at all. She then turned to Lorelei and yelped, once again giving Lorelei those adorable puppy dog eyes.

"Molly, sit!" directed Lorelei, and to her complete surprise, Molly dutifully followed her instructions and sat calmly in front of her. (Admittedly, a few bangs of her tail followed.)

"Good Molly," Hazel murmured as she took a dog biscuit treat from her pocket and handed it to Lorelei, who subsequently popped it into Molly's mouth. Then, turning to Lorelei, Hazel expressed, "I'm just amazed. It's like you and Molly are *meant* to be!"

Feeling rather proud of herself, Lorelei beamed with delight. Maybe she had been a *'doggy'* person all along? They walked along the high street and then took a shortcut up past the play park, which was deserted on this chilly morning. Everyone was trying to keep toasty and snug in this cold spell.

However, the dog walkers would have no choice but to brave the elements, and Lorelei sensed she had a long winter ahead of her and ought to get used to the fresh Cornish air. She'd definitely be investing in a new coat, and walking boots, maybe a snood, and new gloves, of course.

"We'll head to the Upton Towans, a great spot for dog walking."

"Oh, I heard you mention the Towans earlier? The Cornish name for dunes, is it not?"

"Yes, that's right, there's lots of space for Molly to run around and it's nearly empty at this time of year except for other dog walkers, of course."

The area was a fantastic spot of natural beauty, an incredible landscape shaped by shifting sands. As it happened, the region was now regarded as a site of specific scientific interest for its geology and rare wildlife, such as butterflies and glow worms. Lorelei recalled a time where at the holiday park she used to stay at, which was nestled at the edge of the Towans, glow worms could easily be seen in the long grass near the play park and path down to the beach. Sadly, thirty years on, they were more confined to the inner sand dunes but could certainly still be seen at dusk if you knew where to look.

Once entirely on the Towans, Hazel leant down and smoothed Molly's head. "You ready to go for a run, girl?" She unclipped the lead from Molly's harness and off she went like a bolt of lightning, leaping about like the wild pup she was. It was a pleasure to witness such jubilant behaviour from the young Molly. The winding paths around the Towans made them easily accessible, yet still an adventurous place to explore. After walking for close to thirty minutes, the pair made the decision to head back because time was certainly getting on and Hazel had errands to run, including some food shopping and then some Christmas present wrapping.

"Yes, time to be heading back home now. There's much to do this afternoon and I am sure you have things to be getting on with too, Lorelei."

Lorelei sighed. "I suppose I need to pop to the shops myself, to be honest, and there's a few jobs to be done at home." Yet who was she trying to kid? She didn't have an awful lot scheduled for the rest of the day at all and in all honesty would probably spend about half an hour talking to her sister on the phone, then some internet research on dogs followed by procrastinating in front of the TV for the rest of the evening. There wasn't even much work to do around the flat, but Lorelei was so inspired by Hazel's lovely Christmas tree and thought that sometime soon she would make the effort to put a tree up herself.

With Lorelei not having children of her own, the pressure was off when it came to festive decorations, unlike at her sister's house, where Ruby loved the magic of Christmas. (That is, apart from when she was pulling down the tree in a violent rage a few years ago.) Despite all the joy that Christmas would bring, this time of year was not easy for the two sisters. It was the first anniversary of their father's death, which played on their minds a great deal.

It was not long before they were back on the residential street leading back towards Hazel's lovely Victorian Town House and both women were absorbed for a moment in their own thoughts. To Hazel's surprise, her phone started ringing, which woke them both from their absent-minded daydreams.

"Hello?" she answered, listening intently before replying, "Oh my, oh *dear.*" She swallowed and then locked eyes with Lorelei. "Okay, just give me a sec." Touching Lorelei firmly on the upper arm, she sighed arduously. "I've got an emergency — take Molly for a min, will you? I've got to sort something; I'll call you when I'm done!" She stuffed a small bag of puppy treats into Lorelei's hand, along with some poo bags, and with that, she was gone. *Shit* was all that came to Lorelei's mind, and not least because of the poo bags! She was left alone with a dog she barely knew, belonging to a lady she barely knew. *Shit, shit, shit!*

What made matters worse was that with the sight of Hazel darting off at a terrific pace, Molly (clearly distressed) let out a sequence of high-pitched barks and without prior warning hurtled off, spinning Lorelei off her feet for a roller coaster ride behind her. With Molly barking still, Lorelei made her best effort to pull her to a halt, but alas, she was a dog on a mission and could not be stopped. She likely would have eventually gained control, but as chance allowed, she ran just a fraction too close to a curly haired man and in the process subsequently knocked him sideways with his coffee cup flying out of his hands. The dark hot sticky liquid splashed all over his smart jacket, as well as saturating the book he was holding at the time of collision. Spinning around, he saw how Lorelei was struggling with the exuberant canine, but like a true gent he grabbed the lead, their hands briefly meeting, and with a little resistance himself, he managed to bring Molly under control.

Lorelei picked up the book, which had fallen to the pavement and started mopping up the coffee spillage with her scarf. She noted the title.

Shipwrecks & Driftwood

"I'm *so* sorry! Please forgive me, your book, it's *ruined*, I'm so—"

"Please, it's alright, accidents happen," the curly haired man firmly yet softly articulated. He looked at her directly, then glanced at the soggy book in her hands. For a second there was a pause before Lorelei twitched her lips with realisation dawning on her.

"I know this book..." she said, reading the title out loud, "Shipwrecks and Driftwood *written by Danny Kemp...*"

Ignoring her observation and feeling a little bemused himself, he blurted out, "I know this dog! *Molly!*"

Lorelei tilted her head and looked at him with curiosity, slowly putting two and two together. "*Danny?*" she squeaked. Molly tugged on her lead.

"Molly, sit," requested the curly haired man and, of course, he was quite naturally ignored.

Lorelei sighed. "You're doing it *wrong...*" she rolled her eyes and then demonstrated herself. "Molly, sit!" she commanded, and Molly sat most compliantly awaiting her biscuit treat, which Lorelei rewarded her with immediately.

"Wow, you're *good!*" He slowly nodded his head in appreciation of her dog handling skills.

She smiled coyly. "So, tell me, are you Danny Kemp himself?"

"I am indeed, and you are?" his voice was smooth and kind.

"I'm Lorelei. I'm Molly's new dog sitter, and I *really* need to get Molly home."

"I'll walk with you; I know Molly's human mummy."

"I know you do!"

"You do?!"

"Yes, I've heard all about you..."

The pair walked along together, chatting about nothing in particular. It occurred to Lorelei how handsome Danny was with his dark, wavy hair that hung loosely over his ears. He sported designer stubble over his chin, *and that smile!* Hazel was right, he was a looker and had a certain Cornish charm about him. He was tall, slim but not puny, and was dressed in nice clothes, his jeans showcasing the shape of his well-proportioned bottom perfectly.

They reached Hazel's house, and she opened the door before they could even knock, having seen them approach from the large bay window. The emergency had been dealt with and Hazel was free to receive Molly.

"Thank you *so* much Lorelei. You were a real lifesaver then. One of Lilith's guinea pigs had escaped from the hutch in the garden, and we had a real panic trying to capture little Miss Lady Jane!"

"That's a funny name for a guinea pig," Lorelei smiled, reminiscing about a programme called Lovejoy that she used to watch with her mother when she was little.

"Yes, named after Lady Jane in an old eighties TV show. I don't remember it myself. *Lovejoy* I think she said!"

"Did the guinea pig have red fur?" asked Lorelei.

"Yes! How did you guess!?"

Lorelei and Danny looked at each other and burst out laughing.

"Never mind," Lorelei chuckled.

Hazel invited them to stay to try out the iced coffee function on her fancy new machine, but Danny declined since he had to go back home to change out of his coffee-stained shirt. Lorelei made up an excuse that she had to get back to sort out some important paperwork (when, in truth, she had absolutely no intention of going through her mail). Instead, she was planning on jumping into her cosy bed to hide from the outside elements and watch that new space documentary that everyone had been raving about. She was already thinking about picking up a large bar of chocolate to nibble on whilst doing so, *well I've burnt some calories on today's walk*, she justified to herself. The threesome said their goodbyes and went their separate ways.

Later on that evening, Danny sprawled out on his sofa eagerly anticipating the new space documentary presented by a popular young professor, but his mind couldn't help but drifting back to the pretty auburn-haired lady who had quite literally ran into him earlier that day, and he thought to himself how he was really very sure he wanted their paths to cross again.

God help us

Janey stumbled through the front door with her daughter, who was teetering on the edge of an all-encompassing 'meltdown'. Ruby was in a frightful mood and had been since Janey picked her up from the school gates.

"I'm *hungry*. I need something to eat, *now!*" she screamed like some kind of banshee.

"Yes darling, *as I said*, I'm going to get tea in the oven right away—"

"I need something *now!*" Ruby hissed in a low, belligerent tone. Janey drew a deep breath in before slowly exhaling, remembering how everyone had told her to keep calm.

"Okay, well, there's a pear or banana in the fruit bowl. Please help yourself." She turned to the sink to get started on the enormous pile of washing up, wondering why they had not yet had the faulty dishwasher repaired (another thing on a long list of things to get sorted).

"I don't *like* fruit!" Ruby growled, her aggressiveness clearly displayed in her voice and overall demeanour. Janey was frustrated. She hoped it would be possible to diffuse the situation before it got even more out of hand.

"Alright, well, what about a slice of toast to tide you over?"

"*No*, I want crisps!"

"You ate the last packet last night, Ruby."

"I don't want toast! *Why* do you *never* have any food in this house?!" yelled Ruby. More deep breaths were required from Janey. She tried so very hard to keep her composure, she knew getting angry back would not help one tiny bit.

"Darling, there's toast, fruit, even a yoghurt. I've put the oven on, tea won't be long. Why don't you go snuggle up in front of the TV and your dinner will be ready soon." Stamping her foot like some sort of wild animal, Ruby raged until she was red in the face.

"I don't *want* a fucking yoghurt! You're such a *bitch*, why do you never feed me?!"

With patience running thin, Janey attempted to firmly set the expectations. She didn't shout, but slowly enunciated in a clear way. "Right, enough of that, you *do not* speak to me like that. You can apologise right now, young lady!" but ignoring her mother's demands, Ruby continued to argue.

"*No*, I want some food *now*. What kind of a mother lets her daughter starve? A fucking bitch of a mother, that's who!"

Janey scrubbed the pans faster and faster, as her tension rose, and she felt herself starting to lose it. "I told you what's available," she said, still trying to stay calm, which she found really hard when Ruby behaved like this.

"I told you, you stupid cow, I don't want *that*," spat Ruby. Remembering that she just must walk away in such a situation as this, Janey reviewed her approach.

"I don't want to talk to you now." She inhaled again deeply and endeavoured to implement the strategies she'd been taught in the various parenting classes she had attended throughout the years. *Keep Calm, Keep Calm, just sodding keep calm, walk away*, she thought to herself as she abandoned the dishes and made her way into the living room.

It was far from easy, though; it was the hardest thing ever. She checked her wristwatch. Just a few hours and Robert would be home. "Stay cool," she mumbled under her breath. She reached for the smart (and heavy) heating control and gave the room temperature a boost. Then, without thinking very much of it, she left the control on the side of the sofa instead of its usual home, which was high up out of the way on a shelf in the kitchen.

Ruby, who had followed her mother into the living room, now barged past her as she paced up and down the room and back into the kitchen. Ruby was now fully absorbed in the 'red mist' and, in an unprecedented rage, proceeded to tear open the cupboards and then slam them closed again violently.

"Why don't we have any biscuits?" she roared. It was not unusual for Ruby's mood to accelerate from 'mildly annoyed' to 'full-blown rampage' in such a miniscule of time. Janey tried so hard to stay calm and not rise to her daughter's exhausting behaviour, but it took a lot of emotional resilience to do so, and Janey was not always so disciplined. Ruby continued to bellow. "Why do we *never* have any food?"

Handing her daughter a piece of fruit, Janey kindly suggested she eat it, with a decidedly calm voice now edging on the side of sarcasm as she tried to stay pleasant. "Darling, have a lovely juicy pear. The sooner you come out of the kitchen, the sooner I will have tea ready for you."

However, the lovely, juicy offering was not well received at all. Ruby snatched the poor innocent piece of fruit from Janey's hand and threw it with such great force that it exploded on the floor, disseminating into all four corners of the room. The sticky residue was flung up the bottom half of the kitchen cupboards and who knew what other nooks and crannies it had found itself in. Janey couldn't do this anymore.

"You little *shit*! You clean that up right now!" Janey had been pushed so far that she lost her calm manner.

Placing her hands on her hips, Ruby retorted, "*I'm not doing it.*"

"Ruby, if you don't start cleaning this mess up *right now*, I'm telling you, you will not see your mobile phone for a *month!*"

"Yes, I will. You can't take it away from me."

"Yes, I *can*, and I will. Clean it up!"

"I'm not *fucking* doing it, you fucking bitch! Who do you think you are? I'm not your slave! I'm not your cleaner! *You're* the cleaner!"

Though Janey tried to remain calm and be 'the adult', sometimes Ruby pushed the boundaries so far that Janey found it very difficult to remain composed, and sadly this was one of those moments.

"Ruby, I've been at work *all* day. I had to collect you from school because you had a detention, which meant I had to fight through *all* the traffic. How *dare* you behave like this? Just who do you think you are!" Her voice got louder and angrier the more she went on. "Why are you like this? Why do you think you have the right to behave like this!?"

Janey lunged for her daughter's mobile phone, which Ruby held loosely in her hand. Of course, Ruby would not give it up without a fight. She pushed her mother out of the way, throwing her against the fridge. Janey had not managed to take possession of the handset, so she attempted again, and the behaviour became physical.

"Get off me, you nasty cow!" screamed Ruby, desperate to get her mother away from her.

"You do *not* call me that! That's it, I'm having this phone," Janey bellowed, "I'm having this for the next month," she tore the phone out of Ruby's clasp.

"*No, Mummy,* I need it! I need it!" protested Ruby in desperation. For a teenager, in these modern days, their whole life was on their phone, and having no connection to her friends outside of school would be something quite unimaginable for her.

"You should have thought about that before you chose to be so *bloody* horrible!"

"You're the horrible one, *I hate you*!" spat out Ruby with tears now in her eyes.

"That's nice of you to say."

"Well, I do." She was clearly upset. Her eyes told Janey so, but Janey didn't know if it was the thought of being without her phone for a month or the fact that she was remorseful about her behaviour that caused them to well up. *Walk away, don't get wound up anymore,* Janey thought. She did walk away. Janey walked out of the kitchen, through the hallway and halfway up the stairs, but Ruby followed her.

"Give me my fucking mobile phone!" Ruby persisted, still spitting and raging like a wild thing. Trying to pull herself together and working *really* hard on not losing her temper any more than she already had, Janey simply turned around from midway up the stairs and answered.

"No, Ruby." Janey was oblivious that her daughter had picked up the thermostat she had mistakenly left on the arm of the sofa.

"Give it to me, you bitch, or you will regret it!" Ruby demanded. Janey turned her back on her and continued to walk up the remainder of the staircase, which spiralled around to the left.

Ruby's anger had exceeded boiling point, and she had

now escalated to a level where she simply could no longer reign her temper in. "*I fucking hate you!*" And with those wretched words so easily spewed, she raised the thermostat above her head and hurled it directly at her mother's back with enormous effort. She did not miss. Janey buckled over with the shock of the impact. The pain was excruciating, and she screamed.

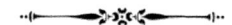

Ruby creeped up the stairs surreptitiously. Her mother had retreated to the bedroom and had been there for quite some time. On all fours, she crawled across the landing, peeping through the slim gap between the door and frame.

"Mum?" she said, in a weak little voice, "Mum?" Then, observing her mum's silent sobbing, she ran onto the bed next to her side. "I'm sorry, Mummy…"

Janey looked out from the edge of her duvet. "This can't go on, this can't go on," wept Janey.

"I know. Why am I such a horrible girl?"

Janey made her daughter her supper while she sat in front of the television watching 'Stranger Things'. When the tea was ready, Ruby sat up at the table and devoured every last scrap of her chicken supreme.

Robert was back from work at about six thirty and walked into a remarkably calm and peaceful household. Not even the lightest shadow lingered from the discord that had befallen the family home earlier that afternoon. Not quite what Robert was expecting, having received dramatic texts from his wife earlier.

I cannot cope — I just want to die!
God help us — we have the child from hell!

He found Janey in the kitchen slumped over the counter looking at her social media news feed on her phone.

"Hello sweet pea, so it's all clearly de-escalated here?"

Looking up from her handset to greet Robert, she sniffed. "Yes. She's upstairs, reading."

Robert rubbed her back gently. "Sounds like you should be upstairs resting, too. Come, I'll take care of dinner." He was such an affectionate man, sensible and logical but also so thoughtful and caring. Janey had always loved his emotional intelligence. Sure, he wasn't that *exciting*, and could be somewhat predictable, which hadn't always made Janey happy; but he had always been there for her, always picking up her pieces, always gluing her back together again.

Janey nuzzled into his chest. "That would be lovely. I would quite like to take a bath."

"Of course; I'll run it for you." Robert slipped off his jacket and rested it on the clothes airer. While his job in the hotel didn't require smart attire, he still wore a shirt and couldn't wait to put a comfortable t-shirt on. He made his way upstairs, loosening his top button as he climbed.

Standing at the door to Ruby's bedroom, he leaned in to listen and peeked through the crack. She was lying on her back with her nose in 'The Book of Dust'. Robert knocked gently on the door.

"Yes?" came the reply.
"Can I come in for a chat?"
"Yes, Dad."
"How was school?"
"Okay…"
"Just, okay?"
"We did drama. That was fun."

"Good. I heard there's been a bit of drama here tonight?"

"Hmmm…"

"Do you want to tell me about it?"

"I got angry."

"Why?"

"I was hungry. Mum wouldn't let me have anything."

"That's not what Mum told me."

Ruby narrowed her eyes and sighed. "Dad, when I'm hungry, I'm *hungry*. I don't want *fruit*."

"Not toast, even?" asked Robert.

Ruby shook her head. "I just wanted something to satisfy me. Mum is so mean. She *wants* me to be hungry."

"That's not true, sweet pea."

"*It is!*" maintained Ruby.

"Relax. You swore at Mum?"

"Yes."

"And?"

"Threw a pear."

"And?"

"Nothing!"

"Ruby…"

"I lost my temper."

"Too right you did. Is it okay to lose your rag?"

"Yes, everyone gets angry."

"Is it alright to *hurt* someone?"

Pushing him away with her foot, she whined. "Dad, stop talking to me like I'm a baby…"

"Stop behaving like one, then. It's not okay to hurt your mother."

"I've said sorry."

"Not good enough. We both love you."

"I know *you* do, not sure about Mum though…"

"Of course she does. I'm going to run Mum a bath. I want you to get ready for bed."

"Dad, I need my phone…"

"Not happening."

"*Go* away!"

"Ruby, you can't have your phone when you swear at your mum, when you throw things at her, *when you hurt people.*"

"Go away!"

Robert left the room, and in doing so, 'The Book of Dust' was thrown at the door by a frustrated fourteen-year-old Ruby. Robert chose to ignore her and began to run a bath for Janey. He mixed some of his wife's essential oil into the hot running water (He had bought it for her last birthday). The oil swirled around, releasing a gorgeous scent of lavender and bergamot. He lit a candle for her too, for he sensed she really needed to relax this evening, and he knew how much Janey loved to soak in the bath. When Robert returned to his wife downstairs, Janey was in a deep telephone conversation with Lorelei.

"You've got a job as a *dog walker*!? That's so…*not you!*" She laughed, while Robert mouthed, "*What?*" as he caught part of the conversation. Janey shrugged her shoulders back at him.

"Lorelei, I'm pleased for you. I just don't know how you will get on with it, but a *writing club?* Is this really Lorelei Logan I'm talking to?" Janey listened as Lorelei filled her in with her exciting news before finally asking her how life was at her end.

"Well, to be honest, I'm at the end of my tether, Sis. Ruby's really hurt me again today. I can't cope with her! Robert's back now. He's run me a bath, but truly Lorelei, I almost wish I was a single mum, so she could be packed off to her father's house for the week. I just can't cope! She's totally off the rails. It's really got to a point where I don't *like* her at all. She's such an evil child. I feel like she's possessed!"

There was a moment's silence on Janey's side as she listened to Lorelei express empathy and offer virtual hugs, but then Lorelei suggested something she hadn't expected.

"How about Ruby coming to stay with me for half term?"

"What? Really?"

"Yes, it would give you and Robert a break! Perhaps you could go away yourselves, maybe back to that cottage in the Lake District that you love?"

Robert had proposed to his wife at Ullswater Lake. It was a special place for the pair. Janey tapped the dining room table to get Roberts' attention.

"Back to Whitbarrow? Well, that would be nice…"

"How about February half term? We'd have to get Christmas out of the way, but it's just around the corner. Why don't you see if you can book the cottage?"

"Well, that would be amazing to have a bit of time just for me and Robert. Thank you so much! What are you planning on doing for Christmas, anyway, Lorelei?"

"I don't know. I was thinking that maybe you could all come down here? I've heard it's lovely in St Ives at Christmas time."

"That's definitely food for thought. Of course, we'd have to rent somewhere to stay, but it really could be a good idea. It would make a change, a new tradition perhaps."

"Absolutely, and listen, go and book a holiday. I'll *definitely* take Ruby off your hands in February half term."

Janey beamed as she filled Robert in with the developments. They both agreed that a break for an entire week was just exactly what they needed.

The best fish finger sandwich in all of Cornwall

December was progressing and everything oozed Christmas. Trees were twinkling in front rooms along the street and St Ives town was beginning to look incredibly festive. Despite this, Lorelei found it difficult to get into the festive mood herself. She'd never much liked Christmas anyway, but it was even harder now because this time of year was riddled with sadness, as she thought so much of her dad's passing. Even now that twelve months had come and gone, there would still be times when her father's death hit her as if she had only just lost him. This feeling had a habit of striking when she was lying in her bed, her mind trailing off in a pre-dream state. She would lose herself in memories weaved among images of moments in time, and before she knew it, she was re-imagining times spent with her father. Then, with an upright jolt, she would open her eyes wide in sudden shock and think to herself, *my daddy's dead*. This had been happening a lot more often recently. At the time of his death, it had taken Lorelei time to figure out how to grieve. She was pragmatic to start with, almost relieved, but just as her sister was accepting his fate, Lorelei fell apart.

"Why are you being so cold?" Janey had accused her sister when he first died. "You're showing no sadness at all; *it's weird.*" It was true, Lorelei had been cold, cool and didn't shed tears until the next day, and never in front of her mother or sister. It was when she spoke to her dear old school friend, who had kindly invited her over for eggy bread after she heard the news, that her tears really started to fall. She hadn't stayed in touch with many school friends, but Louise had been a constant. It had only been the year before that they sat around her big oak table in her Plymouth flat, while Louise recounted the events of her own mother's passing. Little had Lorelei known that she would be relaying details of one of her own parents' departure so soon afterwards.

Lorelei tried to focus on the wonderful memories that she had of her father. For the last ten or so years, they had met around mid-December in a country pub halfway between Bristol and Plymouth, which was their annual Christmas get-together. They'd exchange presents and her dad brought the girls homemade Christmas tree biscuits every time. It wasn't an easy time of year, not by any means.

Lorelei was all set to start dog sitting from the following Monday and, that very evening, she had planned to attend the writing club in Hayle. It was Wednesday morning and, other than a bit of pottering around the flat, she didn't have an awful lot to do. She prepared a cup of tea and some crumpets with butter (the nice, thick and fluffy ones that Warburtons made). The butter sank into all the little tubes and made an absolutely divine breakfast. Lorelei had wished she had some Marmite to go with them. Just a small smudge of it would be quite enough. She reached for her jotter that had found a home on the kitchen work surface and scribbled down a quick shopping list to include Marmite, and more crumpets, of course.

Lorelei settled herself on the armchair in the front room, bringing her warm cup of tea, breakfast and jotter with her. She placed the tea down on the side table, which once belonged to her father and pensively flicked her pen from side to side. *The writing club*, she thought. Perhaps she ought to try her hand at writing something if she were to attend the group. Then she remembered Danny's poetry book, and how she had meant to order it. She decided to wait, in case she could grab a copy directly from Danny at the club that evening. She felt so bad that one of his copies had got drenched in coffee the other day, chuckling as she recalled their 'chance meeting'. He had been such a gentleman, and very kind and understanding, despite the circumstances. She wondered what Danny did for a job? She would have to find out later that evening, she thought to herself, her curious nature revealing itself.

After finishing the last few bites of her third crumpet, she put pen to paper, but all that transcribed was a little doodle. *What shall I write about?* she pondered. *Should it rhyme? Should it be funny or serious?* Many questions ran through Lorelei's mind. How difficult could it be? After a few crossing outs she scribbled down a few lines inspired by the drive her mother and her had so much enjoyed on their way to the Men an Tol the other week. After an hour or so of editing and a few cups of tea later, Lorelei had written two stanzas.

The coast road from St Ives to Lands' End
is the most beautiful stretch, each and every bend.
The St Ives cows have an excellent view,
(the tabby of Porthmeor Farm does too).

The undulating road winds up and around,
bar the infrequent car, there's no other sound.
But sights, oh so many, to feast our eyes on

as we cheerfully relish the journey along.

Wow! Lorelei gasped. *I actually wrote a poem, and it's not that bad.* She praised herself. For a first attempt, she was quite pleased with her efforts, yet still felt anxious about sharing her work.

Lorelei's attention was drawn to her phone, where she had received some notifications on her social media. She had several 'likes' on some photographs that she had uploaded of her flat and the harbour boats. Susan Davis had engaged with the images, as well as her mother and sister. She clicked on Susan's profile. Her profile picture was a beautiful sunset, and after browsing through her page, she could find only landscape pictures and no pictures of Susan herself. She struggled again to remember who she was, assuming that some people just weren't that memorable and soon moved on to pictures her sister had posted of her dinner last night. Once satisfied with her daily dose of the socials, Lorelei was once again twiddling her thumbs and, with only an hour left before it would be a reasonable time for lunch, she decided to go out for a walk.

The temperature had plummeted, and it was definitely hat, scarf and gloves weather with the ground now crispy beneath Lorelei's boots. She wrapped up so that the fresh icy air would not perturb and set out eagerly for her late morning walk. Her first stop would be the convenience store where Mousie spent her days behind the counter serving the community throughout the winter months. It was close to her flat, just a few yards down the street. She burst through the doors with anticipation to tell Mousie that she would be walking Molly from the next week.

"Hello Mousie!" she called from the entrance to the store. With no reply, she then attempted again, "I've got some news, Mousie!"

Mousie was sitting on a high stool behind the counter reading the St Ives Echo. Her head popped up from behind the tabloid. She seemed to have been engrossed in the article she was reading so much that she missed Lorelei's initial greeting. Today she wore a purple cardigan to match her purple streak of hair.

"Oh! Hello deary!" She lifted her reading glasses off her nose and onto her head. She looked rather perplexed and somewhat distracted. "I'm sorry, love. What were you saying?"

"Well, Hazel has agreed that I can look after Molly, and I start on Monday!"

"Well, my love, that's wonderful…" While her words meant well, Lorelei sensed that there was something bothering the usually quite bright and energetic lady because her tone felt deflated as if something wasn't quite as it should be.

"Are you okay, Mousie?"

"Yes, yes, deary…"

"Are you sure? You seem a little preoccupied," asked Lorelei. Mousie began shifting some paper invoices around the counter, appearing increasingly anxious.

"Oh, not to worry," Mousie went on, sounding ever so unsure. Lorelei prompted her again.

"Oh Mousie, you do sound like something is troubling you?"

"Well, I'm sure it's nothing, but I had a customer earlier on, a chap. He seemed a bit," she paused momentarily, "a bit… troubled."

"Oh!?"

"Oh, it's nothing, it was just…"

"*Just* …?"

"It was just a bit peculiar; he was a scruffy so and so, not so dishevelled that he looked like he was homeless, but unshaven, and quite unkempt," explained Mousie. Sensing there was more to tell, Lorelei urged Mousie to continue.

"And?"

Mousie gave in and spilled what was on her mind. "The rascal absolutely stank of alcohol, and twas only 'bout nine o'clock in the morning!"

"Oh dear, some people, huh? He probably had a heavy night, maybe a Christmas party?"

"Yes, pra'bly, but I've never seen him 'round 'ere Lorelei."

Intrigued, Lorelei asked, "But why does it worry you?"

"Oh, it don't matter." Mousie straightened her glasses and shuffled the papers around once more.

"Was he threatening to you?"

"Not 'zackly, he just seemed a bit odd…"

"Oh, this sounds really strange, Mousie, but what did he say, precisely?"

"Nothing really of significance. We just don't normally get such scruffy folk coming in. It was *weird*, and sometimes I get a feeling for people, deary, and I didn't get a nice one about him." She shook her head and tapped on the counter in an attempt to pull herself together. "It be nothing. Anyway. So, you've met Hazel then? You're going to mind that lovely pup, Molly! That is fantastic, brilliant news!"

The two talked more about her meeting with Hazel and what a lovely house she had, and then about how she had met Danny Kemp, and was off to the writing club this evening at 'The Barrel of Blood'. Mousie seemed to shake herself out of her peculiar mood and Lorelei left in good spirits. She had even shared her poem with Mousie, who was ever so impressed, and even suggested she submit it to the local magazine poetry column.

"One step at a time, Mousie, one step at a time!"

Lorelei decided to take a walk up on the island, which wasn't an island at all, but in fact a grassy headland connected to the mainland in St Ives town. Nonetheless, it was a wonderful walk up to the small stone chapel with some stunning views across Porthmeor beach and out to sea. As Lorelei climbed up the hill, she felt the burn in her calves and thought how she really ought to switch her walks to gentle runs to help boost her fitness. Since splitting up with Jay, she had neglected her running routine, but she recalled how well she felt when she used to run a few miles several times a week. Of course, she had the time to do it now and perhaps she could even run with Molly? She paused to gather her breath and suddenly got the feeling that someone was behind her; she spun around but there was no one there to be seen. Shrugging off the sense of someone nearby, onwards she trekked until she was standing by the little chapel of St Nicholas, named so presumably due to St Nicholas being the patron saint of sailors, although she knew little about the chapel's origins. After stopping a while to catch her breath, Lorelei descended the grassy slope towards a bench that she often liked to sit on and had remembered doing so over the years when she had been down to St Ives on vacation. She smiled to herself, so proud that she had fulfilled her dream and could sit on the bench any time she wanted now.

  She was happily lost in nostalgic thoughts when she was disturbed abruptly by the shrill ringing of her mobile. Reaching into her rucksack and cradling her phone, she saw that the handset displayed a number that she was not familiar with. She felt a little uneasy with calls like that; it worried her not knowing who might be on the other end and what they might want. Lorelei also felt slightly unsettled at this time, having suspected that someone was watching her, but she was quite sure that was only because of Mousie's earlier nervousness. She answered the call.

"Lorelei!" came a familiar voice in an animated tone. She definitely recognised the caller but couldn't recall at that precise moment from where.

Lorelei replied nervously. "Uh, yeah? Who's that?"

"Oh, I'm so glad you answered. It's Danny! Do you want to meet for a coffee?"

Lorelei was ever so relieved. *What a pleasant surprise*, she thought, but how did he know her number? "Oh, Danny, hi!"

"I got your number from Hazel; I hope you don't mind me calling you," asked Danny. She should have known, but she wasn't at all cross with Hazel for giving her number out. But even so, she couldn't resist the opportunity to play with him.

"Yes, actually I mind very much, data protection breach from my employer, *noted*!" she snorted, realising her acting may have been a little *too* realistic.

"Oh," Danny stuttered, deflated.

"I'm joking," she quickly confirmed, "of course it's fine. I'm sorry, it was a joke." She giggled, and his disappointment dissipated.

"Oh! Good, you had me for a moment there! So where are you? Do you fancy coffee?"

Lorelei's mind wandered. *No, but I fancy you*, she thought, before in reality replying. "Hmm, not sure about a coffee…" she said, with a little smile in the corner of her mouth.

"No? Ah, that's a shame, maybe another—"

"*I'm absolutely starving*! Do you fancy lunch instead?"

"Oh Lorelei, you had me worried! Yes, it's lunchtime now. I know a great little cafe. I can meet you there in, say, twenty minutes. It's just in the town."

"Okay, where?"
"It's called cafe Java, on the Wharf."
"Great, I'll see you there soon!"

Lorelei was only a few minutes away from Cafe Java on foot and arrived a good ten minutes before Danny. She'd spotted the cafe in passing before and had noted it looked so quirky and cosy. She didn't fancy waiting outside in the freezing weather for him, so made her way through the door. She was greeted by a friendly waitress who pointed behind her at the black board displaying the drink options, and then passed her a menu. In front of her was a mouth-watering display of cakes in a giant glass cabinet. There were chocolate orange brownies with caramel drizzle, rocky road slabs with marshmallows, and crunchy biscuits. In particular, Lorelei had her eye on a gargantuan slice of walnut and coffee cake. Her eyes moved upwards to the drinks menu and, to her delight, the luxury didn't stop at the cakes. The hot chocolate selection was diverse with all manner of syrups to sweeten hot drinks, from salted caramel to toasted marshmallow and even mint.

The cafe itself was decorated with plaques and pictures inspired by Cornwall and times gone by. There were nets and boats adorning the shelves and shells hanging from strings from the ceiling. It was truly a unique space, and it was *warm*. Lorelei made her way up the staircase where there was a large seating area, which was quite hidden away from the entrance. She removed her jacket and scarf, placing it over the back of one of the wooden chairs, and then made herself comfortable at a table by the window. She flicked through the menu whilst waiting for Danny. Her tummy started to rumble despite the crumpets she had devoured for breakfast.

Before long, she had company in the form of a charming poet, and he came bearing a gift.

"For you, lovely Lorelei." He placed a copy of his poetry book '*Shipwrecks and Driftwood*' on the table and pushed it towards her.

"Oh, you shouldn't have! I was going to buy it myself!"

"Well now, you don't have to, and it's my pleasure. I even signed it," he said with a wink.

"Thank you so much," she said while lifting the book and running her hand over its glossy cover. "This book feels really lovely. I can't wait to read your poetry!"

"I really hope you like it; the writing is inspired by this wonderful county that we are both so lucky to live in."

"Truly, *thank you*. This is so generous of you, especially after I ruined your other copy the other day…"

"Yeah — you klutz, ha-ha!"

"Oi!"

"Just messing!" He laughed. "So, are you looking forward to dog sitting Molly?"

"I am indeed," she concurred with an air of confidence.

"Well," he said, pulling his chair in and leaning slightly towards her. "I work locally in Hayle at the accountancy firm, I can always come and walk with you on my lunch breaks if you fancy some company?" he suggested. Lorelei could hardly believe what she was hearing. Danny wanted to see her again!

"Sure, that would be lovely." She grinned. He smiled, feeling relaxed.

"So, what do you make of this cafe?"

"I love it! The cakes look amazing!"

"The sandwiches are great too."

The two of them scanned over the menu cards. Deciding on their food was quite difficult because there was so much to choose from. In the end Lorelei went for a roasted vegetable and goat's cheese flatbread, which came with a side salad and sweet potato crisps. Danny opted for a chunky fish finger sandwich in a ciabatta with tartare sauce. They were about to order two lattes; Lorelei went for gingerbread and Danny couldn't quite decide between popcorn or vanilla, so scrapped the idea completely and went for a spiced chai latte with oat milk instead.

"Do you have family here?" the curious Lorelei began to delve.

"Yes, I've lived here all my life. My mum and dad live in St Ives, down on Tregenna Row, not far from here actually."

"Oh, Tregenna Row, I had to go up there myself recently when my mum came to visit. She'd only gone to the wrong street, and I had to go and collect her. She'd ended up in a lady's house eating saffron cake!"

"No way!" Danny exclaimed.

"Yes! It was pretty hilarious." Though at the time Lorelei had been far from amused, in retrospect she now saw the funny side of her mother's eventful arrival.

"No, I mean, *no way* — that was my mother, Eleanor Travarthen!"

"Seriously?!"

"Yes! She told me all about a woman who was having problems parking her four by four! That was not your mum, was it Lorelei!?"

"Yes, it was! Your mum invited her in! I spoke to her on the phone eventually, when my mum managed to actually call me to tell me where she was, and I met your mother and father when I went to collect my mum!"

"What a coincidence that is!"

"Come to think of it, my mum mentioned that Eleanor had a son who writes poetry…"

"I'd be surprised if she didn't. She's always harping on

about her son being a poet."

"I don't doubt it. She's obviously very proud of you, and rightly so!" Lorelei smiled. She was even feeling proud of Danny herself, and she'd only just met him.

The chatter between them flowed with ease, and Danny emanated warmth and kindness through his mannerisms and tone of voice. Lorelei felt so relaxed with him. He gave her no reason to feel wary or guarded, which was something she wasn't very used to. Lorelei thought to herself that she could fall for him very easily, but she had to be cautious. Even though so far, she felt no reason to be so, she knew people could not always be what they seemed. She tried to remind herself that Jay had been charming in the beginning, too. Besides, she'd only met Danny twice. Why were her thoughts getting so carried away?

"So, Lorelei, how are you enjoying being down here? Do you miss the city?"

"No, I don't, not yet anyway! It's so relaxing and special here."

"Do you mind me asking why you moved?" Now he was being the nosy one, she thought, but she was happy to share and was not ashamed of who she was and where she had come from.

"Of course not. Well, I've always loved the sea and after my divorce, well, I just needed a fresh start. I'd always fantasised about living by the ocean, and, well, after Dad died…" she trailed off, suddenly feeling very selfish, "well, it became a *real* possibility."

"Oh, Lorelei, I'm sorry to hear you lost your dad."

"Thank you. It's been a tough year. I still think of him every day. I still can't believe he's gone. I sometimes even forget he is." She glanced down at her finger and rubbed her ring. She had a little bit of her dad with her all the time in the form of a ring that she had made with a pinch of his ashes. She had always thought that it was a hideous idea when Janey suggested it way before they even knew their dad was ill. In fact, it had been a casual conversation five years or so ago, but cremation jewellery was interestingly more popular than they had realised, and the sisters had no regret in having the rings made.

"That's a pretty ring," remarked Danny, noticing she was fiddling with it.

"Thank you."

"So, you're recently divorced then?"

"Well, yes, but it was a long time coming. What about you? Married? Kids?" she asked.

Danny scoffed, "Me? Oh no, no children, or wife, for that matter."

"You don't like kids?"

"I do. A lot of my friends have children and they're a lot of fun," he paused, "and I'm assuming you don't have children either?"

"Oh no, I mean it just didn't happen, but to be honest, seeing what my sister goes through with her daughter, it's kind of put me off, although I know that not every child is like my niece…"

"Oh, what's she like?"

Again, feeling no desire to hide the truth, Lorelei divulged. "She's aggressive to her parents, particularly my sister Janey. She doesn't listen, she breaks things in a temper. Shall I go on?"

"Oh gosh, sounds hard work!"

"Yeah, she's a lovely girl in a lot of ways, but she has problems with managing her anger. We think she's neuro diverse, maybe ADHD or oppositional defiance disorder, but because she is so intelligent and academic, my sister and her husband just cannot get a diagnosis."

"Oh, I see. How old is she?"

"Just turned fourteen. Don't get me wrong, she's a pleasant girl when she's being good, she just has these issues. She's a bit like Jekyll and Hyde…"

"Sounds challenging for your sister and her husband."

"Yes, it is. That's why I've suggested that Ruby comes and stays here with me in the school holidays, in February. I'd really like to help somehow if I can."

"That is so nice of you. What a kind person you are. Well, maybe I'll meet Ruby when she comes. I would really like to." At that point, Danny's thoughts wandered to another girl he once knew who sounded all too similar to Ruby, but he shut it out, not wanting to attract negative thoughts into his mind when he was having such a lovely lunch date with Lorelei.

The friendly waitress brought their food to the table. It was perfectly presented and both Danny and Lorelei were so pleased with their choices. They were both hungry (Danny more so than Lorelei as he'd skipped breakfast), but either way, the food did not stay on the plates for very long.

"This is delicious," remarked Lorelei in between mouthfuls. "Is yours good?"

"Oh yes, they do the *best* fish finger sandwich in all of Cornwall!"

Lorelei got home around three o'clock in the afternoon. After putting the kettle on, she snuggled on the sofa in her soft cream blanket. Looking around the flat, she decided that her home really could do with some 'Christmas cheer'. She resigned herself to getting the Christmas decorations out and brightening the place up. Her artificial tree was a bit worse for wear and looking a bit tatty to say the least. She thought back to Hazel's house. She had been so impressed with the grandeur of Hazel's Christmas tree and couldn't help but think how amazing it would be if this year she could get a real tree for the first time ever. Well, it would be the first time since she was a little girl when her mum and dad used to get a real tree from the Christmas tree forest. *Yes, that's a great idea.* She then considered the decorations that she already owned and reflected on how they reminded her so much of her old life. With a frown, she grabbed her laptop from the coffee table and googled the nearest Argos and was pleasantly surprised that there was a store in Penzance, only five miles or so away. She opened the shop website and browsed through the Christmas decorations.

Lorelei had a colour scheme formulating in her mind. Yes, she wanted silver and teal. Teal was a colourway that she had always been fond of, and had campaigned for it for her wedding, yet had been overruled by Jay, who wanted a more 'masculine' colour. They went for a standard royal blue instead in the end. Lorelei didn't mind royal blue too much, for it reminded her of the sea, but would have loved the colour teal. Well, she couldn't have it for her wedding, but she *could* have it for her Christmas tree. With passion, Lorelei clicked and reserved teal decorations, including some cute mini baubles with miniature teal and silver stars inside them and some lovely teal and silver Christmas tree beads.

Lorelei had somewhat of an impulsive nature and when realising she could probably nip down to Penzance right there and then to collect her reservations, she thought to herself, *what the heck, let's do it*. So, without further ado, she grabbed her small handbag, made certain her phone and purse were inside, and darted out the door.

During the short journey Lorelei found herself

becoming more and more perplexed with her feelings. She was encumbered with grief, yet at the same time felt happy and excited and she couldn't remember the last time she felt like that. She thought that perhaps when her flat was all decorated, she could invite Hazel around who would surely be impressed with her efforts. Yes, yes, this was all coming together and what a wonderful life Lorelei would have now. She had a job; she had friends; she had met someone (a *man* who she really had a good feeling about, even if it only turned out to be friendship). She hardly recognised the warm fuzzy feelings that engulfed her. Jay had never managed to maintain her happiness for very long and if she thought carefully, she didn't remember ever feeling so relaxed with him, even in those early honeymoon days.

When Lorelei parked up outside the store, she realised that there were a few messages on her phone. There was one from her sister to say that they had booked the cottage for February half term, thanking her with lines of kisses. Then, to her delight, there was a text from Danny. Her heart flipped with exhilaration.

> ***Hi Lorelei, thank you for a wonderful lunch today, you really made my day! I can't wait to see you this evening at the writing club x***

Her heart melted. He felt the same, he just *had* to. Her cheeks began to blush and that unfamiliar feeling once more creeped over her. She was falling for him, and the plummet felt good.

After everything

"Janey, I'm really low. Please, tell me where she is," Jay pathetically pleaded down the handset. He hadn't wanted to call Janey, but he was desperate. Janey's heart pounded, and her anxiety rose.

"I'm not doing that Jay," she said firmly, with determination. There was no way she was going to stoop so low to reveal her sister's location.

"I've made such a mistake to lose her. You of all people know I've not been the husband I should've been, but I need to make it right Janey." He winced as he recalled the years gone by and how abysmally he had treated his ex-wife. Even though it was like an obsession, he felt now she had really wiped her hands of him, he wanted her *even* more.

"Jay, it's *history*," she groaned. "I don't want to be a part of this," Janey insisted.

Though Jay, in hope that Janey would have pity on him, continued to beg. "Make her see me Janey, you owe me this, after all that's happened, please, just try."

Janey sighed and reiterated the message. "She's started a new life. She doesn't *want* to see you!" How much more direct could she be?

Jay guffawed; he could not accept Lorelei no longer had any feelings for him. "I know that's not true; she would definitely want to see me. I need her. I'm in a bad place, Janey, I've let things slip and I don't know how to get out of this *blackness*..." his performance sounded genuine, but Janey spared no sympathy and never would for this man who had done unthinkable things. She despised him.

"Jay, it's not my problem, *please*—"

"—I'm not well, Janey, I need your help," he pleaded without an ounce of shame.

"Look, I'm sorry you're not feeling well, but what do you think I will be able to do?!"

"I need to speak to her. She's my soulmate. I know she can help me find my feet. I've so many wrongs to right, I need her to realise how sorry I am for destroying our marriage..."

"It's over!" cried Janey. "It was over fifteen years ago, you know fine well!"

"She's gone to Cornwall," without listening, he interrogated.

"I'm not saying *anything* Jay..."

"Janey, you don't understand."

"No, you're right, I don't, and I want you to leave *us all alone*!" she screamed.

Seemingly not able to take no for an answer or accept that Janey did not want to help, he continued with his plea. "I know she's down south; I just wish you would contact her on my behalf, make her meet me—"

"—No!" Janey cut him off in mid flow, her anxiety continuing to heighten.

"After everything, you won't even try, *for me*?"

"I can't Jay!"

"I'm not a bad man, Janey..."

She stifled a laugh. "You're a troubled man, that's for sure, and you, *you* have the audacity to call me after everything you have done. You think I will have sympathy? You're crazy!" There was a moment of silence before Jay spoke again. "How's Ruby?"

"She's fine, *keep her out of this*. We're all fine!"

Tessy Braun

Just one more

Lorelei pulled her woolly navy tights over her slim calves and thighs before pulling her knitted jumper dress over her head and down over her waist and knees. It was the perfect winter outfit; snug, warm, and comfortable. She sprayed a few pumps of perfume over her neck and wrists (she'd had the bottle of fragrance for an age, *years* possibly, but hadn't very often bothered to wear it). The scent was somewhat woody which was second to none for the colder months and she adored the subtle notes of vanilla and patchouli.

    Next, she dabbed some hot cherry stain on her cheeks and gently rubbed it in, bringing warmth to her pale skin. She relished in the makeover as she delicately swept a little brown mascara over her upper eyelashes. *Perhaps just a little colour on my lips*, she thought, rolling the subtle shiny gloss over lips that were desperately in need of moisture after all the cold weather (and also desperately in need of some long overdue attention).

    She was all set for her very first meeting with the 'St Ives writing club'. She had planned on driving herself but just a short time earlier, Hazel had sent her a message to say she could pick her up, because she had been visiting her grandma who lived in St Just and would come right past St Ives. Lorelei had not been opposed to this idea at all. If truth be told, she thoroughly fancied an alcoholic drink at tonight's meeting, especially as her nerves were beginning to kick in.

Lorelei thought to herself how Janey would have been much better equipped to attend something like this. Her sister was quite accustomed to attending meetings at work, and she had unquestionably more experience with language and literature than herself. Nevertheless, she would just have to brave it. A phrase she found empowering was 'fake it to make it'. *That's exactly what I will have to do*, she thought to herself, while giving her hair a final style. She wore it down; after having washed and blow dried it and she was very pleased with her voluptuous locks and the nice soft condition her hair seemed to be in. Thick and long, her rich auburn mane shone in the light of her bedroom mirror. She was happy with her style, having made an extra special effort to look pretty in the hope to impress (not in the least, a dark curly haired writer that would be attending the event).

A quick check of the time left Lorelei surprised to see that she had just shy of fifteen minutes until she was to be collected. Yet no sooner than checking her schedule, her phone buzzed with a message to say that Hazel was outside. *Oh no,* thought Lorelei, *this is it!*

She grabbed her tote bag, in which she stuffed Danny's poetry book, her notepad (with the poem she wrote earlier that day) along with her purse, lip gloss, and mobile phone. She trotted down the stairs and flew out the door, where she was met with a splatter of cold rain across her made-up face. Debating whether or not she had time to run back up to the flat to pick up an umbrella, Hazel called to her from her car, leaving her no option, and, besides, she *did* have a long waterproof coat over her arm.

"Come on Lorelei, we don't want to be late!"

Hazel, who looked fiercely fashionable and glamorous with her white fake fur snood and purple cashmere jumper, sat in the driver's seat of her 'Moonwalk Grey Mini Countryman'. The window slid up, but she continued beckoning Lorelei into the passenger seat from behind the glass. The rain was really settling in, and Lorelei made a dash from the door to the curb and jumped in. The interior was immaculate, fitted out with full grey leather and there wasn't a speck of dirt to be seen. Lorelei would not have been able to tell from the lovely condition of the car that Hazel was a dog owner. The stereo played an old yet familiar track.

"Oh, I love REM!" Lorelei exclaimed.

"Me too!" agreed Hazel. "I love all the old bands. I'm not too much of a fan of modern music, really. Do you want your heated seat on?"

"Oh, yes, please!"

"Just hit this button," she said, pointing to the array of illuminated controls on the side of the chair. "You smell amazing, by the way! So, how's your day been?"

"Well, as a matter of fact, it's been rather lovely!"

"Oh, yes? Do tell," Hazel started the engine and pulled out of the little street, paying particular attention to the other cars, and of course, the sometimes invisible stone walls. She was quite particular with her car, well, this one anyway. Lorelei was to learn Hazel had another car that was more of a run-around, and she wasn't so fussy about that little banger, and of course the Ford Focus was the dedicated pup-mobil. Molly certainly hadn't had as much of a sniff inside the Countryman, let alone laid one of her paws inside. Lorelei told Hazel all about her lunch date. *Was it a lunch date?* she second guessed herself.

"Oh my! Lorelei, that sounds *adorable*!" She beamed. "Danny is *so* lovely!"

"Have you known him for a long time?"

"Have I just! Yes, since primary school; Danny and I go back years and years." She sighed internally when she thought of the years gone by and all her memories with Danny.

"Oh wow, that's so lovely. I've not kept in touch with many friends from my childhood, apart from Louise, and I don't see her often."

Briefly rubbing Lorelei's knee in a comforting manner, she empathised. "Well, it's difficult if you're in a big city with a busy career. It's different down here. It's all close-knit."

"My ex-husband hated any close-knit relationships I ever had…"

"Oh, sounds like the narcissistic type?"

"Yeah."

"Let me guess, did he tell you what to wear?"

"Well, he hated me looking too pretty…"

"Accuse you of flirting?"

"How did you know?"

"Let's just say… I know the type."

"Really?"

"Yes, I'm afraid so…!"

"Not your partner?"

"Oh no, before Peter."

"Oh, thank goodness, that's good."

"*But Lorelei*, today I met someone myself, rather a strange encounter…"

"Oh?"

"Yes, I was taking Molly for a run on the beach earlier and this guy was walking on the beach too. Nothing strange about that, I suppose, only he seemed a little 'over-interested' in Molly. He walked alongside me for a while, was friendly enough, but something was just a little bit strange about him and I'm sure he smelled of alcohol."

"This sounds like the same guy that came into Mousie's shop earlier. What did he say to you?"

"Mousie met him too?"

"Uh-huh, I think so. Sounds like the same person…"

"Well, he was friendly… asked me what I did for a living, and I told him how I worked for the newspaper. He seemed interested. He seemed a bit sad, a bit lost."

"This really is weird; I hope he doesn't pop up again." Lorelei suddenly felt quite insecure. This mystery man had given her the jitters. "What did he look like?"

"Scruffy, but not unattractive. Unshaven, didn't look like he'd had a haircut for a while, good teeth, why?"

"I'm just being paranoid, but I was worried that it may have been my ex, but there's no way he would let himself go like that. He's always looked after himself, even though he didn't look after me."

"Have you got a picture of him?"

"No, I've burnt every single photo of him, and there's nothing on my phone. I've blocked him from social media, so can't show you, and there's no way I want to look him up. Anyway, he was always conscious of appearance. It doesn't sound like him."

"Ah, okay, I'm sure it's not."

"No, that would be preposterous."

"If I see him again, I'll ask more questions."

"Thanks, hopefully you won't."

They pulled up on a steep hill not far from 'The Barrel of Blood,' which was a traditional free house with a very unusual name. The ceiling was low, with wooden beams stretching from above the bar to the opposite side of the room. It was a small space, but there was a table at the end of the lounge and an open fire.

"It's a lovely pub Lorelei," said Hazel, "but it's not the ideal location for our meets because sometimes it's busy, but they have 'Rattler' on tap, so the boys like it."

"Rattler?"

"Cornish Cider. Come on, let's get in there, it's almost eight pm."

Lorelei and Hazel were greeted by the friendly landlady as they walked inside. It was warm and inviting and they went straight to the bar to order a drink.

"What would you like?" Hazel asked.

Lorelei thought for a moment and then replied. "I'll have a white wine, please."

"You're not a gin drinker then?!"

"No, not really."

"Oh, it's very fashionable nowadays," Hazel insisted. "I thought you'd be a pink gin kind of girl for some reason. Oh well, can't always be right!"

Lorelei pursed her lips and considered this momentarily. "Well, maybe I am. After all, it's all about change for me, so why not? I'll have a pink gin and tonic, please."

"Let's make it a double!" said Hazel.

"What?!"

Turning to the barmaid, Hazel ordered a large diet coke for herself and a double pink gin with a slimline tonic for Lorelei. The rest of the group were huddled in the corner and gave the pair a nod and a wave. Once they had been served, they joined the others where introductions began.

"Hello you two!" Danny stood up to greet the pair. "Lorelei, welcome!" He gave her a little hug and then the same to Hazel. "Let me introduce you to everyone." He turned to the table, "everyone — this is our lovely newcomer, Lorelei."

There was Mick, who was an older gentleman, probably in his sixties. He was quite skinny and dressed in corduroy trousers and a beige shirt with thin wire glasses over his nose. He looked like the academic type and gave Lorelei a nod and a wink.

"Very pleased to meet you Lorelei," he said in a surprisingly posh voice with no hint of a west country accent.

"My pleasure," she replied. Next there was Tammy, a curvaceous and full bosomed woman with short, mousy-brown hair, which framed her friendly round face. Her eyes were deep sea green with dark specks, and she was very beautiful.

"Hello love!" she said from across the table. Danny went on to explain that Tammy was their spoken word poet.

"Tammy runs a local 'open mic' night and has even been on the radio a few times!"

"That's very *impressive,* Tammy!" said Lorelei.

Tammy blushed. "Oh no, it's nothing."

"She's too humble," remarked Mick, who gave her a playful elbow in the side. Next to be introduced was Flo, who was in her early twenties but could easily have passed for her late teens with her slight frame and youthful looks. She was clearly a fan of body piercings, having a ring through her septum, and a scaffold bar through her right ear as well as numerous studs lined up her left. Lorelei also noted her arms where the ends of a tattoo could be seen crawling out from her three-quarter length sleeves.

"Hey Lorelei, we're so happy to have you here with us!"

That evening the group was small as a few regulars couldn't make it, but Lorelei was quite pleased about that because there were only three names to remember, which couldn't be *that* difficult. *Mick, Tammy, Flo, Mick, Tammy, Flo, Mick, Tammy, Flo*, she repeated in her mind in an attempt to stick it in there somehow. Now, sat down around the table, in between Danny and Hazel, she finally took a sip of her pink gin and Hazel was watching her closely to gauge her reaction.

"You like it, girl?"

"It's divine!" Lorelei nodded with one hundred percent approval. Hazel lifted her palm for a high-five.

Danny and Mick did indeed have a pint of 'Rattler' Cornish cider in front of them and Lorelei admired the decorative snake glass it was served in. *Definitely instagramable*, she thought. Flo preferred a vodka and coke while Tammy lapped up a pint of 'Tribute'. Lorelei lifted her glass again and generously slurped her drink. She really loved the taste; gin was definitely her new 'go-to drink'.

Danny cleared his throat. "So, I thought to begin with we could go around the table and do a bit of an intro, for example, tell the group something about yourself and what your current writing project is." Lorelei's heart started pumping. *Please don't start with me*, she silently prayed.

"Let's start with Mick and go anti clockwise," said Danny, and Lorelei could breathe as she now knew she would be the last to speak.

"Okay, so as you all know, I'm Mick. I'm a physics teacher at Hayle Academy."

Yes, I knew he was an academic, thought Lorelei.

Mick continued. "Well, in terms of writing projects, I'm currently trying to write a poem illustrating the terrible consequences of plastic in our oceans and shorelines."

"That's a very important topic Mick," said Tammy. "I do litter pick walks on the beach once a week with a group to try to help. The amount of plastic that we find is crazy, shocking to be honest." Tammy shook her head with disapproval and Flo nodded enthusiastically.

"That's very admirable that you do that, Tammy. You must let me know the details," said Flo, and Mick nodded.

"Yes indeed, you'll have to share the info. I'm sure we'd all like to help," he said.

"I'll add you to the group on Facebook," said Tammy, with that gorgeous smile of hers. Mick took a sip of his Rattler and continued to explain his writing project.

"So yeah, I'm trying to write a long poem to read at one of your open mic nights, Tammy," he said.

"That will be brilliant. I can't wait to hear it!" chirped Tammy.

"Can you share any of what you've written so far, Mick?" asked Hazel.

"Well, I'm only in the early stages, but I can tell you what it's going to be called."

"Yes, please do," the group insisted.

"Okay, it's going to be called 'The Litter Picker and the Hungry Seagull!'"

Danny noticed Lorelei had almost finished her gin and tonic already. "Same again, beautiful?" He winked at her, and she nodded gratefully. "Anyone else ready for another?" Danny asked.

Flo raised her empty glass. "Please, vodka and coke, Dan." No one else was in requirement so Danny quietly slipped away to the bar, which was very close, and in no time at all he came back with the two drinks that Flo and Lorelei had ordered before they carried on with their round the table speeches.

"Hi, I'm Flo, I'm writing a book. It's a dystopian fantasy. I'm about thirteen thousand words in now!" She smiled and took a big gulp of her vodka mixer.

"Oh, I love fantasy!" said Lorelei, feeling a little more

confident about contributing to the conversation after her first double gin.

"Oh, do you?" said Flo, "Who's your favourite fantasy author?" asked Flo excitedly. Lorelei almost choked on her drink.

"Well, erm, well, I-I can't remember the name…" she mumbled, starting to panic, her face turning red. "Does Harry Potter count?" She giggled, feeling incredibly incompetent and silly, "I mean, J K Rowley, of course."

"You mean, J K *Rowling*," snorted Tammy, who was almost at the bottom of her first pint of ale. "You are funny. I love Harry Potter too!"

Lorelei was thinking back to her early twenties when she had read the Harry Potter books (probably the last time she seriously read). She started to wonder why she was sitting with the writing group after all, then she glanced to her right and realised exactly why. Surrounded by new friends, in a strange place that was beginning to feel like home, she laid her head momentarily on Danny's shoulder. *This was why,* to make new friends who could be like a family to her, and to finally create the happy life that she had craved for so many years. Danny ruffled her hair.

"Don't be embarrassed, beautiful." His smile was infectious.

Hazel was next to speak. "Well, of course you all know that I'm Hazel. I'm concentrating on my poetry at the moment. I've written a new poem. Would you like to hear it?"

"Yes, absolutely!" chimed Tammy and Flo in unison. They looked at each other and said in sync, "Jinx!"

Hazel unlocked her phone and scrolled to find her notes. "Okay, here goes…" She took a deep breath and read the poem out loud.

The darkness drapes its cloak around

and all about there is no sound,

*Then gravel makes a crunching tone
as I park up by my childhood home.*

*I open up my vehicle door,
surrounded by the open moor,*

*and as I lift the boot up high,
I glance up at the country sky,*

*I gasp out loud in shock to see,
the night sky pouring over me*

*and there were planets like red Mars
among the zenith of the stars.*

*In blackened sky, with stars so bright
lies the beauty of the night.*

For a second or so, there was silence. Everyone was just absorbing Hazel's words until Flo broke the stillness.

"Hazel, that is *beautiful*," Flo remarked, quite moved by the piece and Tammy shook her head in awe before adding her own appreciation.

"You're *so* talented, beautifully penned," she said with a touch of envy in her voice.

"Very good," said Mick, rubbing his temples. "Evocative Hazel." He nodded in approval.

"It's no surprise it's so beautiful. You always write so naturally," Danny said softly. "Absolutely stunning."

Lorelei wiped a tear from the corner of her eye. "That really touched me. What a stunning poem," Lorelei said.

Hazel blushed. "Guys, you're so kind. I really appreciate your support. I've really been trying to work on my descriptions. I'm so glad you liked it."

"When do you think your book will be available, Hazel?" asked Mick.

Hazel grinned and squeezed her shoulders up like an excited child. "Hopefully in the new year!" Animating her words with hand gestures, she pointed her forefingers in the air. "Watch this space, everyone!" and she giggled. Lorelei beamed with admiration at her new friends, and what talented writers they all were.

"How do you even go about getting a book published?" she asked, eager to learn as much as possible. Danny went on to explain the options of self-publishing or submitting your manuscript to traditional publishers. In this case Hazel was going to self-publish.

Lorelei listened with great interest. "Wow, I never knew it could be so easy to get your book in print."

"Yes, self-publishing has become really accessible," said Flo, "but for my novel, I'm gonna try to go with a publisher if I can find one that will take me on."

"Yes, definitely try Flo," said Danny, "It took me a while, but eventually I was successful, and there's nothing to say you won't be too."

Lorelei was still repeating Hazel's scrumptious words about the night sky in her mind. The poem had really captured her attention.

She turned to Hazel. "I'm so impressed with your writing. That poem really reminded me of my own childhood home on Dartmoor. I love it."

"Thanks Lorelei. That's really sweet of you to say so."

They were interrupted by Danny's coughing to get the group's attention. "So, Lorelei, tell us about yourself and what you are writing right now?" For a moment silence befell the group, and Lorelei, feeling all eyes upon her, shrank into her seat. A feeling of anxiety wrapped around her, and she almost felt suffocated by the pressure of speaking. After what seemed like an eternity, she squeaked.

"Oh, well, I must admit, I am, ah-hem, extremely new to this, I mean, I do like books…" She tried to compose herself, realising how her nerves had well and truly got the better of her. "I haven't had an awful lot of time for creativity over the last ten or so years," she said, not feeling an ease of the pressure that was mounting on her, and her face turning a bright beetroot colour again, her words fumbling, she continued. "Well, I do want to start with some poetry, and I, well, um, I had a go at writing something, it's not very good, I mean I'm not a writer, really, I just, um, I'm keen to learn more, and, uh …. being new to St Ives, I really wanted to…" she paused. "Um, meet people. I saw the advert for this group, and, well, everything fell together really, I met Hazel, and well," until now she had in the main been looking down, but then she found the confidence to hold her head up, and she ended with a confident, "Well, *Here I am!*"

Her clearly unplanned speech brought smiles around the table. Tammy reached over and touched Lorelei's arm reassuringly. "Well, everyone must start somewhere, and it's great that you are interested in writing. We'll be able to support you a lot!"

Mick nodded enthusiastically. "We'll look after you, guide you…" He was so well spoken, and seemed a true gentleman. "We'll help to answer any questions that you may have." He smiled, looking over his glasses at Lorelei, and nodded as if in approval of her.

"Of course," said Danny. "This is a safe place, Lorelei, and you're among friends."

"Thank you, you're all so lovely, and I'm *so* happy!" She swigged the rest of her drink, and chirped, feeling quite tipsy. "Who'd like another? It's my round!"

"I'll come to the bar with you," said Danny.

"A tribute, please, love," Tammy requested.

"Very kind. A pint of Rattler would be delightful," said Mick. Flo held up her empty glass.

"Vodka and Coke, please." she said.

Hazel looked down at her almost full pint of Coke, having only taken a few sips all evening. "Could you get me some peanuts please?"

"Of course, you remember the order, Danny? My head's feeling a bit fuzzy!"

"Yes, it's all up here," he tapped the side of his head, then took her arm and led her over to the bar. "I'll get these Lorelei. This lot are a thirsty bunch. This is on me."

Once settled back at the table, Lorelei swigged some more gin and reached in her bag for her notepad and addressed the group. "As I was saying, I'm not really *a writer*, but I did try to jot down a poem for this evening." She flicked through the first few pages of her scribbles until she arrived at the poem that she had written up neatly. Everyone looked at her, eager to hear what she had created. The alcohol now gave her a newfound confidence. "So, I wrote this earlier today. It's a poem inspired by the beautiful coastal road between St Ives and Land's End."

Mick raised his hand. "Oh, that's a gorgeous stretch!" he exclaimed. "Definitely my favourite road in the county, and perhaps in the whole of England!"

"Yes, it's stunning," agreed Flo.

"It is," Lorelei continued. "So, I've always had a love for Cornwall, since I was a child. I've adored the ocean and the landscape here, the beaches, the cliffs…" She closed her eyes, imagining the scenery. "When I sat down this morning to write, well, it seemed natural that I would attempt to write about Cornwall."

Danny watched her carefully as she spoke, noting the wonderful animation and passion in her voice. "That's completely relatable Lorelei, I too love writing about this little corner of the world; it's just so magical." He beamed. "All the poems in my book are about Cornwall. It's such an inspirational place."

"So, what did you come up with, darling?" Hazel pressed.

"Well, it's nothing compared to yours Hazel," said Lorelei before beginning to read aloud the piece.

> ***The coast road from St Ives to Land's End***
> ***is the most beautiful stretch, each and every bend.***
> ***The St Ives cows have an excellent view,***
> ***(the tabby of Porthmeor Farm does too).***
>
> ***The undulating road winds up and around,***
> ***bar the infrequent car, there's no other sound.***
> ***But sights, oh so many, to feast our eyes on***
> ***as we cheerfully relish the journey along.***

The group were again struck with momentary silence, which this time was eventually broken by Danny.

"You wrote that just today?" he asked in astonishment.

"Uh, yes," Lorelei nodded slowly.

"Oh Lorelei, that's so lovely," said Tammy.

"The rhyme and metre is very good," agreed Mick. "I'm impressed, especially since this is the first poem you've written."

"It's not finished though, is it?" said Flo. "It feels unfinished?"

"Oh no, I want to write more. I want to write about the ruins of the tin mine, the yellow hotel, the ocean view and much more…"

Mick rubbed his chin in thought. "You really have a talent," he praised.

Danny leaned over and whispered in Lorelei's ear. "He doesn't say that to everyone…."

Tammy looked excited. "Honestly, Lorelei, it was really pleasant to listen to. You read very well, you know! You'll have to come to my open mic night!" Tammy said encouragingly, and it was true, Lorelei's spoken voice was notably strong.

"Well, I'd love to come to be in the audience!" she chuckled, "I'm not so sure about performing, besides, I'll have to do some more writing before I get to that stage!" Trying to contain her blushes from the bombardment of compliments, Lorelei was relieved that it was now time for Danny to speak. He talked about his book, and how the sales were going.

"Rather slow at the moment, unfortunately," he lamented.

"I'm sure it will pick up!" Lorelei comforted him.

"Yes, hopefully," he said.

The group discussed some local events that were in the pipeline, including a literary festival in Truro in the new year, and, of course, Tammy's open mic night, which she ran in Falmouth. Flo told the group more about the vision for her dystopian novel, and Mick harped on about the importance of keeping the ocean clean. He was fervently passionate about the environment, often writing what was known as eco poetry, and he liked to educate people on the importance of the subject.

By now, Lorelei was on her fourth gin and tonic. It was probably just one too many because the room didn't seem quite so stable anymore, and she had slurred her words a few times whilst trying to keep up with the conversation.

"Poetry can be a therapy for me," said Tammy. "I write a lot about my mental health; I find it helps me so much to express myself artistically." The group agreed, and a few of them shared examples. Lorelei had been listening with intent.

"I wonder if I should try to write about my dad's death," said Lorelei, unexpectedly. It was a bit of a bombshell and for a moment, no one knew what to say. Of course, to no one's surprise, the first to comfort her was Danny.

"Oh, Lorelei, I am so sorry about your loss. You said it was last year?" asked Danny.

"Just a year ago, yeah." She gave a brief overview that he had had cancer and it was all just 'too late' for any treatment other than palliative. The bunch were good apples and despite not knowing them that well, Lorelei felt comfortable to bring up the subject. They all thought it could be a useful exercise for Lorelei to get some thoughts down on paper.

"You could write about it, if you felt it would help, Tammy's right, often it's very therapeutic," explained Danny, although he hadn't taken his own advice after his older sister's death, but this wasn't something he'd be bringing up with his writing friends tonight.

Definitely food for thought, thought Lorelei. They chatted away, often going off topic from literature and poetry and instead discussing Flo's next piercing which was going to be a 'daith' (the innermost cartilage fold of the ear), and Flo was convinced it would alleviate her migraines, although the evidence for this was debatable.

"It's based on replicating acupuncture. The piercing is on the pressure point, plus it looks freaking awesome too…!" she grinned.

"It sounds so cool, Flo!" Lorelei reached up to her

own bare ear and felt along her helix where no studs were to be found. Her eyes lit up as she thought of the idea. "Maybe I'll go with you, Flo. I reckon I'd like to get a piercing!"

"*Hell yeah*! What will you get?"

"I like the bar you have in your ear…"

"Oh, awesome, a 'scaffold'. It took about a year for mine to heal, though, but totally worth it."

"Great, it's time that I did something a little…" She thought for a while. "Something a little *crazy!*" She burst into a fit of giggles, the alcohol clearly having a positive effect on her ability to be social.

Hazel glanced up at the big wooden framed clock on the wall and gasped. "Oh, my! I'd better be getting off now. I didn't realise how late it was. Is that okay, Lorelei?"

Lorelei glanced at Danny. She hadn't wanted to leave, but she relied on Hazel for a ride home.

Sensing her dismay and also not wanting her to leave, Danny offered a lifeline. "If you want to stay, I can order you a taxi. Come on, stay out with us!"

Hazel tutted and said quite honestly, "Lorelei, this is part of the reason we're looking to change our meet-up location. They always end up getting drunk, and it all ends up in one big booze up!" she laughed, as although it was the truth, her words were one hundred per cent in jest.

"Well, I've had a wonderful night, and it's been nice to meet everyone," Lorelei said reluctantly, "but, I suppose I *really* should go home with Hazel…" She picked up her bag.

Sensing the disappointment in her voice, Hazel gave her friend a cuddle. "Oh, Lorelei! You should stay out, you don't start work until Monday, so you can lie in tomorrow," she smiled. "You stay out — have fun!"

"Well, if you don't mind, I think I may just stay out for *just* one more…"

"Of course, right, well, I've got to get on. It's been absolutely lovely seeing you all, but I do look forward to the time when we have a place to go, which is *not* a pub!" Hazel teased.

"There's always cans of cider, Hazel," bellowed Mick.

"Hmm, yes, but this always happens. You lot end up getting drunk, and we want to focus on the craft, gentlemen. While we're on the subject, any news on the caravan?"

"I'm working on it." Danny winked at Hazel. "And thank you for letting me keep her for just a little longer." He put his arm around Lorelei and gave her a squeeze.

Lorelei seized up for a slight moment. The terminology he used made her shudder, for she was not a possession to be owned, but after some consideration, she felt it had been used with a good intent. She said goodbye to Hazel, and then turned to her new friends where, in front of her, another gin and tonic had magically appeared as if left by a Cornish Piskie. "Thank you, Tammy!"

Everyone was pretty sloshed by this stage, and Flo came up with a great idea for getting to know each other.

"I know! Let's play two lies and a truth!"

Tessy Braun

The Changeling

In Bristol, whilst her Auntie Lorelei let her hair down with her new friends, Ruby twisted her hair between her thumb and forefinger, wishing it was thicker and more styleable. She sat on her bed in front of her large mirrored built-in wardrobes and stared at her reflection.

Why am I so ugly? she thought to herself. She particularly hated the shape of her nose. *When I'm older, I'll get cosmetic surgery and have it straightened. I'm sure to get enough inheritance money to fix my stupid face when my parents die.* Her mother was blessed with a straight nose, and beautiful Auntie Lorelei had bone structure to die for. Why was she the only one cursed with a crooked witch's nose? Perhaps it suited her personality, because she knew she could be wicked.

Is that why Mummy hates me so much? she silently asked her reflection in the mirror. She imagined she was born a witch or even a goblin and been exchanged at birth — the changeling baby that could never be truly loved by its earthen mother. Ruby always felt different, although she couldn't lie to herself, she could fully understand why her mother may take a disliking to her, considering her frequent volatile behaviour, however Ruby felt the disfavour was more inherent than that.

Though she may think she might try, Ruby's mum didn't do a very good job of hiding her loathing from Ruby's point of view. Ruby had heard the late-night conversations among the sobbing expressions of motherly dejection. She had clearly felt the stabbing words her mother had too often raged at her, "*You little cow, I wish I'd never given birth to you!*" She'd say sorry, later, when they had calmed down, but Ruby recalled the sentiment deeply and the realisation that her mother resented her so much could not be washed away, no matter how hard she tried to eradicate it.

Why am I the way I am? Ruby asked herself again. She certainly didn't want to be aggressive, manipulative, and impulsive. She did possess the skill of rational thinking when she was calm, at least. She also knew how to push and push with no expression of empathy, and mastered the skill to carry on, no matter how hurtful or destructive she became. *I want to be a good girl,* she reflected, *but I was born evil, and that's all there is to it.*

In all truthfulness, it had not surprised Ruby that her mother wanted to send her away to Cornwall to stay with her aunt. Yet she thought her mother to be selfish to want time away and was rather perturbed that her father went along with it all. If it went well, perhaps they'd want her to stay in Cornwall indefinitely. *Would that be so bad?*

It was past ten o'clock and she knew she should sleep, but her mind was so active and showed no signs of slowing down. She lay on her bed, reaching her arm over to the bedside table, tapping rhythmically with her nails on the hard wood surface. Often she found it impossible to physically turn herself off. Bedtimes had always been tricky. She seemed in a permanent state of alertness, which her parents never understood. Ruby reached for the glass of water on the table and accidentally knocked it off. She was clumsy too. She slumped back on the bed, banging her head against the pillow, and then started to hum a repetitive melody to a tune only in her head.

The bedroom door creaked open.

"Are you okay, sweet pea?" Robert's low and calm voice came from the door frame. "I heard a bang."

"I'm not tired…"

"It's late now. Your mother is even asleep!"

"What are you doing?"

"Just watching some TV. Will a hot chocolate help?"

Ruby's eyes lit up. "Marshmallows?"

The two snuck down into the kitchen together to prepare the late-night treat.

"Mint, orange or salted caramel?"

"They're Mum's special ones!" she whispered.

"Our Secret."

They had a bond, and although Ruby knew she could test the boundaries with Robert, and very often did give him an awfully hard time, she felt he was a good dad to her and more often than not he had a way with Ruby that few others did. That was why she was so surprised he had agreed to get rid of her during the February half term. *Mother must have made him do it.* Besides, she was getting used to the idea anyway, and Auntie Lorelei wasn't *that* bad.

Robert handed her a chocolate biscuit, and she beamed.

"Thanks Daddy; love you."

Tessy Braun

Lullaby

"I'll go first," cackled Lorelei. "Okay… so, number one, I was born with a curly pig's tail," she unintentionally snorted. "See, that could be true, right? I'm snorting like a pig now, demonstrating the connection to my ancestry!" She creased with laughter and the others, too, were doubling over in hysterics. "Number two, my name's not *really* Lorelei, it's Esmerelda, I got bullied at school, so changed it by deed poll." She made a sweet little clicking noise with her tongue while she thought of another statement to share with the table. "And finally, a homeless person took great pleasure in peeing all over me, and some of it went in my *eye*!" The four of them were literally crying with laughter, their sides aching from all the giggling.

"Well, I think we can rule the first one out!" said Mick. "In all my teaching days, I've never come across someone being born with a pig's tail. My wife's a doctor, and she's never come across this strange phenomenon either…"

"Well, you never know," said Flo.

"No, it can't be true!" Tammy cried, howling with laughter.

Lorelei let out two more large snorts, this time quite

intentionally. "Yes, you never know!" she said. Everyone was roaring yet again.

"Well, after that, maybe I'll have to reconsider!" chuckled Mick.

Danny turned to Lorelei and looked her right in the eyes. "*Esmerelda...* you know, maybe you *could* be an Esme," he said.

"But," said Flo, "why would you change your name to something equally unusual?" she mused. "You'd think if you were being bullied because you were called Esmeralda, you'd change your name to something really boring, like..." she thought, before responding. "Jane, or something plain like that!"

Lorelei gave Flo a stern look, pretending to be serious and trying not to laugh. "My sister's called Jane!"

Flo pulled a painfully uncomfortable face. "Oh no, I'm sorry! Not to say your sister is plain," she backtracked, feeling terribly awkward.

Mick tapped the table with a beer mat. "But why would a homeless person urinate on her?" he pondered.

Danny slowly nodded. "I know the true statement..."

"You do?" Lorelei asked.

"Yes! You were born with a pig's tail. Your mother told my mother when they met a few weeks ago," he teased.

"Ooh, your parents met *already!*" Flo giggled. "When's the wedding!?" she joked. In the process, she splattered coke from her mouth all over the table.

"Steady on, Flo!" said Mick. Once again, Lorelei's cheeks became flushed until her face donned tomato red.

"Erm, moving on," she said, changing the subject. "So Mick, what do you think? Which is the truth?" Lorelei prompted him to make a guess.

"I think you're called Esmerelda, Esmerelda!" he

concluded.

"And Tammy? What's your verdict?" pressed Lorelei.

"Honestly? You got peed on. That is so *bloody* disgusting!" Tammy pulled a repulsed face and pretended to retch with the mere thought.

"So, tell us Lorelei! Or should I say, Esme!" pleaded Danny.

"Yes, what is the truth?" begged Flo.

Lorelei picked up a cardboard beer mat and ran it on its edge up and down the table, back and forth. "Well, in my early nursing days, I was on shift, well actually, I was on a break. A patient came in, looking worse for wear and absolutely shit-faced. He had been in a fight, a bleeding hand or something. It's hard to remember, but what I do remember is that he took a sodding disliking to me…" Lorelei's cheeks, which were previously scarlet red, were rapidly turning pale as she recollected the misfortunate encounter. "I was just getting up from my chair, walking to the lift and our paths crossed. Then, without any indication he would do so, he got his 'thing' out and started peeing all over me. It all happened so quickly!" Flo's jaw dropped and the others gagged.

"Oh, my freaking *God*, Lorelei, that is vile!" said Flo in disgust.

"Oh yes, it was. I was traumatized! But you know what? Well, us nurses, we're used to seeing *everything* — blood, piss and sick, but back then, I was only newly qualified. It was an enormous shock, to say the least!"

"You've toughened up a lot now, then, Esmerelda?" joked Danny.

"Haha. Sadly, I was never called Esmeralda. I'd have liked that!"

"That was a great laugh Lorelei, who's going next?" said Tammy.

"Danny, you should!" requested Flo.

"Oh, Okay, this is tough." He ran his fingers through his curly hair, which, as usual, hung delightfully over his ears. Lorelei watched as he did so, and all sorts of thoughts ran through her mind such as how she wanted to run her fingers through his hair herself, and she couldn't help but wonder which shampoo and conditioner he used.

"It's fun! I've not played this for years!" said Flo. She was the youngest of the bunch, having only left university a few years ago, where games like this were rife.

"I've never actually played this game!" Lorelei shamefully admitted.

Danny drew in a sharp breath, and without an ounce of dithering, he fluently came out with his options. "Okay, so, number one, I've stood in the place where the fastest ever wind speed in the world has been recorded. Number two, I've met Queen Elizabeth, and lastly, I've got a tattoo of Saturn on my butt cheek!"

"Oh, this is hilarious," chuckled Lorelei.

"So, Danny, I know you're a science nerd, and love space, so you could indeed have the tattoo…" Tammy logically deduced, but Mick shook his head.

"No, Danny wouldn't get a tattoo, he's not that type. Mummy wouldn't approve," he joked.

"Hang on," Danny quipped, "how do you know my mum doesn't like tattoos? Perhaps she has one herself?"

Mick continued to pick at the facts. "I know you've travelled a bit; I'm pretty sure the place you talk of is Mount Washington, and I know you've been to the states, but did you climb Mount Washington?"

Lorelei plummeted down to reality, suddenly remembering that everyone knew Danny (and each other) so very well. It gave her heart a brief little ache, reminding her how much of an outsider she really was.

"What do you think, Lorelei?" asked Danny. She perked up.

"Ooh, it's tricky! It really is. I'm going to go with, well, you've met the Queen?"

Flo shrieked, "No! He's got a 'planet' tattoo on his rear end!" She banged the table. "I'm certain!" For such a petite girl, she had a booming voice.

"Ooh err, how can you be so sure, Flo!?" teased Tammy.

"Oh, it's just a guess!" Flo winked.

"*He's been to Mount Washington*," stated Mick. "We all know Danny's well-travelled. It's got to be that one that's true!" Mick was quite certain.

"Tammy?" said Danny.

"Oh Danny," her smile was to die for, and her cheeks flushed, as she fleshed out the conundrum. "I really don't think you've met the Queen, I think you've got a tattoo of a planet on your bottom. After all, Flo seemed quite sure!"

"Okay, this is God's honest truth. There's *no* Saturn inked on my bottom, but I do love the planets. No, I've not met the Queen, sadly, she seems like a nice lady, but I *have* caught a train up Mount Washington. It was rather windy!"

"Very good Danny, very good!" Mick praised.

"See! I told you I didn't know he had a tattooed butt!" said Flo.

"He *doesn't* Flo!" Tammy squealed.

"Well, no, he may do. All we know is he doesn't have a tattoo of Saturn there!" said Mick.

"I can confirm," said Danny, "I *don't* have a tattoo on my bum."

Lorelei, feeling bold and brave after her fifth gin and tonic, spluttered out, "I can confirm that I *do* have a tattoo, well, down there!" She blushed furiously; she was going to regret this in the morning.

"*Lorelei*," Tammy cried, "you cheeky mare!" she rolled over with laughter, her shapely body jiggling up and down.

"Oh my God, I am so drunk. *What am I saying!*" She leant over and whispered to Tammy discreetly, "My ex-husband's initial," and then to the group, "Anyone know a good tattoo removalist?" The girls burst into tears of laughter. The bell rang for last orders.

"Another?" asked Mick.

"I just couldn't. I've had way too much," confessed Lorelei. The others also declined Mick's kind offer.

"Have we got time for another game?" asked Lorelei.

"Let's pick it up next time," said Flo, letting out a humongous yawn as she checked her wristwatch in horror to see that it was past eleven o'clock.

"Yes, I've got to get home too," echoed Tammy.

"Alright, I guess it's quite late. We should wrap it up. Some of us have jobs to go to tomorrow morning!" Mick gave Lorelei a nod. The comment was clearly directed at her, for she was the only one that didn't have to work the following day. Tammy, Mick, and Flo said their goodbyes, leaving just Danny and Lorelei together at the table.

"So, Esmeralda, we're the last two standing!"

"Indeed, we are. I suppose there's nowhere around here open after hours?"

"No, there isn't. Everything shuts down in Hayle at eleven."

"I've really had way too much, anyway; I feel so drunk!"

"Aww, well, you deserve to let your hair down! Lorelei, I promise it's not always like this…we do focus on writing usually, and usually we drink far less alcohol!"

"Oh, yeah, yeah," said Lorelei sarcastically, the corners of her mouth upturned.

"No, honestly, I think it was a bit of a one-off tonight. Since we had a newbie starting."

Lorelei pouted her lips and raised her eyebrows. "Well, you should have been on your best behaviour then instead, perhaps you've scared me off?" Lorelei made her best effort to look deadly serious, and although Danny suspected she was fooling around, part of him panicked for a moment.

"Oh no, we haven't?" There was a flash of concern in his cider washed voice.

"We'll see!"

They laughed.

"Okay," said Danny, "so we have a few options. I can put you in a taxi home or if you'd like, we could go back to mine, listen to some music, and have another drink." Danny was silently willing Lorelei to accept his invitation.

"Well, I should really go home…"

Conscious not to make Lorelei in the least bit uncomfortable, he reassured her. "It's up to you, absolutely no pressure. We can order that taxi right away," he said. To his delight, it did not take Lorelei long to make up her mind.

"Well, okay, why not, I'll come with you on one condition," she grinned at his bemused face.

"Anything."

"You simply must read me some of your poetry!"

Danny held his hand out. "Deal!" he said, and the two shook on it. The pair stumbled out of the 'Barrel of Blood'. Lorelei, admittedly, more stumblesome than Danny. He, in fact, was practically holding her up as her legs had failed, having turned to jelly. The distance was fair, a good twenty-minute walk, and the rain had not stopped completely. Upon leaving the pub it was light drizzle, but after ten minutes or so it had become heavier, and Lorelei started to wish she had run back in the flat to grab that umbrella after all. She clung onto Danny's arm the whole way and by the time they reached Danny's house, they were like two drowned rats. Lorelei was soaked right through with no chance of drying off, whilst her wet clothes remained against her skin.

Danny showed Lorelei into the house, which was warm and very tidy! Looking at how drenched she was, he offered her a towel, t-shirt, and a pair of his shorts, as it would be unthinkable to remain in her wet attire. He showed her to the bathroom where she dried off and slipped into the comfortable items of offered clothing.

She looked around the bathroom. It was clean. Danny clearly had an interest in grooming, for he had a lot of nice toiletries such as shower gels, shampoos, and moisturisers. She smiled to herself as she noted that the shampoo brand was good old Head and Shoulders. He used an electric toothbrush, Lorelei also noted. *That's good. He has a keen interest in looking after his teeth,* she thought.

His navy-blue bath towel hung on the heated radiator. It was thick and fluffy and matched the hand towel by the sink. Some canvas prints of long exposure waterfalls hung on the wall, which she thought was rather unusual for a bathroom, but they looked great, nonetheless.

Lorelei's head was spinning. She had, without doubt, had too much to drink throughout the evening. Even getting dry and into the clothes she had borrowed was a toilsome undertaking, for she was stumbling around the room, which resulted in knocking a few items down, including Danny's toothbrush into the sink.

Opening the bathroom door, she was all set to join Danny downstairs, although she thought that it might be wiser to have a coffee instead of another alcoholic drink. Lorelei began her teetery descent, but found the stairway walls to be spinning around her. All of a sudden, she felt ever so queasy, and was not quite able to place one foot in front of the other without wobbling to and fro. She tried to steady herself on the banister, whilst precariously making her journey downwards, but to Lorelei's horror, her foot slipped and before she knew it, she was sliding down the stairs on her bottom at considerable speed, bouncing on each step with a thud, thud, thud, and screaming as she went. Danny, who was not far from the hallway, ran out upon hearing the commotion.

"*Lorelei*!" he yelled, whilst flying to the bottom of the stairs at cosmic speed. By some miracle he succeeded in catching her in his arms, and in turn she sent him flying onto the hallway floor where she found herself on top of him, her mouth mere millimetres away from his. She lifted her head, and their eyes locked for a moment between long straggly towel dried hair which hung in a mess over her face.

"Oh, hello," she chortled, "any chance of a coffee?"

That evening there were no more alcoholic drinks, and Lorelei did indeed get her desired cup of coffee. She did, however, insist that Danny read some of his poetry. She *tried* to stay awake, she truly did, but before long her heavy eyelids could no longer resist the urge to close, and with some help from Danny's dulcet tones, she fell deep into a gin infused sleep on Danny's sofa. Danny turned the lights off, not having the heart to wake her, and gently laid a soft blanket over her. He yawned, stretched his arms behind his back and headed up to bed himself, the whole time thinking it quite a flop that his poetry had sent someone to sleep! This really didn't bode well for his writing career at all — perhaps he needed to up his game!

The great escape

It was nine o'clock in the morning. Lorelei nuzzled into her blanket and turned around to face the room. Her mouth was dry, and her head was pounding. She couldn't remember coming home in a taxi and as she slowly recollected the events of the evening, she opened her eyes just a fraction, feeling confused as she didn't recognise the shape of the room, and the chair in the corner was not familiar to her at all.

Whose grey hoodie was hung over the arm of the chair? She scanned the floor, and her heart almost skipped a beat when a pair of men's tan loafers came into her line of sight.

I'm not at home! she thought in disbelief. More fragments of the night's events began to slot together like pieces of a puzzle, and after a short time Lorelei came to remember that she had come back to Danny's house after the writing club. She ran her hands down her legs and gasped. *What am I wearing!?* she asked herself as she realised she was dressed in clothes that were not her own. She looked around to locate her phone, finding it tucked behind a cushion with a small amount of battery life, and a dozen missed calls from Janey. Lorelei had a sinking feeling as she came to terms with the situation. She shuddered and thought to herself how she had to get out of there. This was the most embarrassing state of affairs. She began to devise a plan, noting her long coat hanging from the corner of the armchair, her bag by the leg of the coffee table and her shoes by the door. She would make her escape to wince in humiliation in her *own* home and quite frankly hide away until this awkward feeling had completely vanished *(which would be a very long time*, she thought). She gathered her possessions, carefully checking for her purse and keys, which to her relief were in her bag.

At that moment, she heard movement from upstairs. She hid her head under the blanket again and stayed perfectly still. She then heard the flush pull and a few steps from above before silence again. It seemed that Danny was just going to the toilet and Lorelei could still make her great escape.

Lorelei crept as quietly as possible to the door and wrapped her coat over her tightly. Slipping on her boots, with care, she reached for the latch on the front door and pulled. The door stayed closed. To her dismay, it was *locked*! Her plan to abscond was now just that, a plan, nothing more than a dream that could not be made into a reality unless she could find the keys. She turned around to face the stairs, hoping to find them left somewhere, but instead she turned around to face Danny, standing at the top of the stairs in his fluffy, grey dressing gown.

"Going somewhere beautiful?" he smirked playfully.

"Oh my God, this is *so* embarrassing," she moaned.

"Did you sleep well?"

"I think so. I don't remember."

"I'm sorry, you passed out. I couldn't put you in a taxi like that."

"It's okay."

"Take that coat off and go back to the front room. I'll

make you a coffee!"

Submissively, she did exactly what he said, as if he had some kind of possessive power over her, or perhaps it was the enticement of coffee that forced her to comply. Or perhaps it was something far more ingrained. Nevertheless, she did as requested and retreated to the sofa obediently.

"I'm so sorry. I was so drunk last night. I feel like such a fool!"

"You were a blast. It was fun!"

"I don't even remember much of the evening. That's what's worrying me!"

"Oh, you were just very friendly, a bundle of laughs!"

"You're too kind. I'm *never* drinking again!"

"You say that now. It's Christmas in a few weeks!"

"No, seriously, I feel so ill!"

"We'll see…"

"It was the gin! I'm not usually a gin drinker…"

"See! You just need to adjust to it."

Lorelei shook her head adamantly. "Where's my coffee, sir?" she teased.

"Just coming, ma'am!"

He went to the kitchen and left Lorelei alone for a minute. She took the opportunity to go to the bathroom to freshen up a little. She examined herself in the mirror, noting her tired eyes and the black remnants of mascara. Looking around the bathroom shelf, she found a face scrub and took the liberty to squeeze a pea-sized amount out. She washed her face thoroughly. How she wished she could brush her teeth. *I'm sure he wouldn't mind if I used a bit of that*, she thought as she spotted the mouthwash on the side. She poured a small amount directly into her mouth without touching the side of the bottle with her lips and swirled the minty liquid around.

This, along with a clean face, made her feel slightly more human.

Her hair though, was not at all presentable. She was sure Danny would have a hairbrush somewhere. However, she did see some hair lotion designed to smooth out frizzles, like a conditioner, and she made the executive decision that Danny wouldn't notice if a small pump of the product was taken. She rubbed it into her hands and then through the roots and length of her hair. It untangled her frizzy mane nicely and made it look a lot smoother and neater, and no longer like a creature from the eighties children's TV programme, Fraggle Rock. She made her way back downstairs.

Danny passed her a hot cup of coffee. "It can't compare to Cafe Java, but hopefully it will do the trick."

"Oh, thank you! This is just what I need! Shouldn't you be at work?"

"I should, but I was waiting for you to wake up."

"Oh! I'm really sorry."

"Don't be daft. Drink that coffee and I'll drop you home."

"Oh no, don't. I'm happy to make my own way back."

"Certainly not! I'll take you." he insisted, passing over a bundle of clothes. "All washed and dried!"

"Oh, thank you."

"I'm going to get in the shower, then I can drop you home before going to work."

As soon as Danny was back upstairs, Lorelei quickly got herself dressed, and being so anxious to get home, she scouted around for Danny's front door keys and found them hanging on a hook in the kitchen. She managed to successfully unlock the door and, with her coat over her arm, knowing full well that Danny was still in the shower and wouldn't be able to chase after her, she shouted up to him, "Thanks for the coffee, Danny! I'm going to make my own way home!"

"What!?"

"I'll see you soon, thanks again!" she called, and with that she waltzed out the door, eager to reach the comfort of her own home.

It was a chilly morning, and dry so far, but the wind was strong. She realised she was in a housing estate in Hayle and didn't really know which way to go. Clutching her mobile phone, she swiped the screen to find her GPS app and typed in *Hayle High Street*, for she knew, from there, she'd be able to find a bus stop. It was a short walk before the street became familiar. She walked briskly along the pavement where decorative watering cans hung from decorative lampposts, and the dunes were clearly visible to her right. It wasn't too difficult a task to find a bus stop, and she had only a ten-minute wait until the T2 arrived. The journey was lengthy, much longer than the drive in a car, and it was close to one hour by the time she was hopping off at Upper Stennack in St Ives.

Lorelei pulled her coat tightly around her and fought her way up Tregenna Lane with the wind blowing sharply onto her face, stinging her nose and cheeks. She marched determinedly towards the flat and, after having fiddled around with the key, her fingers frozen and less dexterous than usual, she burst through the door, landing in a heap on the stairs before making the laborious climb upwards.

Lorelei crawled across the landing floor in an exasperated state, as if she were trekking through the desert, before collapsing in a bundle of exhaustion. She managed to reach the soft cushions on the sofa and snuggled into the security of her own nearby blanket. Then, before she knew it, a brief snooze materialised into a deep and well-needed sleep of three hours or so.

When Lorelei finally awoke, she checked her phone for messages and found six more missed calls from Janey, along with a text message and a notification of a voicemail. She sighed, knowing that the call attempts would likely relate to some sort of crisis with Ruby.

Lorelei retrieved the voicemail. It had been left much earlier that day, yet consisted only of her sister sobbing uncontrollably, accompanied by Ruby's deafening screams. The volatile young girl roared her unprecedented abuse in the background, muffling Janey's cries. In that instance, without hesitation, Lorelei called her sister back.

"I'm so sorry it's taken me all morning to get back to you!" Lorelei exclaimed.

"It's okay," said Janey, sounding rather less stressed than Lorelei had expected her to be.

"I've calmed down somewhat, but that little cow, things are getting much worse at home..." explained Janey.

Sighing, Lorelei pushed her forehead with her fingers to relieve her headache (aka hangover). "I've told you before, Ruby really needs *professional* help," she urged, her head still pounding. She left the sofa in pursuit of painkillers.

"I know, Robert and I have been looking into getting her counselling again."

Lorelei took a deep breath. "I think she needs a psychiatrist, or some kind of psychologist. I don't know what she needs, but what I do know is that some very real problems need addressing. Anyway, what on earth happened today?"

"Well, it all started with her waking up on the wrong side of the bed," pausing as if to recollect the order of events, she then continued. "It was about six thirty in the morning, and from the moment she woke up, she was rude to me. Demanding her breakfast, refusing to get dressed. That kind of thing."

Lorelei swallowed a couple of paracetamols with some water. "Nothing different then," she remarked.

"No, but it escalated very badly. Did I tell you I've got a new app, a parental control one, which means I can remotely turn her internet access off?"

"About time!" said Lorelei, who was now multitasking by flicking the kettle to boil and wiping down the kitchen surfaces.

"Yes, well, I did warn her I'd turn it off, you know, I did everything they told me to do."

"Who's they?" asked Lorelei.

"Oh, you know, the various health professionals and our new social worker. Set the boundaries they say, *yes*, we've done that a million times. We *re-set* them just the other day!"

"Go on…"

"Warn her, they say, give her a chance to *change* the behaviour. So, I did. I asked her politely to stop talking to me as if I were a piece of shit on her shoe, not exactly like that, but, yeah, I warned her alright…"

"And then what?"

"I switched her phone off. Oh, it's so good to be able to do that!" Janey let out a slightly manic snigger. "But of course, Lorelei, the decision to do so was not without repercussions."

"Oh God, what happened?"

"She picked up her phone, which no longer worked, and threw it at me, hard as ever, and it hit me on the side of my head…"

"Oh, flip!"

"That wasn't all though. *Ignore* her, they say, *walk*

away…"

"You did?"

"I tried my very best to do just that, but in her unstoppable rage, she continued to launch anything she could get hold of towards me."

"Where was Robert when this was all occurring?"

"He's left early *again*, Lorelei, I can't cope with this. I hate my life. I just want to die!"

"*Don't*. Are you still taking your antidepressants?"

"I wasn't, but I just started again last week."

"Good, you're always able to manage better when you take them."

"Yes, I know. I tried, as I do, to ignore her, but she wouldn't stop. She trashed the bedroom, launched the dirty laundry down the stairs, threw her fist at the walls. And then, after I walked away downstairs (which was very difficult to do, given the fact that she was being so destructive), she followed me, in her hand my Elizabeth Arden hand cream, and she then proceeded to squeeze the tube all over the carpet."

"That girl has no respect," said Lorelei, knowing full well that Ruby knew exactly how to push her mother's buttons. Janey liked to keep her house clean and tidy and was rather obsessed about it.

"I *know*! She smeared it in. I was trying to ignore it, but of course, who could ignore such deliberately malicious damage to one's property?"

"It's disgraceful. What is it that makes her behave like this? Is there anything particularly on her mind at the moment?" asked Lorelei.

"Nothing that she'll confess to me, but to me she's very closed off in general and doesn't like to talk. I'm *convinced* that all these years she's gone undiagnosed with some kind of neurodiversity. Like we have said before, I really suspect something. I've been saying for years that she has oppositional defiance disorder…"

"I'm inclined to agree. She doesn't appear to learn from past consequences."

"Yes, and she is just absolutely incapable of respecting me, and her teachers, for that matter."

"Oh, school's not going well?"

"Well, she's given school detentions most weeks, doesn't do her homework, and always disrupts the class." Running her fingers through her short hair, Janey tugged with frustration. "I can't cope with it anymore. Oh Lorelei, just another four years, then she'll be an adult. Just four years to go, and I'll be free!"

Lorelei sighed as she slumped back down on her sofa. "Have you thought about an ADHD assessment?" she asked.

"I have. It's got to be something like that!"

"It's unfortunate that you and Robert haven't been able to get her the help that she needs. I know Child Services in the NHS are stretched, I really think you need to consider going for a private assessment."

"Yes, you're probably right. You know that we've been bounced back and forth from the school nurse to the paediatrician. It always ends up as a discharge, with no evidence of neurodiversity. Our referrals to the mental health services are rejected. We've done counselling, we've done parenting courses, but nothing works!"

Lorelei was well aware of the efforts and lengths Janey and Robert had gone to help Ruby but couldn't help but think they were missing something. "Honestly, I don't envy you. I don't know how you're still standing. At least you've got your Lake District break after Christmas to look forward to. I'll be having her for that week. Janey, I like Ruby, I really do. She does have a lot of great qualities. I know how tough it is, but don't lose sight of the positives. Hopefully, the break will do everyone good."

"Thanks Lorelei. Sometimes I wish I were a single mum, and at least I'd have a regular break then."

"Robert must be of some support to you," said Lorelei in an effort to encourage her sister.

"He is, when he's there, but so often he's away at the hotel. Oh Lorelei, if I could turn the clocks back—"

"*Don't say it,*" Lorelei snapped.

"But I would, if I could turn the clock back, I'd *never* have had her. She wasn't meant to be—"

"Janey!" protested Lorelei, who was devastated to see how destructive her sister's relationship with Ruby had become.

"She *was* a mistake. There's no beating around the bush. We'd not planned on having a family, at least not at that time. She was a terrible mistake and now I'm paying the price."

It was an awful thing to say, and Janey knew it, but motherhood for her had been one gargantuan battle, and now fourteen years in, there was not the smallest sign of respite.

"You have to get yourself together," said Lorelei. Her sister's lack of passion for a resolution deeply concerned her.

"I can't. Every single day there's a problem with her. My life's a mess. I don't know who I am anymore."

Lorelei had not the heart to mention her carefree night and of her excitement at meeting Danny, so she kept her big news under wraps.

"So, how are you doing anyway, little sis?" asked Janey.

"Me? Oh, well, you know, I'm alright, I'm getting along okay, don't worry about me."

"That's reassuring. So everything's okay?"

"Of course, why?"

"Oh, no reason, I'm just checking. I'm always so swept up in my own woes that often I forget to ask how you're doing yourself."

"Honestly, don't worry about me. Everything is fine." Just as Lorelei was keeping something from her sister, Janey herself chose not to speak of the unexpected conversation she'd had with Jay just the day before. She thought it was best not to worry her sister with Jay's unprecedented reappearance, and as Lorelei had not suggested anything was untoward, she thought best to say nothing, at least at this stage anyway.

"I'm glad you're keeping well; you start your job soon?"

"Yes, on Monday, quite looking forward to it! Have you thought about Christmas? Do you want to come here? It's mid-December, we should make plans soon. Have you spoken to Mum?"

"We'll definitely get together but maybe it would be better at Mum's. There's more space and we can all stay there, rather than renting a cottage in Cornwall, plus we've left it so late, I doubt there will be any availability now."

"That sounds like a perfect idea. I'll call Mum about it later."

The sisters brought their conversation to a close. Lorelei sighed. She wished she could do more to help Janey, but with three hundred miles between them, logistics were not on their side. That being said, she was pleased that she could offer some support in the February half term to allow for Robert and Janey to focus on some well-needed time together in the beautiful Lake District.

Lorelei decided to switch off from everything and submerge herself in mind-numbing day time television, perhaps a program about antiques or DIY. Anything really, just to pass the afternoon away without a need to concentrate.

Before she put her feet up, she checked her social media, where a banner popped up with suggested contacts. She recognised a few faces, probably because she had added Hazel as a friend, so mutual contacts were proposed. She noted the eccentric Mousie on the list with her wide rimmed glasses and knitted cardigan, so she decided to send a friend request. After all, what was the harm? It would be good to connect to people in the area on social media, and she wholeheartedly desired to build a strong network of friends, something she had been without for some time.

As she clicked on the arrows to scroll through the friend suggestions, she spotted Tammy, and even Flo. Eagerly sending out friend requests, she clicked and clicked, but then a profile photo of someone who she had certainly not been expecting to see came up. Lorelei gasped in fright to see the image of Jay staring right back at her. *Why had he come up on her friend suggestions?* They didn't have any mutual friends to the best of her knowledge, and she had certainly not looked at his profile at any point since setting up her new account, and plus, this must be a new one, as she had previously made sure that Jay was blocked. Lorelei shuddered and buried the phone underneath the cushion.

She shook her shoulders at the thought of Jay, and then that uneasy feeling swept over her again, the same one she had felt the other day when she had been out walking in the town. *Why*, despite there being three hundred miles between her and Jay, did he *always* find a way to creep inside her mind again? With that thought, a notification came in on her phone. It was a friend request from *Danny Kemp*! The excitement took the uneasy feeling away and knocked Lorelei into the here and now. She accepted the request with no hesitation and shortly afterwards updated her status to reflect how happy she was to have found such wonderful friends and that she couldn't wait to start walking Molly on Monday. It was a liberating experience to express her true feelings of happiness on social media. It was certainly something that Jay would not have approved of, but that, thankfully, was no longer a concern of hers.

Lorelei moved her phone from under the cushion onto the coffee table and wrapped herself up in the blanket. She enjoyed relaxing for the day, taking advantage of her ability to do so after so many years of working so relentlessly for the National Health Service. It was terribly rare for her to procrastinate, in fact, it really wasn't in her nature at all, but today was different. To do nothing was the only thing that appealed, and the only thing that was absolutely necessary.

It was six o'clock by the time she resurfaced and made her way to the kitchen to make some supper (tomato soup, with grated cheese accompanied by tiger bread with lashings of butter). It wasn't until then that an unread message came to her attention.

Hi beautiful, I've been thinking of you most of the day. Work has been taxing but definitely less onerous, given the fact that you were on my mind the whole time.

I wonder if you'd allow me to take you out to dinner; I know a wonderful Italian restaurant, do let me know, Danny x

Lorelei steadied herself against the kitchen work surface, for such a message sent her heart rushing and her head spinning. She felt quite unstable on her feet with the unexpected rush of adrenaline. *How nice it is to receive such a welcome communication*, she thought, then paused. *Would replying straight away seem too eager?* She paused to reflect on the matter but, noting that the message had been sent hours ago, with confidence she replied most agreeably, accepting his kind invitation without a fraction of hesitation.

A local celebrity

Over the weekend, Lorelei and Danny exchanged messages around the clock. They shared their own views on a variety of very important topics, such as whether mushy peas or curry sauce went best with a chippy tea, or which celebrity talent show was worth watching on a Saturday night. What's more, they could also both be quite inclined to enjoy a particular TV quiz show. It became apparent that they had much in common and they both felt they had known each other for a darn sight longer than a mere seven days.

The weekend smoothly rolled into Monday morning and before she knew it, Lorelei was all set for her first day of looking after Molly. She woke up that morning feeling unusually energised and itching to start the day (perhaps not least because of the positive friendship that was now growing very nicely between herself and Danny). The night before, she had spent time studying the local area on the internet and had devised a plan to take Molly for a run on the beach for their first adventure together.

Lorelei thought back to her childhood days with her granny at Widemouth Bay, near Bude. One particular trip stayed in her memory more than others. Her granny's collie dog came close to being cut off by the incoming tide among the tall sharp rocks on the east side of the bay. She recalled how young Megan had clung to the rocks for what seemed like an unbearable amount of time, yet thankfully succeeded in scrambling to the top. The collie then ran along the sharp tip of the rocks which ran perpendicular to the drop of the cliff. As a little girl, Lorelei had been terrified that day when she helplessly watched that little dog fight for her life. With the tide incoming at such speed, it had not been safe for her granny to attempt a rescue. In any case it would have meant leaving six-year-old Lorelei on the beach alone in danger of being swept away herself. If Lorelei recalled correctly after all these years, she would have said that it had been a winter's day, for she held a vivid recollection of being wrapped up in a warm hat and scarf.

"*Megan!*" she had cried. "Let me go to her, Granny!" Her warm tears ran down her wind-bitten cheeks.

"Lorrie," Granny had held her hand tightly. "Megan will climb," she said. Although her granny sounded relaxed and confident that Megan would find a way out of this precarious situation, looking back now Lorelei could appreciate that she had no way to know this would be the case, but at the time she trusted her granny who was so wise when it came to all sorts of things (especially how to identify sea shells, and little animals in rock pools). Little Lorrie had no choice but to put her faith in her granny, and, of course, in Megan. And when Megan managed to pull herself up by gripping the rocks so tightly with all of her might, she was able to run nimbly across the sharp and pointy rocks straight over to Lorrie with her trademark 'bottom wiggle', and jumped on her affectionately, and rather eagerly but they hadn't cared, for Megan was safe.

Well, thought Lorelei, *such a frightening event would not happen today*. She'd make sure that they would stay far away from the rocks, which were usually prominent around the Gwithian end of the beach. Today she planned to walk up past the play park up to the Towans and then make her way down to the golden stretch of beach, where Molly wouldn't have cause to worry about anything apart from a mile or so of sea rippled sand.

Lorelei showered, dried her hair, and dressed, choosing to layer up with a base layer, t-shirt and fleece. (She'd gone a bit click happy on the internet soon after realising her wardrobe needed urgent updating). Lorelei had just enough time to make porridge oats, to which she added linseeds and raspberries, and a glass of fresh orange juice accompanied her tasty breakfast. (It had crossed Lorelei's mind that she might be offered one of those delicious lattes at Hazel's house, so made the decision to give her own mediocre instant coffee a miss that morning).

Lorelei grabbed her keys and bag and scooted down the stairs, out her blue front door and onto Tregenna Lane with a spring in her step. It was nearly eight o'clock when she jumped in her car and headed to Hazel's house. She thought how nice it was to not have to worry about the morning rush hour, imagining her sister fighting through the traffic in the city right at this very moment.

Hazel's lovely house was now all lit up with Christmas lights and a giant wire reindeer had found a home by the steps leading up to the front door. Lorelei's heart warmed. It was such a lovely time of year and finally she felt she could take pleasure from it. She glanced up into the cloudless sky. *I miss you so much, Dad*, she said in her mind. She just knew he was looking down on her. He'd have been so happy that she'd made the move to Cornwall. He had loved the sea every bit as much as she did herself. Before Lorelei could ring the bell,

Hazel's front door swung open and, to Lorelei's delight, the smell of fresh coffee wafted out.

"Good morning!" chirped Hazel whilst gesturing her in. "Help yourself to a latte, you know how to use the Lattissima pro, right? It's easy. I've got some apfelstrudel capsules. They're to die for!" Hazel plonked Molly's harness and lead on the table along with a pack of puppy treats and poo bags. "Here you are! Oh, and don't forget to dress her in her adorable new *puppy snood*!" Hazel held up the snood and grinned with excitement. Molly really was one pampered pooch. "Her dinner's in the fridge. It's a banquet of duck and chicken with green beans and butternut squash. You could eat it yourself; I tell you!"

"Sounds good!"

"I must go. Any questions?"

Lorelei shook her head and silently added, *apart from how to use the Lattisima!*

"Fantastic!" Hazel reached down to Molly. "You have a wonderful day, my gorgeous pup, and be good for Lorelei — no mischief!" And with that Hazel left for work, leaving Lorelei somewhat dishevelled because she might have been expecting a little more detail on Molly's routine. Molly whined.

"What is it, girl?"

Lorelei's phone pinged, and it was a text from Hazel.

Forgot to say — routine manual is on the coffee table x

Lorelei did manage to get the coffee machine working and made the most divine latte. There were some gorgeous, flavoured coffees to choose from. She thought she'd try the praline one tomorrow, but Hazel was right, the Apfelstrudel one was something special. She read the manual while drinking the barista-quality beverage with Molly happily lying on the rug beside her feet, while the Christmas tree sparkled away.

The manual was comprehensive, but all relatively straightforward. Molly was to have a morning and afternoon walk and much of it was instructions on where to find certain things and emergency vet contact details. Not forgetting the section illustrating all the hazardous items she would have to strictly avoid; she'd never have thought that grapes would be poisonous to dogs! Lorelei started to text Danny, but then her phone rang, and it was him. It was like they were perfectly in sync, reading each other's minds.

"Hi beautiful, how's your first morning going?" his voice was so dreamy, like melted Hotel Chocolat.

She grinned. "It's amazing. Hazel's house is so beautiful and so far, Molly is very good, but I'll be taking her out for a walk soon."

"Fancy some company? How about I grab a couple of bacon rolls from LuLu's?"

"Sounds absolutely perfect, but a veggie option for me, please! Meet you by the park at ten?"

"Awesome, see you then, beautiful!"

Danny wouldn't normally make a habit of nipping out of work outside of his lunch break, but he was so besotted with Lorelei and wanted to see her at every opportunity he had. He was really falling for her, and he wasn't one to plunge himself into relationships with speed.

There was a queue at LuLu's which wasn't surprising as it was a lovely little cafe and morning bacon baps were certainly popular, even off season. A usual mixture of people filled the shop, and Danny noticed a familiar elderly lady cradling a mug of tea. She caught his eye.

"Daniel? It's not little Daniel Kemp, is it?" she croaked with a weak and frail voice. He nodded, trying to work out where he knew the lady from.

"Hello, yes, it's Danny."

"*I knew it!*" she beamed, revealing their connection. "You don't remember me? I used to look after you when you were just a nipper. I'm a friend of your mother's, my name's Evelyn. My my, how you have grown up since I last saw you…you don't remember me?"

"I do, I do! It's just been such a long while. How are you?"

"I'm very well." Evelyn's voice became stronger, "*And I hear you're an author now!*" The entire customer population turned around and stared at Danny. He wanted the ground to open and swallow him whole. It was *so embarrassing*, and regardless of Danny being quite a bold and outgoing person, there were times that he just wanted to grab a bacon sarnie and go. An unremarkable chap sitting on a table to the right of Evelyn devouring a full English breakfast was one of the many people to look up curiously.

"Well, I never!" He held up the book that he was reading. "I'm reading your poetry book right now!" said the unremarkable man.

"Well, that is a coincidence indeed… Mr…?"

"Ellis." He reached out to shake Danny's hand. He didn't look like the poetic type to Danny, but he thought you can never tell.

Danny was honoured. "Well, very nice to meet you, Mr Ellis, and thank you for reading my book."

"Would you sign it for me? I've always been a fan. My wife loves your work too. She holds you in high regards."

Danny was beginning to feel like quite the local celebrity as he scribbled his signature on the inside cover, but catching a glimpse of the time, he had to excuse himself. However, this cringey little moment had given him a boost, seeing that his sales had been low lately. It was great to be recognised like this, even if it was a bit embarrassing and unexpected.

"Please can I get a bacon roll and a spinach and mushroom bap with two lattes to go?" he asked at the counter and then turned to Evelyn.

"I'm so sorry, do forgive me. Please drop in on Mum. She would love to see you."

The unremarkable man returned to his cooked breakfast, shaking his head and muttering to himself in disbelief. Danny exited the café.

Evelyn leaned over to the table where the man was shovelling his bacon and eggs into his mouth ravenously. "Oh, I couldn't have a little look, could I, dear? I used to look after Danny when he was a young boy."

"It's all yours, keep it. I've finished with it anyway and my wife has another copy."

Amazed at his generosity, Evelyn thanked Mr Ellis several times before slipping the book into her shopping trolley and returning to her tea.

"Danny! You've been ages, all okay?"

"Yes, all good. I just met a friend of my mum's who announced to the whole cafe who I was, and then it turned out a gentleman was *actually* reading my book right there and then! He asked for a signature! Crazy!"

Lorelei laughed and elbowed him in the ribs. "You are, like, *famous!* Check you out, Danny Kemp!"

"Don't be daft, you! It was a total one off, believe me!"

Danny passed the wrapped breakfast to Lorelei and kneeled to greet Molly. She was pleased to see him, and so was

Lorelei.

They had the most glorious walk along the beach. The location was stunning, and it was a view that Lorelei had known all her life despite not having personally grown up there. She thought how Danny had more ownership over the place as he was a real local, whereas she was just an 'emmet' (which was how the Cornish would refer to holiday makers), or at least she *used to be*. St Ives Bay was always accompanied by its friend, the little rocky island with the white Godrevy Lighthouse standing tall, watching over the ocean, and also it's seafarers and marine life. It was picture perfect; it was home. They threw the ball for Molly, and her return was so reliable, Hazel had trained her well.

Although it was early in the day and late in the year, the month of December did not deter a shoal of surfers out in the waves that morning. Lorelei shuddered at the thought of it, but winter surfing was often popular. The breakers were bigger than in the summer and the winter surfer would naturally more often bag the big swells all to themselves.

"So, tell me more about yourself. You haven't mentioned a lot about your family other than your mum and dad? Do you have brothers and sisters?" Lorelei asked. Danny visibly tensed, took a pause, and turned his head to the far-reaching ocean.

"Maybe for another day?" he hopefully asked, turning back to her, and squeezing her hand. "I *will* talk about it soon. I just want to enjoy this moment with you. I don't want to feel sad."

She respected his privacy, although felt a little perturbed that she had been so open and honest with him since they had met, and his choosing to keep something from her made her feel a little glum. Whatever it was, it must have been important. She didn't press the matter because she wanted him to speak when he felt he was ready to do so. They continued to walk, and Lorelei continued to throw the ball for Molly. She bounced off energetically, bringing it back every time, eager for more.

"So, this weekend?" Danny asked, "the Italian restaurant, are you still up for that?"

"Absolutely I am! I *love* Italian food!" she declared, imagining an enormous hand cooked pizza, goat's cheese, red peppers. *Hmm, is it lunchtime yet?* she thought.

"Are you a pizza or pasta girl?"

"Pizza *all* the way."

"Spaghetti Bolognese for me, and garlic bread."

"Yummy!" swooned Lorelei.

Danny then posed the most important question. "Pineapple on pizza? I've got to ask…"

"Yes, every time, *love* it!"

Danny wrinkled his nose. "I'm more of a meaty kinda pizza guy."

Lorelei missed meaty toppings, too. She used to love spicy sausage and beef and peperoni on a pizza before she turned vegetarian.

"On the subject of food," she asked, "what's your favourite meal ever?"

"Oh gosh, now that's a question," he mused. "I have to say, I do really have a soft spot for a traditional Sunday lunch, my mum's roast potatoes…" He smacked his lips and pinched his thumb and forefinger together, bringing them to his lips before releasing them. "Delicious!"

"Roast dinner is *definitely* up there, isn't it? Although I'm a veggie now and I really miss the roast chicken or lamb part."

"Slow cooked lamb…" he practically salivated. They continued to walk onwards, barely sharing the beach with a single soul.

"Danny," she said, "what are you doing for Christmas?"

"Well," he said with a bit of a disappointed face, "Mum and Dad are actually going away for Christmas this year."

"So, you don't have plans?" she asked, and Danny shook his head.

"Probably just a quiet one. Why?"

"I was just thinking, if you *didn't* want a quiet one, how about you join me and my family in Devon?" There was an awkward pause, before Lorelei recovered. "I mean, no pressure! I know we don't know each other an awful lot, but I just thought maybe…" she searched for the words. "I just thought it may be nice."

At that moment, Molly broke the awkwardness between them and came bounding back, jumping up onto Danny's legs playfully. He laughed a big, deep belly laugh and knelt on both knees on the wet sand to cuddle Molly.

He looked up at Lorelei. "Lorelei, I'd love to. Thank you so much for asking me." He reached his arms out. "Come here." The three of them huddled together, all arms and a wet nose.

"I'm so glad you moved to Cornwall," he confessed in his low gravelly voice, "I really like you and of course I want to spend Christmas with you!"

Lorelei safely made it back to Hazel's house and Danny returned to the office, and they both had very big smiles on their faces. Things seemed to be moving quickly, but at the same time, it all felt right. Molly was tired after the morning walk. Perhaps it had been a bit much for her. Lorelei realised after sitting down with the 'manual' that Molly's walks didn't have to be very long as she was so young. She glanced at the coffee table where the new snood lay, and she realised she'd also forgotten to dress Molly in it. She felt awful, but Molly was so settled, she curled up in her bed and went to sleep. Lorelei sighed in relief. Despite forgetting the snood and tiring Molly out too much, their first day had gone well.

Lorelei took the opportunity to have a look at Hazel's bookshelf as she had suggested the other week. There were lots of classics, but also a lot of books about the local area. She picked one off the shelf called 'Secret Beaches' and she took a moment to daydream about finding one of those gorgeous, secluded bays. An image popped into her head of her and Danny skinny dipping together. *As if that would ever happen*, she laughed, but those were the kind of memories she wanted to make with Danny, exploring special places that perhaps neither of them had been. She was sure there was still so much of Cornwall that even Danny hadn't ventured into, and even if he had, she wanted him to show her the places he loved and share it all with her.

Before she knew it, Hazel was home, bursting through the front door, chattering about her day in the office and the stories she'd been writing for the paper. Molly was pleased as punch to see her, but when Lorelei put her boots on and headed for the door, she whined immediately, almost like a child's cry.

"Oh, bless." Hazel cocked her head to the side and pursed her lips. "I've truly never seen anything like it. Molly really loves you!"

Tessy Braun

I long for the day I am free

"Mummy, I'm sorry." Ruby looked down empathetically at her mother from the top of her cabin bed. Her pretty eyes, with a definite hint of green, screamed for forgiveness. Janey wanted with all her heart to grant her clemency, but time after time her daughter would repeat this abusive pattern of behaviour. Janey sighed. She was exhausted because just minutes earlier, Ruby's temper had been raging like wildfire and the troubled teen had not the ability to restrain herself from the demons that seemingly took hold of her when the red mist came down.

Holding the side of her face, Janey wept. "Sorry is *no good*, not anymore," she went on. "How can I keep forgiving you?" Janey leaned against the bed.

Tears welled up in Ruby's eyes. "I can't help it, Mummy, it just happens. I can't control it. I'm sorry."

"You know what? It's domestic abuse, Ruby, and I have no choice but to report what you have done to the police." Janey felt the enormous lump that was beginning to form after her head had been crushed between the door and its frame with great force.

"It was an accident, Mummy," she pleaded.

"An accident?! It wasn't an *accident!* You slammed that door quite on purpose!"

"I didn't know your head was going to be there," she smirked.

"Yes, that's the problem. You don't *think*, do you Ruby!? I suppose you didn't mean to kick the door off its hinges, either?"

Glancing at the door, Ruby shrugged. "It's not broken."

"The panel's smashed, and the hinges are hanging off…"

"You can fix it," said Ruby, matter-of-factly.

"Yes, and *you* can pay for it!"

"No!"

"Oh, yes!"

"You're so selfish!" Ruby scowled.

"Pardon?"

"You heard me!" the fourteen-year-old yelled back.

"I can't believe that after what you've just done, you're now acting like this."

"Fuck off!"

"I see. It never takes you too long for you to go back to your usual lovely self."

"You're a bitch! You're the worst mother; you're pathetic!" Ruby sat up and reached for the books that she kept by her pillow and began to hurl them one at a time at her mother with a force to be reckoned with. Janey couldn't contain her own temper, having been pushed to her limit and despite knowing that rising to Ruby's behaviour had not one benefit to it, she lost control.

"You little cow, you are *vile*, you're more than vile, I'm calling the police!"

"No, Mummy, no!"

"Yes, I am! I won't tolerate domestic violence from anyone — who the hell do you think you are!?"

"Mummy, no! They'll take me away! They'll arrest me! Please!" she begged.

"When are you *ever* going to realise that you cannot treat me like this!" cried Janey, and a panic-stricken Ruby replied with promises of redemption.

"I do! I do! I'll change, I won't do it again. Just please, don't call them!"

Janey left the room and made her way downstairs, remembering what 'the professionals' had reiterated to her time and time again, but she could still hear the sobs of her daughter echoing through the walls. Part of her wanted to rush back in and hold her daughter, telling her everything would be alright, but the other part felt terrified that if she did that, how would it end? Would Ruby show her loving side, or would more contact make things even more fractious? The relationship was fraught at the best of times, and for whatever reason, Ruby had lost all respect for her mother many years ago. Janey found it increasingly difficult to empathise with her daughter's emotional needs, and this evening was no exception.

There was a lot to do. The family was spending Christmas together, and ahead of them lay a two-hour drive to their mother's house in Devon. Janey had mostly packed with little help from Robert, who was still busy at work. Tomorrow was Christmas Eve; they'd leave first thing in the morning and Janey was eagerly awaiting her first meeting with Lorelei's new boyfriend.

She'd heard lots about him now. He certainly sounded a nice guy, and she was happy for her sister, though somewhat envious too. Although Robert was well meaning and placid and caring, they were well past the honeymoon stage and the strains of parenting Ruby had at times certainly taken a toll on their relationship. Although Janey couldn't dispute that he had always been the 'cool' one, taking everything in his stride, the logical, calm one of the pair.

Robert worked late that night, and Janey took advantage of this to get various jobs done around the house. Everything was ready for the morning and Janey felt happy she had managed to be so organised despite Ruby's earlier meltdown. Luckily Ruby had kept herself to herself that night and stayed clear out of Janey's way. By nine thirty pm Janey finally sat down. She poured herself a glass of red wine and rewarded herself with some cheese and biscuits. Gorgonzola was her favourite. The Christmas tree looked beautiful; she was sad she wouldn't enjoy it on Christmas day, but no doubt her mother would have made a marvellous effort with the decorations.

Yet Christmas wasn't as it should be, and in all honesty, it never would be the same again for Janey. Her rock, her advisor, her shoulder to lean on, her *father* was gone. There'd be no turning back the clocks. Bittersweet memories began to pour down Janey's face in the form of tears. She sighed as she realised her father never really knew the true extent as to her troubles with Ruby. *Yes,* he was aware she was a difficult child but the violence, the intensity — he hadn't known the half of it, but regardless he loved Ruby so much, his only granddaughter, and Gerald had been so proud of her. The affection was mutual, and Ruby adored her grandad. Since his passing, she even kept a photo of him by her bed. Janey thought to herself that she must try to remember that her father's death had impacted *all* the family members. She sometimes overlooked this because she was the oldest sister and had known her father when it was just the two of them, before Lorelei was born, as if that fact gave her some kind of right to grieve the most. Deep down Janey knew this was absurd, but he was *her* father. Even Lorelei had not bothered much with him when he was alive. *Janey* was the one who had called him every day, instigated visits, written birthday cards, and so on. No, Christmas would not be the same ever again.

Janey stretched, rolled over, then opened her eyes a fraction to see Robert on his side with his back to her. He was gently snoring. She turned to glance at the bedside clock; it was only six-thirty in the morning, and she wanted to go back to sleep but knew that those few hours before Ruby woke were so precious when the house was so still and quiet. She tiptoed out of the bedroom carefully, not waking her husband and heedful not to disturb Ruby, who was sleeping in her bedroom next to theirs.

She pulled a stool up at the breakfast bar and flipped her laptop open before popping a capsule in the coffee Machine (a Christmas gift once bestowed upon her from her dear father). The smell of coffee reminded her of her dad. He had possessed an excellent taste for strong coffee with rich woody notes. Janey's kitchen was wonderful, as was the rest of the house, but the kitchen was the heart of the home. It was spacious, with many cupboards and an island to provide more work surface space. Though it was so comprehensive there was something missing, *perhaps the heart part*, thought Janey.

Thinking of her daughter and reflecting that the grief of losing her grandad may have affected her more than she had let on, she also thought of another person Ruby had lost and that was her uncle Jay, Lorelei's ex-husband.

She was better off without an uncle like that, Janey scorned herself to ever think otherwise. But she couldn't deny how close they were (which made her skin crawl), her daughter often commenting she had wished *he* was her dad, and this made Janey retch. Ruby and Robert did have a bond, of course. Robert was a great father. He was stable, caring, and loving. He was everything apart from available. So many times, Jay had stepped in when Ruby's dad had had to cancel for work commitments. Perhaps in some ways, Jay had been like a dad to Ruby, especially when she was small. Of course, Ruby would have been devastated to lose him, but Janey had made no secret of her hatred of him, and all ties had finally been cut after the divorce. Janey was startled from her thoughts when Ruby plodded into the kitchen in her dressing gown, all sleepy eyed.

"Morning Mummy!" She came over to her mother and kissed her on the cheek. Janey froze and had to remind herself to respond affectionately, for it was such a turnaround from the previous evening.

"Morning, Ruby, breakfast?"

"Have we got those yummy waffles?"

Janey nodded and pointed to the bread bin. Sweet waffles had become a frequent breakfast treat over the last few months, and sometimes they would enjoy them topped with chocolate spread and strawberries.

"Mummy, it's Christmas Eve!" Ruby exclaimed. "*And* we're going to Grandma's!" She did a little skip and a hop, seeming so excited. "I'm going to behave, I promise!"

Janey smiled at her daughter and tried to cling on to some hope that she actually would do as she claimed, but it was a slim chance, if that. Janey shuddered as she thought back to the previous Christmas holidays and remembered Robert's precious blancmange ending up over the walls during one of her daughter's outbursts.

"That's good to hear," Janey spat out with a half-smile. Although Ruby was being polite and well-mannered now, Janey saw straight through it. She had become hardened to the cycle of pleasant behaviour turning to violence. It was like a mirror image of what Lorelei had experienced with Jay throughout her whole marriage and which, of course, eventually led to its demise. *I long for the day I am free,* contemplated Janey, *the day when she is no longer my responsibility, the day when I can start living.*

"Well, eat your breakie up and grab a shower. I want to set off by about ten o'clock. Grandma's doing a Christmas Eve buffet for tea, and remember to pack your earphones, your tablet and anything else to keep you occupied on the journey."

Ruby nodded. "I wonder what Danny will be like, and does Uncle Jay know Auntie Lorrie has a new boyfr—?"

"He's not your uncle Jay anymore, you just remember that!" snapped Janey. She despised that man and didn't want her daughter to have anything to do with him, not even in her own thoughts.

Janey returned to her laptop and started scanning through her emails. *Junk, junk, junk…* updates from school, order receipts from Amazon… then she stopped and her jaw dropped…

1.30am — From: Jay Logan — Subject: Call me, Janey

Tessy Braun

It looks like Superman threw up in here

October 21st 1986

Danny sat on his bed; his Superman duvet wrapped around him. He began to sob. He was a sensitive child with a love of DC Comics, Transformers and Matchbox cars. Danny reached for his journal from under his pillow. He had always liked English as a subject at school, particularly creative writing, which he was showing a promising flare for. His friends had teased him somewhat for his academic preference and thought it rather peculiar that he'd rather be conjuring up some story about aliens in outer space than kicking a ball around the park.

Danny jotted down some words on the blank page. *Alone*, *scared*, *sad*. He lifted his head momentarily from his journal (which, of course, had a Superman cover), and in between his tears, he glanced around his room.

Although he was a sensitive little lad, he was very well liked among his peers and his teachers adored him. He was absolutely no trouble at all for his mother and father (unlike

Beth, who had been quite the opposite in nature). There was a knock on his bedroom door and his mother peered in.

"Hi Daniel, I brought you a snack. You need to keep your strength up, my boy," she said. He looked to see what it was. His mother presented a plate with Golden Wonder Ringos and a Dairylea cheese slice. She slid into his room and sat herself down on the bed beside him.

"Oh Daniel," she said, placing the plate of food down on the bed and cradling him. He started to cry even harder. "There, there," his mother comforted him. "There, there." There was little she could say to her eight-year-old son to make anything better, because nothing could console him. To see him in such distress only added to her own heartache. She cleared her throat. "Daddy will be home soon," she said, and Danny nodded. Daddy was much better at things like this. He was stronger, holding himself together much more successfully than she was. Young Danny had not left his room for three days, apart from to visit the bathroom, and he had barely eaten a morsel since the news broke. He had not even had the desire to play on his Atari 2600, for even Pacman could not lift him out of the darkness that consumed him.

"Will Daddy read to me when he's home?" he asked with a small voice.

Four days earlier

It was four thirty and Beth swung through the patio doors, abandoning her bag on the floor, and kicking her shoes underneath the breakfast bar.

"Mum! I'm home!" she yelled. She skipped over to the fridge and grabbed a carton of Um Bongo before bounding into the living room to find her little brother sitting on the floor, watching an episode of 'Dastardly and Muttley.'

"Hey little bro, how was school?" she asked. Danny flung his arms around his much beloved sister. He always looked forward to her return from 'big school' and although she didn't always display the best behaviour for their parents, she always had Danny's back, and according to him, she was the best big sis ever.

"It was great!" he exclaimed with an added layer of enthusiasm. "We learnt about the ancient Egyptians and hieroglyphics. Did you know how they figured out how to read them?" he went on. "It's so cool, they found this stone—"

"Danny!" she expressed, not caring much for the Rosetta stone, "Let's do something fun tonight, me and some friends are going to go out on a ghost hunt, do you want to come, I'll see if Mum will let you?"

"There's no such thing as ghosts," he said, rolling his eyes, "and besides, Mummy and I were going to watch our new video together." He fumbled around by the side of the television and excitedly revealed the VHS, *Back to the Future*! Beth held her hands to her mouth, and Danny wasn't quite sure if her reaction was genuine or not.

"Oh! That's so exciting! But wouldn't you rather come out this evening and look for the spirits of the dead?" She waved her hands around and made a silly, spooky noise. Danny felt quite privileged that his fourteen-year-old sister was inviting him to hang out with her and her friends. His own friends' siblings hadn't wanted to even be seen with the little ones, but Danny and Beth had a special relationship.

He pushed her playfully. "I *wanna* watch the film with Mummy," he said, and she ruffled his hair.

"Fine little bro, how about a game of Donkey Kong for now then?" He nodded, and they both jumped up and ran up the stairs, knocking into their mother, who was coming down with a basket of ironing.

"Watch it, you two!"

"Sorry Mum!" they said in unison, before tumbling into Danny's room in a heap on the floor, giggling. Beth took one look around at Danny's newly decorated room.

"Ugh! It looks like Superman threw up in here," she said while making a face. He stuck his tongue out at her.

"You're just jealous."

Over the next hour, they played on the console before mum called them down for tea. It was Turkey Twizzlers, a favourite for both Danny and Beth. They gobbled them all up before Beth left to meet her friends. Mum gave her a kiss.

"Be back by eight."

"*Mum*! That's too early…" she protested.

"Okay, nine, then, but *no later*."

Present day

Danny often wondered why he couldn't write about what had happened back in 1986. He was very much aware that writers often used words as therapy, but Danny had almost blocked the horror out, and whenever he had tried to document his feelings or write about the events in his childhood, he would freeze up, and nothing would come out.

It would have affected any child, but Danny had become exceptionally withdrawn following his experience and trauma, which he had largely suppressed. But he'd turned out alright? A good job, a balanced and kind natured personality, yes, but even so, he was plagued by a terrible internal guilt that he was never afforded the time to explore or come to terms with. What had happened had been shut away in a box, and one could argue to an extent this methodology had worked, until now anyway.

He'd thought about it all a bit more lately, with the

prospect of meeting Ruby, who, like Beth, from what he had heard, was somewhat of a free spirit. He truly looked forward to meeting her, maybe part of him felt it would help him connect to his sister. *It's ridiculous*, he thought. Beth was not Ruby, and Ruby was not Beth, but he couldn't help but think that it was fate that brought him and Lorelei together. He couldn't bring his sister back, but he *could* be taken back to 1986 in some small way by building a relationship with a girl so similar to her.

For a reason he couldn't quite explain or justify, he genuinely felt it may help him accept what had happened and draw some sort of closure to it all. He believed that finally he had met in Lorelei, someone who could help him to unpeel the hurt, and after all these years open up to the reality of what happened to his big sister who, unlike him, never got the chance to grow up.

Tessy Braun

Turquoise

Lorelei and Danny were relishing in a lazy lie in at the little St Ives flat. It was such bliss having nothing to get up for. Lorelei snuggled into Danny's warm chest and wrapped her arms around his back. He raised his head and rested it on his hand to look at Lorelei with absolute disbelief she was his. He felt like the luckiest man on planet Earth. This was a love he had never experienced before. She was the best Christmas present he could ever have wished for, and even though 'they' were still *so* new, everything about their relationship seemed right.

"You are *so* beautiful in the morning…" He laid his head down and stroked her hair.

"You are so sexy in the morning," she reciprocated, noting his body responding to her teasing. They caressed each other, Lorelei tracing his jawline and drawing his lips to hers. Everything was so perfect. She was nervous about the day ahead, though, because later that morning they were making the journey to her mother's house for Christmas, and well, family get-togethers didn't have a great track record and had a tendency to become quite intense. Although she had done her best to prepare Danny for how her niece, Ruby, could be so very turbulent, Lorelei was still apprehensive about how the few days at her mother's house would conclude.

"Lorelei, I know we've only known each other for such a short time, but something just tells me we're right." Danny gazed into Lorelei's soft, kind eyes, and kissed her forehead.

"Just brace yourself! You may well feel differently after you've spent a weekend with my family!" she chortled. It may have sounded like a joke, but deep-down Lorelei was horrifically nervous. Jay had always criticised her family and took great pleasure in telling her how they were all crazy, Lorelei included. Of all the family members, Jay had really only seemed to be kind to Ruby, seemingly always to be his favourite. She couldn't do an awful lot wrong, in his opinion, which was quite ironic considering how wild her behaviour could be. Lorelei shuddered, praying Christmas would be a peaceful and happy affair and that she'd not be boyfriend-less by New Year's Eve.

Both sisters, travelling with their respective parties, hit the road. One from the north, and one eastward, both on route to west Devon. Their mother, Iris, lived in a remote village on the edge of Dartmoor. There was nothing there, but it was a beauty spot that attracted many visitors from all around the world.

Ruby sat in the back of the Volvo XC90 while her father took the driving seat and her mother stared out of the window as she left the city behind. As the journey progressed, the tall buildings gave way to green fields and a sense of freedom prevailed.

"Welcome to Devon!" Ruby squeaked as they passed the sign on the M5. "Not long now!"

Lorelei's little yellow car was running well, and she and Danny played games as they journeyed along, spotting different types of vehicles and noting the familiar landmarks. They passed Bodmin Moor and the infamous Jamaica Inn, Danny pointing out the places of interest such as Brown Willy and Rough Tor. (He clarified that 'Rough' rhymed with cow and not buff).

"I saw a wild cat up there once, up near the Inn," Danny chirped.

"You did not!"

"I did so! It crossed the road right in front of my car. I even reported it to the Big Cat Society."

Lorelei laughed. "Yeah right…"

"It's true!"

The journey was pleasant and flew by. It was not long before the couple were approaching the perimeter of Dartmoor National Park, with its rugged granite tors in clear view and then up into the gravel drive of their mother's characteristic bungalow, which was, to the young Lorelei's delight, called 'Pixie's Holt'.

"Real Pixies live here, Danny!"

Janey, Robert, and Ruby had already arrived, and Iris greeted Lorelei and Danny on the driveway.

"Hello dear!" Iris called. "Merry Christmas!" She held her hand out to Danny. "It's so very lovely to meet you!" The pair were ushered into the sitting room where they found Robert relaxed on the leather armchair with a glass of port. The room was beautifully festive with real foliage and red berries around the fireplace that Iris had sourced from the garden.

Lorelei gasped. "Oh Mum, it's absolutely perfect."

She turned to the tree, which also looked stunning with many little hanging ornaments she remembered from when she was a young child, including a little wooden rocking horse. Her father had brought it as a gift from Germany. Janey had been given a wooden decoration too; an angel, and Lorelei searched for it among the branches. The open fire was roaring, and it really felt like Christmas now.

"Janey!" Lorelei cried as she flew into her big sister's arms. "I've missed you, and Robert, hi!" Lorelei composed her excitement for a moment, realising she was forgetting introductions.

"I'm sorry!" she yelped, "Danny, this is my sister, Janey, and her husband Robert, and… where's Ruby?"

Danny hugged Janey and shook Robert's hand.

"Very pleased to meet you," said Robert. "Merry Christmas!" he said. "Let me get you a port. Take a seat, Danny. Make yourself comfortable." Robert insisted.

"Ruby's in the bedroom having a rest…" said Janey.

Ruby had her earbuds in and was listening to relaxing pop music whilst lying on her back on the double bed, her head propped up by a ridiculous number of pillows. Her shoulder-length brown hair had grown a lot since Lorelei had last seen her, and Ruby wore it pinned up in a high ponytail. She wore an oversized jade knitted jumper and stretchy denim jeans.

From where she sat, Ruby was able to see right out into the back garden. In the spring and summer, it would look so pretty, full of wildflowers and greenery, but at this time of year, it looked bleak and bare. This had not gone unnoticed by Ruby. *Bleak and bare, like me*, Ruby had thought. *Life is so pointless*, she thought to herself. *I don't even have a life. I have a mother who hates me, and a father with no time, and I'm a horrible person,* she reflected internally. These things had been reaffirmed many times before and she truly believed her mother didn't like her, didn't expect her to ever be well behaved and didn't have any faith in her whatsoever. *I may as well be the way I am. I'm Ruby, the horrid, vile child.*

She didn't hear the light tap on the bedroom door and nor did she hear the door being pushed open or her auntie Lorelei repeating her name over and over again, until Lorelei was standing right by the side of the bed.

"Ah!" screamed Ruby. "You scared me!"

"Hey, I'm really sorry. I was calling you and I did knock. You okay?"

"Yes."

"It's great to see you. You're looking so grown up now!"

"You're looking so happy now," Ruby retorted. "Is that because you have a new boyfriend, and Uncle Jay's not around? Mum says we're all better off without him, but I still think about him. Most days really, but Mum won't hear anything of it."

Lorelei's heart sank. She didn't want to think about Jay at any time, but especially not now at Christmas, after she had worked so hard to eradicate him from her life. "I am happy, you're right. You know what would make me feel even happier?"

"What?"

"If you come and have some lunch with us, I want you to meet Danny. I think you'll like him."

Reluctantly, Ruby followed her auntie, and they reconvened with the others in the dining room. Iris brought Ruby a glass of fizzy pop and they all sat down around the table, which was laid with big soup bowls, the very deep white ones with decorative handles on the outside. The waft of home cooked soup came from the kitchen. It was French onion.

"Your hair is styled so perfectly, dear." Iris remarked to Janey. Her pixie cut really did suit her. Lorelei thought she'd never be able to pull it off herself, but it did seem to complement her sister's fine features and her bronzed skin tone very well.

"Thank you, Mother, I'm so used to having it short now, I wouldn't go back!"

"I thought we were having a buffet for lunch!" Ruby squealed.

"That's tonight, angel." Iris confirmed. The family tucked ravenously into their soup, which was accompanied by thickly sliced bread and butter.

"This is truly delicious, Iris," Robert remarked with satisfaction, which meant an awful lot to Iris, given the fact Robert's own culinary skills were to be so admired. Ruby sat opposite her father and caught his eye. She looked pained. The soup wasn't to her taste, so she sat there, breaking up the bread into tiny pieces and placing them in her mouth with a glum expression.

"Well, this is nice," Iris said, "all of us together!"

"Not all of us…" lamented Ruby, and Iris gave her a loving look, assuming she was speaking of her grandfather.

"Well, no Ruby, we all think of your grandad, and let's raise a glass to him now."

"No, Granny, I'm not talking about Grandad. I meant Uncle Jay!" Ruby revealed. Lorelei's heart sank with Ruby's shock revelation and Janey through her daughter a scornful look, clearly outraged with Ruby's obstinance. It was an awkward moment.

"I don't think we need to worry about him now, do we?" recovered Iris. "More bread anyone?" She said, offering the bread basket encouragingly to her guests.

Clocking onto the scowl that was still being thrown towards her from her mother, Ruby slammed her fist down on the table. "I've had enough! I don't like this soup anyway, and besides, I'm *not* hungry!" She slammed the table again. "*Or wanted!*" And with that, she stormed out of the dining room resuming her position on the bed among the array of cushions. Her headphones firmly blocking out the outside world with the thumping music numbing her senses and taking her far away from reality. To the relief of everyone, not least Lorelei, the afternoon passed without further incident, and after the lunchtime outburst, Ruby remained in the bedroom.

Early evening approached. Everyone was sitting in the lounge, including Ruby, and Iris rubbed her palms together with a mischievous look on her face.

"Right, I think that since it's Christmas Eve, we can all have just *one* present? What do you think?"

"Presents on Christmas Eve? That's a first in this family," remarked Lorelei.

"Sounds good to me," Ruby said with a smirk.

"But Mum, we haven't even unpacked the presents yet…" said Janey.

"I know, but this is something I've got for each of you. I've missed you all so much, and I just can't wait to give you all a little something." Iris knelt on the floor and reached for an exquisitely wrapped gift from beneath the tree. She handed the gold and red parcel to Danny, with a glint in her eye. "Here you go, dear. I hope you like it."

"Oh, thank you very much!" He seemed surprised, certainly not expecting any presents, at least not ahead of Christmas day.

"Go on, open it!" pressed Iris.

Danny pulled the end of the golden ribbon and gently tore the paper, wondering what on earth it could be.

"One hundred things to see in the night sky. This is fantastic, Iris, thank you!" he ran his hand over the shiny cover of the book.

"Lorelei told us you liked the stars," said Iris.

"I do, I really do, thank you!"

"But that's not all. Look inside."

Danny opened the book, and a small white envelope fell out onto his lap.

"Go on then, open it!" Iris insisted.

"Yes, go on Danny!" pressed Janey.

Danny reached for a sip of his drink. He hadn't felt this excited about Christmas time and receiving gifts since — he began to remember things he really didn't want to remember right at that moment. Pushing those thoughts to the back of his mind, he opened the envelope and pulled out a piece of paper.

"Stargazing experience for two!" His joy was obvious and could not be contained. "This is honestly too much, far too much, but it is a wonderful gift. Thank you, Iris, thank you!"

Robert was next to receive his gift. It was a luxury wine tasting experience accompanied by an expensive looking full-bodied bottle of Shiraz. He beamed with satisfaction, for his mother-in-law knew his taste in wine well.

"Janey, Lorelei, these are for you." Iris passed each daughter over a small package, no less beautifully wrapped than the others. Janey smiled at her mother.

"Oh Mum, thank you!"

"Well, open it first! You might not like it!"

Janey and Lorelei carefully unwrapped their respective parcels to reveal a box, and inside each box, they found a beautiful silver necklace with a bright blue stone pendant.

"Turquoise!" they both exclaimed.

"How beautiful, Mum, I love it!" Lorelei hugged her mother tightly, and Janey expressed how grateful she was too.

"We've always loved turquoise, you remembered!" Janey smiled.

"Yes, I do. I remember you were always trying to raid my jewellery box and fighting over who would wear my turquoise bracelets. Well, now, you have some of your own."

"They're perfect!" Lorelei declared. "What are the properties of this gemstone? Do you know?"

"Of course, they bring luck, peace and protection, so you girls look after them, won't you?!"

"I'll never take it off," Lorelei chirped.

Janey nodded. "Neither will I."

"*Borrrrrring*! Where's *my* present?!" yawned Ruby, exaggerating her boredom by bringing her hand to her mouth back and forth slowly. Despite being very rude, nobody wished for an argument.

"Well, I couldn't very well forget you, could I, Ruby?" Iris passed Ruby a decorative bag with several items inside. "Happy Christmas to my lovely granddaughter."

"Ooh! Look! Lucky me!" She pulled out the most gorgeous fluffy unicorn slippers, with a matching robe and also a selection of luxury hot chocolate and marshmallows.

"Grandma! These are so cool! Can I put them on?"

"Of course," Iris chuckled. "I'm so glad you like them."

"Hmm, banoffee pie white hot chocolate, hmm, not sure about that though, Grandma!"

A wonderful Christmas Eve buffet was served. The table in the dining room was filled with all sorts of seasonal delights, such as smoked salmon with lemon slices, crisps with dips, cooked meats, and an impressive selection of cheese.

"This chutney," Iris announced, "is homemade, my dears…"

Lorelei helped herself to salad, hard-boiled eggs coated in salad cream with a dusting of paprika and a generous helping of carrot and cucumber crudites. Ruby leaned over her aunt, filling her plate with sausage rolls and crisps, whispering in her Auntie Lorelei's ear, "That salmon looks *disgusting…*"

"I heard that, Ruby!" Her mother gave her a stern glare.

"Got any ketchup, Grandma?" Ruby chirped. Everyone laughed. Ruby would eat ketchup with anything.

Later in the evening, everyone was relaxed in the lounge. Lorelei had enjoyed a glass of Irish Cream on ice and Ruby tried out her banoffee pie hot chocolate, which she discovered was really something quite special indeed. The television aired a Christmas special, and everyone felt so relaxed and the warmth from the glowing fire brought much comfort. Lorelei watched the flames dancing and remembered her little ritual that marked the start of her new life — how far she had come since that defining moment in time.

Ruby wriggled, trying to get comfortable on the floor. She'd always struggled to sit still, continually demonstrating such an active personality. She positioned herself on her stomach, reaching her arms out and tapping on the wooden floor.

"Ruby, will you keep still, for goodness' sake," tutted Janey, rolling her eyes at Robert.

Ruby just kicked more. "Blah blah blah blah, not listening," said Ruby, continuing to wriggle around. Lorelei turned to Danny with a sympathetic look, they were both thinking the same, that Janey could be too demanding of her daughter, and really Ruby's 'leg kicking' could have been tolerated, and just maybe Janey's tone could have been a little lighter. Lorelei glanced at her sister. She wasn't watching the show, anyway. She had her nose stuck in her mobile phone.

"Everything okay, Janey?" Lorelei asked, genuinely concerned about her sister.

"What?" Janey snapped, looking up from her phone briefly. "Sorry, yes, I'm just tired. It's a long drive down here." She returned to her phone. What Lorelei couldn't have known is that her sister was distracted by an email that she had received earlier that day, and with all the travelling and family connection, that email had slipped her mind. Janey had not had a chance to properly digest the fact that Jay had sent her a communication asking her to call him, let alone properly read the email.

Jay's unexpected phone call earlier that month still chilled Janey's bones. She thought she had made it crystal clear that she wasn't going to engage with him; so why was he now sending her emails on Christmas Eve of all days? It was just typical of him. He was selfish, and he always had been. The actual body of the email was short, just a few lines begging her to ring him. *What could he want now?* What more could this despicable specimen of a human being, no, he wasn't even a human being… What could he want with her family now? After all the damage he had already done, why was he coming back for more? She wouldn't say anything to Lorelei, she wouldn't want to worry her. So, she'd just have to pretend she was just tired and not anxious about something more serious. Although her anxiety was clearly surfacing, as she was impatient with Ruby, snappy with her sister, and noticeably agitated about something.

Janey was in pain as she thought back to all the heartache Jay had caused them, physically and emotionally. All the times she'd had to pick up the pieces, try to protect her sister from that monster, which she knew very well she'd failed in. He was more of a monster than Lorelei knew — she had been blinded to the full extent of what he was capable of, but Janey would see to it that he couldn't worm his way back into their lives. He was being rather persistent at the moment though, which was *really* starting to worry her.

Robert stroked her arm. "Put that thing away. Let's just enjoy the evening."

"Actually," said Janey, "I think I'll just have an early night. I'm exhausted."

Iris yawned. "I shall be retiring relatively soon myself, dear."

"Well, I'm not tired," Ruby announced, "I'm going to stay up till midnight!" She gave out a ginormous yawn, "I'm not tired at all…"

Janey crawled into bed, she almost sank into the mattress and feather duvet as it was so deep and luxurious. It was always strange being back in her childhood home, and she thought no doubt that Lorelei must feel the same. Janey had moved out when she was only sixteen and had moved to the city to study. She always loved to come back to her mum's on the edge of Dartmoor. It was something about being wrapped around the moorland in the middle of nowhere. Some people might have found it isolating, but to Janey it was like an escape. If only she could go back to her childhood, she often thought. If there was a magic switch, she'd switch it and start all over again. There wouldn't be any debate about that at all.

She thought maybe she was never meant to be a mother, not in this way anyway. (The way it was forced upon her when she wasn't ready.) Robert had been delighted that they were going to be parents, but it wasn't something Janey had chosen for that particular stage in her life. She'd have probably terminated the pregnancy if she had been that little bit braver, but Robert talked her out of it. They were, after all, both professional, employed, no money worries, married and it seemed ideal to the rest of the world, but Janey knew that the truth was far from perfect.

Ruby had in fact behaved well today, apart from being a little cheeky and unruly at times, but the day had come and gone without anything too bad happening, so at least Janey had that to be grateful for, and soon Christmas would be over, and the new year would be upon them.

Janey always loved the new year, the fresh new start, the time for plans, resolutions, rebirth. But what she really was looking forward to was the week away with Robert. She could just feel that hot tub calling and craved for the beautiful hikes they were to embark on up in Cumbria. She just couldn't wait for the downtime, which was all thanks to Lorelei. After all, without her dearest sister, the vacation would not have been possible.

Her eyes were getting tired. There was a little night light plugged in on the edge of the room, so she could make out the shape of the armchair in the corner. She thought she could see her father sitting there. She willed to see him. *Were there such things as ghosts?* She heard his voice comforting her in her mind. "Janey, look after your sister," he would say to her. "You have the rest of your life ahead of you," he would say. "Be grateful for what you have." She tried to listen, but before long tiredness overcame her and she fell into a deep sleep, not even disturbed when Robert came in after having a few more glasses of wine. He wasn't the quietest or nimblest, to say the least. It was only when he started to snore in the early hours that Janey woke and gave him a shove.

"Shut up!!" she scorned, burying her head in the pillow, praying she'd be able to get back to sleep before the house awoke for Christmas morning.

Christmas day came and went without fireworks. Possibly because there were no demands upon Ruby to do anything else but lounge around in her new unicorn slippers and eat the most gorgeous Christmas food whilst watching whatever television she wanted.

There was just one slight hiccup, but it was an accident and was not related to Ruby's behaviour. Ruby had wanted to go to the car to retrieve her book that she'd left in the side pocket of the Volvo. She'd impulsively grabbed Janey's keys and rushed out the door before anyone had a chance to stop her. Ordinarily this may not have been a big problem, but no one had noticed she'd worn flip-flops and when running back up a small set of stone stairs outside her grandma's front door she'd fallen and cut her head open and oh, she screamed. Luckily, nurse Lorelei was there to treat her, and it really was a nasty gash that needed paper stitches, but fortunately Grandma's first aid box was very well equipped.

"Ruby, you shouldn't be wearing flip-flops!" Janey cursed, shaking her head and Ruby scowled back at her mother as she sat on the chair while Lorelei dressed her wound.

Apart from the fall, everything was quite perfect, from breakfast to bedtime, and for one day, everyone felt they could relax and just enjoy being among each other's company. All of Lorelei's family adored Danny, including Ruby, and there was no further mention of Jay, which Lorelei was very pleased about. Everyone was showered with presents, and Ruby particularly felt very much loved. It was hard to choose a favourite, but she did love the little fabric beaded bag that Lorelei had given to her, but the unicorn slippers were certainly up there too.

It could have easily been a complete disaster, but the stars seemed to be aligned. It was a time for everyone to be grateful and even Janey reflected on the things she loved about her daughter. She even felt a romantic closeness to Robert again (which had been lacking for a long while). And if truth be told, Janey felt positive that the next year would bring her a lot of answers and peace, she didn't know how, but she just had this feeling things would start to look up, and that there would be big changes ahead.

Tessy Braun

Mulled Cider

Cornwall

December 31st had arrived, and a feeling of excitement swept over Lorelei at the thought of celebrating at Hazel's New Year's Eve party. She held a sense of satisfaction, knowing that they had survived Christmas, coupled with a sense of exhilaration as it was now, at last, time to welcome the new year. She too, just like Janey, had a feeling it held significant things. Danny had suggested an afternoon walk at Godrevy to blow off the cobwebs, or somehow wash away the troubles of the year, before getting into full-blown party mode, because, "Boy, Hazel knew how to throw a party," he had said, and Lorelei had no doubt about that at all.

Lorelei's outfit hung on the wardrobe door, patiently waiting for her. The dress's sequins anticipating the party as much as she was, glistening in the winter sunbeam. The dress was stunning and underneath the sparkling upper area around the bust, lay a thick flowy net skirt in navy-blue, and Lorelei's elegant silver high heels neatly waited for her size five and a half feet to fill them. Danny would coordinate with his blue suit and a silver tie.

She arrived at Danny's house to collect him for their New Year's Eve walk, for now, laced up securely in her sensible walking boots. The car boot was full of waterproof clothing just in case the heavens decided to open. Giving her little yellow car a toot, she waited for him. In a few moments he emerged from his house, waving a sturdy looking umbrella. He opened the passenger door and jumped in.

"Hi beautiful!" He held up the umbrella. "Heavy-duty in case it chucks down!" he exclaimed proudly. "There's no way this one's getting flipped inside out!"

"Amazing, but I hope we won't need it," replied Lorelei. She turned the engine, and they began their journey along the coast road to Godrevy, passed the holiday park where she used to stay, through the village of Gwithian and then up to the National Trust car park, and from there they'd walk up to Godrevy point where they'd be rewarded with stunning views out to the lighthouse, hoping that, with binoculars they may even be able to spot some grey seals.

The wind was strong and fresh, and the sea battered the rocks violently. Lorelei had long been aware of the relentless power of the sea, and although it was a comforting place, she did not underestimate its fearsome capability. They walked along the coast path, fingers interlinked, absorbing the smell of the sea and the roaring ocean sounds. What was it about the sea that felt so rescuing? Lorelei and Danny shared this connection deeply. It was something ingrained in their souls, in their destiny. As they walked along, Lorelei stole secret glances at Danny, admiring everything about him. How he carried himself, how he dressed, how he made her world so perfect. Danny, catching glimpses of Lorelei's auburn hair blowing in the salty wind, too became lost in thought at what good fortune had befallen him and an excited feeling brewed in his stomach.

They continued to wander peacefully across the headland until, to the couple's interest, they spotted the coastguard helicopter circling from St Ives over the bay. Lorelei recognised its red and white colours and recalled a time where she was bobbing around on her bodyboard when it had once before chopped along this route, flying so low that she could see the crew on board. It had been a training exercise; she wondered if it was the same today, and hoped no one was in trouble.

Lorelei watched the helicopter disappear into the distance and pulled her wild hair away from her face. She took a deep breath while thinking out loud about the evening ahead.

"I'm really looking forward to the party," she said. "So, you said Hazel throws one every year?"

"Yes, it's a tradition that's gone back years, way back to our twenties," Danny revealed.

"And you and Hazel go back a long while, you said?"

"We do. We went to primary school together," he reminisced. "We were very close. She kind of looked out for me."

"That's so nice. I don't stay in touch with anyone from school! Well; apart from Louise, and it's been a while since I spoke to her…" she trailed off, a recurrent curious feeling niggled. She held the distinct inkling that just maybe there had been something more than friendship between Danny and Hazel in the past. It was the way that Hazel had been so smitten when talking about Danny, and the way that he always spoke so fondly of Hazel. "So, were you and Hazel…?"

"What?"

"You know, were you and Hazel," she gulped, "an item?"

Danny thought back to how his best friend had held his hand after his sister's tragic accident, how she'd loved him, how she'd always watched out for him. She'd made him laugh when he cried, always trying to take his mind off the awful events. She had nurtured his writing, encouraged his creativity. He loved Hazel very much, yes, but in a platonic way, and Hazel loved him back.

"An item? Never, but she was there for me, through dark times."

Lorelei let out a sigh of relief; she would have found it a bit weird if they had once been romantically connected.

"We were just kids, but even throughout our adult lives we've been close, but just friends, never more," he reassured Lorelei, supposing it not appropriate to divulge how Hazel was, or had been, very much in love with him, and certainly not in a platonic way.

"And the dark times," Lorelei gently probed, "is it to do with your family? Before Christmas, you didn't want to talk about something?"

"Can we have a sit down?" he pointed to a cluster of small rocks where they'd be sheltered from the wind. They huddled together, with a view of the roaring ocean in front of them.

"Lorelei, I know this must sound really weird, and you've been so open to me, but you're just going to have to trust me on this one. Some really big things happened to me when I was small. I can't even process them properly myself now, but I will tell you this." He hesitated.

"Go on," she gently encouraged.

"I had a sister once." His eyes welled up. "And she died when we were kids…"

"Why didn't you tell me?" she whispered. "Danny, I am so sorry to hear this," she croaked, "I am so sorry," she repeated herself, not knowing what else to say to him, and in disbelief at what she was hearing. It didn't matter, of course, that he had not told her. He was telling her now, and that's all that mattered. She put her arms around his body and held him tight and he sobbed into her shoulder, where he remained for a short time. It was a milestone for Danny to get this off his chest, and now it was, he felt so much better. Especially because Lorelei had taken it so well and hadn't felt angry with him for hiding the truth.

"We're not going to let this dampen the rest of the day, okay?" he said to Lorelei, and explained he didn't want to go into it further at this point. Lorelei respected his wishes.

"That's fine. We don't need to, but we can talk more about this whenever you want."

"I feel relieved you know," he said.

"I feel relieved you've told me, I was worrying about what you were going to say, but it's comforting to know that Hazel helped you navigate through your loss when you were kids." She stopped for a breath. "I just hope I can continue to do that."

Hazel had always loved Danny, and if she could have been with him romantically, she would have. As they had grown up together out of their teens, into young adults, she had expressed her feelings numerous times, but Danny had never felt the same. He only had a sisterly love for Hazel, and in many ways her role was indeed a substitute sibling for him, and for this reason, Danny could never have seen her in a romantic way.

A colony of seagulls squawked above them in a deafening racket and the rain started to spit but didn't quite materialise to anything more than a shower. After an hour, with wind-bitten cheeks they decided enough cobwebs had been blown and took a turn to head back to the car park, and then to Danny's house for it was getting late and they would need plenty of time to get New Year's Eve Party-ready!

Lorelei carefully painted her nails, leaving them shiny and sparkly as she neatly pulled the little brush down each one. She sat on Danny's bed, enjoying the process of glamming up. They played nineties music and reminisced. The conversation that they had had on Godrevy point seemed to fade away and things felt back to normal. Lorelei, who, of course, was naturally curious as to what had happened to Danny's sister, certainly did not want to pry. She wanted Danny to continue to open up to her when he was ready. Danny had snapped quite out of his sad thoughts. It had been a release to get some of his past off his chest, but it didn't change the dynamic between them.

"Your birthday will be coming up in the new year," Danny said. Lorelei sighed, as if she needed reminding. Lorelei closed her eyes. Where had all the years gone? When she didn't reply, Danny remarked, "I was thinking," he paused. "I'd like to take you for a day of relaxation and pampering. How about it, beautiful?"

Lorelei admired her nails, and held them up to the light, imagining spending a whole day at a spa, chillaxing in the jacuzzi, sweating it out in the sauna and de-stressing in the meditation room. She hadn't been to a spa for, what, it must have been ten years or more. She liked the idea a lot.

"I wouldn't say no to that!" She said with a grin.

"And afterwards I can take you out for dinner and we can stay in one of the woodland cabins, and make a weekend of it. This is, after all, a special birthday."

Lorelei had never liked birthdays and, with the big forty looming, she had been trying to bury her head in the sand. It wasn't something she had particularly mentioned to Danny, but he'd wheedled it out of her some time ago.

Lorelei blew her nails and winked at him. "Life begins at forty, right?" And it had for Lorelei. Celebrating this year would be a lot easier for her than previous birthdays that had been scarred with darkness. She thought back to them and reflected on how Jay had always given her roses, and she never really liked them, yet despite her subtle suggestions for her love for tulips or lilies, he never seemed to get the hint. Lorelei reflected how once the forty red roses that had been bestowed upon her ended up as petal mash under Jay's boots, and the thorns on those flowers cut deep. No, birthdays would be different from now on. Lorelei now had hope, and she had Danny.

It was eight pm. Hazel ushered her guests inside, out of the cold, and handed them a glass of prosecco. Party music played through her expensive sound system and the house was, as always, warm and inviting. The Christmas tree, though losing pines, still looked magnificent and the smell of cinnamon and gingerbread wafted. Everyone dressed to impress. Hazel was no exception with a beautiful sea green silky gown with the lowest cut back imaginable. Peter, Hazel's partner, strutted around offering canapes to their hungry guests. Lorelei almost picked one of the mini pancakes with shredded duck, forgetting for a moment that she was a vegetarian — they looked too tempting. In the end, she went for a caramelised mushroom tartlet which looked equally appetising. Molly had gone for a sleepover at Peter's mum's house, which was just as well. There was too much going on and Hazel hadn't wanted any accidents.

Danny and Lorelei floated gracefully into the kitchen

where Hazel was busy warming mulled cider on the stove, careful not to splash any of the spicy hot Christmas drink on her dress. She smiled just as warmly as the cider as she saw them approach. "Oh, just look at how gorgeous you are together!" she exclaimed, noting their matching colour scheme. "I'm thrilled you've both hit it off so well. You both deserve to be happy." Hazel looked fondly at them both, but there was something in her eyes that Lorelei couldn't read; a kind of longing. Though for what, she couldn't tell. Peter sailed through to replenish his tray of canapes, but before doing so deposited the tray on the side and slid his arms around Hazel. Lorelei thought for a second that she saw Hazel flinch, but perhaps she had imagined it.

"Hi," Peter extended a hand to Danny, and then to Lorelei. "It's a pleasure," he purred, in a way that Lorelei found familiar. "What do you think of the canapes? Good, no?" Everyone nodded with approval as Peter used tongs to re-fill the plate. "*Only* the best for Hazel's New Year's Eve party!" he stated, raising his eyebrows with a hint of sarcasm whilst helping himself to a goat's cheese and cranberry bruschetta. "Delicious!"

The others agreed. Hazel had lovingly prepared them that afternoon. She was quite the perfectionist and loved to host. She poured everyone a glass of mulled cider, but Peter excused himself to continue with the canape rounds.

"So," Hazel chirped, "new year's resolutions?" She took a small sip from her glass and nodded with satisfaction. Lorelei and Danny looked at each other with the most tender of expressions, and Lorelei smiled so sweetly.

"I've never been one for new year's resolutions but this coming year…" Lorelei's gaze remained fixed on Danny, and he smiled back at her as she continued. "I just want to focus on being happy. Life is so short, and I feel like I did all the crazy changes this year and so, for the year ahead, I just want to be content." It was a sweet and genuine speech from Lorelei, which Danny followed.

"No stress, no bother. We just want to enjoy life," he said.

"Together." they chimed in unison.

"What about you Hazel?" asked Danny.

"I think, in all honesty, I could do with taking a leaf out of your book Lorelei, and start being a strong, independent woman."

"But you already are," Lorelei insisted.

"I once thought so, but now I'm not so sure."

Bristol

New Year's Eve at the Pritchard's was a much quieter affair. It was just Janey and Ruby because Robert was working at the hotel. So far, the day had passed with no problems, and Janey had very much enjoyed spending time with her daughter. They'd been to the shopping mall and spent some quality time together, which was pretty rare. After a morning of retail therapy, they'd eaten fast food for lunch. Ruby proudly wore her bag, which her Auntie Lorelei had given her for Christmas. She'd hardly taken it off since Christmas day, always wanting to carry it around. She liked the texture of it, and the feeling of the beads when she ran her fingers over them, not to mention the explosion of colours. They had spent a painfully long time in 'Claire's' choosing new earrings and other jewellery, and Ruby had really enjoyed sifting through the rails in search of bargain clothes in the sales. She was over the moon with her purchases, which included some embroidered jeans, more baggy jumpers, and a pair of designer sports trainers.

With Robert being away, it was to be a girlie night, and they'd stopped in the supermarket on the way home to stock up on popcorn, ice cream and sweets (and of course a bottle of prosecco for Janey). Ruby was happy with her fizzy pop and pile of sweet treats, and they planned to order in a pizza for mains.

Ruby had been determined to stay up till midnight to see the new year in with her mum, but it wasn't to be. By ten o'clock, she had fallen asleep on the sofa. Janey left her there. She was too heavy to lift nowadays, so she draped a blanket over her daughter and turned the television down. Janey was on her third flute of prosecco and was feeling quite tipsy and didn't know if she'd make it to midnight herself at this rate. She reflected on the day; it had been a good one, and she had a feeling it was a sign of things to come. Yes, it had been unbearable mothering Ruby over the last fourteen years, but today showed her it wasn't always *that* bad, and surely it was time for her family to have some good fortune. She felt like the coming year would be *the* year that they finally got what they had been craving; answers, understanding, some kind of peace from the whole situation. Janey looked down at her sleeping daughter. She was beautiful, but she didn't see any of herself in her, only her father. As she gazed down at Ruby, she noted how she had inherited his looks and features. And that was all Janey saw, every time she looked at her.

Cornwall

Hazel's party was in full swing; the drinks were flowing, and all but one person was having a fantastic time. Music was blaring, some people were dancing on the makeshift dance floor, others sat down in quieter rooms talking. Lorelei, who was now feeling merry, had been looking for Hazel, who seemed to have disappeared for a notable period.

Hazel had shut herself in her bathroom upstairs. She was trying to clean up her face after a crying episode had ruined her beautiful makeup. Whilst she was happy that her guests were enjoying themselves and that her party was a success, in a disturbing parallel she looked at her own reflection in the mirror, at her tear-stained cheeks, accepting the reality that she was a mess and felt terribly low. She and Peter had argued earlier that day and had had a further altercation just a short time ago. Hazel had always been a strong individual, outgoing and fiercely independent. Her house was her own, and she had never been reliant on a man financially. She had been dating Peter for the last eight months or so, but things really hadn't been how they seemed to the outside world. Lorelei, after checking all the rooms upstairs, realised that the bathroom was occupied. She gently tapped on the door.

"Hazel? Are you in there?" she asked, hearing muffled sobs returned from within.

"Is that you, Lorelei?" she sniffed and when she was satisfied it was, Hazel unlocked the door.

"Oh Hazel, what's wrong?" Lorelei hugged her friend.

"You know what my new year's resolution is?" She blew her nose in a ball of soft toilet tissue. "I'm going to be telling Peter it's over!"

Lorelei's eyes widened in shock. "Hazel, I had no idea things weren't good, well until tonight. I sensed a bit of friction earlier," she admitted, comforting Hazel. "Has something happened?"

"I've been in denial for months!" Hazel lifted her dress to reveal big black bruises on her thighs. "He pushed me into the corner of the table. It's not the first time…"

"Hazel!"

"Yeah, he wasn't happy about the party. He says I've been selfish, and it's all for show."

"What a nasty bastard!"

"I used to think he'd get better, but what you've told me about your ex-husband, it's made me realise Peter isn't going to change either."

"You don't deserve to be treated like this."

"I know, and Lorelei, you've made me realise this!"

"Look, you don't need him!"

"He's just had a go at me again, about the party, and blamed me for taking the mick out of his mother, for leaving Molly with her, but Lorelei, she was so happy to look after Molly when I asked!"

Lorelei knew these tactics so well. It was a narcissist's wicked way of twisting everything you say, trying to make you feel like you're crazy. Lorelei thought back to the day Hazel gave her a ride to the first writing club meet up.

"You said to me before that you knew the abusive type, but when I asked you if it was Peter, you said no."

"We'd only just met. I was embarrassed."

"Look, he's not worthy of you, he's an absolute arse, you're an amazing, strong woman, and you will get through this — don't let him ruin your wonderful New Year's Eve party!"

"You're a good friend Lorelei. Gosh look at the state of me, you're right, let me get my face back on, and let's go back to the party! Go get a very strong drink for me will you, and I'll be back down asap!"

As tempted as she was, Lorelei thought it probably wasn't quite the right time to start questioning Hazel about what happened to Danny's sister, so instead, she nodded. "Of course, one passion fruit martini coming up!"

"And Lorelei, thank you. You are *so* inspiring!"

The countdown had begun, the enormous wall-mounted television had been switched on and turned up and the chimes of Big Ben commenced. Next, the impressive London fireworks display took place, but big bangs could also be heard outside on the streets of Hayle and many people were outside their front doors bashing pots and pans.

"HAPPY NEW YEAR!" clink went the glasses, and beep went all the phones with text messages as new year wishes bombarded the network.

Bristol

Janey and Ruby were both asleep in the front room, full up on pizza and sweets (and Janey on prosecco) when Lorelei's happy new year text came through. Janey didn't see it until the morning, by which time Robert was home. He made her a nice cup of coffee and ran her a bath. Ruby was deadly quiet all day, which was unusual, and they had a delicious roast dinner. *Well*, Janey thought, *what was that proverb? That the first day of the year represented the whole year ahead?* If today was anything to go by, the year ahead held good things.

Tessy Braun

Blue Bear

It was a February Saturday morning, and the skies were grey. Lorelei was busy tidying up her little flat in preparation for Ruby coming to stay for the half term. Ruby's parents had put her on the train from Bristol Temple Meads that morning and they expected her to arrive at Penzance just after two o'clock. Lorelei was in good spirits and was looking forward to finally being able to give tangible support to her sister and Robert. She thought of them preparing to head off to their luxurious holiday village in the Lake District, near Keswick, where they would enjoy a private hot tub and sauna.

For the duration of the stay, Lorelei would give up her bedroom for Ruby and make do with the sofa for her bed. She lovingly took down 'Blue Bear' from the top of the wardrobe and placed the soft, cuddly toy with care on Ruby's bed. Ruby had always loved 'Blue Bear' and his identical twin brother, though would not likely admit to it anymore. The two bears had been in the family for many years. Both Lorelei and Janey had been given them for Christmas when they were children and both sisters had kept each respective bear safe with much love over the years. When Ruby was younger, she was once fond of cuddling 'Blue Bear' when she came to stay at Lorelei's house from time to time. It brought her comfort as a familiar item when she perhaps missed home, just a little bit. Lorelei really hoped that Ruby would be pleased to see the bear when she arrived.

With some time to kill before collecting Ruby, Lorelei took a moment to scroll through her text messages. Reading the latest from Danny, she smiled, and a warm feeling crept over her.

I'm so looking forward to seeing you at lunchtime, and really excited to spend some more time with Ruby xx

Lorelei had previously told Danny all about Ruby's behaviour so he was very much aware of the challenges that Ruby presented to the family, but she hoped that, like Christmas, during a reasonably short period, Ruby would be capable of containing her anger, and she held onto the hope that there wouldn't be any significant issues. Lorelei was sure that Ruby would be grateful for the break, and the change of scene would surely be good for Ruby's mental health. However, even if the worst happened and Ruby exhibited her more challenging side, Lorelei felt sure that Danny's supportive nature would prevail, and he wouldn't be put off. At least, she hoped and prayed this would be the case. Lorelei gave Ruby a quick call, just to make sure that the journey was going to plan and that her young niece was alright.

"Hi Auntie Lorelei," she answered after just a few rings.

"Hi Ruby! I'm so excited to see you. How's the journey going?"

"Oh, I am *so* bored and I'm only one hour in. Can't wait to see you too. What are we going to do later?" Ruby asked.

"Well, I was thinking," she hesitated a little, "and only

if you're not *too* tired, how about we go out to tea?" Lorelei couldn't see, but Ruby was nodding enthusiastically, and a massive smile spread across her face. "Danny knows a nice pub, and they have some pool tables. You like playing pool, don't you?"

"Yes! That will be fun. I can't wait to see Danny again. He's cool."

"Great. Well, I'll see you in Penzance soon!"

From the conversation that Ruby and Lorelei just had, no one would suspect that there were any underlying problems with her behaviour. Lorelei, of course, knew otherwise, but was optimistic and curious to see what living with Ruby for seven days would be like. Lorelei had listened with interest as to the cause of certain eruptions and considered how she may handle them differently if they occurred. She knew well how outrageous Ruby's mood swings could be, but sometimes doubted her sister's ability to react in a calm and measured way. But then again, who could remain calm all the time when dealing with such abusive confrontation? It was soon time to meet Danny for lunch. Lorelei made her way into Hayle town, coming off at the St Erth roundabout and alongside the estuary. She stopped outside Danny's house and gave him a buzz. "Hi, I'm outside," she sang.

"I'll just be a minute," came his reply. He had such an enchanting, gravelly voice. She was excited to see him and looking forward to bathing in his creative energy. It wasn't long before she saw him step outside his front door. He looked *good*, dressed in smart jeans and a navy crew neck, his jacket slung casually over his arm. He opened the passenger door and greeted Lorelei with a kiss.

"Hello beautiful," he said, and she melted. "I missed you."

"Oh, me too, I always do…"

"Let's head down to Penzance. How about we just stop by in the coffee shop in the retail park, and we can grab a panini and cake?"

"Yeah, that makes sense. Finding somewhere to park in the town could be tricky."

"Perfect."

"Oh, and Danny, I spoke to Ruby on the phone, and she was delighted with your suggestion of a pub meal and a game of pool."

Danny beamed, pleased that his idea had been well received. "Brilliant! It'll be really nice to have her here. I'm sure there'll be no drama. We'll just try to keep everything nice and easy."

"Yes," Lorelei agreed, "I think that's the key to it, at least for this week in the short term, I mean." The journey down to Penzance was smooth. They whizzed through the route with no delays, although in another six weeks that would change. The west of England would become a tourist hotspot from spring onwards. The weather for this particular week was not up to much (not that February was ever expected to be a good month) but with spring just around the corner, everyone hoped they'd see the weather change in the not too distant future. Unfortunately, this week, the forecast indicated rain and strong gales.

"How's Mick doing? Have you spoken to him lately?" enquired Lorelei. Mick had missed the last writing club meeting, and the group had been worried about him.

"He's not great, to be honest. He's got a nasty bout of gastroenteritis. He's holding up though."

"Bless him. I must send him a text later."

Danny told Lorelei that apparently there'd been a strange man spotted around the streets of St Ives, and not one of the locals could identify him. Those that had seen him said he seemed a bit 'sketchy,' and reported that he had a can of lager and a cigarette in his hand.

"Hmm, that sounds a bit strange," said Lorelei.

"It's a bit unusual around these parts," agreed Danny. "Not so uncommon in Penzance."

"Perhaps whoever it is, wanted a change of scenery?" she mused, "I hope they're okay, whoever they are." Lorelei gazed out the window and thought a little more on the news. "Come to think of it, I'm sure Hazel mentioned about a random stranger on the beach months ago…"

They pulled up into the car park and noted the wind was gaining momentum when it swung open the car door. With much haste, the two of them made their way into the popular coffee shop chain, looking forward to a bite to eat. They found a seat by the window and Lorelei leaned her back against the glass. The waiter brought over their order of two lattes and two paninis quickly, which was a good thing, as time was ticking on.

"You know, this is *such* a lovely thing you're doing for your sister," remarked Danny, taking her hand in his. "I *really* admire your generosity and kindness."

"Ah, thanks Danny, but it's the least I can do." She stirred her caramel latte. "In some ways I feel guilty that I moved away and left Janey…"

"But she has Robert?"

Nodding, Lorelei replied, "He's a good man. He's just so often away."

"It's not your fault. You're doing what you can to help." Danny reassured her. "Perhaps we can look after Ruby more often in the holidays?"

Lorelei froze. What did he mean by 'we'? *He really must be feeling quite serious about our relationship*, she thought. It made her smile. "Well, let's get this week out of the way first, but yes, maybe we can." Lorelei clasped the giant mug in her hands and took a sip. "That's so good," she said. She had ordered a mozzarella and tomato toasted panini, while Danny had gone for a simple but tasty tuna melt. Danny's gaze crossed from Lorelei to outside the window to the car park and a worried expression on his face alarmed Lorelei.

"*What is it?*"

"My God, Lorelei, it's him, I swear!"

"What do you mean?" she asked. "*Who?!*"

"In the car park, right by your car!"

She turned around, stunned, but saw no one. "Don't tease me, you almost gave me a heart attack!"

"No, really, there was a guy out there! The same dark clothing and messy hair, like Mousie told me," he said. "I'm sure it was the same guy."

"You are *really* freaking me out now."

His voice softened. "Oh Lorelei, I'm sorry, I was just shocked for a moment…"

"I know, but where is he now, and *why* was he hanging around my car?"

For a while now, Lorelei had had a nagging feeling that someone was watching her, and paranoia had increasingly been fed with more unsettling news of a mystery man hanging around the area, especially at a time her niece was coming to stay. It was all very unnerving indeed. All the terrible crimes that had been carried out in Bristol came to her mind, and she shuddered. She couldn't bear the thought of a strange man hanging around. What if he was a murderer or a sex offender? And furthermore, just why had Lorelei felt like someone was watching her? She had an unrelenting thought in her mind; it kept coming back to her, but it couldn't be, *it simply couldn't be him*.

"Don't worry." Danny smoothed her hand. "Perhaps

Hope by the sea

I was mistaken, maybe my mind's playing tricks on me."

"I certainly hope so!"

"Come on, let's talk about something else. So, have you had a chance to write any more poetry?"

"Well, I did write *something*..."

"Oh yeah? Can you show me?" he pressed.

"Sure, well, it's the start of a longer piece that I'm writing. Do you remember what I mentioned?"

"Of course, your dark fairy tale!"

"Yes, and it's very much inspired by Cornish mythology."

"Go on," he prompted.

Lorelei pulled out her jotter from her bag. "I wanted to write a dark story about fairies, but not the sort of fairies that one usually thinks of. Okay, so it starts like this..."

In the little woodland clearing
a bluebell blanket looks endearing.
Though careful as you stroll around,
where flower faeries may be found,
whispering their fairy talk,
peering past the flower stalks.
But in the drooping recurved tips,
inside a wandering child fits
and flower faeries lay their trap
with sticky sticky bluebell sap.

Danny was speechless.

"Well? Is it that bad?!" Lorelei mocked.

"Wow, is there more?"

"Yes..."

And once they've surely captured them
they drag the flower by the stem,
deep into the dingy dell

**they drag and drag that flower bell!
So, tempt ye not by that sweet scent,
and the beauty of those bluebells leant
and swaying in that gentle breeze,
for faeries take just as they please.**

"Well, this is very '*Christina Rosetti*'. It's remarkable, and enchanting," praised Danny. "You must carry on, you're so talented."

Lorelei blushed and looked down into her coffee cup.

"I mean it! This is quite extraordinary considering you'd only started writing a few months ago. I'm *very* impressed!" He reached out and with his hand brought her chin up, so their eyes met, and expressed, "And I'm extremely proud of you."

Lorelei blushed again. "Thanks Danny," she paused, then abruptly changed the subject. "Danny, I'm worried about the man. I don't know why, but for a while now, I've felt like someone's been watching me…"

"Darling, *who* would be watching you?"

"Like someone's after me…"

"What are you talking about?"

"I've tried to push it to the back of my mind, but you say the locals have seen him…"

"It's probably just someone from Falmouth, or Cambourne. No one is after you!"

"But how can you be so sure?"

"Don't you worry, I'll look after you!"

"Danny…" She looked him straight in the eye. "I'm worried," she said. "I think it might be my ex…"

"I thought as much." Unphased, he continued, "If it is him, I won't let you come to harm, but I'm very sure that it's nothing like that. It's just a weirdo from up country. *It's not Jay,* alright?"

She smiled, trying to give him the illusion that she'd been reassured, but really any sense of assurance was far from received.

"Come on, that panini's getting cold, eat up," he commanded.

Lorelei began to chew her panini slowly and slurp her coffee, thinking to herself that it would indeed be preposterous to even imagine that Jay would be after her. It was just that she knew well his obsessive nature and the lengths he would go to get his way if he were up to no good.

The station was quiet as ever. After all, it was the end of the line in a quiet seaside town. Lorelei and Danny waited by the rails for Ruby's train to arrive. Before long, the InterCity chugged in and ground to a halt, and unlike scenes that Lorelei was used to in Bristol, only a handful of passengers disembarked. Momentarily Lorelei panicked when she didn't catch a glimpse of Ruby, but sure enough, she soon saw her niece stepping onto the platform.

"Ruby!" she called as the teen dragged her holdall awkwardly over her shoulder. She wore denim shorts, with purple leggings underneath and white pumps on her feet. On her top, she adorned an oversized knitted cardigan.

"Did you not bring a coat, Ruby?"

"*My coat!*" she cried, "I've left it on the train!" Ruby threw the holdall to Danny. "I've got to go back!"

Lorelei had quite forgotten what an absent-minded child she was, or how 'careless' she was, as Janey would often describe her. Ruby came jogging back down the platform with her faux style leather jacket.

"That's better. Come here, give me a hug," she said as she embraced the young girl, who was evidently exhausted after a long journey. Ruby turned to Danny and gave him a hug, too.

"Are Mum and Dad there yet?" she asked.

"Do you know, I don't think they are yet," said Lorelei, checking her phone. "It takes a lot longer to get to the Lake District from Bristol than it does to get from Bristol to Penzance."

"Hmm, Is it near Scotland?" asked Ruby.

"Yes, not far at all," said Danny, "and your mum and dad have gone to the North Lakes, so that's really close to Scotland," he explained.

"Can we call Mum when they're there? I miss her already," said Ruby, suddenly feeling a little despondent.

"Of course, of course," reassured Lorelei. "We'll definitely call them, but I bet they'll call before we do. They will be missing you too."

"I doubt Mum will be missing me. She couldn't wait to get away. She needed a break from me, that's what she said…"

"Oh Ruby, she will *definitely* miss you," Lorelei comforted, saddened by how Ruby felt.

"Well, come on then," Danny hurried them along. "Let's make a move back, get you unpacked and settled in." They got in the car, belted up, and began the journey home. Ruby, sitting in the back, gazed out of the window, quite absorbed by the countryside views.

"Where am I sleeping?"

"Well, you've got my room for the week," said Lorelei.

"So, where will *you* sleep?"

"I'll be in the lounge."

"You can sleep in with me if you like. I don't mind."

"We'll see. I want you to have your own privacy. I'm

fine on the sofa!"

"Will Danny stay?"

"Oh no, there's not enough room."

"Oh, okay. I wouldn't mind if he did."

Danny and Lorelei exchanged a glance. They'd already spoken about this and had decided it was best that they kept to their own respective properties for the night time while Ruby was staying, but it was sweet how she was so inviting of Danny's company, nonetheless. It was indeed hard to imagine how such a sweet and harmonious girl could ever turn into such a monster. Lorelei had never felt very maternal, and her biological clock had nearly passed that stage, but for the first time in her life, she actually felt motherly and had a very real feeling of what it would have been like to have her own family; a mum, a dad, a daughter, and it felt good. She was sure she'd never have her own child, not now. It was all too late, but it was nice to have a niece.

As they approached the north, joining the coast road to St Ives, Ruby beamed with delight when she saw the ocean in a 'V' shape between the houses. Despite her reservations, she was so excited to be on holiday with her auntie, although Ruby would find it hard to share her enthusiasm with her parents. She hated to be seen to love anything that was remotely to do with the outdoors, or for that matter, anything other than her mobile phone. Yet in her heart she loved the ocean so much and knew she was lucky to have the opportunity to come to St Ives for half term. In fact, she rather fancied the idea of escaping there for good, just like her auntie had. She often fantasised about it herself, daydreaming about what she would do and who she would meet. She wondered if she'd meet a friend here this week, someone who she might stay in touch with, a pen pal perhaps. She could do with some new friends, she thought to herself. In fact, she didn't really want to go home at all. *Perhaps she would stay indefinitely; her mother probably wouldn't mind that at all.*

Before long, they arrived outside Lorelei's flat.

"You live above an art gallery?"

"I sure do!"

Ruby gazed into the window at the wonderful brightly coloured paintings of boats and Cornish harbour scenes.

"I like art. I think I would like to paint like this," she mused as her eyes trailed over the many bold impressions. *It can't be that difficult,* she thought. "Six hundred pounds! These are expensive, Auntie Lorelei!"

"Yep, you'll find lots of art galleries in St Ives," Lorelei remarked.

"There's a special light in this part of the world, Ruby," Danny said, pulling Ruby's holdall over his own shoulder.

"A special light?"

"Yes, it draws artists here from around the world. It's quite extraordinary."

"Maybe you can do some painting while you're down here, Ruby," suggested Lorelei.

"I'd like that. The weather's not great, but I'm sure the sea is still cool, especially if there was a storm…"

"You could maybe write a poem about the sea too," added Danny.

Ruby looked in wonder. "So many ideas of what to do. It's not like at home. I'm usually just on my social media!"

"There's more to life than YouTube and Instagram," said Danny, and Ruby nodded. She was beginning to realise that perhaps Danny was right.

Lorelei showed Ruby her room while Danny put the kettle on

and poured Ruby a glass of juice. He could hear the two of them from the kitchen.

"*Blue Bear*!" shrieked Ruby. Danny smiled, thinking about how he was looking forward to the week ahead. He'd taken some annual leave so he could support Lorelei and make sure they were both okay during the visit.

Lorelei was forever grateful for Danny's help. He meant the world to her. If it were not for the strange man that had been spotted, she could honestly say she'd never felt happier or more content.

Ruby unpacked her belongings and for the remainder of the afternoon, she had a rest in her room. It was three o'clock when Lorelei finally received a call from her sister.

"Hi Janey! You've arrived safely then?"

"Oh yes, Lorelei, what a journey! It was worth it though, as soon as we saw the south lakes from the motorway. Is everything okay?"

"Yes, everything is perfectly fine." She listened. "No, no, everything is good, don't you worry, I'll just pass you over to Ruby."

Lorelei tapped on the door, but there came no reply. "Ruby?" she called, but still no answer. Lorelei carefully opened the door. "Oh," she sighed with relief. "She's asleep Janey! Bless her, she must have been so tired from the journey."

"Okay, well, not to worry. I'll speak to her another time. Thanks so much for having her. I owe you, sis."

"Not at all. It's the least I can do for my big sister, who's helped me out *so* many times before. I'm just happy I can help."

"And you're *sure* everything's okay? No concerns — about *anything*?"

"Not one bit. Now you enjoy your break. You deserve

it."

Lorelei quietly snuck into the front room where Danny lay on the sofa, looking utterly irresistible. Lorelei couldn't quite get over how handsome a creature he was. She was beginning to love every part of him, and not least his physical appearance. His figure was well defined, not overly muscular but sculpted just enough for her liking. Lorelei brought one finger across her lips.

"Shh, Ruby's asleep." She climbed on the sofa with him, and ran her hands inside his jumper and, as she had come to learn his t-shirt was always tucked snuggly into his jeans. With one swift move, she pulled it out and slid her hand up onto his warm chest, which was covered in soft, curly hair.

"Oh, I could just…" he murmured, before she kissed him on the lips.

"I know…"

But knowing that they had a young guest in the room next door, the desire they both felt was curtailed, and after a quick cuddle, they turned their attention to the television.

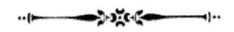

Ruby appeared in the doorway. "I'm hungry."

"Oh, hi! You're awake!" Lorelei cheerfully replied.

"Yes, and I said, *I'm starving!*" Ruby declared. Danny checked the time; it was gone half-past five.

"Do you want to head out to tea then?" he said.

"I'm starving hungry, I need something *now*." Looking at her auntie she begged, "*Please!*"

"We're going out for tea, if that's what you still want to do," said Lorelei.

"Yes, I want to! You promised we would!" snapped Ruby.

"Okay, Ruby, we *are* going out. We didn't say we

weren't." said Lorelei.

"Good. I just need something to eat, just a *snack*!"

Danny had quickly nipped to get the fruit bowl and offered it to Ruby.

"No, not *fruit*. I don't want *fruit*. I need a biscuit or something nice like that!"

Lorelei knew that food was often the catalyst for Ruby's temper tantrums, and she was starting to panic that this could be the start of one.

"Ruby, of course, you can have a snack. Come with me." Lorelei led her niece to the kitchen and retrieved a box with several items in it, such as cereal bars and dried fruit. "You can choose something from here. Is there anything you like?" asked Lorelei.

"I hate dried fruit." She turned her nose up at the offer in disgust.

Danny thought for a moment before asking. "Have you tried dried cranberries? They're so delicious, they're like a chewy sweet."

"No, but I hate raisins."

"They're nothing like raisins. They taste completely different. Try them," he suggested. Lorelei poured a small amount into a little ramekin bowl and gestured for Ruby to try.

"Oh, I don't know, they look disgusting…"

"Just try. If you don't like them, have a snack bar instead," said Lorelei. Ruby's face screwed up as she picked up a juicy looking cranberry, and as she brought it to her mouth, she winced as if she was in pain.

"Go on!" encouraged Danny, who had picked a few up himself. "They're delicious!" he said as he threw a handful into his mouth.

"Okay, here goes…" Ruby said. She placed the fruit in her mouth, and for a moment, there was silence. Her eyes popped wide in the strangest expression before she burst into laughter. "They're okay! I like them!"

"Okay!" Danny said, and he and Lorelei high-fived. "So, you nibble on those, let's say, we leave for the Ship Inn at six o'clock?"

The Ship was busy. It was a Saturday night, after all. The three of them grabbed a table in the restaurant area and studied the menu. All the expected pub favourites were there, including a tasty section of dishes from the sea. Lorelei salivated over the meat grills and fish and chips but forced her way past to the vegan and vegetarian options where she found an appealing halloumi burger, fries, and slaw.

"You *could* have fish. Fish is good for you," said Ruby.

"I know, I may have to start eating fish now that I live by the sea!" Her childish humour inspired her to make fish mouth movements in jest, and Ruby giggled.

"I like you Auntie Lorelei. You're funnier than Mum. Mum's always angry, or sad."

Ruby picked Hunter's chicken, which was one of her all-time favourite meals, and Danny chose a rack of ribs. The service was second to none, and the food was delicious. For pudding, all three indulged in ice cream sundaes, with chocolate brownies and sauce. Lorelei had enjoyed two glasses of wine, and Danny a few ciders. They finished the evening with some pool in the games room. It had been some time since Lorelei had played, and admittedly, it took her a few rounds to warm up. Ruby had played pool herself a few times before, but needed a bit of a refresher, which Danny was happy to provide. They seemed to have formed a really positive bond. They had fun, and the evening was thoroughly enjoyable, though all the time in the back of Lorelei's mind was that nagging feeling that something wasn't quite right, and she couldn't quite put her finger on it.

They walked back to the flat around nine o'clock. Luckily, it was a short distance, taking them around twenty minutes at a slow pace. Once they were back, Ruby got ready for bed with no fuss. She snuggled under the blanket, cuddling Blue Bear. She felt safe, like she belonged there at her Auntie Lorelei's, a lot more than she did in her own house in Bristol. Perhaps she and her auntie had more in common than she initially thought. They both needed to escape from something.

Danny and Lorelei, both craving each other's touch, hovered in the kitchen whilst Ruby fell asleep. They made some tea and Danny muttered about booking a taxi back to Hayle, though Lorelei wasn't listening in the slightest. Instead, she took his chin in her hands and kissed his lips.

"I'm so very happy I met you," she said. Kissing him again and again.

"I'm—", she kissed him. "so glad—" and kissed him "I met you—", again she kissed him, "too!" he finally managed to express between kisses. He grabbed her waist and pulled her in tightly.

"I've fallen for you, Lorelei, and tonight, you are incredibly irresistible…" He kissed her neck, and his hands began to wander south, and this time Lorelei had not the care to resist. With his touch, he stripped away her anxiety and stress, leaving only her wild instincts, which focused on him, and the way they both felt right there and then. He tapped her bum and whispered, "Other room."

Once in the lounge, he peeled off her stretchy jeans, leg by leg, and lowered himself to meet her navel, kissing her soft belly, down and down until his tongue slid inside of her knickers. She let out a faint moan and allowed herself to enjoy the moment and all that followed.

The Taxi was ordered and would be outside in five minutes.

"Stay..." Lorelei murmured.

"I can't. It wouldn't be right. I'll be back in the morning, beautiful."

Lorelei nodded. "You're right, I know..."

"I love you," he said, for the first time ever, "I do..."

She beamed up at him. "Ditto."

Once Danny had left, Lorelei made up her bed on the sofa, brushed her teeth and changed into her pyjamas. But before she snuggled into her duvet, ready to close her eyes, her phone beeped with an incoming text message. It would be Danny to say he was home. She swiped the screen to display the text, but to her absolute horror, it was not from him.

"Lor, it's Jay, I need to see you."

I'm not your baby girl

Lorelei froze. She knew it, she just *knew* it. As soon as there was the slightest possibility of happiness in her life, Jay would be back. A feeling of sickness in the pit of her stomach swamped all the feelings of contentment that she had felt just a short moment ago. Her pulse raced, and the adrenaline had a sudden sobering effect. She stared at the phone, feeling numb all over. She couldn't contemplate phoning Danny; he'd only just left, and although she fully intended to fill him in the next day, she really did not want to trouble him right now. Her phone buzzed again, startling her, but this time the message was from Danny. She sighed. It was just to let her know he was back at his house and to wish her a good night's sleep. Signed off with, she counted, *one, two, three, four, five, six kisses*.

She took a deep breath and attempted to pull herself together, but her concentration was broken by her phone's persistent ringing. She cursed herself for failing to turn the volume down. In an attempt to prevent Ruby from being woken, she fumbled around with the buttons on the side of the handset, thankfully managing to reduce the ear-piercing ringtone.

"Hello?" she said in a quiet, low voice.

"Lor, it's me, Jay." He paused, awaiting a reply, but Lorelei said nothing, so he continued. "Won't you talk to me, baby girl?"

"What the *hell* do you want?" she hissed. "*Why* are you calling me?!"

"I'm in a right state, Lor. I've made mistakes in my life. Please hear me out!"

"Are you out of your mind?" she exclaimed.

Taking her question as rhetorical, he went on. "Since we split up—"

"*Divorced,*" she sharply corrected him.

He cleared his throat. "Okay, since we went our separate ways, things have been, well, y'know, difficult…" He took a deep breath, "I've realised how it was all a mistake, baby girl." The purr was distinctive, and she flinched every time she heard the once affectionate term.

"What the bloody hell are you talking about? Look, I can't talk now."

"Why? It's not like *he's* there…"

"Who's *he*?"

"Lor, I know you've got a new boyfriend." He paused, and Lorelei gasped. He really had been stalking her. He went on, "And I actually understand the reasoning behind it. I mean, it must have been hard for you to be alone, and in a way, I don't blame you, *but I'm here now.*"

"*What!?*" she screwed her face up in utter disgust and disbelief.

"You don't have to be with a stranger. I wanna make things right, baby girl," he said, slurring his words.

"Have you been drinking?!"

"Lor, please, I love you, and I want my wife back—"

"I am *not* your wife! Now, listen to me! What the hell do you want?"

Now sniffling somewhat, Jay whimpered. "I need to see you, I need to show you how sorry I am, I need to…" He tried to string his sentence together, "I need to sort my shit out, but I need help, I need *your* help baby girl." He was evidently very emotional, but Lorelei was sure he was under the influence.

"What in God's name is wrong with you? You sound drunk!"

"Lor, you know I liked a drink, but I've fallen into a bad place. It's like, I now realise what it's like to be truly depressed," he groaned, and Lorelei rolled her eyes.

"*Where are you…?*" she slowly queried, with a note of hesitation in her voice.

"Don't be cross, Lor, but I'm in Cornwall," he said. Lorelei gulped as Jay carried on. "In your neighbourhood to be more precise," he sniggered, "and I couldn't be more precise than that."

Lorelei's blood began to boil. *"I knew it*, I just knew it!"

"Lor, I've been living out of my car for months. I've been trying to find you, then trying to find the right moment to show myself." As he explained, it slowly dawned upon her that all this time he'd been there, watching her, creeping around, stalking her, infecting her new life, poisoning her fresh start. All those times she had felt uneasy but brushed it away — he had been there. She gagged as she steadied herself.

"I've a good mind to call the police right now," she threatened.

"Please don't do that. Surely you still feel there's something there between us?"

"Don't do this," she said, trying to keep her tone as unemotional and level-headed as possible when inside, she was an emotional wreck.

"Won't you let me in?" he pleaded. Shaking with a rollercoaster of emotions, she surreptitiously peeked through the curtains and scanned the road below. She gasped. There was a figure sitting on the wall outside. *It was Jay.*

"It's gone ten o'clock. I'm going to bed now, and besides…"

"You've got Ruby, I know…" he sighed.

"Of course you know Ruby is here!" she growled. "This is beyond a joke, this is serious, this is what I call harassment!"

"I'm sorry for everything, and don't worry about Ruby. She always liked me, we had a bond. It wasn't meant to be like this."

"Well, sorry to say, but it *is* like this. What are you doing living out of your car? What about your job? Your house?"

"It's all gone. I've made mistakes, I've lost my job, got into debt, the landlord evicted me!" He wept.

Lorelei, feeling somewhat sorry for him at this point, to her utter bemusement, offered him an olive branch. "Look, I will book you somewhere to stay, only for a few nights, and then you need to go!"

"Oh Lor, thank you, I knew you still cared, that I still meant something to you—"

"Just wait a flipping second," she spat. "I'll help you get on your feet, and I'll talk to you *tomorrow* but then you are going back to Bristol. I've moved on, *I've changed*, I'm not your baby girl anymore!"

Lorelei hadn't noticed the teenage girl behind the living room door, secretly listening to the entire fraught conversation. Ruby did not allow her presence to be known, and instead quietly retreated to her room once she had heard the conversation draw to an end. She lay on her bed with her knees to her chest, clutching Blue Bear, the whole time trying to fathom the relevance of the words she had just heard. She hadn't mentioned to her mum or Auntie Lorelei that she'd been talking to Uncle Jay via text messages over the last week. He'd told her to keep it a secret. It was going to be a surprise. He would see her again this week, but she was told to not, under any circumstance, tell a living soul about it.

      Ruby now worried that the surprise wasn't one that Auntie Lorelei had happily received. She cried fiercely, her tears running down her cheeks. Had she been wrong to give Uncle Jay Auntie Lorelei's telephone number? Ruby feared for what repercussions may come her way. Her mother had told her that Jay was a 'bad man', and that she should count her blessings that he was not a member of their family anymore. Yet Ruby had indeed, as Jay said, always been fond of her uncle, apart, of course, from when she learnt he had been unkind to Auntie Lorelei. That wasn't nice, so she had made a choice to do what her mother said and try to forget about him. Until that week, of course. He'd told her how sorry he was, and how he missed her so much. However convincing Uncle Jay had been, she now knew she'd made a mistake, and she didn't feel at all comfortable with the tone of the telephone call she had eavesdropped on. Ruby wiped tears away as she dreaded what the morning may bring. She silently sobbed herself to sleep, and in the lounge just across the hallway, Lorelei did just the same.

Tessy Braun

Simply, no photographs

Morning came, and when Ruby awoke, Lorelei was already up and was pottering around in the kitchen. Ruby rubbed her eyes and sat up in bed. Sniffing the air, she could smell something cooking. It smelled sweet, freshly made, and she could almost taste the hot maple syrup that she knew Auntie Lorelei's pancakes always came with. Reaching to the nearby dressing table for her gown, Ruby then slid on her matching unicorn slippers and crept into the kitchen. She was so bewitched by the gorgeous smell of the breakfast that she almost forgot what had happened the night before.

"Pancakes!" she said to her aunt.

"Good morning, Ruby," said Lorelei as cheerfully as she could. Lorelei opened the fridge and poured Ruby a glass of apple and mango juice. "Here you are. You'll like this."

Ruby gulped it down. "I do, it's really nice."

"I know how much you enjoyed pancakes before, and I had all the ingredients, so I thought, why ever not?"

"Thank you, I *do* really like them!"

Lorelei dished up three small pancakes, American style, stacked one on top of the other, and drizzled maple syrup over them. She then garnished the dish with raspberries and blueberries. Ruby sat up at the breakfast bar about to devour her restaurant style treat. She suddenly jumped down.

"Oh! I need to take a picture of this!" she cried, returning a short moment later with her mobile phone. She took a photo of the breakfast, before tucking in. "What are we doing today?" she asked. Lorelei thought for a second, deliberating whether she should say anything about Jay, knowing she had promised to talk to him later.

"I don't know. The weather's awful today; there's wet weather forecast all week, I'm afraid," said Lorelei. Ruby's phone pinged and as she picked it up, a panic-stricken look of horror shot across her face; she quickly dropped the phone on the breakfast bar. Noticing her obvious change of expression, Lorelei asked if she was alright.

"Yes, *fine*, why wouldn't I be?" Ruby, quite evidently agitated, snapped back at her, rolling her eyes. She started coughing after stuffing a rather too large fork full of pancakes into her mouth, but the coughing transformed into wailing.

"Ruby, what is the *matter*?"

The tears flooded down her face and her breathing became quick and hysterical. "It's all my fault!"

"What's all your fault?!"

"That h-he, that he…" she struggled to get her words out. "That he's here!"

Lorelei's heart sank as she began to put two and two together. "Oh no Ruby, no…"

"*Yes, it's Uncle Jay.*" She handed over her mobile phone to Lorelei. "See for yourself." Lorelei took the handset and read the text message that Ruby had just received.

Your Auntie knows I am here. I'll see you later today x

Lorelei drew in a deep breath. "You've—he's, he's been using *you* to get to *me*," she stuttered in disbelief. "Just how long has this been going on for?" she demanded. Between the sobs Ruby managed to relay information about their communication over the last week, and in the end let Lorelei read through all the messages they had exchanged. Lorelei then revealed to Ruby that Jay had been in touch late the night before, and that she knew he was not at his home in Bristol.

"I'm not mad at you, okay?" said Lorelei with certainty. Ruby nodded.

"I'm sorry," she said, "he was so nice to me."

"He *has* been nice to you, yes, but he's manipulated you, too."

"I'm an idiot. I'm a stupid, stupid idiot! I can't believe I fell for this; I can't believe I was so dumb to give Jay your number!"

"Ruby, you're not stupid. Don't blame yourself!"

"Are you gonna tell Mum? Please don't, she'll kill me," she begged.

Considering carefully what Ruby said, Lorelei tried to reassure her niece. "Your mum won't kill you; she'll understand."

"Who are you trying to kid? She absolutely hates Jay. She always has, even when you too were together. She never liked him, it was obvious."

Lorelei nodded; it was true. Ruby was right. They may have got on in the early years, but Janey had a massive chip on her shoulder when it came to Jay. Lorelei supposed it was because her sister hated to see how he twisted and manipulated everything and, of course, the violence. Of course, it was natural that Janey hated him.

Ruby tilted her head and looked inquisitively at her aunt. "Auntie Lorelei, Mum says he's a bad man. What did he actually do to you?"

"He had a temper."

"Like me, then?"

"Well, yes, you can have a temper, that's true."

"And what else?"

Lorelei thought for a moment. It was hard to explain to a child. "He used to make me think I was in the wrong, and that things were always my fault, when they weren't really my fault at all."

"Go on…"

"His language wasn't always kind, and he'd twist my words around."

"Did he hurt you?"

"Physically? Yes."

"I do that to my mum. That makes me a bad person too."

"Don't say that. Come here, you." The two of them hugged, and Lorelei stroked Ruby's hair. "We'll sort this out, don't worry."

"Will we have to see him?"

"I will, but you don't need to."

"What will I do when he comes?"

"You can go to Danny's house."

"Auntie Lorelei, I don't even know Danny that well," whined Ruby, "and I don't want to leave you alone with Jay!" Lorelei smiled at how protective Ruby was being. "It's not a good idea," said Ruby, "not after what you've just told me."

"That's very sweet of you. Look, I don't want him to ruin our day. I say we go out somewhere. Let's just get in the car, *drive* somewhere. The rain's not settling in until later. I'll make some sandwiches."

"Alright, that sounds good, just you and me? What about Danny?"

"I'll text him and say we're having some 'girl time' today."

Ruby smiled and thought to herself, that it sounded nice.

"Mum and I don't really spend much time together; I don't think she likes me much."

"That's really not true Ruby, it's really not…"

The pancakes were eaten, and Lorelei put a packed lunch together. She'd also called Danny to let him know about their plans for the day. They were going to go for a walk to the Lizard, which was a peninsula ending in the most southerly point of the British Isles. Lorelei was correct in saying that the weather was not up to much at all, for light rain was forecast in the morning before heavier rain settled in over the region later that evening. They were ready to go, and Lorelei giggled as Ruby slid her feet into her flip-flops.

"Those are really not appropriate footwear for this season. Didn't we learn that on Christmas day?" Lorelei teased.

"But we're going to the beach!"

"Yes, but it's February, and it's raining…"

Ruby shrugged her shoulders. "So?"

Under Lorelei's instruction, she put some socks on and reached for her only slightly more appropriate pumps.

"Those are going to get wrecked. They're white. What size are you?"

It turned out quite nicely that Lorelei and Ruby shared the same shoe size. Lorelei loaned her niece a pair of walking boots, which was met with some opposition, and agreed only with the promise that there would be no photographs posted on social media from the day, or at least any photographs that caught her in these 'most unfashionable' and 'ugly' shoes.

It would take around forty minutes to get to Gunwalloe

Church Cove. There were plenty of more local places to walk, but Lorelei did not want to run the risk of bumping into Jay while they were out. She wanted to escape from him that morning, knowing full well that she had committed to seeing him later that day — somewhere where there was zero chance he'd have the opportunity to ruin special time with Ruby.

Before they left, she sent Jay a text informing him that if he wanted to come over to the flat at two thirty, they could discuss the next steps. She regretted all the decisions she made last night when she invited him. She had initially felt sorry for him, but now, after sleeping on the matter, she was upset with herself for letting those feelings creep in. However, even an abusive husband of eighteen years was hard to shut off completely, especially one that had such hard times befell upon him, and who appeared in such a sorry state. Lorelei, being an ex nurse, had compassion for any human being and always demonstrated a caring nature. It seemed Jay had played upon this essence of her personality, knowing that she would indeed, care.

Ruby caught a glimpse of herself in the wing mirror and her wild green eyes stared back at her. There was something quite fierce about her, feral even. She'd never felt that she belonged or had found herself. She had grown up with a sense that she was resented, and just a mere inconvenience to her parents, well, her mother mostly.

"Auntie Lorelei, what will happen with Jay later on?"

"Oh, I'm just going to have a chat with him, give him some dinner, and book him into a Travelodge."

"So, if you're booking him into a hotel, where has he been staying until now?"

"He's not been staying anywhere, Ruby. He's been sleeping in his car."

"*In his car?*"

"Yep, he just needs me to help him get on his feet. He's not staying, don't worry."

For the rest of the journey, they talked about nothing of great importance, but the conversation meant a lot to Ruby. Lorelei asked about what music Ruby liked and what television programs interested her.

"You used to play the violin; do you miss it?" asked Lorelei.

"I wish I hadn't quit, but Mum made me practice for hours *every* day, and even before school; it was too much. It stressed me out, *big time*."

Lorelei, thinking what a shame it was that she stopped playing, didn't want to make a fuss about it. "Well, you can always pick it back up again."

Ruby smiled, thinking to herself how Auntie Lorelei was so chilled out and didn't place any demands or expectations on her. For the first time ever, Ruby felt relaxed, and the pressure finally seemed off. They buttoned their coats and set off on foot down the path towards Gunwalloe Church cove. They walked side by side on to the beach.

"I bet you're glad you wore my walking boots now!" remarked Lorelei.

Ruby smiled. "I guess you were right!"

"So Ruby, I suppose since you've said a few things about Mum, I thought it may be good to have a chat. I'm really worried about how things are at home, and the things Mum tells me."

"I know."

"Tell me, why do you think it is the way it is?"

"I don't know. I get so angry; Mum and I don't get on."

"What about Dad?"

"He's okay; he's calmer with me."

"How so?"

"Well, Mum, she goes mad at me, and I know what I do winds her up, but she loses it too…"

"Well, it's hard for Mum, when you get in a rage, that is."

"Yeah, but she gets in a rage, too. She's angry, and she has that hate in her eyes. She doesn't like me. In fact, she hates me…"

The Lake District

"I miss her; that sounds strange doesn't it, Robert?" Janey sank her head and neck back into the forceful jets of the hot tub in the garden of their holiday home. The air was chilly but thankfully the rain had held off up in the Lake District, or at least it had until then, and the heat of the hot tub was at a lovely 38 degrees Celsius. "I think it's the guilt too, Robert."

"How so, dear?" he asked.

"The guilt of being here, and relaxing. The guilt of knowing I've bundled Ruby off to Cornwall. It's as if I've done something terribly selfish, and well, wrong."

Robert touched her leg under the bubbles, leaned over, and kissed her cheek affectionately. "We're not selfish to have a break. You deserve it more than anyone."

"When we're together, I try to love her, to give her happiness. She never stops, she never learns from past mistakes, she's only ever angry with me, she's only ever disrespectful *to me*, in the main."

"You don't have to tell me, darling, I know."

"Yes, but I feel that sometimes you don't see it; you miss it, and she's better, and calmed down by the time you're back."

"But I know how she can be," he reassured her.

"I know." Janey ducked under the water and back out again. "When we're together, me and Ruby, I try *so* hard, but we can never get along. I spend all my time resenting her, wishing for the years to go by, praying I will survive. That I," she corrected herself, "that *we*, will have some kind of life when she is grown. Only four more years, I keep thinking." Robert passed Janey her can of dark fruit cider, and she took a slurp. "Christ, this is good stuff, isn't it?" she said, and Robert agreed. "But, Robert, now I've got rid of her for the week, I feel different, like there's something wrong, like I can't protect her."

"Janey, there's no harm in this, no harm at all. Let's just try to enjoy this time together. It's so rare for us to have time to relax like this."

"You're right, you're right, I'll try to stop worrying."

"You need to, yes. I know it's easier said than done for you," he teased, "you, Janey Pritchard, who worries about everything. Anyway, you must try to enjoy the moment."

They looked with wonder up into the sky. It wasn't completely clear, but there were some gaps in the cloud.

"We'll have to come back out here tomorrow night," said Robert. "When it's dark; I'd love to do a bit of stargazing." Robert, like Danny, was quite the nerd when it came to science and the night sky. "We haven't done that for a while, have we?" he remarked.

"Not for ages. The last time I recall was when we were in Dubai," Janey remembered with nostalgia. Robert laughed, as he also remembered the night in question.

"The desert safari, yes," he said. Janey moved closer to him.

"That was a moment to remember, out in the desert, getting drunk!" she reminisced.

"But they weren't supposed to give us alcohol," chuckled Robert as he said, "That was lucky for us. I think the host fancied you and that's why we got given tickets for the bar."

"Do you remember those tourists? You were giving them a lesson in astrology?"

"I do, I do," he laughed.

"Happy memories, they were," Janey croaked, feeling a little teary.

"We can go away on holiday again, somewhere abroad, in the future."

"It's not the same with Ruby…"

"We can do it in years to come, like you suggested, when she's grown up. For goodness' sake, Janey, in four years she'll be eighteen, she'll soon be an adult, and have her own life. We'll be able to have a special holiday then."

Janey nodded. "You always wanted to chase a total eclipse…"

The two chatted about memories they had, weaving a spiral of nostalgia about times gone by, and dreaming up possible future child-free adventures.

Cornwall

As they walked over the sand, Lorelei told Ruby that she had no doubt that her mother loved her, it was just that she found it difficult too, and dealing with Ruby's violent outbursts was tough on Janey, not to mention for anyone else witness to them.

"You seem to be pretty chill down here with me so far?"

Ruby nodded and explained how she felt relaxed, and that any sense of expectation seemed to have lifted. "It's almost as though Mum *expects* me to be bad," she explained, and then, changing the subject, Ruby moaned, "Auntie Lorelei, I hope you can help Uncle Jay…"

"You do?"

"Yes, because he must be very sad if he's come all the way to see you and has been sleeping in his car. That's not normal behaviour for a grown man…"

Lorelei couldn't help but chuckle to herself. Ruby's very fair and straight up observation seemed humorous for a fourteen-year-old. Lorelei put her arm around Ruby's shoulder.

"Come on, let's not waste our time thinking of him. Let's just enjoy this lovely sea air." Lorelei took an exaggerated deep breath in, and exhaled, "ahhhhh."

"This *freezing* cold sea air, you mean," Ruby corrected her auntie, but Lorelei reached in her coat pocket and brought out a woollen hat.

"Here, put this on."

"You *really* are trying to make me look stupid, aren't you?"

The two of them walked across the bay, crossing over the little stream by hopping across the stones, which wobbled as they leapt across. There were no other souls around.

"Do you think you will stay with Danny?" Lorelei was taken by surprise by Ruby's question.

"Who can tell?"

"You'd like to, though?"

Lorelei pursed her lips and nodded her head, while considering how to reply in a diplomatic way.

"It would be fair to say, at the moment, he makes me happy."

"I can see you getting married to him; in the summer on the beach!"

"Ruby! *Don't!* —"

"It was just an image I had."

"Well, I don't think I'll marry again…"

"I hope I'll find a nice husband when I'm older, one that will take care of me, but Auntie, *why* did you stay with Uncle Jay for so long?"

"Sometimes, when things are the way they are, for so long, it becomes normal. It took me a long time to break free from him, but I did in the end."

"But now he's back…"

"He won't be back for long. We're going to help him, because that's the right thing to do, but he'll be gone again in no time."

"Good."

"And in the summer, you can come and stay again, when the weather is better!" Lorelei grinned and Ruby beamed.

"Sounds good to me!"

After walking across the cove, they made their way up onto the coastal path before looping back to the car. Because the wind was picking up, they ate their sandwiches in the relative comfort of the car before starting the journey back. They listened to a CD of old sea shanties by a local Cornish band, "The Fisherman's Friends". Conversation dwindled, but they enjoyed the music. Within fifteen minutes, Ruby had closed her eyes and fallen asleep.

Lorelei took note of the time and panicked when she realised she expected to see Jay not long after they would arrive home. A plethora of feelings were thrust upon her. For one, *guilt*, for she had still not informed Danny about Jay's unexpected reappearance, yet she also felt a sinful curiosity at the prospect of seeing Jay again. It wasn't her nerves getting the better of her; it was more so the way her feelings were making her nervous. She was worried that seeing Jay would bring back emotions she hadn't felt for a long time.

Lorelei cussed herself, but she almost felt glad that he had come crawling back, desperately, in need of *her* help. Besides these feelings, she was angry and absolutely seething inside. She didn't want him back in her life, not for one second. The more she started thinking about it, the more the rage built up. She tried to think of more pleasant things, like Danny, and their intimacy the other day, and how he told her he loved her, but it didn't work, and her mind kept returning to the present circumstances.

Ruby stirred and twisted around in her seat just as they were negotiating the curiously narrow streets of St Ives. She stretched her arms out and yawned. "Oh, we're almost home."

As they drove up Tregenna Lane, a man was perched on the wall opposite Lorelei's flat, and from his posture and stance, there was no doubt who it was. Ruby drew a sharp breath in. "Auntie Lorelei, he's there!"

Tessy Braun

A merry dance

Lorelei turned the key, and the engine silenced. She laid her hand softly on Ruby's knee before they turned to each other and exchanged reassuring, and somewhat fearful, looks. At that moment, the age gap between them seemed to disappear; they were two women terrified of what this man's presence would bring, an ex-husband for one, and an uncle for the other. Lorelei had to put their roles into perspective, for Ruby was only a child, and although in some ways seemed grown up, she was far from it. She had to be strong for Ruby; she had to protect her. It was sometimes easy to forget Ruby was just fourteen, *sometimes*, anyway.

"Don't worry, okay? Just go straight to your room. I'll just have a quick chat with him. Everything will be sorted."

Ruby nodded. She really would try to do just that, but it pained her to admit that she still felt something for her poor old uncle and now she saw him leaning upon the wall the sentiment was growing stronger, seeing him look so sad and downtrodden. Yet divulging her compassion to Lorelei was not an easy feat, especially now that she understood, to a degree, the downfall of their marriage. Yet surely Lorelei had to understand? Ruby had known Jay all her life. He was, after all, like family to her.

"Just go straight to your room, okay?" Lorelei repeated, this time a little more sternly, as if she may well have had an inkling into the thoughts whirling around in Ruby's mind. The two of them gingerly stepped out of the car, and with an air of trepidation, slowly walked towards the wall where he leant. Jay lunged forward, his black holdall now over his shoulder. With his dirty clothes and messy hair, he looked in a sorry state. Ruby's heart skipped a beat, and then, in what almost seemed like slow motion, Jay held his arms out, and to Lorelei's astonishment, Ruby ran straight into them like a lamb to the slaughter.

"Ruby!" he cried, half laughing, half crying, as he invited the young girl into his clutch. He looked up to Lorelei with hopeful eyes, hoping that his ex-wife would greet him in the same way, but she threw him a scornful look instead, and for a moment his viridescent eyes fixed upon hers. To say he looked dishevelled was an understatement. Ruby knew she should not have embraced him. She knew it would displease her aunt, but his actions made her feel loved and wanted. Seeing him, for the first time in such a long time, conjured up all sorts of emotions, and his affection brought a feeling of validation.

It pained Lorelei to see such warmth between them. He'd always had a soft spot for Ruby, she'd always been aware of that, but to see his dirty hands on her, watching Jay lure her in, it stirred an unhealthy notion within. Ruby was no more his possession than she was his.

Lorelei gestured to the pair to make their way towards the flat. With two hands on Ruby's shoulders, she directed her niece ahead of her. "*Why on earth did you do that!*" she scolded Ruby under her breath.

Once they were up in the flat, Ruby disappeared

sheepishly into the bedroom. Lorelei covered her nose with her hand and held her breath for a moment. He smelt *really* bad, a sensory cocktail of sweat, cigarettes, and alcohol.

"Do you have any clean clothes to change into?" enquired Lorelei, hoping so very much that he did.

"I don't think so," he said, as he fished around in his bag.

Feeling impatient, she snapped. "Oh, give it here." Lorelei took the offensive contents of his bag straight to the washing machine. She looked him up and down and shook her head. "You're going to have to have a shower to start with. Sorry to say, but it looks like you could really do with a freshen up!"

He gave her a reminiscent look as they simultaneously thought of the times they had showered together. However, Lorelei dismissed the feeling of sentimentality creeping over her.

He looked her up and down. "Lor, you don't know how good it is to see you!" His breath was heavy, and his words had conviction. He had that way about him, that voice. It somehow got under her skin. She knew very well he was so bad for her, yet somehow, she was drawn to him. She resisted.

"*Stop*, just stop it."

He frowned. "Aren't you happy to see me, baby girl?" he continued to tease her, "Not just a fraction?"

Lorelei pursed her lips together, her skin turning mottled in an instant. It outraged her he was under the delusion he could still torment her. "Jay, this isn't a game. Do you have any idea how serious this is!" She pointed toward the bathroom. "Please take a shower, you absolutely stink!"

Lorelei steered him into the washroom, handing him a towel, before instructing him to toss his dirty clothes outside the door. While Jay enjoyed a well required hot shower for the first time in many weeks, Lorelei went straight to the kitchen and poured herself a double gin and tonic. She'd become quite accustomed to gin since the first writing group meeting she had attended before Christmas, with a now well-developed taste for it. It would be rare now to find herself without a bottle of Cornish Rock Gin in the pantry, quite preferring the spirit to wine nowadays. For good measure, she threw in a dash of sparkling pomegranate gin liqueur. God knew she needed it.

Breathe, she thought to herself. Just *breathe*. With Jay's clothes tumbling around in the washing machine, she reached for her phone and came to realise she had missed a call from Danny. Oh Danny, sweet Danny, she wished he were here instead of *him*. She didn't even want to think 'his' name, and she wished she wasn't in this awful situation. For who would have thought it? Her ex-husband in her shower, and his socks and pants swishing around inside of her washing machine like some kind of merry dance.

While she wallowed in the mess she found herself in, she saw that Danny had sent her a picture. She furrowed her eyebrows. It seemed he had been to the supermarket. She scrolled through the various photo messages, including a display of sweets and other delicious goodies.

> ***Looking forward to movie night. What time would you like me? x***

Lorelei gasped. With all the drama unfolding, she had failed to remember their plans for the evening. She began composing a reply, but then suddenly stopped. *I don't need to tell him*, she thought. *I could get Jay sorted and dropped to a hotel, all by six o'clock. It will be fine.* Janey had been busy sending photographs, too. Lorelei flicked through the selfies she had received of them at Buttermere in the Lake District. She had to admit, they looked so happy, both kitted out in all their expensive wet weather hiking gear. Janey ended the message with "Is everything okay?" Lorelei thought she would reply to that one later too, once this ghastly situation was resolved. She didn't want to tell any untruths.

Lorelei generously gulped her drink and almost spilled it as Ruby walked into the room without her realising. Ruby's affection towards Jay earlier had certainly irritated her, but she tried to hide her disappointment. Nevertheless, Ruby wasn't stupid in the least and knew she had crossed the line. She looked sad as she watched the juice pour into the tumbler. Lorelei, feeling sorry for the girl, tried her best to empathise.

"Look, I *know* you're fond of him," she said, giving Ruby's back a gentle rub. Ruby let out a sniffle, and a tear ran down her cheek.

"I shouldn't have hugged him," she squeaked, significantly emotional about the whole to-do.

Lorelei let out a sigh before taking another swig of gin. "I knew this wouldn't be easy. You seeing your Uncle Jay after all this time, especially with him in this…" she scratched her head. "State."

"I just want you to help him," Ruby whined, reflecting on how *different* he was to the uncle she used to know. She hated to see him in such a way.

"I know, I know." Lorelei took another gulp of the gin cocktail, and she winced because it really was very strong. "Ruby, you feel like this because you're a kind-hearted girl." In her mind, Lorelei added *sometimes* to her sentence. She placed her drink on the counter and gave Ruby another light touch on her shoulder this time. "Hey, look, Danny's bringing a film over later; we'll have a movie night and get a takeaway pizza; he's ever so thoughtful. He's bought some sweets for us too."

Ruby rolled her eyes and gave her aunt a stern look.

"Movie night?" She raised her hands in frustration. "Haven't we got more important things to focus on!?" Ruby felt cantankerous inside. She had grown to recognise the sensation, and it was hard to control. She felt trapped, almost like she would explode. The feeling shot through her body like lightning. "I want to go out!" she cried.

Lorelei was starting to feel somewhat irritated herself. Ruby's moods and temperament were so changeable.

"What?! We can't go out *right now*. I need to sort things out, don't I?" said Lorelei.

Ruby put her head in her hands, and then, with her fingers, she scratched and pulled her hair. "I'm feeling *claustrophobic*… There's nowhere to go; this place is so ridiculously tiny!" Ruby's home in Bristol was far bigger than the family needed. It was a far cry from Lorelei's little St Ives flat. Her parents' income allowed the size of the property, and it meant Ruby was privileged when it came to space.

"Well, I'm sorry Ruby, we've been out all morning. Why don't you put something on the TV or do something creative, I don't know, some art?" She tried to explain to Ruby that she found writing a diary, or scrapbooking could be extremely therapeutic, but Ruby yawned and mumbled something under her breath which Lorelei did not like the sound of or appreciate very much at all. It was something resembling "Fucking art."

"What did you say?!"

"I didn't say *anything*," protested Ruby, as she stood up and proceeded to pace around the kitchen.

"I heard you perfectly well. There's no need to swear or be rude to me when I'm merely trying to suggest something for you to do!"

Ruby pulled the fridge door and swung it open on its hinges, grabbing the bottle of juice, and slamming it down in a temper on the work surface.

"You're starting to sound like Mum. I *thought you were nice!*"

Lorelei bit her tongue, despite feeling the urge to react. She knew she needed Ruby on her side and couldn't face dealing with her first meltdown at that particular moment.

"Come on Ruby, don't be cross. Take a deep breath." Lorelei thought back to her experience as a nurse when she had to help people in a state of panic. "Breathe in through your nose, and out through your mouth," she explained to Ruby, but that didn't go down too well.

"Oh, shut up Auntie Lorelei! Just shut up!"

How dare this child talk to her like this? *Just ignore,* she quietly encouraged herself. She turned away from Ruby and began to take the wet washing out of the machine and bundle it into the tumble drier.

"Oh, so you're doing Uncle Jay's washing now, are you?" Ruby smirked sarcastically. "Didn't take long to fall back into your old 'wife' role!"

Still biting her tongue (although it was getting increasingly more difficult), Lorelei ignored her niece and continued to take out the washing

"Oh, I wish I'd never come here!" hissed Ruby behind Lorelei's back, and she dropped her glass down on the work surface with such force it cracked. Ruby retreated to her room, slamming the door behind her, and the walls shook. In that moment Lorelei decided to retreat into the front room, but not forgetting to refill her drink beforehand, knowing she probably shouldn't have any more but boy, did she need it. She curled herself into a fetal position on the sofa, tucking her legs up and reaching for the comforting fluffy blanket and she started to feel a lot more empathetic towards Janey than she ever had before.

Just as Lorelei had made herself comfortable, Jay appeared in the doorway with only her own pink towel tied around his waist. "So, she's still our old Ruby then, getting in a flap? Nothing's changed there then!" He leant on the door frame. Lorelei couldn't help smirking at him. The pink towel was quite fetching. For someone who had been downward spiralling, he had kept in far a more reasonable shape than one may have expected. Perhaps he'd put a little weight on here and there, but he still looked good.

Coming to her senses, she snapped. "Bloody hell, put some clothes on!" She was aghast to see him flaunting himself around; it was quite unwelcome, given the circumstances, but somehow, she couldn't stop looking.

"*I would* Lor, but you just put them all in the wash…"

She jumped up. "Right, you'll just have to wait! Maybe I've got something you'll fit into." She returned a few moments later with an oversized t-shirt and a pair of Danny's 'sleepy shorts' and threw them at him. "Just put those on!"

It was almost half-past three and there had been three more missed calls from Danny, and more text messages from Janey. Janey pressed to know how things were going, and Danny pressed to get a time that he should arrive. The pressure was certainly manifesting, as Lorelei got no closer to resolving the situation. In a short time, Jay's clothes would be dry, so hopefully by five o'clock she could have him dressed, fed and out of there.

"Lor, try to relax, I can see you're so tense," he said. She just hated how he proclaimed to know precisely how she was feeling. He had been good at doing that in the past. How dare he assume how she was feeling, especially now!

"And steady on that booze, baby girl," he lectured her, as he gawped at the near-empty bottle. "It's not like you to drink spirits, anyway. You were always more classy, a wine drinker; what was it, Sauvignon Blanc?"

The one that tastes like fruit, thought Lorelei. Yeah, she drank a bottle of that in celebration when she finally received the divorce papers.

"Yes, but things change, don't they?" she reminded him with venom in her voice. Her heart sank. It suddenly occurred to her that now she had been drinking, taking Jay to a hotel would no longer be possible. *Oh rats,* what had she been thinking? She realised that she would have no other choice but to call Danny. She would have to ask him for help after all.

"Have you got a little drinkie for me, Lor? Any beers in? Surely *he* must drink beer?" he asked, without being able to hold himself back from the snide remark about her new lover, but Lorelei, although a fine one to talk, didn't think Jay should be consuming any alcohol.

"It's not a good idea, I'll make you a coffee, besides he doesn't drink beer, he drinks cider."

Jay settled for a coffee, accepting defeat, and not protesting for something stronger. Perhaps he had realised it was time to stop.

"Right, so let's get down to business." she began with resolve to stay in control and not have him distract her. However, he *was* distracting, sitting there, and she couldn't quite help glance down at his muscular thighs and calves. *Danny is much skinnier,* she thought.

"Business? Is that all I am to you?" he asked in a pathetic voice, no doubt fishing for some reassurance (that was what narcissists do).

"Jay, *why* did you come here?" she asked, her voice exasperated because she hated him for coming back. Lorelei had a new life now, and he wasn't a part of it. He began to pour his heart out again, professing his undying love, begging her to take him back.

"What we had was too good to be thrown away, don't you see?" He went on. "It was a mistake, baby girl," he purred. She shuddered. *Yes*, she thought, it certainly was a mistake. The entire eighteen years of their marriage had been a *mistake*. She had no doubt about that at all. Yet his words tugged on her heartstrings, and she was beginning to find it difficult to resist moving over to him and reaching out to touch him one more time. She scolded herself. *Stop these thoughts; don't go back there.*

"Jay," she said, trying her hardest to avoid looking into those hypnotising and apologetic eyes. Trying her very best not to be caught in his trap for one last time. "Jay, I've moved on, there is no 'us'; it's over."

But she couldn't do it. Despite all her best intentions to avoid his eyes, she succumbed and looked at him. His eyes welled up. *Probably crocodile tears, trying to make me feel guilty,* she justified in her mind.

"No, no, I can't accept this is the end. It was all my fault. I didn't treat you the way I should of," he said. Lorelei corrected him silently. *It's 'should have'* she thought. It had always been a bugbear of hers.

"But you know I always loved you," he whispered. Jay was persistent. She gave him credit for that. "I've surely not come all this way for nothing? I just know there's something still there between us, and that we can make it work." He wiped his tears away with the back of his hand. They were now flooding down his face. It was strange, Lorelei had never actually seen him cry in all of those years together. He'd often well up and look sad, but these tears were *proper* tears. It was uncomfortable to see a grown man in such torment, especially Jay. He'd always been more of a 'man's man'. Her heart ached to see it, and her empathetic nature took hold of her logical brain, as it so often did. It was the nurse in her, but she couldn't go back to the past. She wouldn't.

"No, Jay! I'm sorry, I *don't* feel the same," she tried to explain. "Our relationship wasn't healthy, and I don't think it ever could be." She pursed her lips together. "I'm not being funny, but I'm gonna have to call Danny in a minute…"

Jay notably tensed. "Oh, Danny? The new *cider* drinking love interest!" His tone rapidly changing, bitterness engulfing him. "What exactly has he got that I haven't!? Like I'd be threatened by him anyway, *Danny the writer*, more like a little Jessie. He's *nothing!*"

"You've certainly done your homework," remarked Lorelei with disbelief that he evidently knew about Danny's writing pastime.

"He signed a copy of his book that I bought but I gave the crappy piece of shit to some old hag in a coffee shop months ago!" Jay's true colours began to show, but it wasn't long before his soft and gentle manner returned. *Jekyll and Hyde-esque.*

"I *know* we can be happy again. I'm going to *love* you and look after you…" He slid forward in the armchair and before Lorelei knew it, he was at her knees looking up like a lost puppy dog. He leaned forward to get closer to Lorelei and slid his hand over her thigh. Lorelei's heart skipped a beat, and a feeling of lust pulsed through her. *That touch.* She'd forgotten how good it was. He leaned forward an inch closer until she could feel his breath upon her face. She pushed him away, without determination, and let out a weak cry.

"*No,*" she said, but her pleas weren't strong enough. He continued to seduce her, kissing her neck, squeezing her thigh. Ruby, who had yet again been watching from the door, could not let this happen and in that instant, she burst in screaming from the top of her lungs.

"Stop!" she bellowed. "Don't touch my auntie!" The

anger in her eyes penetrated him like a laser, and for a moment, they made a strange connection. He backed down and submissively returned to the armchair with a look of shame upon his face. "Ruby, you don't understand. You couldn't. You're only fifteen," he dismissed her.

"*Fourteen*!" she corrected him.

Lorelei requested Ruby go back to her room and let her deal with the situation, but Jay interrupted her.

"No," he said, "maybe Ruby *should* stay here," he muttered, rubbing his temples, and breathing deeply, but before he could say more, Lorelei's fiery niece could not bite her tongue.

"I know what you're really like, my mum's told me all about you!" she shouted. "And you've been using *me* to get to my auntie; you tricked me!" Her heart was beating so fast, and she started to shake.

"Your *mother?* What exactly has your mother told you about me?" Jay probed.

"Stop! Just stop this!" cried Lorelei. "This arguing isn't helping!" The two of them ignored her attempts to calm the situation.

"Mum's told me how you're not family to us!"

"Oh, has she now, well your mother is not quite telling the truth there," he sniggered and shook his head.

"Just stop, you two!" pleaded Lorelei, and in another attempt to put a stop to the argument, she grabbed Ruby's arm and pulled her out of the living room.

"A word with you, *please!*" commanded Lorelei, but Ruby resisted. It was then that Lorelei came to realise how strong her niece really was. Ruby launched her down onto the arm of the sofa with such force that Lorelei was sent tumbling into the coffee table hitting her head on the corner. Jay dived towards Lorelei and helped her back up, and then turned to

Ruby.

"Don't you do that to your aunt, you silly little girl," Jay reprimanded her, but Ruby paid no attention to his attempt to parent her.

"Silly little girl!? How dare you! You are nothing to me, you are *nothing* to Auntie Lorelei! Look at you! You're pathetic! Coming here all dirty and disgusting, you're a joke!" Ruby continued to hurl abuse at him. It was clear to Lorelei that Jay was starting to lose his temper because he was no longer crying like a baby, and his face had turned red with purple veins bulging on the side of his head. She noted he was flexing his fingers on his right hand without even realising. A sure sign to Lorelei that he was about to blow.

"Aren't you going to do something about this Lor?" he bellowed.

"Can you *please* be quiet, and stop shouting, both of you!" Lorelei pleaded yet again, holding her head, which was bleeding from the knock, though it was somewhat in vain, for the two of them were undeniably in full swing.

The tumble dryer made a tone to indicate the cycle was complete and Lorelei expressed that at least he could get bloody dressed in his own clothes now. Lorelei darted out into the kitchen, pulling Ruby out with her, but this time with a firmer grip anticipating her strength.

"Get off me!" she squirmed and flailed her arms around.

"Do you want me to call your mother?" Lorelei roared and upon this threat, Ruby complied, and once in the kitchen, she demanded that Ruby stay just there.

"Auntie Lorelei, your head!" she gasped as she saw the gash on her forehead. With one hand holding her head, Lorelei grabbed the clothes with the other, which were warm to the touch, and brought them back into the front room for

Jay, instructing him to get dressed, and quickly. She returned to the kitchen, where Ruby was struggling to stay calm.

"How dare he! How dare he!" she repeated, fuming.

Lorelei was losing patience rapidly. "Oh, Ruby! Why did you start talking to him again? *Why* did you get his hopes up by running over to him today when we saw him by the wall!?" Lorelei reached for the first aid box from the cupboard and rummaged around to find a dressing for the cut on her head. Meanwhile, Ruby's temper was bubbling out of control.

"I've missed him! He always used to be kind to me! But now I know what a low life he is! It was a mistake. I'm sorry, I'm such an idiot! *I want to go home!*"

Jay burst in, interrupting them with more persistent begging, "Lor, can't we just start again?" he pathetically mumbled, but Ruby took matters into her own hands.

"It's too late now, you complete, utter fuckwit! Don't you understand that!?" screamed Ruby, allowing no time for Lorelei to speak for herself and wondering where she had heard language like that before. "You're not wanted, you're disgusting! Go back to Bristol!" Turning to her aunt, she insisted, "Auntie Lorelei, give him some money for petrol and tell him to get the hell out of here. Tell him to leave us alone!"

Lorelei considered her proposal, and it didn't take her long to come to a conclusion. "She's right, Jay. I was gonna book you into a hotel for tonight, but there's absolutely no point. You need to go back…"

"I've got nowhere to go!" he yelled.

"It's no longer my problem. I can't deal with this. I'll give you some money. How much do you need? I'll give you a couple of grand. You can get a place to live, you can get yourself sorted, that's all I can do!"

He shook his head in perplexity that she was trying to 'buy him off'. He hadn't thought it would be an easy feat to win Lorelei back, but he hadn't anticipated it being impossible.

"You heard her!" said Ruby. "Take the money and fuck off you horrible man, you make me sick!"

Jay was confused. He looked sad again. "You were pleased to see me Ruby, you were! What's changed?"

There was an uncomfortable silence as Ruby contemplated her feelings, not something she was ever very good at doing. She gulped. "When I saw you try to touch Auntie Lorelei, it reminded me about everything Mum told me…"

"What exactly did your mother tell you?"

"Never mind, but enough to know you're not worthy to be part of our family!"

Jay slowly shook his head. His breathing was laboured, as if he was carefully considering his next words. He raised his hand and banged it down on the arm of the sofa and bellowed, not so much in anger, but in agony.

"I'm more family than you know!"

There was a deathly silence for just a few moments before Ruby broke it. "What is that supposed to mean?"

He started to weep. "Nothing…" He retreated into the living room, but Ruby followed him despite Lorelei telling her to stay put.

"He's just manipulating you, trying to warp your mind and confuse you," she told Ruby. *Oh God, what was Janey going to say when she found out?* She hated Jay, and now he was messing with her daughter, who already had so many issues of her own. Jay sat with his head in his hands, breathing deeply, looking as though he was teetering on the edge of a nervous breakdown. Lorelei took the risk of sitting down next to him. She pulled his hands down away from his face.

"You're not fit to drive. I'm going to call the Travelodge after all and book you in tonight. I'm going to transfer you some cash, and you need to go. You need to restart your life." She was trying to be gentle and kind to him, yet firm at the same time. He nodded, perhaps finally admitting defeat, or maybe too tempted by the prospect of receiving a few thousand pounds for a new start. Yet Ruby wouldn't stop and continued to interrogate him.

"What did you mean about *family*?"

Jay looked up at the young girl. He was proud of her. She was strong and determined, just like him. She had passion, flare. "Well, maybe it's about time that you both knew the truth," he said, "since everyone has moved on, and I'm going to have to move on too, perhaps this is the only opportunity I'll ever have to tell the truth!" He stood up and peered out onto the street below. Lorelei was sick of the lies, the manipulation, the attention seeking.

"Jay, just stop it. It's all finished," she said.

"No, don't stop it, say it!" demanded Ruby. "If he's got something to say, let him!"

He turned to Ruby. "I've always been so fond of you; we've always had a special bond, haven't we?"

"Not anymore!" Ruby snorted.

"There's a reason for our connection, our special relationship…" As he went on, something in Ruby clicked, a puzzle fitting together. It was like she had known all along.

"Since there's obviously no going back for me and Lor, it's best the truth is out…"

"What are you saying?" asked Lorelei. Her skin went red as the blood rushed through her veins. He turned to Ruby, his green eyes locking with hers, his voice now gentle.

"Ruby, now, I don't want you to get even more cross but it's important you know." His voice began to wobble, "Ruby, I'm not your uncle…"

She gasped, trying to understand what exactly was

unfolding.
"I'm your father…"

Tessy Braun

You're that smulk!

Jay, Danny, and Lorelei gathered around the breakfast bar in Lorelei's small kitchen. Lorelei tapped persistently on Ruby's mobile phone screen, feeling furious that she had chosen to storm out of the flat leaving it behind. At first, when Ruby left, it was just late afternoon, but true to the forecast the bad weather had come in and it was now nearly seven o'clock, so concerns over her safety were rapidly increasing.

After Jay's unanticipated announcement leading to Ruby running off, Lorelei had called Danny for help. The three of them, now officially acquainted in such unfortunate circumstances, tried to formulate a plan of action. Lorelei paced the kitchen back and forth.

"I need to go look for her. It's been hours now. We must go and look for her!" Lorelei insisted. The effect of the gin was wearing off and her head started to pound. She rubbed her forehead to ease the pain.

"She's just gone to blow the cobwebs off, she'll be back," said Jay, somewhat dismissing the seriousness of the situation, or maybe just trying to make Lorelei feel less anxious as tensions were rising.

"In this weather?! For this long?" cried Lorelei. "Without her phone?" she held up the mobile, evidencing the fact, before dropping it back down on the counter, and then hopelessly dropping her head down with frustration. "We should have gone after her to start with." Lorelei couldn't believe that they hadn't, but Jay had insisted Ruby just needed some time to cool down. "I'll have to call Janey," she moaned.

"Let's not do that quite yet," replied Danny. "I'm sure Jay's right. She just needed some space," he reassured. "It's only just getting dark now. She'll be back any minute, I'm sure of it." His kind intentions caused only aggravation.

"I think this is a bit more than 'she just needs to cool down!'" snapped Lorelei. "She's just been told that her father is *not* her father, and that her uncle's her dad. Do you have any idea!?" Lorelei turned to Jay, scowling at him with a hatred stronger than she'd ever felt before.

"You had an affair with my sister! You've lied about this for fourteen years!"

"Lorrie—"

"Don't 'Lorrie' me, I'm not finished with you, but right now, the only thing that matters is *my* niece."

"Yeah, and *my* daughter!"

"As if we could forget! You're the cause of all of this, yet you're still trying to wind me up!"

"Lorelei." Danny put an arm around her. "I know this isn't easy, but we need to focus on Ruby right now." He was right, and Lorelei knew it. Arguing with Jay wouldn't help anything, and it wouldn't bring Ruby home. Pragmatic Danny began to collate the facts.

"Did she take anything? Her purse? Money?" he enquired. Lorelei shrugged her shoulders. They checked the flat for Ruby's bag, but it couldn't be seen. They drew the conclusion that she had taken it with her, along with her purse.

"Maybe she's caught the bus somewhere?" suggested Jay.

"Like *where*? She doesn't know the area," said Lorelei, rolling her eyes at his stupid comment.

"Well, at least she's got some money. Maybe she's gone to a cafe?" Jay continued to speculate.

"But what's open at this time?!" Lorelei cried in exasperation. "The pubs are, but cafes?" Glancing at the clock, she sighed. "They'll all be closed by now."

"What was she wearing?" asked Danny.

Lorelei turned to face Danny and took his hands in hers, all the time hating herself for failing to go after Ruby when she ran out. Instinctively, she had started to, but Jay had held her back. Tears built in her eyes as she thought about Danny's question.

"She's got her coat." Lorelei buried her head in his shoulder and sobbed. He held her back tightly, kissing her head. She released herself from his grip, trying to recall the particulars. Jay turned away, seeing how close the two of them were, really hit home. Lorelei was with another man, and truly had moved on.

"At least I think she's got her coat; I can't see it anywhere here." Lorelei left the kitchen to check which shoes were left on the landing. There were the walking boots that Lorelei had lent her that morning, some white pumps, and her beloved unicorn slippers strewn across the floor. Lorelei frantically tried to remember what other footwear Ruby had brought with her.

"Oh!" she moaned as it dawned on her. "She's got those bloody flip flops on!" Lorelei knew how much Ruby adored her designer flip flops but couldn't understand it.

"Why she even brought them here, I have no idea. It's February for God's sake!"

Jay coughed uncomfortably, and Lorelei followed his gaze down to his own footwear, realising his feet were encased in a pair of black sliders, not wildly different to Ruby's footwear of choice.

"Oh, yes," she nodded sarcastically, "just goes to show you're as stupid as each other, like father, like daughter, it seems!" At that moment Lorelei could not contain the trauma that had unfolded, and she burst into inconsolable tears. "This is a bloody nightmare!" she sobbed. "I was supposed to have Ruby stay here to take the pressure off Janey, and now look what's happened!" Then, turning to Jay, she hissed, "Why do you have to turn up and destroy everything?!" and with half tears, half spitting rage, she screamed at Jay, "Get out! Get away!"

"Lor, it was a long time ago," referring to the obvious intimacy fourteen years ago between him and Janey. "Please, it didn't mean anything," he said.

Lorelei, for the first time since learning of her husband's affair with her sister, considered that Jay was not the only guilty party here, as she reflected on Janey's part in all of this. But Janey had always hated Jay. She'd never had any respect or time for him. It didn't make sense. Her sister wasn't here, though, and Jay was. Unluckily for him, he faced the full brunt of Lorelei's anger as she lunged at him, her arms flailing about in a furious rage. Jay was surprised how strong she was. Every time he had been violent to her in the past, she had never retaliated.

Danny stepped in and dragged Lorelei off Jay. To see her so distraught was upsetting to no end, but he also knew that while they argued, nothing good would come out of the situation.

"Lorelei, I'm here for you. Once this is all over, we'll get away from all of this, but for now, focus."

She fell into his arms again, for there was no question about his ability to make her feel safe, the safest she had ever felt. Although despite Danny's reassurances, he was inwardly very concerned for Ruby. It wasn't a nice evening to be out in the elements, and he knew that from personal experience.

"Look, she'll be back soon. However, if she's not, we'll have to call the police." Danny spoke in a calm manner; he was able to think more clearly than Lorelei and Jay. "There's no point in you two arguing! Not now anyway. We need to get Ruby home safely. That's our goal right now, okay?"

What he said must have sunk in. Lorelei dried her eyes, and Jay once again apologised. He did truly wish that things had been different. The guilt of what had happened between him and Janey, and the burden of knowing all these years that Ruby was his little girl had manifested a lot of unhealthy emotions, and coupled with his relationship with his own father, made way for some very mixed-up feelings. Watching Ruby grow up under the illusion that Robert was her father, and just 'being there' as Ruby's uncle had been unbearable.

"That's fine," she said. "You're right, Danny. You stay here at the flat. Call me if Ruby comes back," said Lorelei.

"Which she will." He nodded in a positive affirmation.

"I'm sure, but Jay and I will go out looking for her," she paused, and then said firmly, "but Danny, I think we should call the police now."

"Let's give it another hour, then I *will* call them."

Glancing again at Jay's footwear, she sneered. "Put some sensible shoes on for God's sake," said Lorelei. He nodded submissively and retrieved some trainers from his holdall. Meanwhile Lorelei buttoned up, put her own sensible walking boots on, and grabbed a torch. She secured her own mobile phone safely in the inner netted pocket of her rucksack for safekeeping.

They headed outside to face the wind, which was certainly picking up its pace. Their first port of call was to look around the town. They would enquire in any establishment that was open, and Mousie's shop was first. Mousie was closing the shutters behind the counter, which was home to the cigarettes and spirits. She was about to shut the front up and count the tills.

"Oh 'ello, Lorelei!" she beamed, but quickly noted the distress strewn across Lorelei's face. "Whatever be the matter? And, who be this?" Mousie's eyes narrowed as she tried to recollect where she had seen this man before. "I recognise you!" she whispered as she scrutinised the fellow.

"Mousie, this is Jay." Lorelei coughed shamefully. "My ex-husband." She took a deep breath and gathered her thoughts. "Mousie, have you seen a young girl? It's my niece. She's missing."

Mousie furrowed her brows and adjusted her glasses. "Your young maid, missing, you say? Scarpered?" she looked Jay up and down. "You're that 'smulk' I saw hangin' round…"

Lorelei sighed. "Mousie, never mind about that, have you seen a teenage girl?" she pressed, without the energy or inclination to fully explain the situation and why she was standing in Mousie's shop with the drunkard that had been seen lurking around town for the last few months.

Mousie shook her head. "No." She frowned, as if trying to think very clearly. "No deary, I've not. Whatever's happened?"

Lorelei's feet were fidgety, and she was anxious to

continue the search. It was clear that Ruby had not been seen in the little shop. "We've had a family issue; she ran off at about five o'clock."

"Your maid gone off in a teasy? The weather's turning bad; not good for anyone to be out in the dark like this. I can see why you're worried, deary…"

"Yes, we are rather," said Lorelei, with a tremble in her voice. She tightened the straps of her rucksack and bent over to tie her lace.

"Go down the local pubs," said Mousie. "See if anyone heard anything. Someone *must* 'ave seen her; tis a small town!"

Jay, who was not paying full attention to their conversation, was instead eyeing up the booze behind the checkout. "Are you still serving? I'll have a bottle of that whiskey, just the small one."

Lorelei looked at him with pure displeasure. "Jay!" she cried, appalled that at a time like this he was thinking about alcohol. "Why can't you just go without a drink!?" she pressed her lips together and shook her head in disgust at his self-centred attitude. He was so greedy; nothing like Danny, who was always kind and selfless.

"Hark at her!" His Somerset accent was evident. "She was pouring gin down her throat earlier!" Mousie did not look impressed at all. She exhaled and shook her head from side to side, her eyes piercing in Jay's direction.

"*What?*" He raised his hands in defence. "Perhaps we could all do with a little drink later, that's all I was thinking." Although secretly he had intended to have a swig or two right out of the bottle as soon as they left the premises! Mousie reached for the lone bottle of whisky and cautiously handed it over to Jay.

"It's on the house."

As they turned towards the door, she muttered under her breath, "With that scoggan around, I think you're going to need it. Trouble if I ever saw it!"

A fine Chianti

After more enquiries, they received the hopeful news of a potential sighting. A lady called Martha distinctively remembered seeing 'a young maid' fitting Ruby's description, running past her house toward the island. Jay and Lorelei ran across the car park, up onto the grassy headland where Lorelei had so often liked to walk. The wind and rain beat down ferociously. Cold icy bullets stung their cheeks, yet they fought on relentlessly.

"*Ruby!*" they cried, one after the other, praying to hear their calls answered but nothing other than the howling wind responded.

"She wouldn't have come up here, would she?!" Jay bellowed, the hood of his jacket flapping around in the wind. It really was wild up there. Lorelei sheltered her head with her hood, securing the toggles around her neck.

"Well, who else did Martha see from her bedroom window?" asked Lorelei. "She saw a young girl running past. It must have been Ruby!"

An hour had passed since the sighting, and it was now gone eight o'clock according to Jay's wristwatch. Daylight had been lost for a good sixty minutes. They trudged on upwards towards the chapel, where they hoped to find Ruby sheltering from the elements. It felt like an eternity, but when they finally reached the little stone church, they circled around it over and over again, becoming quite disorientated, the whole while calling out her name.

Turning to Lorelei, Jay grabbed her shoulders, and in desperation bawled. "Lor, where is she?!" It was only now that they were outside facing the full force of the Atlantic weather front that Jay seemed to appreciate how dangerous it could be for a teenager out there, especially one with limited local knowledge.

"I don't know! I don't know! Don't touch me!" Lorelei wailed, "I'm only breathing the same air as you right now so we can find Ruby!"

"I'm sorry," he said, feeling ashamed of his over-familiarity towards Lorelei. It was all such an emotional rollercoaster, but he now knew that the chances for them to rekindle were slimmer than he had ever imagined.

"Oh God," Lorelei moaned, "what on earth will Janey say when she finds out Ruby's run away?!" she yelled over the wind. Jay attempted to reassure her.

"She'll be back. She might even be back at your flat already!" he claimed, although the conviction in his voice was somewhat lacking. Lorelei shook her head repeatedly.

"No, Danny would have definitely called me if she'd come back. Can we just focus on finding her, please!"

After a thorough evaluation, they concluded that Ruby was not by the chapel, so they made their way to the path that circled the island, never ceasing to call her name. Their efforts reaped no rewards. Above their cries, not far behind them, came footsteps.

"Wait! *Wait up!*" came voices, and once close enough to converse, one gentleman spoke out.

"We've heard about your maid who's missing," he panted. "We've come to help!"

To Lorelei and Jay's astonishment, a group of four members of the public approached them, all seemingly in a position to help them search for Ruby. Lorelei spotted Mousie among them straight away, but did not recognise the others, although it was hard to tell in the darkness. They came armed with powerful flashlights and clothing suitable for treacherous weather.

"Mousie, did you organise this?" called Lorelei through the wind and rain.

"I'lltellywott, we all come together in times of need, we do, and your Ruby ain't no exception!"

Lorelei's phone rang. She raced to retrieve it from her bag, now wishing it hadn't been packed away so snugly in the netted pocket. "It's Danny!" she exclaimed. "Perhaps she's home!" A wave of anticipation rippled through her, sending shivers down her neck and spine. She willed to hear the good news. The others waited with bated breath.

"Answer it! Quick!" pressed Jay.

"Danny? Tell me she's back!?" Her face dropped. "The police?" Listening intently, she replied, "Okay, yes, of course, we'll carry on searching." She told Danny she loved him and ended the call. "They're sending the police out," Lorelei updated the group. Almost numb, she stood there staring out into the distance. Jay, sensing Lorelei's lack of hope and clear despondent reaction, took the opportunity to gain control.

"Come on!" he bellowed. "Martha Brian saw a young girl head up here an hour ago. It *must* have been Ruby! You three go that way," he directed Bobby, Mabel, and Trevor. "And Mousie, come with us and we'll cover the island in no time!"

There was no such sign of Ruby on the headland, and if there had been, what would she be doing there? It was dark, cold, and raining something awful by then. It was no condition for a pleasant evening walk. If truth be told, it would have been truly inconceivable for anyone to come up there at that time of night in those weather conditions. With no news, the two groups reconvened and carried on past the peninsula, onwards towards Porthmeor beach.

"Where do we go now?" Jay asked. "Should we check the beach?"

Lorelei gasped, knowing how fierce the water was and not for a moment imagining Ruby would have gone near it. "No! *Surely not…*" she said, her voice trembling. Jay sighed.

"We had better check the beach, just in case," he insisted. He had a nagging feeling, call it a sixth sense even. He didn't know why, but he knew they should eliminate the beach. Then, addressing Mousie, Trevor and Mabel, Jay firmly instructed, "You three go inland, back in the town," then turning to Bobby, "you come with us Bob, we'll check the beach out, just in case."

Mousie reluctantly accepted the instruction. "Sure, but I really think after that, we should head back home, the police will want to talk to you," said Mousie, drenched from head to toe, but still looking quirky and rather sensible with her rain drop covered round glasses.

The larger of the gentlemen, Bobby Penrose, who was to remain with Jay and Lorelei, put his foot forward and with his walking pole hit a rock. "Yeah, Mousie, but since we're 'ere, Jay's a righten, we may s'well check the beach."

"I'm not so sure," the other lady, Mabel Cox, spoke out.

"We can't do much more," sighed Trevor Paynter. "Go home Lorelei. The police will know what to do next."

"Our Mabel's right, we're pra'bly wasting our time out 'ere. We should let the professionals take the lead dreckly."

They continued to debate the best course of action, and there seemed to be a clear divide.

Danny rang again. "Lorelei, the police are on their way to your flat. I'll drive round to the Island car park and get you," he explained. Lorelei nodded and let out a weak acknowledgment.

"Okay," she said, and then ended the call.

"Stop!" shouted one of the group. It was Bobby. "I've found somefin!" he pointed his flashlight onto the path where he had been pushing his walking pole back and forth, and the light revealed a piece of sodden material. Jay, who was more agile than the others, crouched down to retrieve it and on closer inspection, they identified the material as a small fabric bag with colourful beads sown into it.

"It's hers!" shouted Lorelei. "It's *definitely* hers!" She howled into the darkness. It was indeed the little bag that Lorelei had given Ruby at Christmas. She knew it all too well and she could see that the thin rope strap had broken.

"This way! She can't be far off," Jay bellowed. "You lot, go back to the town; it's too dangerous up here," but the party insisted on trudging on.

"Ruby!" they yelled desperately into the night.

Lorelei called Danny back, explaining what they had found. "I must stay. I have to keep looking," she insisted.

"I was just about to call you," said Danny. "There's been a change of plan. They're sending out the Coastguard helicopter. I'm coming now."

By now, everyone had progressed onto the coastal path and were dangerously close to the cliff edge. They were, however, well lit, Trevor with a headlamp and the others with hand torches, but even so the ground was unsteady beneath their feet with uneven granite rocks and moss-covered boulders jutting out everywhere. Each step was a danger in its own right, but each member of the search party was determined to find Ruby.

Aware of a distant humming and small point of light in the sky, Lorelei clung tightly to Jay's arm, quite forgetting her hatred of him for just that moment in time. Before long, the lashing sound of the rain was overpowered by the swish-swash of rotary wing blades chopping through the storm. The light from the aircraft lit up the area like a beacon in the night sky, rendering their own torches quite obsolete. Everyone raised their arms up to shield their eyes from the blinding light. Time stopped in that moment and despite the frantic whirring of the blades, Lorelei felt detached, and all she could hear was that distant murmur while she watched the events unfolding before her eyes. *Had someone called Janey and Robert?* Surely, they should have, but of course, it would be her responsibility. Ruby *would* be found, she thought, perhaps injured, a broken leg or fractured arm, but she'd be okay, she kept telling herself. There was no need to make any phone calls just yet.

The Lake District

The steamy hot water ran down Janey's back as she stood in the shower. She enjoyed the pressure of the water on her back. It was much stronger than her shower at home in Bristol. Well, she'd have expected it to be, given the extortionate price they paid for a week in the cottage. After a long session in the hot tub, she was looking forward to putting her pyjamas on and settling down to watch a film with her husband.

Tonight, it would be 'Apollo 13'. They both loved space *and* movies based on true stories, so it was a perfect choice, and she couldn't wait to cuddle up with Robert. They had pizza on the menu along with garlic bread and with no 'Ruby-tantrums', it was the absolute epitome of nights.

Janey stepped out of the bath and reached for her towel. It had been a long day, like it so often was, but without the stress and with a lot more fresh air and walking. They had hiked up Buttermere, and it had been a challenge, to say the least, but the rewards were gargantuan. The views were just amazing from the summit, and Janey had felt on top of the world. If she had been able to, she would have jumped off, arms widespread, sprouting marvellous white wings, and she'd have glided down over the lake like a magnificent bird.

"You look *so* relaxed darling," remarked Robert as Janey entered the lounge. The cottage was upside down, with the living room and kitchen upstairs, and bedrooms on the ground floor. Janey touched Robert's back as she walked past him into the kitchen.

"I am," she said with a smile.

Robert had started the dinner and left a wine glass with the bottle opened on the work surface. She poured the wine generously; it was a deep rich colour, the colour of blood. Janey had always had a palate for a fine chianti and tonight was no exception. She took a sip, relishing the fruity notes. It was a very good bottle indeed.

Robert cut the pizza and placed the garlic bread in a bowl before carrying it into the lounge. They would eat whilst watching the film rather than sitting formally at the table. Before long, they were ready to start the movie. Robert laid his hand lightly upon hers and rubbed it gently. "You really deserve this break, Janey." He kissed her, "we'll have to buy your sister a gift for allowing us the respite."

Janey nodded. They had been lucky, she thought. Very lucky.

Tessy Braun

Flood Lights

The helicopter hovered for a few minutes before making its way a few hundred metres to the west, its light still illuminating the coastline. It stopped, not quite as far as Clodgy Point, and the beam scanned the rocks. Lorelei ran towards where the helicopter hung in the air, its blades chopping away frantically. Jay grabbed her arm. "Stop, you're going to slip!"

Lorelei's heart was racing. In fact, that was an understatement — it was quite literally popping out of her chest. The coastguard had found something, she just knew it. Ruby was in trouble, and she needed to reach her. Why else would the aircraft be suspended in the air like that? She turned around, then realised how far ahead she had run, losing sight of the others, yet to her amazement, Jay was still by her side. She turned to him and this time she grabbed his shoulders, looking desperately into his eyes. Neither of the pair could feel the rain running down their faces; the adrenaline had numbed the sensation.

"Lor, I'm sorry. I'm sorry!" he begged yet again for forgiveness.

"How could you have kept this dirty secret from me? *For all these years?*"

"Forgive me," he pleaded, as his mind trailed back to that hot summer's day.

She drew a breath in, and her jaw tensed. "It was when I went to Lucy's wedding, wasn't it!" she growled, her voice low and raspy. "That weekend; the *only* weekend I went away, ever."

He nodded slowly. What came next could certainly not have been expected. Lorelei supported herself with his shoulders. She lifted her knee, intending to give him the blow he well deserved, but instead, at the last minute, she changed her mind, leaned in, and kissed him. She kissed him hard, in a way that she had kissed no one else, and he kissed her back just as intensely.

"*You are a dirty fucking viper fish,*" she muttered; an insult had never sounded so sexy. Jay's eyes were wide, in shock, to say the least, but he liked her aggression. She was feisty tonight; he had not seen her so before. He leaned in for more, but as he did, she drew her leg back and forced her knee hard between his legs, crippling him, before running off towards the light.

Cowering in pain in the dark, he cried, "You fucking bitch!" before reaching into his pocket for the whisky, downing it from the bottle as he watched her disappear into the darkness. Bobby, Mabel, Trevor and Mousie came up behind him.

"Hold up," panted Bobby, "where's Lorelei gone off on her own to?"

Swigging once more, Jay shrugged his shoulders, returned the bottle to his pocket, and started to sob. "I think they've found something, I couldn't stop her," he mumbled, losing his train of thought, "I need to go after her." It was clear that Bobby was struggling with the terrain, and Mabel was shivering like nobody's business.

"You should go home," said Jay. "It's too dangerous; the more of us out here, the more risk. You can leave me to catch up with Lorelei. I'll be quicker on my own."

The others agreed, after all, there was nothing else that they could do. The search team had launched, and it would be the sensible thing to do for all intents and purposes.

"Thank you for all you've done," he gave them reassuring looks, "I'll be alright, get home and get warm."

Danny, who had now reached the Island car park, was trekking at speed across Porthmeor beach in search of Lorelei. It annoyed him that she hadn't waited for him, but he couldn't leave her out there on her own, and they had to find Ruby.

Once out on the cliff, he called out Lorelei's name, but it seemed to be swallowed up by the fearsome gusts of the Atlantic, and he couldn't see any lights at all in the distance. At least the rain had eased, he thought, yet the wind was still ferocious. He moved quickly but carefully and could only pray that Lorelei was taking the same care.

Further along the way, Jay was also on a mission to find Lorelei, though he was closer to that objective than Danny. He stopped for a moment; he could no longer see the coast guard, nor hear it. Perhaps it had been a false alarm, and the rescue team had found nothing after all. His heart was pounding and, to steady his nerves, he knocked back more of the whisky, grimacing as he swigged and wishing he had asked Mousie for a bigger bottle.

He was going to have serious words with Ruby once this was all over and done with. *If she was found, he thought*, surely, she would be. She would be in so much trouble once they got her home. *How dare* she try to scare them all! Perhaps she wasn't even up on the cliff, perhaps she had met someone and ended up back at their place. There *were* other explanations. Alright, Jay mused in his head, *Bobby found her bag*, but it didn't mean she was still up there on the cliff.

A few hundred feet ahead, he saw a light, and as he got closer, he made out the foreboding shape of the chopper at ground level, along with the murky shadows of people between the cliff edge and the aircraft. He upped his pace to reach them. The clouds cleared, and for a moment the wind seemed to settle.

"Lorelei!" he cried. A man walked towards him.

"I'm afraid the area's out-of-bounds, Sir."

"Out of bounds? Why? I'm looking for my daughter," he trailed off, "and my, my wife."

"Jay!" Lorelei bellowed. "They won't let me near the edge, I *have* to see…"

"I'm afraid it's too dangerous, madam."

"We *have* to see!" Jay pushed past the paramedic, pulling Lorelei with him by the arm. She was drenched, shivering and he held her close to his body as they slowly approached the edge of the cliff.

"Don't go any further!" warned the paramedics with conviction, but Jay and Lorelei did not listen. Standing so close to the edge, and shaking with fear of what they may find, they scanned the rocks below. Lorelei held her torch out.

"There's nothing, I don't see anything!" she yelled.

"Stop!" the response team shouted again. The man shone his powerful torch onto the pair, who were dangerously becoming closer and closer to the drop.

"Lorelei, get down on your knees," Jay instructed. She obeyed him like she had done so for so many years, yet for a just cause for the first time. They crawled towards the edge; Lorelei's right arm outstretched with the torch pointing downwards. As they lay on the precipice, acrophobia kicked in, and waves of sickness rippled through her stomach. The rescue team followed, powerless to stop them, for any kind of struggle could have been catastrophic.

"It's too dangerous," they shouted, "come away from the edge."

"Will you just shine your God damn light down there; we need to see what you've found," Jay raged.

"Come back!" the rescue team persisted.

Ignoring their request, Jay and Lorelei continued to scan the rocks below, but Lorelei's torch was dying and was not fit for purpose, and soon the pitiful light began to fade. "Fuck!" She banged the torch onto a nearby rock. "It's no good!"

She tilted her head sideways, engaging in eye contact with Jay, thanks to the back light provided by the rescue team. Within seconds, the RNLI Lifeboat powered through the weather from St Ives and the vessel's flood lights gave the visibility they required. Lorelei gasped and then wailed. "It's her…!"

Jay let out a visceral moan. It was wild and frightening. He blinked, aghast, taking in the image of her little body strewn across the rocks.

Danny was making haste. He had tried to call Lorelei several times without success. The signal could be terrible in west Cornwall, that, he was fully aware of, but it was ringing, so why on earth was she not answering? Surely, she knew how desperately worried he would be? In the few months he had known Lorelei, he had fallen so deeply in love and had become happier than he could ever have imagined, yet tonight everything was falling apart. He was crushed when he found out that Lorelei's ex-husband had resurfaced from the past, and knowing she had disappeared into the night with him was utter torment. In addition, a lump had been manifesting in Danny's stomach ever since he was aware Ruby was missing. The whole thing brought terrible memories back from his own childhood and, since the events had started, he had been unsuccessfully trying to fight off the familiarity of the situation. Thinking back to when he was just eight years old and how poor Beth had been lost on such a comparable night. He had shut it all out for so many years, not being able to talk to anyone about the tragic loss of his sister. The events this evening uncovered years of suppression of the reality that his own sister came to peril in this very stretch of the ocean.

The Lake District

Janey snuggled into Robert's chest, feeling the comfort of his arm around her. He felt strong and protective. She had not felt this relaxed for as long as she could remember. They would have to do this more often; it was good for the soul, and it was definitely good for their relationship. She reached her hand out for her phone, which was resting on the arm of the sofa.

"Sorry darling." She wriggled away from him just an inch. "I'm sure Lorelei must have texted back by now. I've been trying to reach her all afternoon."

Cradling her handset, she cuddled back into Robert's warm embrace, opened her phone with a four-digit pin and sighed when she saw no messages waiting for her.

"That's strange. Why hasn't she replied?"

"They're probably having too much fun," said

Robert, stroking her hair. "Give her a ring in the morning."

Before resuming the film, Janey sent a text to Ruby's phone, not really expecting a reply. After all, she knew how terrible a communicator her daughter could be, although she had expected more from her sister if she were to tell the truth; but again, she also knew how carefree Lorelei could be. She only had to think back to their childhood, where it was evident that Lorelei was the wild one of the two.

Sweet dreams Ruby, I love you x

She hit send, with hope it would reach Ruby before sleep arrived. Then, nuzzling into Robert once more, she intended to enjoy the night. She meant to put her phone on charge, but Robert smelled *so good* that evening, she put it off. She wasn't quite sure what it was, but she knew for sure that the Lake District air had done something magical for her marriage, and tonight she had absolutely no complaints about her husband. He had been more attentive than ever, and this special time together had been well overdue.

Cornwall

Ruby lay face down, her limbs unnaturally distributed and her arms twisted around like a disregarded rag doll. With a knotted stomach and the taste of vomit rising in Lorelei's throat, she groaned. There was no question of mistaken identity. She shook repeatedly as she recognised Ruby's clothes. Jay screamed down to his daughter, willing her to rise, yet despite his fervent efforts, she lay there motionless on the granite.

Ruby, sit up! Climb! Climb up from the rocks! The words whirled around Lorelei's head in a peculiar parallel to the moment she was on the beach with Granny, but unlike Megan,

Ruby did not climb. Lorelei howled, and Jay didn't stop shouting down to her, refusing to believe she was not more than merely injured. The rescue crew approached the two of them and ushered them away from the cliff edge.

"You should both go home," a well-meaning man urged. Jay agreed that the advice was sound. He drew a breath in and stared out into the wind and rain.

Turning to Lorelei, he encouraged the man's judgement. "We have no choice. We've seen what we needed to see. There's nothing more we can do…"

Lorelei and Jay were escorted back to the town, reconvening with Danny on the way. Lorelei ran into his arms, weeping.

"She's gone, she's gone!"

The Lake District

Janey's eyes were closing despite gentle nudges by Robert in an attempt to keep her awake. It wasn't even ten o'clock, but perhaps she'd done well, considering all the walking they'd done that day. He slid away from her side and carefully carried her to the bedroom as her mobile phone slipped from her grasp into the crevices of the sofa. She was only half asleep, but didn't complain. It had, after all, been a long day.

Robert returned to the lounge and found himself a TV channel of game show replays. He poured himself a further glass of wine and rested his feet on the coffee table. He was so relaxed. The break had finally helped him to switch off from the stresses of his job and everyday life; he smiled as he reflected. It had been much needed time for him and Janey to re-connect. He absorbed himself in QI and other light entertainment shows before padding into the bedroom to join his sleeping wife, misplacing his own mobile phone, and not caring at all.

Around twenty minutes later Janey's phone rang from the depth of the sofa cushion, though its muffled ring undisturbed the couple, who by now were soundly sleeping after relishing in the delights of a Ruby-free vacation.

Cornwall

Danny held Lorelei by her shoulders at arm's length and looked directly into her eyes. "What do you mean, 'she's gone!?'"

Lorelei's whimpers gave way to feral howls as she saw the image of Ruby on the rocks in her mind again. The flood lights flashing as they searched, the beating of the helicopter's blade, and the rain all replaying in her mind, relentlessly around and around. Failing to vocalise reality to Danny, Lorelei could only see the events repeating in her head like her own personal horror movie.

Danny turned to Jay. "What the hell has happened, mate?"

As Jay imparted to him the details of the tragedy, Danny fell to his knees. History was repeating itself, catching up with him, reminding him that however much he loved the sea, it would always be his enemy. It was always going to *take, take, take*. But why had he not foreseen this? Why had he not warned Ruby to stay away from the cliffs? He, if anyone, should have known how important it was to educate her. *He could have prevented this.* Images of his own sister raced through his mind. The resemblance was uncanny. How could this have happened again?!

Danny suddenly transported back to his eight-year-old self, punishing himself for not coming with Beth that night, because perhaps, just perhaps, he could have saved her.

All the guilt and pain streamed back to him. He tried to pull himself away from his own selfish thoughts, into the here and now, and process the incomprehensible news he was hearing.

"Janey!?" he gasped, "does she know?"

"I tried to call her," Jay explained, "but it's late and there was no reply."

While they conversed, Lorelei's stomach churned with a sickness she had never before felt, yet even though she gagged and strained, nothing came up. They hadn't eaten for hours. Her head whirled, and for a moment she felt disconnected from reality, like she was not actually there, but she was reminded she was, when the wave of sickness came over her once again. *What the hell had happened?* She tried to process the events. She held images of her and Jay embracing. How could she have done this to Danny? She was sure she kissed Jay at the very least. But this was the least of her worries. Her niece had been killed, and on *her* watch. Had it been a tragic accident or had Ruby thrown herself off? Ruby had been so happy earlier that day at Gunwalloe Church Cove; she was looking forward to her future, dreaming about falling in love. Could the information that had been thrust upon her that day have caused her to take her own life? Either way, Lorelei concluded it was ultimately her fault. If she had not suggested Ruby came to stay in Cornwall with her, she'd still be alive. If she had gone after Ruby when she ran out of the little St Ives flat, this wouldn't have happened. How could she carry on now? Knowing what she knew, and knowing Janey would be destroyed. Could she even ever see her sister again now that she knew the ugly truth, and would Janey ever forgive her? Could anything ever be the same again?

Her mind was a mess. Nothing of what had happened made sense. While Jay and Danny exchanged more words and Jay recounted again the events of the last hour, Lorelei tilted her head and stared into the sky. The rain had cleared, giving way to a parting in the clouds to reveal a stunning galaxy of stars. She thought of her father. *What would he be thinking now? My life has been a disaster*, she thought, and just as things seemed to take a u-turn, fate would have it turn one eighty degrees, all the newfound goodness snatched away. With the return of Jay came destruction and in that very moment, she just wanted to run away. She hadn't run in so long, and lord knows she certainly didn't have the natural energy, but something fuelled her, giving her legs a power she'd not experienced before.

Lorelei ran into the night, and for a second or two, Danny and Jay didn't even notice she had gone. She ran and ran until she was quite off the cliff path and onto the sandy Porthmeor beach. The rain started again as she ran down to the dark water's edge and screamed at the waves. Lorelei couldn't see too well, but she could hear the roar of the breakers, and she could feel the icy rain beating down on her face. She waded into the water, unclear if she would stop, considering it may be better for her own life to be taken as the comeuppance she deserved.

She then felt the thud of Danny as he caught up with her and grabbed her upper body tightly and pulled her out of the water. Turning to face him, she wailed, grabbing him back just as firmly. She never wanted to let go.

Tessy Braun

A slight wobble

Two months later — Bristol

The last bag was thrown in the Volvo XC90. Janey checked her watch; it was nine fifteen in the morning precisely. *Not bad at all*. She should be in the Lake District by mid-afternoon.

Meanwhile, Robert sat at the breakfast bar in the heart of the now almost empty five-bedroom house. From the kitchen window, he observed the 'For sale' sign in the garden just in front of their beloved Volvo. He contemplated on whether he would take it off the market when she was gone. How could he bear to leave this place?

Janey took a deep breath. She knew she had to say her farewells to Robert; she owed him that at least. His life had been turned upside down too — it wasn't *just* hers. One day he had a daughter and the next he didn't, not only because she had died in such tragic circumstances, on his own sister-in-law's watch, but also because he had to face the fact, he never actually had a daughter in the first place. Janey had begged Robert to believe her when she told him how Jay had raped her that weekend, when Lorelei went to her best friend's wedding. *Why wouldn't he believe her?* Surely, he knew how much resentment and hatred she had for that evil bastard long before all this stinking mess happened.

All those years ago Janey had chosen to cover up the truth, whatever the actual truth was, but she had kept it from him either way, and it was a secret that Robert just couldn't forgive. He couldn't come to terms with the reality of it all, so they had no choice but to separate. After all, the only thing that really held them together was now gone and this time, the cracks could not simply be glued back together. She crept in the front door and slinked into the beautiful kitchen, laying eyes on Robert, who was slumped over the breakfast bar.

"Oh Robert," she murmured, placing a sympathetic hand on his back, "how did it come to this?" she asked. He wriggled away from her touch uncomfortably.

"Don't make this harder than it has to be," he said, straightening his back and sighing deeply, "just let me know when you've arrived in Keswick safely," he said, keeping to the practicalities of the situation, "and drive carefully, you must take a break halfway."

She nodded. "I will." she promised, although had no intention of doing so. She looked around the kitchen. It was idyllic, every mod con one could imagine; from a posh coffee machine to a pressure cooker, from a waffle maker to an American-style freezer, but Janey just couldn't see past the smashed plates, kicked in cupboard doors, angry voices, tears and all the ghosts her wild daughter had left behind. It was haunted with such visions of a life with Ruby, and she couldn't imagine staying there any longer and found it completely impossible to understand how Robert wanted to do just that.

"Well, this is it then…" her voice was shaky, but she knew it was the right decision. However much she had wanted to work things out with Robert, he couldn't accept the situation and she had to accept that. She turned and took a step towards the hallway.

"*Janey!*" gasped Robert in a grief-stricken manner.

"Yes?"

"I believe you!" His eyes filled with unshed tears. There was silence for a moment. Janey didn't quite know how to respond. It was too late. None of this made a difference to her future. She still had to go to Keswick and start again, she still wanted to.

"Thank you, Robert. It doesn't matter though; what happened, happened, and the consequences, you and I will have to live with forever." she swallowed. "If I'd have told you fourteen years ago, we could have dealt with it, and none of this would have ever happened." She shook her head. "I take full responsibility for all of this," she confessed, true sincerity trickling. "And just because you say you now believe me, well, that's good, but it doesn't change anything. We're still as broken as we were before."

For a moment she paused, brought her hand up to her neck where she wore the silver necklace with the turquoise pendant that her mother had given both her and her sister for Christmas. She held the stone, which was cold between her thumb and forefinger, and thought of Lorelei. What a catastrophe it all was, with the whole family split apart, but wearing the necklace had brought some comfort and she held a little hope that maybe one day Lorelei could bring herself to forgive her for the secret that she had kept all these years. However, she doubted she'd ever be afforded clemency over this tragic series of events. Even her mother struggled with accepting it all, and Janey was thankful her father hadn't lived to witness her fall from favour.

Two months on from Ruby's tragic loss, and Janey still didn't know how she should feel. At first, she had held her sister accountable for the cause of her death. After all, if Lorelei had never suggested to take Ruby for the holiday, it wouldn't have happened. Then, she had terrible feelings of relief, and almost felt grateful that she could now have her fresh start that she'd always dreamed of, but a rush of agonising guilt followed this fleeting reflection. Then there was Jay. If he had not obsessively followed Lorelei, Ruby would be none the wiser of her parentage and would still be alive. If Jay had just not blurted it out in such circumstances… and then she circled back to Lorelei, if she had just run after her daughter, and not left her for hours alone, outside, in the storm, she'd still be alive. What had she been thinking? Who in their right mind would just let that happen? But then she recalled Lorelei's pleas that Jay had insisted she needed space to cool down. Who was to blame? It was still a question that Janey couldn't answer.

Sometimes the moment comes for one to make life-changing decisions; yet occasionally in reality, there's no decision to make, and the latter was true for Janey Pritchard. As she prepared to pull away from the driveway, she didn't cry. She couldn't; there were no tears left, just numbness. She swallowed as she took one final glance back at what really was never truly a happy family home. It had been a home riddled with too many secrets, too much anger and destruction, but it didn't matter now. Ruby was gone, her marriage was over, and the word 'family' was a mere concept of the past.

Janey pulled the seatbelt over her shoulder, securely clipping herself in, noting in the rear-view mirror how thin she had got over the last few months. It was no wonder really as she'd fallen into the darkest depression she'd experienced in all her life, deeming her appetite non-existent. She perhaps managed a piece of fruit, or tinned peaches, for lunch, but Robert had struggled to get her to eat anything else.

With the engine started, Janey checked her mirrors, again catching her own tired dark eyes in the sun visa. "Janey, you *can* do this," she positively affirmed to herself out loud (with a slight wobble). She manoeuvred the vehicle with care out of the driveway, saying goodbye to her immaculate tulip and daffodil display which had delighted her every springtime, but after that, she didn't look back. Her eyes and heart focused forward; it was the only way for this to be. As she drove by the familiar landmarks of the city, she felt drenched in the sweet sense of relief, until the south of England was behind her. Despite all the questions that still hung over her, this was the beginning of her new life, and she looked to the future with shallow confidence, but deep hope, that she could escape.

Tessy Braun

The turning tide

Cornwall

It was surprisingly hot for late April and Lorelei sat on her new favourite Cornish beach, Porthcurno. It lay to the east of the Minack, the marvellous theatre carved out of the granite cliff, with a view of the wild Atlantic. Although she'd never seen a show there, she'd walked the upper circle and stalls, and sat in the box, taking in the incredible vista. In the past, she'd often looked down from the edge of the cliff to the white sands of Porthcurno beach, but never actually made her way down there, even as a child or young adult, until recent weeks following Ruby's death. The water was tropical turquoise blue, and ever since Danny had insisted that she visit this beach, she loved to sit and watch the waves roll up and crash back down again onto the bright shell-laden sand. It was a true paradise, and a wonderful place for inspiration, but today she wasn't writing poetry, but a letter instead.

An email would have been quicker, that's true, but a handwritten letter was so much more fitting. She remembered her father writing her letters when she was at university before emails were even a thing. She was alone today, but it was a *good* alone. She had been alone quite a lot of the time since Ruby had died. Thinking time had been required, that was for sure. Everything changed after that wretched black and stormy night in February, and not only had she lost her niece in the most permanent of ways, but she'd lost her sister, too.

Lorelei had never expected that Janey would take the news without laying blame on her. She took full responsibility for her actions, which led to Ruby's demise, and it was something she would have to live with for the rest of her life. Danny did his best to comfort her and help her realise this wasn't the case. Telling her repeatedly that no one could have known that Ruby would have ended up on the cliff. Reminding her she hadn't been the one that caused her to run out that night and that they had all been there, and all three of them could have made the decision to go and look for Ruby sooner than they did. He tried to get her to realise it wasn't her fault, but regardless of that, Janey, as Ruby's mother, would not feel the same. Even though most of the time Janey had struggled being Ruby's mother when she was alive, it hadn't meant the grief of losing her would be any less, and Janey had taken it very badly. The sisters had barely spoken since the funeral.

There was naturally the added layer of betrayal from Lorelei's point of view, too. The big elephant in the room surrounding Jay, and how he had come to father Janey's child. Jay had not stayed around the last few months, and Lorelei had certainly not wanted to speak to him about it. The friction between Lorelei and Janey had meant they hadn't had a conversation, both too stubborn to reunite. Iris had passed on information though, and the latest was that Janey had told her mother that their affair had not been consensual. Lorelei knew Jay was a bastard, but was he capable of such an act?

Nevertheless, with the changing of the seasons and the daffodils orchestrating the start of spring, things seemed to shift, and Lorelei felt ready to try to repair the damage.

She put pen to paper, *Dear Janey*, but then was lost for words, so she replaced the notepad in her satchel and lay down on her back watching the fluffy clouds float by against the beautiful blue sky. She stretched her arms out in the sand as if she were one crucified, and asked the Gods to help her with this darn letter, which she didn't know how to begin. With arms outstretched still, she sieved the sand through her fingers and stretched her arms up and down a little, enjoying the sensation of the warm grains falling through her fingers, and then she felt something small and hard, like a pencil tip. Slowly turning her head to her right side, she gently pulled the object out of the sand. It was a feather. A stunning white feather hidden in the sand.

"Dad…" She looked up into the heavens, stunned, but euphoric, and muttered under her breath, "If ever I needed proof that you're always there watching over me." She exhaled, "A *white* feather; this is a sign that the tide is turning."

She lightly touched the silver chain that she wore every single day and pressed the turquoise pendant onto her skin, while hoping Janey was wearing her necklace, too.

By the time Lorelei left the beach, the letter of reconciliation was written and sealed in the envelope. If she hurried a little, she thought, she may just get to the post office at St. Buryan in time for it to go off to her sister that very afternoon.

Tessy Braun

The conceivable truth

The elder, and usually more sensible, of the sisters had not taken Robert's advice to stop for a short break. The adrenaline had carried her along motorway junction after motorway junction, and before she knew it, she was so close to her destination. She had made excellent progress along the M6 with the impressive Lake District fells now visible, spanning out slightly to her left in the far-off distance. She and Robert had always loved this first little glance of the mountains. It was an exciting landmark of the journey. Traffic had been quiet, and the sun was surprisingly still shining this far north, fortunately the entire country basked in this warm springtime spell.

        She'd been listening to a podcast that had kept her mind busy. It was all about mindfulness and well-being and featured breathing exercises and meditation that helped to calm her nerves and relieve the anxious feeling. As she journeyed, she tried to push the torturous thoughts out of her mind that had gnawed away at her, not only for the last few months since her secret was out, but since the very day of Ruby's conception. From the very day she felt the brunt of Jay's abusive behaviour herself, which she knew very well her little sister had been made to endure for eighteen years.

It was that day fifteen years ago that she began to truly detest him, for she then knew what a monster he really was, and what he was really capable of doing. *Why had she lied?* Why had she not just told the truth when it happened? The weekend when Lorelei went to Lucy's wedding, that was the afternoon her life changed. Holding the secret of Jay's actions on that stifling hot afternoon had been the very trigger of her long-lasting anxiety, and never talking to anyone about it (not even her therapist at the time), had catapulted her mental health into a downward spiral over all these years. From the event itself, to finding out she had become pregnant, to the horrible reality of knowing she was carrying *his* baby.

Seeing how overjoyed Robert was when she told him she was expecting and how attentive he was for the entire three trimesters had been unbearable. He would touch her bump and lovingly talk to the growing baby, and when he was with her in the delivery suite, he held 'his child' for the very first time, loving both of them so much, unknowing that it wasn't his child at all. *How could she have done this to this poor, innocent man?*

Looking back now, with hindsight, she knew the right thing would have been to tell her sister that her husband was not *just* a dirty fucking viper fish, but a rapist, and a liar of the highest degree, but then what did that make Janey? No wonder Lorelei had cut all ties and never wanted to speak to her again. No wonder she'd been forced to abandon her life in Bristol that she and Robert had worked so hard for.

Through all of Janey's motherhood she had resented her daughter. Throughout Ruby's childhood, all she had been able to see in those innocent little eyes was Jay, and all she saw in Ruby's volatile behaviour was her father's destructive nature. She had wanted to escape; she had *hated* being a mother, for her it was a cycle of abuse, but Janey convinced herself that all this was her comeuppance, for the lies and deceit she put everyone through. Iris had been over the moon to become a grandmother, Lorelei had been delighted to be an auntie, and really none of it was as it seemed. At that time, Janey had never wanted to be a mother. She had felt robbed of what her life should have been. She could have aborted this '*imposter*', she could have stopped it all. But she didn't. Then, throughout Ruby's short little life, she wished and wished for the years to go by, so she could finally be free, but she now felt she'd wished too hard. As it is often said, 'be careful what you wish for'. That was the most recent guilt, that feeling that she had been the cause of *all* of this because she had wished it on Ruby, and subconsciously willed something tragic to happen. She imagined her father looking down on her from the heavens, aghast at what she had done. Then, as if someone had punched her in the stomach, she almost buckled over at the wheel, with the thought that he somehow knew what had happened. That wasn't a possibility of course, because there was no 'heaven'. It was all bullshit but, even so, the shame Janey felt was insufferable.

Janey tried to return to the podcast, but her unruly thoughts were beating her up once again and her mind was drawn to that scorching Saturday afternoon fifteen years ago…

Jay had called Janey while she was relaxing at home in the sunshine. It was unusual, but not completely unheard of. This time he had wanted help with the gardening as some of Lorelei's newly bedded flowers appeared to be in a sorry state, and he didn't want Lorelei to return with them all shrivelled up and dead.

Knowing how Janey had particularly green fingers, he asked her if she wouldn't mind popping around to give him a hand. It was a beautiful day, and she wore a floaty mid-thigh length flowery skirt, in purple and pinks, reminding her of the lupins and foxgloves she had grown in her own lovely garden.

After rescuing the flowers and helping him tidy up the borders, which had been thirsty work in this heat, he asked her if she wanted a lemonade. They entered through the back garden, and he locked the doors, which wasn't unusual really because anyone could just walk in through the back gate if he didn't. Janey hadn't felt nervous about this or thought anything of it. It was the kind of house where most people entered through the back, so you wouldn't just leave the doors unlocked. He poured a very welcoming glass of fizzy pop and even offered to lace it with something stronger, which Janey half considered but declined because, after all, she had brought the car. She had longed for the refreshing drink after the hard work in the garden, but could never have anticipated what was going to happen next.

While she was washing the glasses up in the sink, he came behind her and placed his hands on her back, giving her shoulders a gentle rub. It was a strange thing for him to do.

"You've been my saviour today," he purred. "I really would've been in Lorelei's bad books if the garden had gone to pot under my watch," he said with a smirk. She didn't like his closeness and shuffled her shoulders as though to shake him off.

"That's no problem at all," she brushed it off, rather aware, and very perturbed at his inappropriate body language. She spat out a quick, "Goodness," and then catching a glimpse of the time on the wall clock which Janey recognised from her father's apartment, she clarified, "I really *must* be making a move now, Robert will be wondering where I am."

Hope by the sea

"Shush," he murmured, seductively, more obviously leaning into her back now, and moving his hands to her waist. *What the flip was going on?* she thought, her heart pounding, feeling his hot breath on the side of her face. She could smell the dirty stench of alcohol on his breath, and she could also feel the metal of his belt buckle against her, where he had swept up her floral dress.

"What on earth?! *Get off!*", more forcibly, she elbowed him away, but he was stronger and persistent in his objective and that was it. She closed her eyes, realising that she couldn't stop him. She winced, powerless to break from his grasp, and silent tears fell from her eyes. Afterwards, he sat on the wicker armchair in the conservatory with his head in his hands and he cried to her.

"Don't tell her Janey, *I'm sorry*," he groaned, his eyes desperate, watery and evil. Then his tone changed, and she noticed his fists clenching. "Don't tell anyone, *ever*. If you do, I'll fucking kill you."

Janey opened the window of the car, plummeting back to reality, shouting out loud, "Fuck you; fuck you Jay Logan," and then she slapped herself hard in the face, dangerously swerving into the middle lane. Luckily there were no cars in it. Robert was right. She should have taken a break. She was over two hundred miles away from her past in Bristol, and she still couldn't shift that dirty filthy afternoon from her head, and all that happened afterwards, or *because* of it.

She turned the radio on instead, trying to distract herself, but then visions of her father in his coffin came into her head, then images of Ruby's little body replaced that of her fathers, then thoughts of her sister dominated. How she wished very much there could be some kind of reconciliation in the future, for without it she wasn't sure how she could carry on living.

Hope by the sea

A few more grey hairs

A week had passed since Janey had left, and Robert had kept himself busy at work, doing extra hours in the kitchens and regularly finishing late. He couldn't stand to be in the house alone on an evening, much preferring to come home after nine, and head straight to bed. Not always his own, though. He often found himself drawn to Ruby's bedroom, where not one detail had changed since her passing. The last book she was reading was still on her bedside table, alongside the framed photograph of Gerald, her pile of ironed clothes, still on the stool, and her dressing gown still hung over her headboard. He'd sometimes curl up as small as he could on her bed and howl.

When he had first discovered the truth, his world had come tumbling down and he didn't know who he was anymore. He didn't know who *Janey* was anymore. Everything collapsed around him, and to some extent he erased the fact that he had ever had a daughter, because it was the easiest thing to do. The truth was (which he was now coming very much to terms with) that frankly, it didn't matter who had been Ruby's biological father; it made no difference at all. It didn't take away fourteen years of loving and nurturing this little girl who knew him only as her daddy for her *whole* life, apart from the last six hours or so. He could cry now; properly, deeply, animalistically, because now that Janey was gone, and it was just him and the echoes of Ruby's presence rattling around in the big empty house, Robert could finally allow himself to grieve.

One evening he returned, exasperated with the amount of post that was building up that he just didn't have the desire to face. With a sigh, he lifted the mountain of white envelopes, and one immediately caught his attention. He recognised the handwriting straight away as Lorelei's. It was addressed to Janey. He smiled. The sisters had fallen out under the most terrible circumstances. *Could this be the start of a reconciliation?* he thought. It was certainly a positive sign to see this communication, and he couldn't help but think the intimacy of a handwritten letter was not likely to be something more formal.

He touched his face. His beard had grown a lot, and it was about time he spruced himself up a bit. He was very aware he'd let himself go over the last few months, not least to say stopped eating healthily and piled more than a few pounds on. There were also quite a few more greys coming through on his facial hair and his head — well they say stress can cause this and he certainly had been under a lot of that.

Throughout their marriage he had always done everything he possibly could have for Janey. They had a stable relationship; she wanted for nothing. He supported her to his very best ability through her anxiety and depression. *Yes,* there had always been a slight friction over his time away in the hotel trade, but when he was with his family, he was the model husband; everyone saw it. Janey was the unstable one; he was her rock. So why, he asked himself, did he let her down at the very last hurdle? The truth was that he couldn't cope with the reality of the lies; he turned away and couldn't deal with it. *He* was the reason they were separating and getting a divorce, because he couldn't accept what had happened, and although he had told her he did, he simply couldn't understand a reality in which Jay had forced himself upon her. If that was the case, why was he so involved with Ruby whilst she was growing up? Why did Jay step in so often when he was away at work? Surely, Janey wouldn't have wanted to be with him *ever* if he had done the unthinkable? So *why* did she allow him to be part of her daughter's life? How could she have managed to be around him so often and why was it only after Lorelei divorced him that her bitterness towards him grew so strong? Or perhaps he just missed it all; perhaps he never saw it. Either way, he now knew what a mistake he had made and if he had realised this sooner, perhaps he could have stopped her going to the Lakes.

He put the envelope in a larger white jiffy bag and scribbled Janey's forwarding address on the front. He'd post it tomorrow morning. If he and Janey had no chance in hell of reconciliation, he hoped that the sisters, at least, could make peace.

Tessy Braun

A Cornish Steak Pasty

Danny ran his fingers through his soft curls and noted that his hair had become much longer. It bounced way down past his ears to the curve of his jaw, but it was still silky soft and bobbed lightly over the side of his face. Gazing out over St Ives Bay from the Hayle side of the beach near the Bluff Inn, he reflected on how lucky he was to live there, and reaffirmed to himself that, despite all the tragedy these waters had brought, he never wanted to leave.

He had nestled himself high up in the dunes. In his hand he gripped a warm Cornish Steak pasty that he'd picked up for his lunch from the high street, and his stomach rumbled in anticipation of taking his first bite. Before he did, he took in his surroundings once more. It was a tremendously impressive view, and from a photograph alone one could be mistaken to believe it was somewhere else far more tropical in the world, like the Caribbean, and not little old Cornwall on the British Isles.

There was no doubt at all that he was in love with Cornwall, obsessed with her unrivalled golden beaches and rugged coastlines. He knew also, with more certainty than ever before, that he was in love with Lorelei and there wasn't anything that could ever change that fact. He took a bite of his lunch. The pastry was cooked to perfection, giving way to the hearty root vegetables and well-seasoned chunks of tender steak, and he thought more about her. It was because of Lorelei that he could now not only talk about his big sister Beth, and the terrible way he had lost her, but he could now also write about her. Not one piece of his poetry or prose had documented what had happened. Lorelei had given him inner strength when he had watched her create poems about Ruby. He saw how it was a wonderful medicine for the soul, enabling Lorelei to accept and let go. It was because of Lorelei that he felt alive every morning, despite the pain of both Beth and Ruby's passing. She was the sweetest, most caring, empathetic, gorgeous human being that he had ever known, and he wasn't about to let her slip away. He couldn't.

He ravenously devoured the traditional Cornish lunch and tucked the greasy crinkled paper bag into his jean shorts pocket and returned his attention to the sea. On this side of the beach, the waves were gentle and unassuming. The soothing ripples were translucent blue and made the water look so inviting and, with the sun beating down on his back when it wasn't even the month of May, he sensed they were in for a fine spell, and he hoped for a long, settled summer. One thing for sure was it was too nice a day to not dip his feet in the water, after all, it looked so appealing.

He jumped from the sandy spot on the dunes and headed down to the beach, kicking off his canvas shoes when he reached the warm, soft sand. There was no one else around. The holidaymakers who flocked to the coast for Easter had now gone home, and the locals had their place to themselves again. As Danny gingerly stepped into the sea, the baby waves nipped at his toes and he was reminded how the wild Atlantic Ocean, although looking inviting, had some warming up to do before swimming without a wetsuit would be a pleasant experience. Even so, Danny let the waves crash onto his shins, the water splashing up, catching the hem of his shorts. With resolve he waded deeper, rolling his shorts up as much as he could, and to his surprise it felt nice, and he started to feel free.

He glanced behind him, where there was still no one about in the immediate vicinity, and an impulse struck him so peculiarly in that moment. He turned to the beach and ran back onto the wet sand, peeled off his t-shirt and hurled it a few metres ahead, and then did the same with his shorts. Then, with a sharp inhalation of breath, he darted back into the sea. (He had his tight black boxer shorts on, this wasn't Pedn Vounder beach on the south coast after all.) Danny ran into the sea that day, gentle as it was, and threw himself into the water, which was more like a blue lagoon the way it had been pooling up into the estuary mouth. He swam with strong arms in the front crawl stroke and his body tingled with the cold sensation and his mind felt liberated, like he could do anything, like nothing could ever hurt him again.

It was then he knew *exactly* what he was to do; he wanted to marry Lorelei. He did not know whether or not she would accept, considering all the trauma she had been through. Would she even want to marry again after Jay? Perhaps she would be horrified and run all the way across the River Tamar into Devon, but Danny had never felt love like this for a girl and he didn't think he ever would again, so it was decided, and he knew exactly where and how he would do it.

Tessy Braun

Epilogue, five years later

Robert

In the end, Robert had taken the property off the market and ended up staying in the big old house in Bristol. It was five years later, and he still couldn't bring himself to leave. Being there made him feel closer to Ruby, and he now cared even less that he hadn't been her biological father. He had accepted everything for what it was, but still left her room untouched. He still loved Janey, he still wished she loved him, but knew reconciliation was impossible, so he focused on other things like cooking and a newfound love of photography.

He often went to Ruby's grave where little trinkets were left, and fresh flowers appeared every day, not left by him, and one day he encountered Jay kneeling by the headstone, weeping. It was a shock, around a year after Ruby died, and Robert felt great anger when faced with him. While he wasn't usually a hot-headed man, seeing Jay for the first time since the funeral meant he had not found it easy to stay cool. He managed to keep his composure and, in the end, the two men sat on a nearby bench and talked it out. Robert learned that Jay had got treatment for his alcoholism and now frequented St Mary's church as a regular in the congregation. Turning to God had apparently changed his life. He remarked that, where no one else in the world accepted him, he had found a place in God's house. He was convincing, and Robert hoped he truly had gained the help he needed.

Jay also revealed to him that Janey and Lorelei's father had known the truth all along. Jay claimed that he had told him so when Ruby was born. Quite what he had told him wasn't clear, and whether he was telling the truth to Robert was also unclear, but that was a final nail in the coffin. Robert was now tormented by the possibility that Gerald knew about Ruby's parentage all along and made the conscious decision to keep it from him. If it had been true, and Gerald had said nothing and allowed Robert to believe Ruby was his, was it a blessing or a curse? He did not know, but he knew it would be one final blow for Janey, that her father had indeed learned of her 'disgrace'. He didn't tell Janey. He saw no point in doing so, and whether this was right or wrong, he didn't know.

Janey

Janey remained in the Lake District. She loved it in the North of the country and had made a close circle of friends through the support groups that she had attended for her anxiety and depression. They helped her through the most difficult of times and without them Janey knew she may not have made it to the light at the other end of the tunnel. She had a new therapist, Marie, and although still a work in progress, she had helped her to process the loss of her daughter, and her health anxiety was better than it had ever been.

The landscape in Cumbria offered her much space for reflection, and she made a regular hobby of walking the fells, sometimes alone, sometimes with a group of ramblers. Though even when she was alone, high up on Catbells or Coniston old man, she had the distinct feeling her daughter accompanied her. Thoughts of her failing Ruby still haunted her to the core, and it still tormented her, not knowing for certain whether Ruby's fall was intentional or not. Had she thrown herself off that cliff, or had she slipped? Janey had discussed with Marie the feelings of guilt that she had experienced, the notion that she had willed this to happen, how she had wished for escape like her sister but never dreamed her wishes would be granted in this tragic way. She missed Ruby deeply. No one should have to bury their own child. She would never truly get over what had happened, yet she felt her daughter's presence on the mountains, and it brought great comfort.

Janey and Lorelei, although now living at opposite ends of the United Kingdom, were reunited through the power of their turquoise, and not least the letter initiated by Lorelei from Porthcurno beach five years ago. It would take a day to drive the four hundred and fifty miles between them but every few months they made the great journey to spend time with one another, and although Janey wasn't anywhere in the frame of mind for new relationships or commitments, she was delighted for her sister to have tied the knot with Danny and what's more, happy for them that they now had a little girl together.

Danny, Lorelei, and Hope

Lorelei had said yes when Danny proposed on the most stunning of spring days at the Minack. It was a warm day with no need for long sleeves or jackets. The far-reaching views were magnificent out to sea, when he went down on one knee on the theatre's stone stage, reciting a romantic poem that he had especially written for the occasion. The backdrop was incredible and a few scattered onlookers who sat in the upper circles cheered when she fell into his arms crying, "Yes!"

He had then pointed over to a beach in the distance, past Porthcurno and declared that was where they were heading next. It was Pedn Vounder, a naturist beach which was extremely difficult to access, and it took some skill and a lot of nerve to climb down to the golden sands. Despite this, both agreed it was very much worth the effort. Lorelei had felt a strong déjà vu, and then remembered why it felt familiar. She'd read about this beach at Hazel's house in the book of secret beaches, way back on the first day she looked after Molly, and she had at the time fantasised about being there with Danny. She had never mentioned this to Danny — how they were so aligned. No one was there and, to mark their engagement, Danny said he wanted to show her how cold-water swimming could be so rejuvenating. Whilst shy at first, Lorelei thought, *what the heck!* They abandoned their clothes by the rocks and scampered into the water laughing and truly embracing this intimate moment, representing to them both a fresh new start to their lives. They had been married six months later, on the beach, with a colourway of teal.

Hope was now three years old. She was such an adorable happy little girl, with curly dark hair just like her father's. Hope was certainly free-spirited and had already become a natural water baby with a unique imagination, often giggling and laughing in her own company when no one else was around. The pregnancy had been quite a surprise for the newlyweds, especially as Lorelei was to be an older mother, and having a baby post forty had certainly not been in the 'life-plan'.

However, neither was a train wreck of a first marriage and the death of a niece, so she just embraced it, and she felt so blessed to now have a child of her own, although her heart ached tremendously for her sister who could no longer say the same.

Lorelei continued to support Hazel by walking Molly, but in the main she focused on being a full-time mother to beautiful Hope, yet she and Hazel had become very close friends over the years. Lorelei had moved into Danny's house where there was certainly room for the three of them for the time being, while Hope was small, but in years to come they knew they would have to move somewhere bigger but neither had desire to move away from Cornwall. Hope enjoyed the garden space where Lorelei had nurtured a colourful display of wildflowers, and Lorelei, although very much missing her little St Ives flat, relished in the luxury of a garden once more.

Lorelei had stayed true to her word and now had a scaffold piercing on one ear and a daith on the other. Flo was very impressed and had even come with her to hold her hand at the body piercing studio in Truro.

Flo, Tammy and Mick

Flo's dystopian novel was now published traditionally and was a top ranked seller on Amazon. Tammy continued her spoken word poetry nights and acquired a regular spot on a local radio station to read out poems and promote other artist's work, and Mick, sadly hadn't been in great health and led a quiet life still working away on his eco poetry.

Hazel and Mousie

Hazel still worked for the newspaper, but her new poetry book had been a success, and she was now writing fiction with a much more chilled out Molly who no longer required round-the-clock supervision.

It goes without saying that Hazel had removed Peter from her life years ago and was enjoying free, independent living. Hazel also regularly took Molly to visit Mousie, who was now retired and focused on her painting pastime. Lorelei had been so inspired by Mousie's artwork and now practiced herself, and the caravan, when not being used for the writing meets, was a perfect place to escape to for mum and daughter, with fantastic dune and ocean views over the bay.

Iris

Iris remained on the edge of Dartmoor, growing older but too stubborn to admit she would have to downsize to something more manageable soon. She loved it there, where neighbours could not be heard, traffic was non-existent, and only the sound of birds and the bleating of sheep carried through the air. Lorelei tried to visit her mother as often as she could. Iris was in good health for her age and was a very proud grandma to Hope, although of course there was a huge gap in her heart where Ruby was missed so much. It was a dark cloud that hung over the entire family and of course always would, but time would be a healer, and one must continue living after darkness, for if not, what is left?

Lorelei and Danny kept their memories of Ruby and Beth alive with photographs displayed around the house, and Hope was growing up knowing who these special girls were. It was strange, as Lorelei had never known Beth herself, but over the years Danny had opened up, and Lorelei felt close to Beth through Danny's stories of their time as children. Of course, the same was true for Lorelei and Janey's father. Danny had never met him, but likewise, felt a strong connection through his wife's memories.

On the anniversaries of Beth and Ruby's passing, Danny and Lorelei would take Hope by the sea at Porthmeor and leave flowers on the rocks to be swept away by the sea, in an offering to pay respects to the two girls. Not roses, never roses, but colourful tulips and coronations that would be taken by the rolling waves, just as the girls were. The flowers would sometimes be found washed up on the beach in the following days, a curious sight for passers-by who often took arty photos and wondered what their meaning was.

Life is a short journey, and no one really knows when it's going to draw to an end. Like many others, Lorelei and Janey now know this with the most personal experiences and certainty. Twenty years from now, you'll look back and wish to be returned to this very moment, no matter how mundane it seems, no matter how depressed you have been, no matter what tragedy has befallen you. There comes a time in life when one must take control, grab hold of the chances one gets and live one's life for the very moment you're in, and under no circumstances allow the past to prevent you from moving on.

Ruby

Ruby had slipped on that fateful February night; she'd worn the flip-flops that had sparked suitability concerns by Lorelei just a day earlier. When running out of the little St Ives flat on that rainy February day five years ago, she'd not thought of the implications of wearing such inappropriate footwear. She'd been angry and in no frame of mind for clear thinking as she ran high up onto the coastal path.

In her heated rage she'd run too close to the edge, which was blurred with rain and wind, and she'd not meant to slip despite how distraught she'd been. The truth was that she'd not thrown herself off that cliff. It had indeed been a tragic accident and, from the heavens, Ruby tried to make this known to her family. She willed them to be happy and carry on living their lives and, with this willing, they seemed to respond. She could see them not merely existing, but now enjoying life and moving forward.

Only Hope seemed to see her, but she loved playing with the little girl and making her laugh. She sensed her mother felt her, when it was just the two of them on the Cumbrian fells. Ruby wished she'd had the chance to climb the mountains, to feel the pull in her thighs, to breathe the fresh cold air into her lungs. She wished she'd had the chance to make good her relationship with her mother.

She was now, nevertheless, at peace, reunited with her beloved grandad, grateful to have met Beth, and the three of them watched over their family, who they missed so very much, from afar, in their own celestial way.

About the author

Tessy is an author and poet from Dartmoor in the south-west of England, now living in Bristol.

Being a mother, writer, detectorist, witch, *and* call centre manager — it's no wonder this novel took nearly five years to come to fruition.

Though now focusing on fiction, poetry was Tessy's first love, and she has published a number of collections in addition to two short story books.

Honest reviews are welcome on Amazon / social media, and if you were able to leave your thoughts after reading this novel, the author would be exceptionally grateful.

Printed in Great Britain
by Amazon